Dragon
Fire

Also by Lisa McMann

» » « «

THE UNWANTEDS SERIES

» » « «

THE UNWANTEDS QUESTS SERIES

» » « «

FOR OLDER READERS:

ANN

THE UNWANTEDS QUESTS

Dragon Fire

Aladdin
NEW YORK   LONDON   TORONTO   SYDNEY   NEW DELHI

ALADDIN

An imprint of Simon & Schuster Children's Publishing Division

1230 Avenue of the Americas, New York, New York 10020

First Aladdin hardcover edition February 2020

For information about special discounts for bulk purchases, please contact Simon & Schuster Special Salesat 1-866-506-1949 or business@simonandschuster.com.

The Simon & Schuster Speakers Bureau can bring authors to your live event. For more information or to book an event, contact the Simon & Schuster Speakers Bureau at 1-866-248-3049 or visit our website at www.simonspeakers.com.

Book design by Karin Paprocki

The text of this book was set in Truesdell.

Manufactured in the United States of America 1219 FFG

2 4 6 8 10 9 7 5 3 1

Library of Congress Cataloging-in-Publication Data

Names: McMann, Lisa, author.

Title: Dragon fire / Lisa McMann.

Description: First Aladdin hardcover edition. | New York : Aladdin, 2020. | Series: The unwanteds quests | Summary: Leaving Dev to face the Revinir alone, Thisbe leads a group to Artimé to help Fifer, Aaron, and his allies combat the reckless new head mage, Frieda Stubbs.

Identifiers: LCCN 2019028735 (print) | LCCN 2019028736 (eBook) |

ISBN 9781534416048 (hardcover) | ISBN 9781534416062 (eBook)

Subjects: CYAC: Fantasy. | Magic—Fiction. | Brothers and sisters—Fiction. | Twins—Fiction.

Classification: LCC PZ7.M478757 Dsr 2020 (print) | LCC PZ7.M478757 (eBook) | DDC [Fic]—dc23

LC record available at https://lccn.loc.gov/2019028735

LC eBook record available at https://lccn.loc.gov/2019028736

Contents

To the dreamers and the creative ones
(that's you): Dare to do your thing.

Abandoned

When Dev awoke to a loud slam in the castle turret, the Revinir was standing over him, her dragon tail snaking out through the open set of doors. Her eyes flashed in anger. Smoke drifted from her nostrils and traveled out the window's iron bars, and flames curled around her teeth and licked her lips. Her scales shone iridescent in the moonlight, and her long, curved dragon claws gripped tiny vials of broth.

Dev gasped and scrambled to his feet. He pressed his back against the wall, and a sickly wave washed through him. There was nowhere for him to go. Through the barred window he

LISA McMANN

could see a great number of dragons in flight, circling a little too close for comfort. Some looked in at him with dull eyes—they were under the Revinir's mind control and would attack him at her command.

"Where are they?" the Revinir demanded in a horrible voice. She leaned closer. "Where?" Her wretched, fiery breath caused Dev to squint and turn his head to one side to protect his eyes.

His whole body began trembling uncontrollably, and he squirmed against the wall, trying to put a little more space between him and the Revinir. He knew she was asking about Thisbe and Rohan and the other black-eyed slaves who'd managed to escape the catacombs. And he knew they'd fled Grimere on the backs of two ghost dragons. Leaving him behind. He didn't reply.

"Tell me where Thisbe and Rohan went!" The Revinir loomed closer. "Answer me! Did they go to the forest to find the twin? Is Fifer there?" She grabbed Dev's shoulders and shook him. The points of her claws broke his skin.

Dev winced. He was almost as furious at Thisbe for leaving him behind as the Revinir was for tricking her and escaping.

But Dev wasn't about to give Thisbe up, even after what she'd done. That was out of the question. He yelped as the Revinir dug her claws deeper into his shoulder, then yanked himself out of the dragon-woman's grasp. He dropped to the floor and started crawling in a wild attempt to slip past her to the doors. But she slammed her foot down on his back, flattening him and pressing so hard that he was having trouble breathing. He could feel his heartbeat reverberate in his empty stomach as his spine sagged under the weight.

Dev struggled to free his arms, then covered the back of his head to protect it. His nose pressed uncomfortably against the sooty, uneven line of mortar between the stones, which scraped his tender skin. He gasped and coughed, trying to get enough air and sucking in some ash particles left over from the recent fire. He couldn't answer the Revinir now even if he wanted to. Gray spots formed and floated in his line of sight, and his body began to buck and twist on its own, trying to survive.

That's really all Dev had fought for every day for as long as he could remember. To survive. But this was the first time he felt like he might not make it.

The Revinir whirled, jerking her tail inside the room and

reaching for the doors she'd entered through. She grabbed them and slammed them shut so Dev couldn't escape. Then she lifted her foot. "Don't try that again," she said.

Freed, Dev inhaled a ragged breath and coughed violently. He curled up on his side and took in a few more desperate breaths. With each, a searing pain cut through his chest, making him wonder if the Revinir had cracked some of his ribs. Eventually the gray spots vanished. Dev looked up at the dragon-woman, not hiding all the hatred he had in his heart for her.

"I know how to get you to tell me the truth," the Revinir muttered. She shoved two vials of dragon-bone broth at Dev. "Sit up and drink these. Now!"

Dev felt his muscles go weak again. He'd known this was coming. Ignoring the pain in his chest, he gingerly rolled and sat up. As he did so, he could feel the vial of ancestor broth in his pocket. Thisbe had slipped it to him before he'd come to the castle. "Just in case," she'd said. Dev knew it would work as an antidote to the dragon-bone broth. The only problem was that once he was back under the Revinir's mind control, he wouldn't know to take it . . . *and* he might accidentally confess to her that he had it, which would have horrible consequences.

Was there any way he could fake drinking the stuff that the Revinir was handing him? Or perhaps do some sort of sleight-of-hand trick with the one in his pocket?

He coughed again to buy himself an extra second. The movement brought with it another ripping pain in his side. As he made a show of wiping his nose and eyes on his sleeve, his other hand went to the pocket and slid the vial out. He palmed it, keeping it hidden.

"Good grief," said the Revinir with disgust. "Do you have to go on and on with your dramatics? There's no way to avoid this. You're stuck here with me, and you'll drink this broth now. Or . . ." She looked around recklessly, and her eyes landed on the window. "Or I'll throw you from this tower to your death. Does that help you decide what to do?" She shook the vials and shoved them closer to Dev, then attempted a soothing voice that only grated on Dev's nerves even more. "Come, now. You'll feel so much better once it's done."

Dev reached up with his free hand and took the vials. But he needed his other hand to uncork them. Panicking, he slid Thisbe's ancestor broth under his leg so the Revinir wouldn't see it and uncorked the first vial. Thinking frantically, he realized

LISA McMANN

he should have tried to make the switch when he'd taken them from her, not after he'd uncorked them. Now it was too late—it would be too obvious. His hands began to tremble.

"Drink it!" shouted the Revinir, her voice pitching upward and dropping all pretense of gentleness. "Or out you go!" She hesitated as the reckless look grew more exaggerated on her face. Then she went to the window bars and placed both clawed front feet on them. Bracing one giant rear foot against the wall for leverage, she yanked hard. With an explosive grunt, she ripped the bars out and stumbled backward with them, leaving Dev openmouthed and staring, speechless and horrified by her strength. Then the Revinir threw the bars out the opening and ducked her head to look out after them, watching them go. They made a clatter on the way down, followed by a faint splash into the moat far below.

In the moment of distraction, and with the Revinir looking out the open space, Dev regained some of his senses and moved to switch the two corked bottles. But with his trembling hands, he bobbled the uncorked one and sent it skittering across the floor, leaking dragon-bone broth as it rolled. He uttered an oath under his breath.

The Revinir turned sharply and saw the mess. She snarled at Dev and started toward him. "You did that on purpose!"

"No!" cried Dev. "I didn't mean to do it! You—you just have me so scared!"

The Revinir's face wrinkled in disgust. "You're such a simpering baby. Completely useless to me. Not one person in this world cares about you, which does me no good at all. I need an evil one that people care about. This isn't easy!" The Revinir grabbed Dev by the back of his shirt and picked him up, shaking him. The two other vials went flying and crashed to the floor, shattering.

The Revinir looked puzzled for a moment as she realized there'd been one more vial than what she'd handed him. Then her grip tightened. She lifted Dev to eye level and stared at him. "What is going on?" she said in a dark voice.

Dev held his ribs and didn't answer.

"Is the extra one a dose of dragon-bone broth that you should have taken in the catacombs? Is that why you aren't under my spell?"

Dev froze. "Yes," he said too quickly.

The dragon-woman studied him suspiciously. "You're

LISA McMANN

lying," she said, sniffing him. "You sneaky boy." Still holding him by the shirt, she wrinkled her dragonlike snout and bent down to smell the remains of the broken vials, first one, then the other. She went back and forth again, stopping on the second. "That's *ancestor* broth," she said. "I thought we'd destroyed it all long ago."

"There must have been an old one mixed in by mistake—"

"Lies!" The Revinir shook Dev to silence him. "Did she . . . ?" she wondered aloud, her eyes clouded with contempt. But there was reluctant admiration, too.

Dev whimpered in pain. He slumped and didn't try to lie any further—not with him hanging precariously from her grasp. Besides, it wouldn't help. It was clear she was already beginning to piece together what Thisbe and Rohan had done to break the spells that the black-eyed slaves had been under for the past months. It was only a matter of time before she figured it out. The ache in Dev's side throbbed with every movement, every breath.

"I see what's happened now." The Revinir moved to the window, taking Dev with her, and sneered, "That little . . ." She snorted angrily. "I *knew* it! Thisbe lied to me, and I didn't detect it. The ancestor broth *does* affect the black-eyed slaves. Doesn't it?" She shook Dev again. "How is she able to trick me?"

Dev couldn't concentrate on anything she was asking. He could only stare out the window at the circling dragons while his stomach tied itself in knots. Any second he could be flying out toward death, either from the fall, or from one or several dragons tearing him up at the Revinir's command.

He squeezed his eyes shut, mentally checking out. Totally giving up as the Revinir continued interrogating him. In that moment he realized that not only was he about to die, but he'd also just accidentally let the Revinir know that the ancestor broth was actually powerful for the right people. He'd messed things up for Thisbe and the others.

It didn't matter now. They were long gone. "They went to the forest," Dev mumbled, trying to at least throw the dragon-woman off Thisbe's scent for a while. Perhaps it would help a little. But they were all doomed. It didn't matter how powerful Thisbe was. The Revinir was more powerful. She was unbeatable.

"You are all rats," the Revinir said. "I will find Thisbe Stowe if it's the last thing I do, and you're not going to help her escape

LISA McMANN

this time!" She lifted Dev higher and held him above her head. "I don't need you. Nobody does!"

"Aaah!" Dev cried. "Help!" As he twisted and screamed, the Revinir let out an earsplitting roar. Three images exploded in front of Dev's eyes. *Rushing river with a forked tree branch. Palace. Gray man.* Then the Revinir threw him, sending him sailing out the turret window.

Three dragons, their mouths open, answered the Revinir's call and swooped in.

No Longer Alone

Landing in a dragon's mouth wasn't at all comfortable, but for a split second Dev felt relief: At least he wasn't falling anymore. Then a double row of sharp teeth pierced the skin of his back and another double row clamped down over his chest, and his fear of imminent death returned. On top of that, the flashing images were disorienting, and he could feel the pull of the horrible dragon-woman's roar. Luckily, he'd avoided drinking the dragon-bone broth and was not under her mind control. It wasn't much of a victory to hold on to, but it was something.

With his head hanging outside the dragon's mouth, Dev

LISA McMANN

tugged and twisted, trying to unhook his body and clothing from the sharp teeth and jump out before the dragon really crunched down. He thought he had a chance of survival if he got away now and landed in the moat.

But the dragon pressed firmly enough to immobilize Dev despite his struggles. Frightful, uncontrollable sobs of fear and pain and panic escaped the boy's chest. But after a while they stopped, replaced by a sense of despair and numbness. It was almost as if the dragon were paralyzing not only his limbs, but also his brain. Had he been poisoned by the dragon's bite? Was this what it felt like to approach death? When would the creature press harder and pulverize Dev's bones into tiny pieces?

He closed his eyes and let his head loll back. The wind sliced through his dark brown hair and whistled around his ears. Heat from the dragon's throat made his skin burn. His legs, back, and chest ached where the dragon's teeth had pierced him, and blood soaked into his clothing. The thought crossed his mind that he might bleed to death before the dragon decided to eat him. Maybe that wasn't all bad. It seemed like a less violent way to die.

After a while, Dev lost consciousness.

The dragon flew on.

Across the Sea

There were moments when Thisbe Stowe felt like she was on holiday: training with swords on the back of a pillowy ghost dragon who was flying leisurely through the night over a beautiful green sea. She loved the zing and clash of the metal and the way the muscles in her back and shoulders were on fire for being alive. She respected the instinctive connection between her brain and her hands that took over when she was sparring with the other black-eyed children. She had a knack for traditional combat—even Kaylee Jones had said so once. Navigating the cushiony surface of the dragon and keeping balance

LISA McMANN

while speeding along made the workout even tougher and more satisfying.

But the joy of it all couldn't take Thisbe's mind off the many problems at hand. She was plagued by the guilt of leaving Dev behind—unrelenting questions about his status pounded between her ears and twisted her insides. It was wrenching not knowing where he was or how much danger he was in. Sure, he was clever and scrappy and had managed to survive a lot of terrible situations. But was he fierce enough to keep himself alive in the presence of the Revinir, who was growing more powerful by the day? And had he realized yet that Thisbe and the others had abandoned him? How would that make him feel? The knot of guilt and worry tightened in her stomach.

Thisbe also feared for the state of Artimé—Florence had told her in the new send spell that their beloved magical land, once safe and carefree and filled with loving people, was somehow in the midst of a civil war. A civil war! It seemed so unfathomable that it was hard for Thisbe to picture it, even though she'd witnessed some of Frieda Stubbs's shenanigans. How had things escalated so quickly and violently?

Added to that, and looming large at the top of everyone's

list of worries, was the threat of the Revinir being able to find them anywhere they went. How long before the dragon-woman would have full control of the land of the dragons? And when would she come looking for them? No one knew where she would strike next. And few knew how far the land stretched beyond Grimere and the palace where Ashguard the curmudgeon was rumored to have lived. Thisbe made a mental note to ask Maiven about it later.

And then there was Fifer. Thoughts of her twin brought a deeply unsettled feeling. Their relationship had become frayed in the past months. It was practically in tatters. And Thisbe had snuck away with Drock without telling Fifer—without saying good-bye. Everything about that felt awful. What if something terrible was happening to Fifer in Artimé now . . . and she and Thisbe hadn't patched things up between them? It would be just like what had happened with Alex. A wave of nausea went through her, and she had to take a moment to catch her breath.

While Thisbe was dwelling on all of these problems, another one came ringing in their ears. Everyone but Rohan and Maiven Taveer froze in the middle of combat practice.

They simultaneously cringed and looked in the same direction, behind them at the land of the dragons. Maiven glanced curiously at Thisbe. "What's happening? Is it the Revinir?"

Thisbe nodded. She squeezed her eyes shut as images of Grimere's fraught history pounded her mind. Her scales stood up sharply. "She sent out a dragon call again. I wonder who for this time. I hope it's not us." The Revinir's roar could be heard by anyone who'd drunk at least one vial of dragon-bone broth. She looked at Prindi, Reza, Asha, and the others. "Is everyone okay?"

"Do you think she discovered we're gone?" asked Reza, a bit fearful.

Prindi nodded. "That's what I think."

"Or she's done something with Dev," said Thisbe. Guilt pounded her again, and she wished she could stop the horrible way it felt. "What if he's told her our plan and she's angry?"

"He hardly knew the plan," Rohan pointed out. "And I don't think he'd do that if he could help it."

"You don't know Dev like I do," said Thisbe, but then she cringed and felt even more terrible for saying it.

"Thisbe," Rohan chided.

"I know," said Thisbe quietly. "Dev wouldn't willingly do anything to harm us."

"He might have inadvertently given us up, but you have to remember who he's stuck dealing with. I couldn't guarantee I'd keep any secrets if I were face-to-face with the Revinir." He turned and quickly translated the gist of the conversation to the black-eyed children, who didn't have a solid grasp on Thisbe's language.

"What if she comes after us?" asked Asha in the common language of Grimere.

Thisbe, who was learning to speak it, could understand some of the girl's words and figured out what she was asking. She answered haltingly in the same language. "We will fight her."

Asha looked solemnly at Thisbe. "We'll die."

"No we won't!" said Thisbe. In her haste to combat Asha's fears, she slid back into her familiar tongue. "We can't talk like that. Besides, I don't see anyone coming behind us. Do you?" She turned to the ghost dragon flying beside them. "Quince, can you detect anyone following us?"

Quince's huge head pivoted to glance behind them as he

flew. He stared for a long moment; then his eyes narrowed. "What am I looking for?"

"To see if the Revinir is following," Thisbe reminded him gently.

"Right. No, there's no one behind us. No one following."

"Thank you," said Thisbe, then turned to Maiven. "We'll fight, won't we?" she asked the queen.

"We most definitely will," said the stately woman, her back rigid and chin lifted defiantly. "So we should be prepared for anything. If you're ready, let's run this again."

Maiven Taveer, who once reigned as the military commander and queen of Grimere—and still did, according to this group—was also the Stowe children's maternal grandmother. In the time after her lengthy captivity, she'd returned to her family's abandoned home outside Dragonsmarche, where she'd stashed many of her important belongings back when things had started looking dangerous for her in Grimere. She'd discovered them unharmed under layers of dust.

Now she was dressed in her old commander uniform: a charcoal-colored military jacket and pants with tall black boots.

A bandolier hung from each of her shoulders crosswise, making an X over her body, front and back. The bandoliers held nearly a dozen weapons. Perched on her head was a purple felt cap with a small visor, and in one hand she carried a swagger stick to help her keep balance when the dragon ride got rough. Maiven looked smart and tough as she tirelessly trained the future rulers. There was little resemblance left to the feeble old woman Thisbe had known in the dungeon. Once freed, Maiven had quickly regained her strength. Only her wise words, soothing voice, and white hair in a thick plait down her back reminded Thisbe that this was the same person she'd met in that dark cell.

Thisbe smoothed down the scales on her arms and studied the others, who wore expressions of fear and fatigue. "Perhaps we should take a break first," she said, and sheathed her sword. "And try to sleep. All right, Maiven?"

"Of course, my dear."

Thisbe was the best swordsperson of all the former slaves, having had years of training in Artimé. First she'd studied stage combat with Samheed Burkesh, the theater instructor, and then she'd taken general sword fighting classes and trained privately with Florence. Rohan was slightly better than the others as he'd had more time to get used to carrying the weapon after escaping the catacombs with Thisbe. But he was still no match for her.

As Gorgrun continued flying, Thisbe sat down for a chance to catch her breath. She looked out in front of them to try to gauge their location, but it was difficult in the dark. She'd made this journey several times by now and knew that the Island of Fire would be the first island they'd come to, halfway into the trip. But the ghost dragons weren't very fast fliers, so it would be a while.

As the group rested, Thisbe mentioned the islands they'd be passing and told the others about the volcano transportation system. She explained how the one in the crater lake west of Grimere worked in conjunction with this one. Then she and Rohan laid out their theory about the meteors that had hit the land, causing multiple problems for the people of Grimere decades before and creating the crater lake. Maiven knew all about the meteors, but she had been surprised to learn of the unusual undersea workings of the volcano. She knew nothing of the Revinir's initial journey through the volcanos years ago, when she was known as Queen Eagala. No one else seemed to know much about it either. The sneaky dragon-woman had managed to keep that a secret.

They slept a few hours, then woke at sunrise and sparred some more. When they took another break, Maiven asked Thisbe and Rohan, "Do you suppose the second meteor struck in this sea and became the impetus for the Island of Fire volcano?"

"I've never read about that happening in our history books," said Thisbe, who wasn't sure what "impetus" meant, but she could guess based on the rest of the conversation. "Though that would explain the connection." She told them how the people of Quill hadn't been allowed to write anything down or tell stories for many decades because of High Priest Justine's heavy-handed rule and fear of creativity, so much of their history had been lost.

"There would have to have been several more meteors to create all of the volcano portals you mentioned going past," Rohan mused. He took a swig of water from his canteen and wiped his lips on the cuff of his sleeve. "We only know of two from our books, but just the one volcano formed."

LISA McMANN

"The other place we ended up in felt like a totally different world, unconnected from us," Thisbe explained. "It seems to me like no one around here would have known if a meteorite had struck there and formed some sort of volcano." She shuddered. "I don't really have any desire to go back to hang out with that giant eel."

"Giant eel?" asked Maiven.

Thisbe described the gray world for Maiven and told her what had happened there. "The eels have been in these waters too. They must travel through the volcanos. But that lake in the gray world seemed like it might be their home base. There wasn't anything else alive around there that we could see, except for some plants."

Maiven furrowed her brow. "I don't wish to visit that world, thank you," she said. "We have enough darkness in our own right now to contend with." She tapped her lips, then murmured, "We need tea." A moment later Reza was heating up a tin vessel of water with his fiery breath for Maiven to make tea. Everyone took a moment to refresh and rejuvenate while enjoying the scenery.

Rohan wore a thoughtful look. "Maiven," he said, "when

the Revinir had us and the dragons working together in the castle while under her mind control, did that mean the proper leaders had taken over Grimere again? And if so, why didn't the ghost dragons die?"

"Clearly not," said Maiven. "As Gorgrun and Quince might be able to tell you, the true leaders will only be able to retake control when the black-eyed humans and the dragons are in their fully functioning minds. Then the dragons must choose a leader."

"And what about the black-eyed people?" asked Prindi. "Do they choose a leader too?"

"We already have one," said Rohan. "Maiven Taveer is our queen."

Prindi was abashed. "I meant to ask if there was a process or ritual for the official choosing," she said quietly.

Maiven reached over and took the girl's hand, smiling warmly. "I understood what you meant. Yes, there will be an official declaration by all of us. And you don't need to choose me."

No one could imagine choosing anyone else. Rohan clarified: "So there can be no retaking of the land of the dragons by the two proper ruling bodies unless the dragons and black-eyed families, in their sound minds, have made their choices?"

"That's correct," said Maiven. "But there's one more step. The dragon ruler and the human ruler must approve of each other, too, and pledge to work together."

The children nodded, glad to finally understand how things worked. "I don't think the Revinir knows all of that," said Thisbe. "And nobody had better tell her. It's a relief that she can't just take over as the ruling dragon like she seems to be focused on doing."

"Nobody would vote for her," said Gorgrun, who had been listening. "Not once they find out what she did to them."

"Ours is a good system of checks and balances," said Maiven. "And it can be a wonderful process, finding new leaders from all corners of our land."

That reminded Thisbe of the other question she had for Maiven about what lay beyond the land of the dragons. But Maiven dabbed the corners of her mouth and stood up. "Back at it," she said cheerfully, like she enjoyed every moment of the training. "Afterward Thisbe will teach us a few magical spells."

» » « «

They continued training until their arms shook and their muscles could take no more. Thisbe tried and failed to put her other fears and worries aside—in fact, the closer they got to Artimé, the more fear she felt in her gut about Fifer. Thisbe had experienced a lot of things going wrong in her life by now, and a certain feeling of dread remained present most of the time. After having a couple of things go *right* for once in the past few days, Thisbe could only imagine that her luck would soon turn bad again. And the memory of Alex and being at odds with him when he'd died weighed heavily. The thought of losing another sibling in the same manner was becoming all-consuming.

When at last they put their weapons down and settled in to learn about magic, Thisbe shoved her concerns to the back of her mind—she had to focus and get this nonmagical team ready to fight in a magical land. She rummaged around the supplies for a specific box she'd packed, which contained craft-type items from Maiven's house, like paper and colored pencils and extra dragon scales and feathers and even a few colorful jewels that had been lying about. As she passed the items around, Thisbe instructed the future rulers to create small gifts for each other so they could learn to send seek spells.

Once gifts were constructed and exchanged, Thisbe taught the others how to concentrate on the person who'd given them the gift, and then she demonstrated with Rohan. By evening, all of them had succeeded with Artimé's simplest spell.

Under the moonlight, Maiven lit a lantern and turned to her books, while Thisbe went with the others to the tail end of Gorgrun and taught them how to throw a glass spell. After much effort, Rohan, Prindi, Asha, and Reza all managed to do that as well. While Rohan worked with the remaining ones on the glass spell, Thisbe moved on to teach invisible hooks. Though they didn't need light for this spell, since it was invisible, it was nevertheless a hard one to demonstrate, for they were in constant motion and there was no solid wall at which to throw the hooks—only Gorgrun's cloudlike body. After casting, they'd have to get down on their knees and slide their hands from side to side, looking for the hook. And though the old dragon didn't seem to mind being struck with spells, they were still difficult to find after a successful throw.

Next Thisbe pulled her precious components from her pockets. She only had a few left. But knowing she'd be able

LISA McMANN

to stock up again once she reached Artimé, she quickly went through the specifications for each spell, including the verbal component for each—being careful, of course, not to teach any lethal iterations of the spells. She demonstrated scatter-clips, using Rohan as a fake enemy and sending him flying past Maiven and sticking into the back of Gorgrun's neck. Rohan went so deep into the pillowy softness that he almost disappeared, and for a moment in the darkness Thisbe worried that he'd flown completely off the dragon's back. But she didn't hear a splash, and he soon shouted for help, so Thisbe quickly located him and showed the others how to release a spell. Rohan emerged from the ethereal dragon skin and began to breathe more easily.

With their first full day of slower-than-usual travel behind them, Maiven studied late into the night by candlelight. Thisbe's worries quickly resurfaced. She found herself dwelling on Fifer, hoping she was okay, and wondering what she might say to her when they met again. Was Fifer as angry with Thisbe as Thisbe had been with her? Should she wait for Fifer to apologize for being weird and awful? Because Fifer was the one who'd basically caused all the problems between them—at least that was how Thisbe felt. Relationships were hard, even with identical twins. Thisbe stared at the sky, trying to sort her jumbled thoughts and ease her mind.

The other black-eyed teenagers went to sleep, knowing that the next day they needed to train even more. Soon they would arrive in a strange land and might need their hastily learned skills to break up a civil war.

Civil War

The sun rose in Artimé, revealing that Frieda Stubbs and her supporters had clearly lost their minds. They were slowly but surely destroying the mansion and the property surrounding it, and terrorizing the Artiméans who didn't join them in their way of thinking.

Fifer Stowe was certainly losing her mind too, watching what Frieda's people were doing and knowing all of this was happening in the name of her dead brother, Alex . . . and her living one, Aaron. After watching from afar on the Island of Legends following a trip to Warbler to research Queen Eagala's past, Fifer and Sky set out for the shore of Artimé in Scarlet's

LISA McMANN

skiff. They'd hesitated to return, knowing Fifer's life was in danger after Frieda Stubbs's reckless threats. But they couldn't stay away while their friends were in the midst of the fight. They sat in the boat for a few moments, taking in the puzzling and frightening scene, looking for allies, and trying to decide how best to go about helping.

One of the worst parts of it all was how disorganized and muddled everything seemed to be. Fifer had experienced and led battles before, and it had always been obvious who the enemy was. Whether it was the green- and blue-uniformed soldiers or the Revinir herself, there was no mistaking friend or foe. But here? There were no identifying uniforms. No line drawn down the middle of Artimé's lawn separating the Frieda Stubbs supporters from the Aaron Stowe supporters, so that people could see who stood with whom.

There was definitely a visible small contingent on the lawn that Fifer and Sky knew they could trust: Aaron Stowe, the Ranger-Holiday family, Samheed and Lani Burkesh-Haluki. Henry and Thatcher Haluki and their children, Ibrahim and Clementi and the rest. Sky's brother, Crow, and Scarlet from Warbler. And Claire Morning and Gunnar Haluki from Quill.

Statues Florence and Ms. Octavia, of course. But where was Simber? And who else was with them? What methods were they using to determine who to attack? Maybe they were merely defending themselves and going solely after Frieda Stubbs.

"Do you see her?" Sky asked, holding her hand up to shield her eyes from the bright sunrise and peering at the mansion and lawn.

"Who do you mean?" asked Fifer. "Frieda?"

"Yes."

"All I can see," said Fifer angrily, "is our precious mansion being torn to shreds by people who have clearly become an unruly and dangerous mob. It's bad enough when *I* go around breaking all the windows accidentally. But this is a brawl, inside and out. Look there, through the front windows. Dining chairs scattered in the entryway, glass everywhere, statues hobbling around with broken limbs." She shook her head. "Where do we start?"

"I could really use a weapon," Sky said. She didn't use much magic. "I'm feeling pretty vulnerable here without one. I have my dagger," she said, patting the sheath at her hip, "but I think a sword would be a little more helpful."

"Samheed keeps tons of extra swords in the theater—all the ones that used to belong to the pirates that you fought off years ago. Shall we try to get there?" Fifer eyed the path to the mansion. "I think we have a decent chance if we can make it to the tubes."

The three main tubes in the mansion weren't too far inside the entryway. They were positioned to the right of the staircase, on the wall between the hospital ward and the dining room. There was no telling what or who would be blocking Fifer and Sky's path to them, though. "Let's go for it," said Sky, swinging a leg over the edge of the boat and dangling it above the shallow water. "Right now, before the doorway gets blocked."

Fifer nodded. "I'll lead in case we get attacked." She checked her vest pockets for components, then climbed out of the skiff. Sky hopped out right behind her. Fifer used a magical anchor on the boat, and the two sloshed the short distance to land, hoping the dissenters were too busy being horrible to notice them. Keeping their heads down, they snaked between skirmishes and made it to the main entrance of the mansion. Fifer pushed open the door and peered inside, with Sky looking over her shoulder. They both gasped at the ruinous mess.

The black-and-white marble floors were covered with debris. Chandeliers had crashed to the floor, and the tiki statue was pinned beneath one of them. The bannisters leading up the elegant staircase were broken in places and hanging precariously. The two heavy marble pedestals, which Florence and Simber sometimes stood upon to keep an eye on everything on both floors, were toppled over and cracked. In the dining room, tables were upended, and there was broken glass everywhere. The hospital ward was teeming with walking wounded, but no one was there to help them.

"Oh dear," whispered Fifer, moving inside. "Quick—let's free the tiki." She and Sky ran for the poor statue, whose top head had a nasty gash in the wood. Together they lifted the fixture off him and shoved it aside, then helped him up to his base.

"Thank you," said the tiki. He shuddered, and tiny bits of glass from the chandelier fell off his head.

"Florence should be able to fix your injury once things settle down," Fifer told him.

"Is it very bad?" the statue asked, turning all six of his eyes toward the gash but not quite able to see it.

"Oh yes," Fifer assured him, for she knew the tiki statue was quite dramatic. "You'll have a big story to tell the others."

Rattled, yet pleased, the statue nodded his appreciation. He moved away and into Ms. Octavia's classroom to hide.

Through the broken windows, Fifer could hear Frieda Stubbs on the lawn bellowing to anyone who would listen. "The Revinir is an enormous, evil, dragon-monster, as big as a real dragon!" she shouted, even though she'd never seen the Revinir and had no idea of her size. "She killed our beloved Alex Stowe, and now she's after the rest of the Stowe siblings. I drove her away once before, but I'm warning you—she'll return and come after all of us if you don't listen to me!"

Fifer and Sky exchanged sickened glances. Frieda had clearly taken her fearmongering up a notch in the days since they'd last been here. And despite Frieda's dubious claims, people were listening. Fifer scanned the area quickly, then started toward the tubes. "We'll deal with her after we have weapons. Come on. These tubes seem unharmed."

Sky followed.

Once inside the first one, though, Fifer discovered all the buttons had been smashed to bits, as if someone had taken a magical sledgehammer and assigned it to the control panel. There was one person she could think of who had a fondness for that new component: Frieda Stubbs. She'd used several of them to break down a wall in her apartment in order to make it bigger after she became head mage.

Fifer moved to check the middle tube and saw the same thing had happened to it. "Oh no," she breathed. "What is Frieda trying to do?"

"Here," said Sky, going to the third one. "This one looks intact. Thank goodness." She stepped in, making room for Fifer so they could stick together, and pushed the button that would take them to the theater. In an instant they were swept into quiet darkness, and in another instant they were inside the dimly lit auditorium.

Fifer exited the tube and looked up, expecting to see hundreds of swords and other weapons lining the walls, like they'd been for as long as Fifer could remember. But all the weapons were gone—not a single one remained. "Wh-what?" she sputtered, looking all around. "Where are they?"

"Oh no!" Sky lamented. "Frieda's been here. I was suspicious when I saw all the people on the lawn with swords—that seemed like a lot. It looks like Frieda has taken them all." She wrinkled her nose, consternated. "Any other ideas?"

"Backstage!" Fifer said. "I know where there's one." She took off down the sloping aisle, her steps echoing in the empty space, and leaped up the stairs two at a time and onto the stage. There she fumbled with the heavy velvet curtains, looking for the center opening. Once through, she began feeling her way in the darkness. When she hit the solid wall of the prop room exterior, she slid her hand sideways to locate the doorframe, then fumbled for the doorknob. Finding it, she swung open the door and flipped on the light to make the path easier for Sky to navigate.

Fifer saw something move out of the corner of her eye. "Aah!" she cried.

A man with a peg leg and a ship captain's hat blinked back at her. He drew his sword. "Arrr," he growled. "Move away!"

"Captain Ahab—I'm Fifer Stowe!" Fifer exclaimed, eyeing his sword and raising her hand, ready to throw a component at him if necessary. "Please don't hurt me."

Sky's footsteps approached, and a moment later she reached Fifer. "Oh!" she said when she saw the statue's weapon raised, but then she relaxed. "Hello, sir. I haven't seen you in a long time."

"Yaaar," said Captain Ahab. "Where is she?"

Fifer frowned. "You mean Frieda Stubbs?"

"I mean the whale! Where's that beautiful blue whale?"

"Not this again," Sky muttered. "Hey, Captain, Spike Furious is far away at sea doing good deeds, but she most certainly sends her love. And . . . could I please borrow your sword for a while?"

"Please," Fifer added earnestly. "It's very important. We're trying to save Artimé."

"From pirates?"

"No," said Fifer, faltering. "From . . . ourselves. Or so it seems."

The old captain statue snarled obstinately, then seemed to soften. After a moment he lowered the sword, then stumped over to Sky and handed it to her.

"Thank you," said Sky earnestly. "We'll bring it back."

"And we'll tell Spike you asked about her," said Fifer. Sky

LISA McMANN

and Fifer filed out, with Fifer switching off the light and closing the prop room door before the captain could growl at them again.

"Where is Spike, anyway?" asked Sky as they carefully retraced their steps in the dark.

"Lhasa told me that Spike spotted Issie's baby in our world again. So she and Talon and Issie have gone searching for her. If they can't find her in our sea, they're going to try the volcano network." She frowned and reached for the opening in the curtain. "It would be nice to have Talon's help right now, but I guess I can't blame them for going after Isobel since she's been lost for seven hundred years."

"Brave to go into the volcanos," murmured Sky. "Can you picture Spike Furious being spit out of a volcano and doing a big belly flop in a different world?"

"I just hope all the volcanos are in water," said Fifer, "or she'll be in trouble." As they went through the curtain opening, the painting of the giant set of doors on the back wall, which was mostly just for decoration, pushed out slightly and became a three-dimensional, usable door. That meant that someone had just put up Ms. Octavia's magical 3-D drawing to allow one of the large statues access to the theater. Three-D doors were very difficult to produce, but they were crucial for statues like Simber and Florence, who couldn't fit inside the tube.

Fifer and Sky squinted from the overhead spotlight's glare and watched to see who was using it. The door opened and Simber appeared.

"I'll be back shorrrtly," the stone cheetah said over his shoulder as he entered.

"Search everywhere!" called Frieda Stubbs from the other side, but Fifer couldn't see her. She and Sky scrambled back behind the curtain in case the new head mage was following Simber inside.

Simber growled low, annoyed, and kept coming. The 3-D door swung shut behind him, and he lumbered down the aisle. "Anybody in herrre?" He sampled the air. "If so, you might not want to tell me." He stopped and sniffed again. "Fiferrr? Is that you?"

Fifer and Sky emerged from behind the curtain and went down the stage steps.

Simber spotted them and started toward them. "What arrre you doing in herrre? You'rrre in dangerrr!"

LISA McMANN

"Hi, Simber," said Fifer, moving swiftly up the aisle with Sky coming behind her. "What's going on here? Everything is in an uproar! Sky and I returned from Warbler and saw the fighting on the lawn. And we heard Frieda saying some pretty horrible lies. We snuck inside to get Sky a sword—"

"Stop," the big cat muttered. "Don't tell me anything morrre."

Fifer reached the winged-cheetah statue and pulled short of giving him a hug. "What? Why?"

"Because I worrrk forrr Frrrieda now! You know this."

"But, Simber, I—" She let out an exasperated breath. "That doesn't affect our friendship, does it? What are you saying? Did she order you to, like, *attack* us or something?"

"Fiferrr," said Simber. His eyes darted uneasily around the shadows of the auditorium. "You need to get out of herrre. You'rrre not safe. Find Aarrron and tell him to leave too. Go to the Island of Shipwrrrecks. You too, Sky—all of you. Life herrre has changed in an instant. And I fearrr it's neverrr going to be the same again."

Fifer stared, horrified and mystified by Simber's words and struck by the heavyheartedness in his voice. "But—"

Just then a scraping sound came from the back wall. A moment later the huge double doors flattened and returned to being a painting. The three of them stared. "What just happened?" asked Sky. "Did Frieda take the drawing down?"

Simber let out an angry roar, then charged toward the painting. He stopped short of slamming into the wall and shouted, "Put that drrrawing back up! Frrrieda! The doorrr!"

But it was to no avail—whoever had taken it down wasn't actually on the other side of the wall. They were somewhere in the physical mansion, far away. Simber let out another roar, which shook the seats and made the stage curtain tremble. "Come back herrrre!" he shouted.

"What's happening?" Fifer whispered to Sky.

"I don't know," said Sky, "but I think someone accidentally locked Simber in here."

"We'll get help," Fifer said to Simber. "Just sit tight. We'll find the 3-D drawing and put it back up while you . . . do whatever it is you are supposed to be doing in here."

Simber let out another angry, bloodcurdling roar.

Fifer covered her ears. "It's going to be fine!"

"No it isn't!" shouted Simber. "You don't underrrstand.

LISA McMANN

She's done this on purrrpose." He began pacing behind the back row of seats. "Just . . . go. Get out of herrre."

"She— On purpose?" said Fifer. "I'm sorry, Simber— what?"

Simber turned as his angry expression morphed into one of defeat. "I'm surrre of it. Frrrieda locked me in herrre so I wouldn't join Aarrron's side—*yourrr* side. She trrricked me. Earrrlierrr I admitted to herrr that I would have a difficult time harrrming any of the people on Aarrron's team. So she sent me herrre to see if anyone was hiding. It was a trrrap, don't you see? And now I'm stuck, unable to do anything. My head mage doesn't trrrust me."

"Oh, Simber," said Sky. "I mean, does that really matter? She's your head mage, but she's horrible. Why do you care that she doesn't trust you?"

"I'm so . . . conflicted," Simber moaned. "I was crrreated to serrrve the head mage . . . but . . . she's . . . " The statue growled angrily again, then said, "This is Aarrron's fault for handing herrr the rrrobe." He broke into a gallop along the wall in frustration, even though he knew that wouldn't solve anything. Finally he skidded to a stop and sank to the floor, giving up. "Please listen to me. Get out of herrre now beforrre she finds you."

"But what about you?" asked Fifer, distressed.

"I'll be fine," said Simber. He stared at the floor for a long moment. "Just . . . stay safe and tell Florrrence I'm sorrry." He sniffed, then looked up. "And if you surrrvive, don't forrrget me in herrre when this is all overrr."

A Siege

Shaken, Fifer and Sky left Simber in the theater and returned to the mansion via the tube. Hearing a crowd in the vast entryway, they crept over to the bottom of the staircase, keeping their faces hidden behind the large baluster that still stood, although precariously, and peered around it. Then they heard a familiar, unpleasant voice—Frieda Stubbs was gearing up to speak to her people, most of whom were gathered in the large open space. Fifer and Sky looked through the spindles and listened. They could see the 3-D door drawing rolled up at her feet.

"Greetings, my good people," Frieda began. "As you are all

LISA McMANN

becoming aware, the remaining Stowes are a menace to our island. I've been aware of this for years, because I knew their mysterious mother better than anyone." She narrowed her eyes. "Nadia Stowe was not the quiet, demur Necessary she appeared to be. She was a pirate who snuck into our world. Her children, except for Alex, are worse than she ever was. I tolerated them through all of Aaron's disastrous choices, through Fifer and Thisbe's uncontrollable and dangerous dark magic. I trusted Alex to rein them in, and he did his best. Unfortunately, the girls stirred up a bee's nest far bigger than anyone ever imagined in the land of the dragons. And when Alex died, killed by the evil Revinir, this situation escalated. Now the three remaining siblings have brought danger to Artimé—more danger than this island has ever seen."

The group was utterly silent, taking in this revelation.

Frieda continued. "Against Alex's wishes, the twin girls engaged with the Revinir, ruler of the land of the dragons. They set off a chain of events that will eventually destroy Artimé. And Quill. And our entire world."

Several people scoffed. Surely she was exaggerating.

Frieda's most ardent supporters shushed the doubters, and

LISA McMANN

the head mage went on. "Hear me out," she said, sounding deceptively rational for once. "Thisbe and Fifer awakened a beast. This Revinir isn't the woman Alex sent packing back when she was Queen Eagala—not anymore. Now she has transformed into a dragon-monster. She's got all of the other dragons from far and wide under her command, even *our own dragons*, which is also the Stowes' fault—they've left us with no allies who can fight this army. Plus, the Revinir is furious at Thisbe and Fifer."

Fifer frowned from behind the bannister. *Well, she's angry at Thisbe, anyway,* she thought, but that was a minor inaccuracy compared to all of the other exaggerations and lies Frieda was telling. But that wasn't even the point! The issue wasn't that the Revinir was angry at them. It was that she wanted to abduct and control Thisbe. The dragon-woman didn't seem to care about Fifer at all. But Frieda was making things up to convince her supporters that Fifer was dangerous to have around too. Fifer didn't like it. She wrinkled her nose and pushed up on her tiptoes to try to see better.

Sky pulled her back down and gave her a warning look.

"As you know, the Revinir was on her way here. I scared

her away once. But with Fifer and Aaron skulking around, you can bet she'll return with her fleet of bloodthirsty dragons." She paused briefly to let the words sink in, then asked, "Do you know what we have to do to make sure that doesn't happen?" She looked sidelong at a man named Garrit who often accompanied her, as if to give him a cue to speak up.

"Get rid of the Stowes!" cried Garrit, pumping his fist in the air. "Sacrifice *them* to save our world!"

Frieda's other crewmembers repeated the cry.

The rest of the people stared at Frieda and her staunchest supporters with drawn faces and open mouths. Some of them nodded fearfully. "We don't want that Revinir beast to come back," said someone from the crowd. "Dragons?" said another. "We can't fight dragons!"

"If the Revinir comes back, why can't we just throw Fifer and Aaron at her?" asked one of the skeptical ones.

"We don't want that monster anywhere near our land!" said another. "Do you really trust a dragon-monster to take just those two? What if she's not satisfied with that? I'm not willing to chance it. Let's do away with the Stowes now, before it's too late!"

Fifer sucked in a breath. She could hardly believe what she was hearing. Some of the people calling to do away with her were acquaintances she'd been friendly with all her life—or at least that's how Fifer had seen their interactions. Maybe they'd always been scared of her magic.

"Fifer and Aaron have too many friends here who will protect them," Frieda went on. "Which makes them our enemies too, right?"

Garrit frowned and elbowed Frieda, like she wasn't supposed to go that far, but Frieda ignored him.

Not everybody in the crowd was buying this line of thinking, but an alarming number of people were. Fifer clutched her shirt placket and exchanged another glance with Sky. This was surreal and escalating quickly. Now the people weren't just mad at the girls and Aaron, but Frieda had just lumped in all of their friends as enemies of Artimé too. It was so backward that Fifer could hardly believe this was happening.

"What can we do?" asked someone whose face was etched with fear. "We have to stop the Revinir and the dragons from killing us all!"

"We have to fight anyone who opposes our plan to remove

Aaron, Fifer, and Thisbe," said another firmly. "This is no joking matter. These are our lives we're talking about."

"And if we remove them, their friends will fight us," said another.

"No doubt," said Frieda Stubbs, jumping on that theme. "We must fight first if we're going to save our people."

"This means war," said Garrit. The way he said it made chills go down Fifer's spine. "For the good of Artimé."

"For the good of Artimé!" echoed several others.

Frieda wore a strange smile as she addressed the crowd of dissenters once more. "I think we should clear every single one of the traitors out of this place and take control of the mansion as you suggest: for the good and safety of Artimé. Don't let any of our opposition in through these doors to stock up on food, water, and especially components! If they resist or try to force their way in, sideline them. And if you see any of the Stowes, bring them to me so I can take care of them myself."

Frieda smirked, as if imagining that scenario, then continued. "Now, everyone take your places guarding the doors and windows. My personal search team will comb the mansion to scare up anyone who might be hiding. Be ready for attacks from both directions—inside and out. The Revinir could show up at any moment!"

The people scattered, some near panic as they searched the skies through the window for the ominous dragon-monster woman none of them had actually ever seen before.

Fifer gripped the stair spindles and sank lower, keeping her eye on the people in the crowd. There were still some who cringed or shifted uncomfortably at Frieda's harsh language, as if they felt some sense of appall at fighting against their fellow Artiméans or even kicking them out of the mansion. Some of them took the threat of war seriously, having fought before. And none of them had ever been through a civil war before. Fighting neighbor against neighbor, Unwanted against Unwanted? The thought was horrific. It went against everything Artimé stood for. It defied all the principles that Mr. Today had employed when building it. Added to that, the very people Frieda wanted them to fight against had been the same ones who'd saved Artimé time and time again.

But nobody spoke up, so Frieda's words stood without opposition. And slowly those words found a comfortable spot inside the minds of the listeners and seemed a little bit more normal than they'd seemed a moment before.

Not to Fifer and Sky, though. Sky turned and whispered to Fifer, "It's a reverse siege. They want to keep us locked out of the mansion instead of barricading us inside." Begrudgingly she added, "It's actually a really clever plan—for them. I hope Florence and the others saw this coming and gathered as many components as they could." She glanced over her shoulder, measuring their options as to the best escape route. "We have to get you out of here before somebody follows through on that reckless threat and hands you over to Frieda. Simber was right to be so concerned. I can hardly believe I'm saying this, but I have no doubt that woman will harm you, Fifer, if she gets a chance. Don't take her words lightly."

Fifer's heart raced. "But if we leave, Frieda wins—she's driving us out. We don't want to make that mistake again! This is *our* world! *Our* home! And what about Simber? The 3-D door is right there at Frieda's feet! We can get him out. We need him!"

"Fifer, no! She just gave the dissenters permission to attack us, and some of them are in such a frenzy that they might not hesitate to use lethal spells. If Frieda or some crazy follower of hers kills you, she wins too . . . and I lose. Again. You and I alone are not strong enough to defeat them. Let's be smart. Come on. Follow me." Sky grabbed Fifer's hand, and the two, staying low, slipped through the dining room and to one of the windows that had been shattered in a skirmish. Fifer froze the guard standing there with his back to them. Then the two jumped through to the lawn. They got up and ran for the fountain, beyond which they could see Lani and Samheed standing with Florence, having a heated conversation without being attacked. The spats and skirmishes around them had diminished significantly due to the meeting inside the mansion. Fifer and Sky soon reached them.

"He'll help us when he can," Florence was saying passionately. "I believe that. I don't care who the new head mage is now—Simber won't turn his back on me. Or any of us. It doesn't matter what he's instilled with. Following a bad leader is not in his nature. It can't be! Or I'll take him out with my own bare hands!"

Lani saw the two coming and reached out to embrace Fifer. "We're so glad you're back. Some terrible things are happening."

"Yeah," said Sky, "we figured that out." She patted Ahab's sword. "I'm ready to fight."

Lani flashed a grim smile. "That's good. But, Fifer, you'd better not linger—I think Aaron wants you to go to the Island of Shipwrecks before Frieda sees you."

"Thanks, but I'm not going anywhere." Fifer spoke firmly and didn't elaborate further, having more important news to share. "Simber's locked in the theater."

"What?" said Florence. "How?"

"Frieda sent him in through the 3-D door. Once he was inside, she took the door down, and now he's trapped."

Samheed blew out an impatient breath. "Well, of course she did." He shook his head angrily. "She doesn't trust that he's fully with her, and she knows she can't fight him."

"Where's the 3-D drawing?" asked Florence.

"Frieda has it," said Fifer. "She's surrounded by her dissenters. They're planning to banish all of us from the mansion. Aaron and me and all of our friends. You."

"It's like a siege," said Sky. "Only they're going to keep us out, not in."

Florence closed one eye and looked at the sky, her nose

wrinkling. "That's . . . crazy. Isn't it? How does that hurt us, exactly?"

"We have water," said Samheed, pointing to the fountain. "We can get food from Quill. So I'm not sure their idea is going to work."

"Components," said Fifer grimly. "We don't have access to them. What we have on us is it."

"And we're severely outnumbered," said Sky.

Florence studied the newcomers. "We need that door drawing back so we can get Simber out. It could take days for Octavia to draw a new one." Florence glanced around the lawn looking for allies, seeing a few small groups of people, creatures, and statues standing together. "Where is everybody?"

"All of Frieda's supporters have gone inside," said Sky. "They're being assigned duties now to guard the windows and doors."

"But where's the rest of *us*?" asked Florence, growing alarmed. "Our allies? Is this *it*?"

The others looked all around. There were perhaps twenty-five or thirty of them remaining outside on the torn-up lawn.

Something caught Sky's eye, and she turned. A few small

groups of people were leaving the mansion carrying rucksacks and travel bags, heading for the lagoon where Artimé's ships were anchored. "Looks like some of the people aren't buying what Frieda is saying, and they're leaving."

"Should we go after them?" asked Fifer. "Convince them to stay and help us?"

"I'll do it," said Lani. "They might not want to be seen talking to you, Fifer."

Fifer grimaced. What Lani said hurt, but Fifer knew it was true. Lani rolled swiftly across the lawn, trying to catch up to the departing groups before they made it to the lagoon.

Florence turned to study the mansion. Now stationed at every window and door were Frieda's people, glaring out at them. Some of them seemed scared or unsure. But others wore expressions filled with spite, warning those who sided with Aaron to never return to the mansion they called home.

"Gather everyone who's firmly with us," said Florence, her voice quiet. "Be discreet. We'll meet near the rock's lair in an hour."

Samheed, Sky, and Fifer all nodded. "I'll relay the instructions to Lani," said Samheed.

"Good. I need to talk to Panther and the rock. I'll see you out there." Florence turned and strode purposefully out of sight of the mansion toward the entrance to Quill, where the gate once stood. When she reached the road, she turned sharply to the right and headed for the jungle.

"Why is she going the long way around?" asked Sky, watching her go.

"Maybe she doesn't want the people inside to know what we're doing," Fifer guessed. "Let's talk to everyone and sneak into the jungle by way of the lagoon. We have to figure out how to beat Frieda Stubbs without anyone . . ." She trailed off. "Dying," she was going to say.

Sky nodded, looking increasingly troubled. She and Samheed and Fifer did as Florence had told them. But no one had any idea how they were going to manage taking on the majority of Artimé's people, who were all extremely well trained to fight. Trained by the very people and statues they were now ready to attack. This was not going to be easy.

A Stealthy Invasion

An hour later the last of the stragglers, having followed a path from the lagoon through the jungle, reached the base of an enormous living rock. The rock had come alive after Mr. Today had enchanted it many years before. Its mouth was a large cavern from which Florence had been carved. Fifer, Thisbe, and Crow and all the other young children of Artimé had once been kept safe inside the rock's mouth during the battle against Queen Eagala and the pirates.

The mass of stone mostly stayed in the jungle, though, watching over its sometimes-frightening occupants. Panther,

LISA McMANN

who was half-wild, lived there, as did a little dog with very sharp teeth who'd put a number of puncture wounds in Aaron's arms over the years. A giant scorpion resided much deeper inside the jungle. That creature had nearly done Fifer and Thisbe in once, and no one was ever safe from it. Luckily, it loved the darkness and rarely visited this area, where bits of sunlight filtered through the treetops.

Florence scanned the group, sizing up her team. Sean, Carina, and Seth were there with young Lukas and Ava. Lani and Samheed too. Aaron, but not Kaylee, who was keeping Daniel safe on the Island of Shipwrecks. Henry and Thatcher, with Ibrahim and Clementi and their other teenage children. Fifer and Sky, and Fifer's birds hovering above. Claire Morning and Gunnar Haluki. Crow and Scarlet. Ms. Octavia, the octogator instructor, Fox, Kitten, and a few other statues who'd snuck out of the mansion before the siege. A spare handful of other staunch Aaron supporters filled in the gaps. Lani hadn't managed to convince any of the departing Artiméans to stay— they'd wanted no part of a civil war. They set off for Warbler to wait it out.

The toothy dog wasn't present as far as anyone could see,

though his body had a camouflage quality to it that made it hard to spot him in the jungle. But Panther paced restlessly a short distance away. She wasn't nearly as ferocious and dangerous as she used to be, but it was safer for everyone, including her, if she kept her distance, especially now that she was agitated over the news Florence had given her about Simber being trapped. Florence had warned Panther that she'd take her down in an instant if she threatened anyone present, and Panther respected that.

"So this is it, then," said Aaron, bringing everyone to silence. "Thank you for sticking with us even though it looks like our side is sorely lacking in numbers. But some of Artimé's best fighters are in this group, and that makes me feel confident." He didn't sound as confident as he said he was. "Florence, what thoughts do you have about our immediate future? We've been driven out of the mansion—what do you advise? Go quietly? Or fight?"

"It will be nearly impossible to fight them," Florence began, and a few in the crowd, like Carina and Fifer, reacted by stepping forward and beginning to protest. But Florence held up her hand to explain. "We certainly can't beat them.

Their numbers are too large, and they have all the extra components."

Others began to shift uncomfortably. What was Florence saying? Didn't she think they had a chance?

The warrior trainer seemed troubled—more conflicted than she'd ever been in the past when leading up to a battle. "We also must remember," she went on, "that like us, they are people of Artimé. The majority of them were Unwanted too. They were thrown out of Quill. Rescued and accepted into our world by Marcus Today and Alex and all of us. And . . . I think many of them have gotten caught up in the fearmongering. Not all of them are thinking straight. They're not making decisions of their own accord like they've been taught to do from the moment they set foot in Artimé, because Frieda Stubbs is completely different from any ruler our land has ever seen. She's disorienting and chaotic. Some of the people have been swayed by friends or coerced by Frieda's lies."

Florence paused, then went on. "I'm not sure why this is happening now—perhaps the Revinir scare uncovered some insecurities and brought back the memories of our past battles. It could be that the thought of fighting the Revinir and potentially losing loved ones after years of peace was too much for some of them to handle, so they're grasping at what seems to them a better option. We're all still traumatized from the last time things went wrong. So I have empathy. For some of them."

Fifer nodded. "I refuse to believe that all of those people have fully turned against the world that saved them when the people of Quill sent them away."

"I agree," said Lani. "I believe some are making a mistake, and they'll see it soon enough. We just have to figure out how to show them."

Aaron kept his eyes on the ground.

Samheed glanced at him and shifted uneasily. "I hope you're right, Lani. But I'm equally sure that *some* people refuse to see the truth even when it's right in front of them." His voice held a weight that seemed to imply he wasn't just talking about Frieda Stubbs and the dissenters.

Sensing it, Aaron turned and saw Samheed staring at him. Aaron's face flushed, and he looked hastily away. "Despite the current state of mind of the dissenters," he said, "and the fact that they are mostly Unwanteds too, we can't just do nothing.

We have to try. We won't walk away from Artimé."

"What do you mean?" Florence pressed. "Do you think we should go in and fight for the mansion? Against all of those people?"

Aaron lifted his gaze and saw that Florence was sincerely asking his opinion. "If we don't go after Frieda Stubbs forcefully and immediately, her power will only grow, and her support will strengthen. The unsure members of her party will assume they're doing right if no one opposes them, and they'll become more confident in their decision to join her. Right now Frieda has free rein to say and do whatever she wants without anyone contradicting her. And, knowing her, she'll take every opportunity to do so as long as she is not being challenged." He paused, then muttered, "Believe me. I know how her mind works."

Samheed's eyes flickered. "Are you tempted—" He stopped abruptly when Lani's elbow sank into his flesh. "Ouch. Never mind."

Aaron turned sharply. "Am I what?"

"Never mind, I said."

Aaron studied Samheed with a highly skeptical expression.

LISA McMANN

"Am I tempted to join forces with Frieda? Is that what you were going to say?"

"No! I—"

Lani frowned at Samheed. "Is it, Sam? I'd actually like to know too."

"Lani, seriously. I don't want to get jabbed in the ribs again."

Lani glared at her husband. "You need to stop."

"Stop what?" Samheed said, sounding exasperated.

"Get. Over. It," said Lani.

"No. Please go on," said Aaron haughtily. "You've held on to this . . . this undercurrent of distrust for me all these years, and it has come roaring back lately, though I don't know what I've done to make you disapprove of me this time. So let's just address this. Get it out so we can move on and be done with it."

Samheed closed his eyes, then opened them and said, "I'm sorry, Aaron. I just wonder how you . . . feel. Are you struggling? About what Frieda is doing, I mean. You know—being evil and taking control like this. Does it . . . ?" He sighed. "Does it bring back . . . ?"

Aaron lifted his chin and waited, eyes flashing.

Samheed glanced around the group and saw that everyone was looking skeptically at him. He gulped, then confessed, "I think it's the playwright in me, always questioning characters' motives. I guess I want to know if this situation brings back any desires to be that way again. I'm sorry that I'm worried about it, and I wish I weren't. It's just a feeling that won't go away."

Aaron was quiet for a long moment. He'd certainly had temptations and desires for power over the years since he'd turned his life around. He'd punished himself mentally quite a lot for it too. And he laid much of the blame on the government of Quill and the High Priest Justine, who'd been so influential on him in that year after the Purge. Frieda was doing the same thing now in Artimé with the others. But being asked outright like this, in front of everybody, brought out his defensive side. He glanced at Florence and Claire, and then at the others as Fifer sidled over and slipped her hand into his in support.

"I'm not a character in one of your scripts, Samheed," Aaron answered evenly. "I have no desire to be like that anymore. And I'm insulted and hurt that you think I do. I'm not sure what more I have to do to convince you that I've changed.

It's been . . . so long." He shook his head slightly. "To be honest, I'm tired of apologizing for the same things year after year after year, but I believe I must do it, because what I did was terrible. That is the cost of my actions. So I apologize again to everyone here—I'm sorry for how I hurt Artimé." He hesitated. "But sometimes I feel like if you haven't been able to let it go and forgive me by now, Samheed, I doubt you ever will. And as much as I want to be your friend and comrade, well . . . perhaps . . . perhaps it would be better if we no longer spent time together."

Samheed's eyes widened. "Oh, come on, Aaron. No. I didn't mean—"

Aaron raised his hand. "Please, Samheed. Don't say anything more." He turned away. "I understand now how it's got to be for you, and I will accept it because I must. I hope we can coexist without making any of our mutual friends uncomfortable."

Samheed stared at him. Then he shook his head and blew out a breath. Lani folded her arms over her chest, clearly frustrated. Fifer looked anxiously from her brother to her instructor, unsure what to make of them. She'd never quite understood the animosity between the two, and they'd done

LISA McMANN

well to hide it from the younger generation until now. Fifer stayed still, not sure what to do besides keep out of it. The rest of them shifted uncomfortably. It had been a conversation ill-timed and not suited for extra ears to hear, yet it had happened, and there was no taking it back.

Carina was first to break the silence. "Okay," she said decidedly, resting her hands on the shoulders of her younger two children. "That's enough. Moving on. We have an issue to deal with here that takes precedence over . . . whatever that was." She turned to Aaron. "You were saying that we should declare our opposition to Frieda Stubbs loud and clear."

"That is my position," Aaron said stiffly.

"I support that." Carina didn't look at Samheed, but it was clear to everyone that she'd just made a statement. "I'm not sure how we're going to do it, though."

"I have an idea," Aaron said quietly. He stared hard into the jungle, deep in thought, and after a moment, a flicker of recognition crossed his face. In his youth, he'd spent some time sneaking from the tube in Quill to the one in the head mage's kitchenette and on to the one in the jungle, befriending Panther during his visits. And he could just barely see the jungle tube in some brush not far away. "Hmm." He turned to Carina. "Yes. And I think we should attack immediately, since they won't be expecting us to."

Florence looked concerned. "How? We barely have enough people to surround the mansion."

Fifer glanced at her brother and saw him staring out into the jungle again. She followed his gaze and caught a glimpse of the tube in the clearing. "Oooh," she said, almost as if she could read Aaron's thoughts. "I see. We'll surprise them," she said slowly. "And on the way we can get more components."

Aaron pivoted to his sister with a small smile and a nod. "Exactly."

In the Cavelands

Dev opened his eyes and blinked at the sky a few times, trying to remember where he was and what had happened to him. With a sick feeling welling up inside, he recalled being thrown from the castle tower window and his ride in the grip of the dragon's mouth. Was he dead now? This . . . didn't seem anything like what he'd imagined death to be.

After a moment he was certain he could not possibly be dead with his body aching and head pounding like it was. His thirst was intense, and his stomach was trying to communicate either hunger or the need to vomit—he wasn't sure which. He

LISA McMANN

heard something snuffling some distance away but could see no one. Dev tried to move, but his limbs wouldn't obey, so he let his lids droop.

When the snuffling noises grew louder and an oven full of hot breath blasted him, Dev's eyes flew open again. Looming over him was a shocking sight. One dark purple dragon and two silvery ghost dragons stared down. A huge drop of something disgusting fell from one of the ghost dragon's nostrils and sizzled on Dev's arm. Steam rose up from it, and the dull burning pain it created joined the various other pains Dev already endured. "*Krech,*" he whispered, but the word from the common language caught in his parched throat, and only a scratchy noise came out. He closed his cracked lips and let his head sink to one side, too exhausted and injured to be frightened.

"Is he dead?" one of the ghost dragons asked.

"Maybe he's a ghost human," said the other, taking a claw and poking Dev in the side. Dev recoiled.

"He's alive," said the dark purple. He pursed his lips and blew a narrow stream of hot air, as if painting Dev's body in long, sweeping motions, paying extra attention to the bloody parts.

LISA McMANN

Dev lifted his head, squinted, and worked up the effort to speak. This dragon was familiar. "Drock? Is that you?"

"It is," said Drock when he stopped to take in a breath. "Do you suppose you can roll over? I can turn you if you aren't able to do it yourself."

"I—I can do it," said Dev. He preferred the dragon never touch him again if possible. Of the five dragons he'd tended to in the castle dungeon, Drock had been the most unpredictable and troublesome, and they'd shared a mutual wariness of each other. He struggled and rolled to his side, feeling a bit stronger already, though he wasn't sure why.

"That's far enough." Drock started to blow on Dev's back and legs as he'd done before.

The air felt scorching to Dev, but somehow comforting, too. And healing, if that were possible. "Are you . . . ?" He closed his eyes and drifted off to sleep for a moment, enveloped in the warm, magical dragon breath.

"There," said Drock after a few moments, startling Dev awake. "You'll be feeling better soon."

"How are you making me feel better?"

"I can heal the wounds I caused easily enough," said Drock.

He pulled back to take a good look at the boy and seemed satisfied. "When you're ready to walk, there's a cave nearby where you can find shelter. The river is there." Drock pointed with his tail to some large, smooth rocks and a line of trees not far away.

Dev blinked. His mind, still fuzzy, was having a hard time putting together what was happening. Wasn't Drock under the Revinir's spell? "Aren't you supposed to destroy me? Or eat me? The Revinir . . . the Revinir roared . . ."

"No, I won't eat you," said Drock. "And neither will the ghost dragons. They are the only ones you can trust." He stepped away as if to signal his imminent departure.

"Wait," said Dev, feeling desperate for answers. "What happened? I blacked out."

The dark purple dragon glanced worriedly over his shoulder toward the edge of the forest, then looked back at Dev. "I'd heard you were summoned to the castle, so I was keeping an eye on you when I saw you approach on the back of one of the mind-controlled dragons. I was concerned when you didn't leave, so I searched the castle exterior and discovered you in the tower. When the Revinir roared her command and threw you out of the window, I was circling below. I swooped in and caught you. And I carried you here to the cavelands."

Dev shook his head slightly. It was hard to imagine how he'd been lucky enough to survive. Luck didn't usually come his way.

Drock went on. "You'll be safer here than anywhere else, at least for a while. The ghost dragons will take care of you if they remember you're here—you must remind them if you need anything. But I know you are capable of caring for yourself once you're up and on your feet. Though," he continued, holding his face close to Dev, "there's an injury I can't heal inside your chest."

"My cracked ribs," said Dev.

Drock lifted his head and looked into Dev's eyes with sympathy. "Perhaps that's it." He edged a few steps away. "I recommend you stay here. Don't return to Grimere."

Gingerly Dev pushed himself up to sitting and took shallow breaths. "You're not under her spell."

"No."

"Why doesn't she affect you?"

"She does. Just not as much as she affects the others."

Drock glanced over his shoulder again and sniffed the air, then settled down on his haunches as the two ghost dragons who'd been there earlier wandered by. "I am in control of my mind so far, though I've been pretending to heed her call for my own safety. And for Thisbe's. And . . . now yours."

"So, go back to that," said Dev, his mind clearing a bit. "You saved me . . . intentionally? *Me?*"

Drock tilted his head and studied the boy. "Yes, Dev," he said quietly. "I told you I had my eye on you. To save you if I could. With the others gone, I knew you'd take the brunt of the Revinir's wrath. And she's going to continue to be very angry once she finds out she'll never legitimately rule this land. So I'm going to do what I can to help you."

Perhaps it was the intense trauma he'd endured, or the rare bit of warmth in Drock's voice that caused Dev's chest to tighten and his face to convulse. A tear leaked from his eye, then a small stream of them. He coughed and choked and curled up in a failed attempt to hold everything in and keep the pain from killing him. After a moment he caught the emotion back up inside him and wiped his tears on his ragged, blood-stained sleeve. Then he whispered, "Why would you do that?"

Drock seemed taken aback by the question. He lowered his chin to the ground to align with Dev's gaze, and the two faced each other on the rolling hill for a long moment. "Because you're on your own, like me," he said. "And because you deserve to be saved."

Surprise Attack

Two by two, the teens and adults and statues who could fit into the jungle tube went inside, pressed a button, and disappeared. Even Sky went along, though she'd be stuck in the secret hallway, unable to go out with the others who were magical enough to see the exit to the balcony. But she could at least get the scoop for Florence and report back, since the Magical Warrior trainer was too large for the tube.

Soon only Florence remained to watch Ava and Lukas in the jungle and anxiously await Sky's report. While she waited, she consulted with Panther and the rock about what was happening

LISA McMANN

in Artimé, giving them a little more background on the events that had led to Frieda and the dissenters' rise to power.

The others arrived via the tube to the slightly secret hallway kitchenette, which was across from the head mage's office. Like most people in Artimé, Frieda Stubbs couldn't access anything in that hallway, which gave this minority group some wry satisfaction in this dark time.

They filtered out of the kitchenette into the hallway and grew somber as they crossed over it and stepped into the office. It had hardly been touched since Alex's departure to the land of the dragons. The desk held two neat piles of books and a stack of papers that had belonged to the former head mage. No one had been able to bear clearing things off since his death. Sky's face was drawn as she remained by the door and peered at Alex's things while watching the others mill around.

Fifer touched Sky's arm, and Sky gave Fifer a small smile. "Shall we start by gathering components?" Fifer asked, leading her a few steps inside the office. "I know where some are."

Sky swallowed hard and nodded. "I can bring the extras back to Florence," she said, pointing to the deflated rucksack on her back. Her eyes strayed to Alex's desk.

"Great," said Fifer. She hesitated, eyes filling, then blinked hard and continued a few steps farther into the room and looked around. Sky followed. Everyone was quiet in the absence of their great former leader, missing him even more now. What would he do in this situation? Certainly he would fight for the mansion, to preserve Artimé—there was no doubt about that. They all knew it. They moved with purpose, but each one paused here or there, by the desk or a chair, or near Alex's beloved, haphazardly piled books and artwork from his earlier years. Remembering their friend.

"Did Alex ever draw a 3-D door to the theater?" asked Samheed.

"No," said Lani. "He didn't need to. We always used the one Ms. Octavia drew."

"And now Frieda has stolen it," said Ms. Octavia passionately, her glasses bobbling as she wrinkled up her alligator snout. "Technically it's my property."

"We'll get it back," said Aaron. "I promise."

Ms. Octavia folded two of her octopus arms over her chest and muttered something under her breath. They all began to gather up everything useful they could carry in their packs,

LISA McMANN

for they weren't sure when they'd return . . . if ever.

Fifer felt a pang cross through her, thinking Thisbe might never have the chance to see this. She closed her eyes. Things were so unsettled with Thisbe. Would Fifer's twin ever come back? Was she okay? As focused as Fifer was on this task, her mind strayed to the fights and misunderstandings between her and Thisbe. Things were bad, but Fifer felt powerless to do anything. It seemed like Thisbe was the one being distant after she sneaked off without telling anyone but Aaron.

When they finished in the office, Lani took the lead, rolling down the hallway in the direction of the mansion's balcony, which overlooked the entryway. "Did Alex leave an extra robe up here anywhere? We might want to take possession of it before someone else does."

"Yes," said Fifer. "Florence told me there's one hanging in his living quarters."

"Good to know. Alex stored even more components in there. I suppose we'll have to go in after them." Lani's expression was grim. Going into the office was one thing, but entering Alex's personal apartment felt so . . . invasive. And sad. Lani had kept her emotions in check so far, because of the severity of the task before them, but this wasn't going to be easy.

Lani stopped in front of Alex's door and peered out toward the main mansion, looking for any sign of Frieda or the dissenters. "Be careful not to get too close to the balcony," Lani said over her shoulder. "I'm not sure if anyone in Frieda's group is magical enough to see into this hallway, but if they are, we don't want them to know we're coming." She hesitated, then added, "I really wish Florence were here. I'm worried we're not going to make much of a splash without someone big on our side."

Aaron frowned. "We'll do what we can. Attack to let them know we won't go quietly, then retreat to the jungle to plan our next move. All we need to do right now is let Frieda know she's not going to take over unopposed. And hopefully bring some of the more reasonable people back to reality and open their eyes to what's happening." He glanced across the hall from Alex's apartment at the door to the Museum of Large. While Lani went into the living quarters with Samheed, Carina, and Sean, Aaron touched Fifer's shoulder. "I can't stand to go in there just yet," he said to her in a low voice. "Let's check something out in here."

Fifer nodded, relieved to not have to enter Alex's room and experience all the sadness there. She followed Aaron. The Museum of Large was a lovely storage place. True to its name, it housed large things that couldn't fit anywhere else, like the gray shack that was now reassembled after it had exploded, as well as Mr. Today's personal library, which Lani had painstakingly organized once Artimé was finally at peace. A pirate ship rested nearby too—Alex had put one up here as a spare, a precaution in case their other ships were ever stolen or sunk by enemies in the future. He'd prepared them for almost everything imaginable except his death.

Once inside, Aaron headed for the gray shack while Fifer searched the room for weapons and spell components. Finding neither, she stopped in front of a large frozen statue of a mastodon. His name was Ol' Tater, and he was the only frozen statue in Artimé because he was so destructive and dangerous. Mr. Today had created him many decades ago but sadly had to put him to sleep and keep him in the Museum of Large. The beast occasionally came to life—sometimes by accident when the world was restored after a head mage's death. Other times he could be awakened when Artimé needed him, as when the pirates and Queen Eagala had attacked the island of Quill when Fifer and Thisbe were two years old. To put him back to sleep, one needed to perform a singing spell.

"We could definitely make a statement with Ol' Tater," Fifer remarked to Aaron when he started heading back to the hallway.

"That thought crossed my mind." Aaron paused. "He's so unpredictable, though."

"True," Fifer admitted. "He could come after *us* —that's the last thing we need."

They exited the museum to find Lani and the others finished in Alex's living quarters and tiptoeing toward the balcony.

"Is anyone there?" Fifer whispered, catching up to Lani.

"Not lingering outside the hallway," Lani said. "It looks like they're all downstairs at the windows and doors, looking for us."

"This is our best chance to surprise them," said Aaron. "Let's talk strategy."

The group sketched out a plan of attack while Lani divvied up the spell components she'd gathered from Alex's apartment.

She handed Alex's extra robe to Sky. "Can you bring this back to Florence?"

Sky took it. She shook out the wrinkles, then lovingly folded it. She held it to her chest and crossed her arms over it. "I wonder if the best place to keep this is in Florence's quiver," she mused. "That way we'll always know where to find it, even if Florence gets frozen. And Frieda won't think to look there."

"That's a brilliant idea," Fifer said, and the others nodded.

Sky gave them an encouraging smile. "I'll watch you all go, then head back to give Florence a report."

Lani nodded and looked at Aaron. "Are you ready?"

Aaron nodded. "Is everyone clear on the plan?"

The group expressed their affirmation. Aaron and Fifer led them to the opening.

To Sky, it appeared like they were all standing up against a solid wall. But she'd been up here before, and she knew they didn't see it—they could walk right through it as if it wasn't there.

On Aaron's command, with Fifer and Lani right beside, they slipped through the wall and disappeared. When everyone was gone, Sky pressed her ear to the wall, but she could hear nothing. Then she stepped away quickly, realizing anyone with the magical ability to see the hallway would be able to see her, too.

After a moment, she retreated to the kitchenette. Still carrying the robe and her now-bulging rucksack full of components, she entered the tube and pressed the button that would take her back to the jungle.

It would be quite some time before she and Florence discovered what happened next.

A Critical Mistake

Fifer, Aaron, and Lani burst through what looked like a mirror to most of the people on the other side of the not-really-a-secret-anymore hallway. The rest of their team was right behind, and before the dissenters could react, Fifer and the others began to fire spells over the bannister. After the first round left several dissenters flattened, frozen, or pinned to the wall, Fifer and Aaron charged halfway down the stairs yelling "Run!" and "Get out of the mansion, quickly!" to try to confuse Frieda's followers. Some of them didn't hesitate to leap out of the broken windows and through the doors.

Others in the surprise-attack group followed to back up the leaders, firing spells as they went.

Fifer didn't see Frieda Stubbs, but one of Frieda's top dissenters was surprisingly quick to react. "There they are!" she shouted. "On the stairs! Get them!" She fired freeze spells, and the rest began doing the same, some of them rushing all together to barricade the bottom of the stairs so Aaron's group couldn't advance. Florence had taught them well.

Aaron and Fifer dodged the first round and fired more spells as they pressed forward, using the parts of the railings that still stood as cover. But Frieda's people swarmed the main floor around the stairs, finding the open spaces and taking aim. Right behind Fifer, Carina was hit by a freeze spell, and she fell into Aaron, knocking him off balance. Then Samheed and Sean were hit, and they tumbled down a few steps. Fifer darted and scrambled to release the spells so her teammates could continue fighting, but as soon as she released them, they were struck by more. Then she was hit by scatterclips and went flying back, stacking Carina and Ms. Octavia behind her, all three sailing to the balcony and sticking to the wall between the girls' and boys' hallways. Seth quickly ran up and released

LISA McMANN

them; then he, Fifer, and Carina charged down the stairs again, firing spells as they went.

Ms. Octavia descended a few steps but preferred to stay near the top of the staircase so that she could employ all eight of her tentacles in various directions. Two or three tentacles she used to power herself forward and dodge the flying components. With the rest she sent clay shackles and various confusion spells down the stairs on both sides.

More dissenters came together at the bottom of the staircase, making an impenetrable mass. Soon they began to climb, forcing Aaron and Fifer to retreat in order to find new cover in the curve of the bannisters. Other dissenters emerged from the various classrooms on the main floor and forced the attacking party to retreat up the steps even more.

Just as Fifer was about to call her people to retreat and escape back down the secret hallway to the jungle, a group of dissenters, with Frieda Stubbs among them, flowed out from the second-floor living quarters onto the balcony. They blockaded the top of the steps, trapping the attackers on the stairs.

To Fifer's chagrin, she and her team were stuck in the kind

of trap Florence had warned them about time and again. But this was the first time they'd actually fought against people who were also trained by her. All they could do was fight their way out of it. Spell components filled the air like a bizarre and colorful blizzard. People and statues dropped left and right. The scramble to release the spells was equally dangerous as fighting, for taking one's eyes off their foes, even for a split second, could mean death if a dissenter chose to use a lethal spell. Fifer knew Frieda could try to put an end to her or Aaron at any second.

Now fully surrounding Fifer and Aaron's team, the dissenters worked together to send dozens more freeze spells at them. There was no place to run or hide, and several in Fifer's group were hit. One spell whizzed by Fifer's ear and struck Aaron. He froze on the spot and tumbled down the stairs, and others were hit and piled on top of him.

"Aaron!" Fifer cried out, and dove down after him, firing more components with one hand. She released the spell on him and squirmed again to avoid another wave of airborne components. Aaron revived, then was immediately hit again.

LISA McMANN

"No!" screamed Fifer. It was hopeless. Fifer whirled around and saw that she and Seth were the last ones standing, and the parties at the top and bottom of the stairs were advancing toward them. Seth and Fifer exchanged a frightened glance as they both realized just how much trouble they were in. As others of their party, all frozen, slid and tumbled down the stairs, Fifer abandoned her attempt to release the spells and instead let out a loud shriek.

Frieda and the dissenters paused to cover their heads, but all the glass in the entire mansion was already broken. Instead, flocks of red-and-purple falcons came soaring in through the windows. Shimmer and a few others carried the hammock by its ropes. Seth took the momentary reprieve to release spells on Carina, Sean, and Ms. Octavia, but as soon as he finished, more components came soaring at them again.

"Come on!" Fifer yelled to Seth and anyone else who remained standing. She dove into the hammock and scrambled around to make room, staying low so she wouldn't get struck.

But Seth and the others didn't come. After an agonizing second, Fifer peeked out and saw that they were all frozen, and Seth had been hit by a freeze spell *and* shackles. Now everyone on Frieda's side was trying to launch components high enough to arc and land in her hammock.

"Retreat!" Fifer called out to Shimmer. There was nothing else she could do. The birds took her out of the mansion, and Fifer pelted as many dissenters as she could on her way. As the falcons carried her through an upper window, she could see that the dissenters were storming the stairs. They picked up and dragged the frozen bodies of Fifer's friends over to the single tube that was still functioning.

"Circle around and stay close to the mansion!" Fifer commanded the birds once they were outside. "I need to see what they're doing." Through the windows as she passed by, Fifer could see Frieda's people stacking two or three frozen friends into the tube at a time and pushing a button. Fifer breathed a sigh of relief—at least they weren't trying to hurt them. But then she looked closer to see which buttons they were pushing. They were sending her friends to the library and the lounge, which seemed very strange. As each couple or three-some disappeared, the dissenters loaded more frozen bodies inside.

Growing more distressed, Fifer circled around again,

staying high up and peering through the second-floor windows of the entryway, trying to understand what was happening. Finally the last of her friends were being stacked and sent to the library. "What?" she muttered. Were there people down in those remote rooms to guard them or something? Was this just a way to contain them?

Frieda, who'd retreated to the hallway when the fighting got rough, reappeared and came thundering down the stairs. "Destroy the tube!" she shouted when the last bodies disappeared. She produced magical sledgehammers and handed them off. A few dissenters cast the spells, and the magical sledgehammers began pounding the control panel, sending bits and pieces flying. Soon the whole tube began rocking off its base.

Fifer gasped. "What are you doing?" she cried. "Now there's no way for them to—" She clutched her head as she realized what Frieda had done. On purpose. "No!"

Frieda Stubbs had trapped all of Fifer's friends and team members in the remote expansions of the magical mansion, just like she'd trapped Simber in the theater. Only this was much more serious. These were humans who, unlike Simber, needed food and water to survive.

With Florence and Sky far off in the jungle, Fifer was the only one left to show Frieda Stubbs that she wouldn't get away with this. But as the grim realization of what had just happened came over her, Fifer began to panic.

One Small Victory

Fifer wasn't sure what to do. If she retreated now with the birds, would Frieda Stubbs feel even more emboldened? It seemed like that would make this already horrible situation even worse.

And what about all of Fifer's friends who'd been frozen and sent to magical rooms with no way to escape? How was she going to get them out of there? They would thaw naturally in a matter of minutes, so being temporarily frozen wasn't the problem—being trapped forever in the library and lounge definitely was, though. "Think, Fifer," she muttered as she flew around the perimeter of the mansion.

The people in the lounge might be able to survive for a while with the food and drink to be found there, so that was a bit of a relief for some of them, at least. But what about the ones in the library? They'd have plenty of books to read to pass the time, which normally was sufficient in Fifer's mind. But there wasn't any water or food in there. How long would it take to repair one of the tubes? And how long would it be before Fifer or anyone else could get to it so they could try? This was a serious problem

Fifer and her birds circled the mansion again, staying just out of range of the dissenters' spell-casting ability, as she struggled to figure out what to do. What would Alex do? Or Aaron? Or even Thisbe?

"*Spirrr!*" sang Shimmer, sounding urgent.

Fifer looked at the bird. "What is it?"

The falcon pointed its beak at one of the windows.

Fifer focused in that direction, not sure what she was looking for. And then she spied a tiny white spot on the sill. "Is that Kitten?"

"*Spirrr!*" said Shimmer again, and jabbed its wing in the same direction.

LISA McMANN

"Something else?" Fifer stared past Kitten through the window. There on the floor, forgotten in the melee, was the 3-D door drawing rolled up like a scroll. It looked relatively unharmed. "We have to get it," murmured Fifer. Her heart began to race. She commanded the birds to circle again while she searched her spell components, trying to figure out her best options for this stealthy, dangerous move. If Fifer got nailed by a spell and captured like the others, Florence and Sky would have no idea where everyone had gone. But if Fifer could get the drawing, they could at least free Simber to help them. And they needed help now more than ever. She had to succeed.

Fifer looked closer at the white spot on the windowsill. "It *is* Kitten!" she whispered to Shimmer. "She must have snuck out of someone's pocket when they were being sent to the remote rooms. We have to save her, too."

It was settled—Fifer had to get the 3-D drawing. But it was going to be a precarious situation. They'd have to swoop in through the large side window, and Fifer would somehow grab Kitten without getting hit by flying components, then jump out of the hammock and grab the scroll. Unfortunately, from inside the hammock, there was no way Fifer would be able to lean out far enough to reach the floor—the sides were too tall. And she didn't trust asking any birds to pick it up, because if the drawing ripped or got poked through with beak holes, the door wouldn't work.

Fifer wasn't sure how she was going to do that without getting struck from all directions—especially knowing she had to leave the safety of the hammock. If she could at least get the 3-D drawing inside the hammock before she got hit, Shimmer and the other birds could take it to Florence.

They swung around, and Fifer saw the scroll was still lying unattended. But half of Frieda's dissenters were hanging out the windows and doors, staring at her and taking aim. How was she supposed to do this?

"We might have to go through the upper windows so their spells have less of a chance of hitting us," Fifer told Shimmer. "If we choose that route, can you send some of the falcons down to get Kitten before the dissenters discover her? That will also cause a distraction and allow us to swoop down and grab the 3-D door."

The head falcon let out a vocal agreement. Fifer pulled out the components she planned to use to clear a path. "Let's aim straight for Kitten's window. I'll start firing as soon as we get close enough. If I manage to knock everyone out of the way, we'll keep going. If more keep coming, we go to plan B. Got it?"

Shimmer bobbed its head and let out a command, and soon the entourage was soaring fast toward the window.

Fifer kept mostly hidden and protected behind the canvas hammock, and as soon as she got close enough, she began throwing handfuls of scatterclips at each person standing at the window. One by one they flew backward, banging into other dissenters and dragging them all the way to the opposite wall and pinning them there.

But it didn't take long for the opponents to react. From all windows, they flung components at the approaching hammock, knocking a few birds down in the process. Fifer ducked and waited to see which plan Shimmer would choose. As she sat, she noticed a small rip in the hammock fabric that was large enough for Fifer to poke her finger through. Blindly she started sending freeze spells, knowing there was no wrong target and hoping she landed some of them.

"*Spirrr!*" cried Shimmer. The army of falcons shifted sharply as components pelted the outside of Fifer's barrier. As she felt the birds rise, she pointed down, hoping she could knock out a few more dissenters. Moments later the birds continued forward through the upper window, and Fifer could see the elaborate mansion ceiling of the vast entryway not far above her. Gilded chains hung down with no chandeliers attached.

Fifer scrambled to her knees to peer over the edge of the hammock and send out a line of shackle spells, hitting several people from behind. "Did anyone get Kitten?" Fifer asked, but the birds were too preoccupied with navigating to respond. A few more of them were hit, and with each loss, the hammock dropped a little. With renewed fear for the birds as well as her own safety, Fifer shouted, "Hurry!"

Now, as the birds began to descend, the young mage pulled out her heart attack spells. She needed a serious spell that would also cause a distraction. She hated to use it on Artiméans because of how traumatic it was to experience, but she knew the people would be fine again in about fifteen minutes—as long as she didn't use three or more of them in one throw. This time she aimed at the people nearest the scroll, shouting "Heart attack!" with each toss. Neatly she took several of them down, and they began shaking and shuddering. Those around them came running to tend to them.

LISA McMANN

"Now!" Fifer said in a harsh whisper as she fired off even more.

Shimmer gave the command. Fifer rose to her feet as the birds swooped lower. From all sides, the dissenters sent off a variety of components, but Fifer dodged and ducked, avoiding them. The birds weren't so lucky, though—several more of them were hit by freeze spells. They fell to the mansion floor and dropped their ropes. Without warning, Fifer plunged down, hit hard, and rolled out.

With a frantic lunge, Fifer reached for the drawing and threw it into the hammock. Realizing she was too heavy for the few remaining birds, she commanded Shimmer to escape with the hammock. She put up a glass barrier behind her, which would stop some of the dissenters until they had a chance to release the spells. Then she released a component directly in front of her while dodging another round of fire. A green mossy carpet popped out before her. Fifer climbed onto it, commanding it to rise quickly, exit, and go to meet Shimmer in the jungle. The carpet shot forward and climbed up toward the upper windows while Fifer hung on to the edges for dear life.

Lying flat as the carpet rose to the ceiling, Fifer peered over the side. Components were still flying, some of them hitting the bottom of the carpet and falling back down, which thankfully didn't affect Fifer. "Please hurry," she urged it.

As they neared their chosen exit, Frieda Stubbs raced up the stairs to the balcony. "I told you all to capture the Stowes and bring them to me!" she hollered. "You messed up with Aaron, and now you're messing up with Fifer, too!" Before Fifer's carpet could get through the window, Frieda pulled three heart attack components from her pocket and launched them at the girl. The heart-shaped components sailed through the air. Midway they sprouted white, feathery wings to help them reach their target.

Fifer gasped. "No!" she cried. "What are you—are you serious? Help!" She pulled the corner of the magic carpet and curled it over her head to shield herself as the carpet lurched through the window and rose farther.

Two of the components found their mark. The third smashed into the window frame and fell to the floor, undetonated. Fifer, stricken with a double heart attack, felt an unbearable searing pain pierce through her chest and arms. She fell to one side and began to shake and shudder until she rolled right

LISA McMANN

off the carpet and dropped swiftly toward the lawn, unable to do a thing about it.

The carpet swooped down to collect its rider. At the last second it reached her, catching her convulsing body just in time before she hit the ground. It followed through on its instructions and carried Fifer away from the mansion, racing after the few remaining birds toward the jungle.

Trapped

Samheed, Fox, Ms. Octavia, Clementi, and Aaron woke up from being frozen and found themselves lying haphazardly just outside the tube on the main floor of the library. Aaron sat up and rubbed an egg-size lump on his head. He wasn't sure how he'd gotten it. He tried to figure out what had happened and how he'd ended up in the library, of all places. The last thing he remembered was fighting next to Fifer on the stairs.

But where was she now? He looked around frantically at the other four, then beyond them at the aisles of books. "Fifer?" he

LISA McMANN

called out, getting shakily to his feet. "Where is everybody else?" He began searching the vast room. "Fifer!"

No one answered, but Fox realized that his fighting mate was gone too. "Kitten LaRue is missing!" He began running in a circle and then stopped. "Kitten! LaRuuue!" he howled. There was no answer from her, either, which put Fox into a great depression. "We have to find her! Oh, I just know she's dead."

"She still has lives left," said Clementi distractedly, while testing her aching limbs to see if she was in one piece.

But her words didn't console Fox, and he began running around in a circle again, this time near the picture-books display, which was Kitten's favorite section. "Kitten LaRooo000o!"

"The others must have escaped," Clementi said to Ms. Octavia and Samheed. As Aaron returned to the group, Clementi got up and went through the shadows to the tube, then paused at the opening and glanced back at the others, who were getting up too. "Should I try it? What if they're waiting to ambush us outside the main tubes in the mansion?"

Samheed walked over while pulling a few components from his vest. "We could just surface quickly to take a peek, and then immediately push the button to come back here," he said.

"That's a good idea," said Ms. Octavia. She searched the floor for her glasses.

"I'll go with you, Clementi," said Samheed. "Is that all right with"—he looked over the small group he was with, and his eyes flickered when they landed on Aaron—"everyone?"

Aaron gingerly touched the lump on his head again and grimaced. "Why don't you just go alone? If you don't come back, we'll have our answer."

Samheed shot him a dirty look. "Rude. But funny," he admitted.

"I don't think we have a choice," said Ms. Octavia. "We need to figure out what the status is and help if our friends are still fighting out there."

"Yes, that's what I was thinking—especially if they're still fighting," said Clementi. "They'll need us."

Clementi's urgency brought Aaron to the tube as well, and he felt sheepish for being snide to Samheed when things were in such chaos. "I'll go with you too, Clementi."

"We're all set, thanks," said Samheed, who stepped into the tube with the young mage.

"You guys need to knock it off," Clementi said. "You're both

LISA McMANN

being a distraction. This is serious." She glanced at Samheed. "Ready?"

"Yep," said Samheed.

Clementi pressed the button to the mansion. Everyone expected them to disappear, but nothing happened. She pressed it again. And again.

"It's not working," she said, peering at the control panel. "Does anybody have a magical highlighter?"

"Is there another button?" asked Samheed. "I haven't used this library since I was trying to foil Aaron, way back when we were thirteen—I prefer the one in the Museum of Large. Where can this tube take us? Individual rooms? Or just the remote spots?"

Ms. Octavia handed Clementi a highlighter.

"There's definitely no direct line to individual rooms from the remote places," said Clementi. She lit the component. "I've only ever gone to the mansion entryway from here. There's no other option." She bent to study the control panel and noticed gray words flashing on the black screen. "'System failure in primary tubes,'" she read. "'All social tubes are down. Shelter in place and wait for head mage.'" She reread it to make sure she wasn't hallucinating. "I've never seen anything like that."

Fox stopped running and joined them. "What?" he said with a whine. "We're doomed?"

"Let me see, please," said Ms. Octavia, pulling Samheed out of the tube. Clementi stepped aside too and handed the octogator her highlighter. The instructor read the screen, then began pushing the button several times in a row. A light turned on, and the panel brightness increased, but nobody went anywhere.

Aaron came over and peered through the glass from the outside. "This is strange," he said lightly, but his face was alarmed. "Is there another tube somewhere in this library? On a different floor, perhaps?"

"No," said Clementi and Ms. Octavia together. "There are more floors," Clementi clarified, "but this is the only way out."

Aaron blew out a breath as he started to realize the vastness of their predicament. "We're trapped down here unless someone knows how to fix the main tubes, which we can't get to. And we're supposed to count on the head mage. Great. Does anyone here know how to fix the system? I wonder if we can do something from this tube to get things working. I . . . I fixed the one on the Island of Shipwrecks, but this is a different situation."

Samheed looked dazed. "Lani might be able to finagle something, or at least find the right book on it. Or Claire. But . . ."

"But what?" asked Ms. Octavia.

"What if they don't know we're in here? What if they don't think to test our tube?"

Clementi's eyes widened. "So they might not know to reset this one? Is that how the tubes work? Each line has to be tested?"

"I don't know," said Samheed apologetically. "I'm just . . . worried. I don't like to be trapped. It brings back bad memories." He dropped down into a nearby chair and put his head in his hands.

Aaron studied the panel, which was completely intact. There were no necessary parts to connect like in the one on the scientists' island, which is the kind of fixing Aaron was good at. This tube control panel wasn't broken—it was the main tubes that were causing the problem. Was there anything Aaron could do from here? It didn't seem like it.

"I'm not sure how we're going to figure this out," said Aaron. "And I have no faith in our head mage to be able to fix it, or to come to our rescue even if she managed to. Where do we start?"

Samheed looked up. "I wonder if there's a way to override the error from here. Again, none of us know the answer." He rose from the chair and postulated, "It has become clear to me that Artimé has a flaw that has been exploited. Nobody seems to have a clue about how these tubes actually work."

Clementi smirked at the theater professor and said sarcastically, "If only there were a place we could go to look for information."

Aaron turned to her. "What?" And then: "Oh."

"We're in the library," Clementi explained for the ones who weren't tracking with her. She took the highlighter back from Ms. Octavia and started looking at the walls, trying to find the master light component. "There's bound to be something in writing about the tubes on one of these three floors, don't you think?" She stopped near the stairwell and touched a small button on the wall. "Illuminate," she said, and the room burst into brightness, lighting up thousands of books.

"Well, that's a point I hadn't gotten to yet," said Samheed, though he flashed an embarrassed grin at Clementi. A memory struck him, and he turned to look at the sign that pointed out what subjects could be found on each floor. He studied

LISA McMANN

it. "There are loads of maps up on the third floor, I remember. Perhaps there's a blueprint of some sort that will give us some insight." He started up, and then stopped abruptly and turned to the others. "There's also a lighted drafting table up there. Alex used it to work on his first 3-D door." He paused and looked curiously at Ms. Octavia. "Is there any chance you could replicate a 3-D door from memory?"

"Which door?"

"Any door that'll get us out of here."

Ms. Octavia lifted her snout, thinking hard. "I highly doubt it'll work. 3-D doors are extremely difficult to get right even when you have a picture for reference. And it could take days of work before we know if we're successful." She tapped her jutting chin. "But then again, we also don't know how long we'll be stuck here."

"Exactly," said Aaron in a low voice. "So I say it's worth a try."

Ms. Octavia nodded and set her glasses on her snout, then headed for the stairs. "No time to waste."

A New Dilemma

Fifer, still weak and shaking from the heart attack spells, sat up somewhere in the jungle, her magic carpet already gone with a *poof*. The hammock was on the ground nearby with the 3-D drawing still rolled up and sitting in the middle of it. A few birds perched above in the trees. After a moment of simply breathing, Fifer tested her arms, pressing her palms into the soft, mossy jungle floor, then pushed herself up. She stood, then picked up the drawing and began limping slowly through the jungle, trying to find a path, and pausing now and then to catch her breath. Her knees continued to quake from her near-death experience.

LISA McMANN

It was surprisingly hard for Fifer to wrap her mind around the fact that Frieda Stubbs had tried to kill her. Sure, there had been threats. But this was a solid attempt, and it made Fifer wonder if the woman had truly gone crazy. Frieda had launched three heart attack spells at Fifer without so much as a blink. That made her inhuman in Fifer's mind. Fifer didn't really know what had happened after the first component had struck her. But the coldness of the act was chilling—someone from Artimé, an Unwanted, had tried to kill her. *Her*. It was a good thing Frieda hadn't noticed that Aaron had been sent through the tube with the others, or she might have gone after him, too. Frieda Stubbs had gone from reckless to dangerous. And she was leading people in that direction right along with her.

Kitten was fine. One of the falcons had scooped her up from the windowsill and carried her out to where Fifer's magic carpet had run out of steam. Now the tiny white cat nestled on Fifer's shoulder, purring as she slept. But Fifer was far from content. Everything was in an uproar. When her mind cleared, she stopped for a moment to examine the drawing that she'd risked so much to procure. Luckily, it appeared unscathed, despite the battle raging around it. Satisfied, Fifer continued, carrying it carefully under her arm. They needed Simber now more than ever . . . as long as he was actually their ally.

Above the treetops, Shimmer flew with the rest of the falcons that hadn't been struck by freeze spells. They carried the empty hammock. Slowly their numbers grew as the spells they'd been hit with wore off. Those who hadn't been injured, killed, or captured in the mansion battle rejoined the flock.

Fifer felt physically miserable, but she didn't want to tax the birds so soon after they'd been traumatized, so she didn't call for the hammock. Being hit by two heart attack spells had been one of the most painful experiences of her life. The effects lingered longer than with a single hit, which she'd experienced once before in warrior training. Each step she took sent pins and needles radiating through her. It had been such a close call, and her mind kept circling around the question: What if the third component hadn't somehow missed her? Would she really have died?

Death was tough to think about. And while she was unfortunately familiar with the deaths of others by now, it didn't seem real that Fifer herself could have actually been so close to it. Being extraordinarily magical, she felt invincible most of the time. Maybe it was foolish to feel that way. She'd had her share of near misses too.

She also wondered if it was Frieda Stubbs's poor magic skills that had saved her. Fifer viewed the heart attack spell with a new reverence now, and she knew she'd be way more thoughtful in the future when launching that one at anyone who had a shred of goodness in them.

Slowly Fifer's strength returned. She spotted the path she needed to take that would lead to the area where the rock lived. She picked up speed. What was she going to tell Florence and Sky? And poor Ava and Lukas, who would be waiting for their parents and Seth to return—how was she going to explain to little children what had happened?

This whole surprise attack had been a big mistake. They'd underestimated Frieda and the dissenters. And they'd gotten trapped on the stairs, which was so amateurish that Fifer didn't even want to tell Florence that part. They'd made the false assumption that all of Frieda's people were downstairs because of the meeting. Not one of Fifer's team had thought to keep watch behind them, just in case—either that or they'd all thought someone else was doing it. Fifer muttered angrily under her breath and stomped the jungle path, bringing the pins-and-needles feeling back. She hated making mistakes. She wouldn't make that one again.

The jungle grew shadier, and Fifer knew she had to be getting close. Florence and Sky would be so shocked to see that she was the only one who had escaped. She was pretty sure that all of their friends were trapped indefinitely, but at least they'd be able to get Simber out soon, now that they had the drawing. He would be a huge help. Their biggest hope. He had to be.

Without warning, Fifer stumbled on a vine and plunged forward. Kitten and the 3-D drawing went flying, and Fifer face-planted on the jungle floor. "Oof," she muttered. She caught her breath, then pushed herself up, arms shaking again. "Are you okay, Kitten?" she asked, wiping the leaves and dirt off her clothes.

"Mewmewmew," said Kitten sweetly, and ran up Fifer's leg to get back to her spot.

Fifer picked up the 3-D door, cringing as she examined it. The dirt shook off easily enough, but there was a small ripple and a tear in the paper. After everything the scroll had been through today, *this* was how it got wrecked? "Not good," Fifer said, smoothing the ripple but unable to do anything about the tear. "I hope we can fix it."

There was nothing more she or Kitten could do right now. A door with a little rip in it was better than no door at all. She continued on, finally making it to the clearing and the jungle tube where Florence, Sky, and Ava and Lukas waited, looking anxious after so much time had passed.

When they saw Fifer coming, they ran to greet her. "What happened?" Florence demanded. "Where's everyone else? Why didn't you come back through the tube?"

"Where's our mom?" asked Lukas.

"And dad?" asked Ava.

"Are you okay?" asked Sky.

"I'm okay," Fifer confirmed. Keeping the children in mind, she explained everything from the time her team left the secret hallway: Conducting their surprise attack, getting trapped on the staircase, and everyone dropping faster than Fifer could perform release spells on them. She told them how she'd escaped, and how she'd watched from the hammock as the dissenters sent everyone to the library and lounge and then destroyed the only remaining main tube that actually worked. "We were lucky Frieda wasn't present for most of it. When she showed up, she tried to, um . . ." She glanced at Ava and Lukas, then continued. "Tried to take me out permanently with three heart attack components." She paused. "Only two of them hit."

Florence was quiet. Her face fell with every detail. "I didn't expect this level of severity. Or this much organization," she said, beginning to pace. "How did you get trapped like that? You are all seasoned fighters. How many times . . . ?" She frowned and mercifully trailed off.

"We . . . made a mistake. We didn't think anyone was in the hallways on the second floor," Fifer explained, feeling the shame rise in her neck and face. "I guess we thought that since Frieda had recently been holding a meeting in the entryway, everyone would still be down there. So we were planning to do some damage and then retreat. But . . . that didn't go as planned. Everybody wanted to be fighting, not looking out."

Florence let out a deep sigh and shook her head. "Did I not teach you stubborn alpha mages anything?"

"But," Fifer said with a glimmer of hope in her voice, "I

managed to steal the 3-D theater door. Unfortunately," she added, "it sustained a small tear." Fifer chose not to mention that the rip happened due to her tripping over her own feet. She and the others were already looking incompetent enough in Florence's eyes at the moment.

"Good," said Florence. "How did you get it?"

Striving to get back in Florence's good graces, Fifer explained how she'd managed to steal it while still under attack. "I know it was a big risk, because if I'd been hit . . . well, among other unpleasant things, it would have taken longer for you to learn about what happened. I took the chance because we need Simber."

"That was dangerous," Florence said. "But I'm glad you did it. Having Simber back with us will be a big relief."

"Not that he's 'with' us, exactly," Sky warned. "He told Fifer and me outright that he works for Frieda now, and we shouldn't tell him things that could compromise him. He said he's bound by the constraints of magic that Mr. Today instilled in him, and that he must be loyal to the head mage. I'm not sure that's something he can change—it's just ingrained."

Fifer looked troubled. "Well, sure, that's how he was made,

but this is a terrible mage. I would hope he could get over those feelings of loyalty to somebody who's not worthy of it. Won't his sense of right and wrong win out? I mean, he told Frieda he wouldn't hurt us. But he didn't say he would work with us, either. Do you mean we shouldn't even try to release him?" After all Fifer had gone through to get the 3-D door, she wasn't keen on doing nothing with it.

"I didn't say that," Sky said. "But . . ." She frowned. "Can we trust him to help us? Or will he be one more enemy? Florence, you'd know better than me."

Florence looked troubled. "Your concerns are valid, Sky. I find it a relief that he told Frieda he wouldn't hurt us. And her locking him up in the theater means she doesn't trust him, or else she'd certainly use him to fight us." She paused to think. "He's got to have some type of strength in him that will help him overcome his loyalty to Frieda. Something good inside him that senses what's right for Artimé and all of the people he loves. I mean, he knew better than anyone what Marcus Today intended this world to be. But now I'm worried." She hesitated and looked down, shaking her head slightly. "I can't believe I'm questioning my dearest friend. I've known him every day of my life."

"Simber wouldn't turn against us," said Ava decisively, looking up from her spot on the ground. "He couldn't." Lukas nodded sleepily in agreement, but they both looked scared. Sky knelt to reassure them, then invited them to sit down with their backs against a tree so she could tell them a story.

Fifer and Florence stood grim and unsure, talking through what could happen if they freed Simber. Fifer was overwhelmed by their tiny army. *If only Thisbe would return to help this land— her homeland!* Fifer thought. Then she felt a twinge of guilt, because that's exactly what Thisbe had done by going with the Revinir. But wasn't Thisbe able to return by now? Where was she? They needed help!

Finally Fifer threw her hands up in exasperation. "Look. If we can't fix the 3-D door, we won't be able to get to Simber anyway. So we may as well not stand here forever wondering. The clock is ticking on our friends trapped in the library. They won't have any food or water like the lounge people have access to. I say we chance it and free Simber first, because we're definitely not going to get anywhere without him."

Sky left the children to pick their favorite leaves at the base of the tree and returned to Fifer and Florence. "Do you know who's in the library?" she asked, her expression worried. "Did you see who they were sending there?"

"They didn't send as many there as to the lounge. I saw Aaron and Clementi. And Samheed. Maybe a couple of others."

Florence looked up. "Aaron and Samheed? Well, that'll be interesting at least. Forced to work together after that argument they had. I look forward to hearing that story once they're out of there."

"Here's hoping we can get them out," said Sky. "Do you have any more of those new send components so we can communicate with Aaron and the others?"

"I made a few more after the one I sent to Thisbe, but they're in Octavia's classroom," said Florence grimly. "I didn't think to tell the group to grab them for me."

"We wouldn't have been able to reach her classroom anyway," said Fifer.

"We also didn't expect to be separated like this," Sky said. She blew out an exasperated breath. "We have to figure out how to get everyone out of there."

"One thing at a time." Florence reached for the 3-D door

LISA McMANN

and unrolled it carefully to examine the tear. It went a few inches into the drawing, which meant the door wouldn't expand and rise off the paper to form a real door. "Okay," she said. "This is definitely a problem. Since we can't access the mansion to get supplies to fix this, the nearest place to find what we need is in Quill. And you're going to have do some serious searching to find art supplies there."

"We could break into Claire's house," said Sky. "I'll bet she has plenty."

"Great idea." Fifer emitted a short, shrill whistle to call for the hammock, then turned to Florence as her birds, now fully recovered, laid the canvas down and gathered around them. "Sky and I will take the hammock to Quill—it'll be faster. We'll meet you back here."

"Don't bother," said Florence. "We can't do anything with that door out here—there's nothing smooth enough to attach the drawing to. The kids and I will meet you at the old Quillitary building. We can use the exterior wall there. And while I work on fixing the drawing, you two and the children can get some sleep in the barracks. By morning I'll have a plan for our next move." Florence gave them a weak but encouraging smile.

Fifer and Sky agreed to the plan. They got into the hammock, and the birds took them up through the trees.

Florence, Ava, and Lukas watched them go. After a moment Florence turned and called out to Panther and the rock to let them know what to do next if summoned. Then she hoisted the children up, one in each arm, and started the trek toward the Quillitary grounds, each step causing the land to tremor slightly. Heavyhearted, she knew that even with Simber on their side, the small group of them who weren't trapped didn't stand a chance against an army so brainwashed they couldn't tell right from wrong.

Meanwhile in the Lounge

S eth went behind the lounge bar and tried to figure
out how to get the orange-cream dispenser to work.

"What are you doing?" asked Ibrahim in a hushed
voice. He didn't want to disturb Lani and Carina,
who were nearby, deep in conversation about how they were
going to escape their entrapment. Others sat in the booths
in small groups, brainstorming. Sean brooded by himself, no
doubt worried about Ava and Lukas.

"If we can't get out of here, we may as well eat something,"
Seth replied, jiggling a tap handle. It clicked and stuck forward,
and orange cream started pouring out onto the floor. "Crud!"

he cried, and Ibrahim ran for a tall soda glass and a towel.

Seth filled the glass, then pushed the handle into the upright position, stopping the flow. "That was easier than I expected," he said. "I could totally work here." He licked the sticky mess off the back of his hand and offered Ibrahim the first sip from the glass. "I used to help in the kitchen sometimes, you know. Thisbe and Fifer and me. We sent the room service food up the elevator to the proper rooms."

"I'm not sure that qualifies you to work here, but okay," said Ibrahim. "I mean, licking orange cream off your hand might be a bit of a turnoff to your customers." He slurped on the drink and nodded approvingly. "Are you any good at food design?"

"Food design?" Seth had never heard that term before, but he nodded. "Sure. I'm good at a lot of things. Pottery, um, food design, like you mentioned, and . . . other food-related things."

"Pottery is food related?"

"Obviously." Seth rummaged under the counter and brought out a ceramic serving bowl with fruit in it. "See? Pottery. Food."

Ibrahim's thick, tented eyebrows were the most expressive part of his face, and when he raised one, as he did now, his

LISA McMANN

skepticism was glaringly obvious. He grabbed a piece of fruit and polished it on his shirt.

"Hey, Seth, Ibrahim," said Carina. "Can you bring that fruit bowl over here? And anything else you can find. We need fuel for our minds to figure out how to get out of here."

Seth and Ibrahim searched the cabinets and found loaves of bread, nuts, and other snacks. Seth filled several glasses with the orange-cream drink and put them on a large round tray, then carefully brought it over to where Lani, Carina, and the others sat. There were close to twenty-five people and statues milling around.

"Has anyone figured out who's not here?" Lani asked. "Samheed, for one." She seemed a bit worried, understandably so. "Who else is missing from our team?"

"Fifer," said Seth. "And Aaron."

"Octavia's not here, is she?" asked Claire, scanning the room.

"No," said Henry, who was sitting with Thatcher and the rest of their family. "Clementi is missing too."

"What about Fox and Kitten?" asked the ostrich statue grumpily. "Everyone always forgets the statues."

Claire looked like she wasn't about to take any sass from the

LISA McMANN

ostrich, as she'd been the one to note Ms. Octavia's absence a moment ago. But Gunnar Haluki nudged her, so she closed her lips firmly and ignored the bird instead. "Does anybody know what caused the tube system failure? I can't even get Earl to surface on the tube's blackboard. I don't know if all of the blackboards are broken too, or if Earl is under Frieda's command not to speak to us."

"I was hoping you'd know how to fix it," said Carina.

"I have no idea how," said Claire. "This has never happened before."

"I assume something must have gone wrong with the main tubes," said Lani.

"Yes, it has," said Sean, looking up from his seat nearby. "Two of the tubes were already destroyed—did anybody else notice that when we were fighting? I was trying to figure out a new plan of escape and saw that the control panels were smashed."

"Monsters," Claire muttered. "Why did they have to destroy everything? What's the point in doing that? After everything Artimé has done for them—it's just absurd. And uncouth. My father would be horrified, and so hurt."

"It doesn't make sense, especially since they decided to take over the mansion," said Seth. "What good does that do? Talk about a lack of foresight. Now they're stuck with the ruins."

Sean smiled grimly. "And we're stuck in here."

"They had enough foresight to organize and trap us," said Ibrahim glumly. "Florence is going to be livid when she finds out."

"Where do you think the others are?" asked Seth. "I hope they're not . . ." His face turned gray. Alex's death was still fresh on his mind. What if Frieda Stubbs had killed Aaron and Fifer, like she'd threatened to do? Was that too far-fetched to worry about at this point? Would she really go through with her threats, or was it all just fearmongering blather? He could feel his chest tighten. *Where are they? And Clementi, too?* He couldn't think about it. "I really hope they escaped," he murmured. His stomach gurgled, and suddenly the thought of orange cream made him nauseous.

"I think they're fine," said Carina reassuringly, despite the worry in her eyes. "My guess? The dissenters probably just shoved our frozen bodies out of the tube into the piles we found ourselves in when we woke up. When they couldn't fit any more on top of the pile of people in here, I'll bet you any-thing they sent the rest to the theater or the library."

LISA McMANN

Seth gave his mother a grateful look. "I hope you're right." He took in a deep breath and let it out slowly. It was calming to have a new image to dwell on. Carina was always so good at sensing when Seth's anxiety was high and he needed help with it. But he was still worried. He had to focus on something else. "So," he said with another measured breath, "how do we fix the tube?" When nobody said anything immediately, he offered, "Remember, Aaron fixed one once. Maybe he's already working on it."

"No doubt he is," declared Lani with assurance she didn't feel. She pressed her fingers to her temples, massaging them as if she had a headache. Then she looked up. "Who's our best artist in here? Anyone especially good with drawing or painting?"

Henry glanced at Ibrahim. "Ib? You're pretty good."

"I'm better at dance," Ibrahim said, looking worried. "Why? What kind of drawing do you need?"

"A 3-D door," said Lani. "From memory."

Ibrahim stared. "I—we haven't started that in art class yet. I don't have the faintest idea about how to do it."

Lani patted his hand reassuringly. "That's okay. I didn't expect any of us could do that. It's very difficult. I figured it was worth asking."

"Here's hoping Octavia's already started on one," said Claire. "Wherever she is. But for now, I say we may as well get some sleep while we can."

Many of the others agreed, but Sean stayed seated at his table, staring listlessly at the tubes. Soon Carina joined him, and they sat together silently, feeling helpless and hoping their younger ones were handling everything okay.

Before Seth lay down to rest, he went over to his mother and Sean. "You know," he said quietly, "Florence is the best babysitter in all of Artimé. I speak from experience. Ava and Lukas are probably having a total blast hanging out with her."

Sean looked up, eyes glistening, and put his hand on Seth's forearm. "Thanks, Seth," he said earnestly. "You really know how to make a guy feel better. When did you learn how to do that?"

Seth glanced warmly at his mom, then back at Sean. "I dunno," he said lightly. "I must have figured it out somewhere." He left his mother and Sean to themselves and found a place to lie down on the floor, though he wasn't sure he'd be able to sleep. He may have eased Sean's fears, but now all Seth hoped for was to feel just as good about Fifer being alive.

Seeing Things

To Dev's great relief it was quiet in the cavelands, and the ghost dragons weren't the least bit fierce. They wandered aimlessly as if waiting for something that they couldn't quite remember. By nightfall, Dev was moving around and feeling a bit better, though his ribs still ached badly. He was strong enough to draw water from the river to drink, but fishing was out of the question. Every slight movement made some part of him hurt.

But at least he wasn't dead, he kept reminding himself. Eventually, when he grew hungry enough, he worked up the courage to ask for help with fishing from a passing dragon

LISA McMANN

named Astrid. She obliged without argument and said she'd deliver it to wherever Dev decided to sleep for the night. He found an empty cave nearby and watched for Astrid to come back so he could flag her down in case she forgot who she was bringing it to. When the ghost dragon returned with a nice plump fish, she started a fire for him with one breath so he wouldn't have to and left him to settle in and cook his dinner.

The peaceful environment gave Dev plenty of time to think about his narrow escape from death, as well as his predicament going forward. Did the Revinir think he was dead? He certainly hoped so. And would he stay here in the cavelands? While this sort of quiet boredom was nice for the moment, he didn't think he could stand it for long. But Drock had practically ordered him not to return to Grimere, and for once Dev felt strongly that he should not challenge that directive. Maybe it was the near-death experience that had him wanting to obey, or his increased fear of the Revinir now that he was back in control of his own mind. Or perhaps it was the compassion that the dark purple dragon had shown him. The memory of Drock's kindness warmed him. Dev wasn't quite sure how to accept that sort of gift, since he'd rarely seen such generosity directed toward him.

Eventually Dev's mind wandered to the images that had flashed before his eyes when he was falling from the window, which had been caused by the Revinir's roar. He'd experienced them a few times since taking the ancestor broth, whenever the Revinir sent out her call. But it always seemed like he'd been on the run and too busy trying not to get caught to contemplate them.

Not so, now. He had all the time in the world to think them through. The only problem was that he wasn't sure what the images stood for. He'd never seen anything like them before in his life that he could remember.

He'd heard Thisbe talking about this phenomenon briefly in the catacombs—before he went to sacrifice himself to give the others a chance to escape. And he remembered the first time it had happened—it was in the kitchen, around the time he'd recognized Thisbe was back working with him. Maybe he'd seen them before that, but if so, he didn't have any recollection of it. It was like he'd come back to life in that moment after Thisbe fed him the ancestor broth.

She'd saved him, really. He knew that. Saved him from being under the Revinir's mind control forever. She'd risked

LISA McMANN

coming back to Grimere, getting sent to the catacombs, and being taken captive again just for him. For the others, too, of course, but she didn't know them very well. And he could tell how glad she'd been to see him recognize her, which made him feel like he had a real friend for the first time ever, even though that feeling was short-lived. So him saving her right back? Well, Dev thought it shouldn't be feeling as bad as it did. It felt lonely, like his insides had been shredded by Drock's teeth too. Maybe the brokenness inside him that Drock said he couldn't fix wasn't his ribs after all. "It's just that they all left me," he muttered, staring at the embers of the fire.

He lay down on the hard ground. The images lined his mind, easy enough to pull up now that he had time to focus on them. The most intriguing one was that of a glorious palace, with five bulb-topped towers, one in each corner of the structure and the largest in the middle. The palace was shimmering and colorful, like something out of a storybook. It was boldly painted, purple and orange and red, and it stood slightly raised on a hill with inviting roads and paths leading to it from all directions, and lush grass and flowers in between. People strolled along paths through an orchard from a village nearby, and carts hurried up and down the roads. The scene looked so pleasant, like a place without any cares. Where no one had to worry about being punished for someone else's mistakes. Where friends were a normal part of life. Where food was abundant, and no one was excluded from eating it.

It seemed like a dreamland to Dev. Too good to be true. And certainly it was, for in the corner of the image, Dev could see a small flaming rock with a lengthy tail of fire in the sky, heading straight for the palace. One more thing that was too good to be true.

When Dev slept, he erased the meteor from the image in his dreams and wandered the land outside the palace, traversing the paths that led to the glorious entrance and waiting to be invited inside.

A Rough Landing

Gorgrun and Quince flew over Warbler during the second night and had the island of Quill and Artimé in their sights before dawn. They steered toward it. Their riders woke, having missed Warbler Island completely while they slept. Thisbe got up feeling agitated and anxious, with all of her worries multiplying the closer they got to Fifer in Artimé and the farther they got from Dev in Grimere.

But Thisbe had work to do, and soon she and Maiven had the others fueling up with breakfast and on their feet to practice breathing fire, work on their sword fighting techniques, and review the magical spells Thisbe had taught them. The former slaves were quick learners, and slowly but surely things were coming together. Thisbe's confidence rose when she could see her home island. Her scales tingled in anticipation, and she wanted to urge Gorgrun and Quince to fly faster. Florence would be surprised and pleased to see the small army she was bringing. Thisbe hoped they weren't too late to help.

As they approached the Island of Legends off the coast of Quill, everyone took a break to look down on the beautiful, living crab named Karkinos, who had a lush forest covering his shell. Thisbe, in a combination of both languages, described the scene before them. "There's a shiny rooster on the top of the tallest tree at the center of the forest," she explained, like a tour guide. "Do you see him glinting in the sunlight? His name is Vido. He shouts out weird wisdom quotes if you get close enough. And hidden in the trees are hundreds of drop bears. They are adorably cute but really dangerous. There's a smelly hibagon, too, but he stays hidden, because if you catch his gaze, you'll fall in love with him."

The team tittered with that revelation. Thisbe smiled and waited, then continued when they quieted. "Often on the

LISA McMANN

beach you'll see Lhasa the snow lion, and Talon the bronze giant, who is the caretaker of Karkinos the crab. But I don't see either of them right now. Oh, and Issie the sea monster! She's the mother of Isobel, who helped me and my friends return here safely through the volcano system. I've been trying to get them to find each other, because Issie keeps crying for her baby. It's really sad. But they don't seem to understand. Talon talked about going in search of her—I hope he has."

Maiven and the other children peppered Thisbe with questions, but soon her attention turned toward Artimé, and she faltered with the answers. She strained her eyes to detect what was happening, imagining all sorts of bloody battles going on across the lawn like she'd read about in Lani's books. But she could see nothing but the mansion and the fountains and the jungle. No human or statue activity, not any movement anywhere. They got closer, and Thisbe could see signs of past skirmishes, for sure—some of the grass was torn up, and piles of glass next to the mansion caught the light. She noticed Scarlet's skiff anchored in front of the mansion, which was uncommon, but not suspect.

"I wonder if the whole battle is over already," said Thisbe, her heart pounding. If so, what was the outcome? She rested a hand on the hilt of her sword and kept looking for any sign of life. While Thisbe never wanted to see any Artiméans in battle against one another, or discover that anyone had been hurt, this calm scene was almost disappointing—they'd come all this way at Florence's request. "If it *is* over," Thisbe mused, "it would have been nice of Florence to let us know."

The others eyed Thisbe, gauging her mood, and watched the island grow larger.

"Are you able to send Florence the new send spell?" Rohan asked. "Ask her what's happening? We don't exactly want to go flying in there with the dragons spraying fire if everything has been settled."

"No," Thisbe lamented. "I wish I could. When I sent my reply, the spell component went with it—my guess is it'll only come back to me if Florence replies to my response. If I had my own supply of send components I could start a new message, but it's a brand-new spell, just developed after I left." She paused. "Maybe she hasn't made any more components. I'm sure she's been busy."

Asha said something to Rohan in the common language

LISA McMANN

intended to be translated, but Thisbe thought she understood. "Are you wondering if I should send her the regular seek spell?" Thisbe asked. "I could, but that might be confusing—it's been known mainly as a call for help. I don't want Florence to worry about me right now, or receive a brightly lit spell that could give away her location in case she's in danger or hiding somewhere." She wrinkled her nose and studied the island as they drew close, trying to see through the mansion windows. She could barely make out the outlines of people standing just inside, not moving. "This is strange. They must still be fighting, but nothing's actually happening right now. Unless . . . it's over? But if the war is over, why is nobody on the lawn on such a beautiful morning? It's not normal."

Quince turned his head. "What is it that we are doing again?" he asked. "Is this where Pan lives?"

"No," said Thisbe patiently, for there was no other way to be with the ghost dragons. "Pan is back in the land of the dragons under the Revinir's mind control. When she's in this world, she lives one island farther east, the tall cylindrical one. We're here to stop a civil war on *this* island. Remember?"

"Oh, yes," said Quince. "Though I don't see a war. Where is it?"

"Um," said Thisbe, "I'm not . . . sure." She and Maiven exchanged a pained look.

"What shall we do, Thisbe?" asked Maiven gently. "This is your decision."

"I—I'm thinking." Thisbe leaned forward, knowing she had about ten seconds to come up with a plan before they'd actually be on top of the island. "Gorgrun and Quince, can you circle around please?" called Thisbe, feeling desperate for time to think. Certainly someone would have seen the dragons approaching by now—there was no way to sneak up on them. Where was Simber? The island was too eerily quiet and calm. Something wasn't right. Simber should be here. *Something wasn't right.*

Thisbe began to panic. "Be on your guard!" she shouted. "Prepare your spells, humans! Gorgrun, swoop in so we can get a better look inside the mansion, but don't land just yet."

"Do you want us to torch the structure?" asked Quince.

"No!" cried Thisbe, clutching her shirt. "Goodness. No. That would be terrible. Hold your dragon fire! Let's just swing wide around the mansion for a look."

LISA McMANN

Gorgrun complied with Thisbe's instructions, swooping low over the beach and lawn. As they passed the windows, Thisbe shaded her eyes, ready with components. She peered inside, trying to see if she recognized anyone standing there. Cries of fright rose at the nearness of these unfamiliar ghost dragons. "They're here! The evil dragon-monsters have come!" Through the noise, Thisbe heard a louder call to attack. Fearful dissenters launched components from every window.

"Look out!" Thisbe cried, but her warning came too late as three of her friends were hit with scatterclip spells. With nothing immediately behind them to stick to, the three sailed backward off the dragon and flew all the way to the fountain on the lawn, smacking into the sculpture and sticking there.

Rohan dodged flying components and sent a glass spell at one of the mansion windows, sealing it up nicely and forcing the person inside to find a new place to work from or take the time to release the spell. Thisbe peppered the visible dissenters with backward bobbly head, fire step, and pin cushion components, introducing all sorts of confusion and distraction into the mansion. They soared around the other side and did the same. One of the other children from Grimere managed to place a glass spell too, and earned high praise from Thisbe as the dragon rose out of range.

"Let's quickly grab the ones we lost," Thisbe called out to Gorgrun. "You can land on the lawn by the fountain. We'll be far enough from the mansion that their magic won't reach us unless they come outside. And if that happens, we'll see them coming. I'll release the spells on our friends, and we can figure out what to do next."

Thisbe was deeply puzzled and very worried. What had happened here in her absence? Where were all of her allies? She didn't recognize anyone in the windows. Where was Simber, for crying out loud? He was always at the forefront of battle. And Florence—the Magical Warrior trainer would never shy away from a fight. She was the lead. And what about Fifer and Aaron and Seth and the others? Were they hiding somewhere? Or had they somehow been . . . overcome? A sick feeling came over her. She couldn't lose Fifer the way she'd lost Alex. *Where is she?*

As Thisbe released the scatterclip spells and helped the three board Gorgrun's back again, she grew more and more alarmed about her missing friends. If they had been overtaken by Frieda

LISA McMANN

Stubbs and the dissenters, where were they? Somewhere inside the mansion? Or . . . dead . . . even the statues? Killed by fellow Artiméans? If not, what were they doing? Where had they gone? Were they in hiding? Had Thisbe and the dragons unwittingly bungled something?

Thisbe had a hundred more questions and no answers. "Let's retreat!" Thisbe called. Gorgrun and Quince thundered across the lawn and rose up over the water. "Circle the entire island, please. I want to have a look at what's going on elsewhere." Maybe they'd see someone they actually knew.

As the dragons left the dissenters hanging out of the mansion windows, watching the giant ghost creatures fly away, Thisbe ripped her fingers through her short curls.

"Perhaps we should torch the place after all," Quince called out in an upbeat voice. "It didn't seem like you cared about any of the people in there."

Thisbe stared at the back of Quince's head. "Didn't you tell me once that you couldn't cause the deaths of people?" she said. "That's what you told Rohan and me when you brought us to the castle the first time."

"That's only in the land of the dragons," said Gorgrun.

"Our motherland. That rule has to do with the black-eyed rulers and the dragons, and the way the rulership is transferred from one generation of dragons to the next. We cannot do the work for the next generation—they must prove themselves worthy by performing the takeover."

"Oh," said Thisbe, glancing at Rohan and Asha, who were nearest her. "That'll never happen as long as they're mind controlled."

"The Revinir is a dragon," Rohan pointed out. "And she has taken over."

"There's no way any of us black-eyed people would approve the partnership and pledge to work with her," said Thisbe. "The transfer can't happen until there are two agreed-upon leaders. Right, Maiven?"

"Correct," said Maiven.

It gave them some comfort. But it didn't diminish the Revinir's power.

Turning back to address Gorgrun's question about torching the place, Thisbe called out to him. "I'm not sure where my allies are at the moment, so I don't want to set any fires, in case they're inside." She didn't want to torch the mansion,

LISA McMANN

regardless, she added silently. The mansion was more than a home. It was a symbol of goodness. Of life and love and safety for children being purged from their families in the only world they'd ever known. Losing the mansion would be the end of something so many Unwanteds had come to find tremendous comfort within.

"Besides," said Thisbe, who was still justifying her decision, "the people who attacked us are Artiméans. They're our own people." She blew out a breath and looked down at the jungle, wondering if any of her allies were hiding there. "This is a very confusing situation," she added. "All of these people should be our friends. But now they're enemies. I don't understand what happened."

"War is strange," Quince said in a somber voice. "We've seen enough of it, haven't we, Gorgrun? Maiven? I remember that well enough."

"Indeed," Maiven murmured. Quince curved inland and Gorgrun followed. Soon they were flying above one of the four quadrants of Quill, casting vast shadows over the land and striking fear in the people who were out and about, apparently unaware of the strife in nearby Artimé.

Maiven approached Thisbe. "What are you thinking about?" she asked her quietly. "Is there any way I can help?"

Maiven's humble offer reminded Thisbe that the woman standing beside her was a great warrior. Thisbe had become so used to dealing with problems on her own that she'd nearly forgotten she had wisdom at her fingertips. She swiped her hands down her arms to resettle her scales as images swept through the back of her mind of the rogue usurpers and the battles in Grimere. "Thank you, Grandmother," Thisbe said. "I'll take any advice you wish to offer."

Maiven touched Thisbe's hand. "I think you're smart to circle the island. Is it strange that life seems casual below us here compared to your magical mansion area?"

"I think it points to the fact that Quill isn't involved in this war," Thisbe said. "They don't seem to know it's happening. That's not totally surprising—the two entities work independently."

"I see," said Maiven. "And what are we looking for?"

"Large statues. You know what Simber looks like. Florence is a very tall, muscular, ebony-colored stone warrior woman with a quiver and arrows on her back. You can't miss her."

LISA McMANN

"And you don't think they're part of the group in the mansion?"

"No," said Thisbe decisively. "Unless they're somehow being held against their will. I can't imagine how, though."

Both of them studied the ground below, looking for any sign of Simber or Florence or the others. Talking to Maiven had calmed Thisbe enough to think things through, but the fear for Thisbe and Aaron remained. She fingered a small folded drawing in her pocket, which Florence had scribbled for her when she was training. Then she pulled it out and opened it. "I think we need to risk sending a seek spell to Florence," she said. "At least that'll tell us where she is. I don't want to waste time searching the whole island if she's in the mansion."

"Are you sure? You said earlier that it might also worry her. Or reveal to others that you're looking for her, thus putting her in danger."

"It could do both," Thisbe admitted. "But the people who fired on us already know we're here. As for worrying her—well, that's the least of our problems right now. Besides, she knows we're coming, so she should be expecting us."

"Well thought out," said Maiven. "I say it's worth the risk."

With that, Thisbe made up her mind. She held the drawing, closed her eyes, and concentrated. A moment later a ball of light shot out and soared straight and true to a spot in Quill not far from the border of Artimé. Thisbe and the others followed the trail of fading light with their eyes, and Gorgrun started after it. Then Thisbe gasped when she saw a most peculiar sight.

"There!" Thisbe cried. "I see them! Gorgrun, Quince, head straight for that open area near the building, where that tall statue and four humans are dancing and waving."

A Grand Attack

The first person Thisbe saw was Fifer. Her heart caught in her throat. Her sister was alive! Relief flooded her, but the animosity between them immediately resurfaced. Fifer looked disheveled and didn't seem terribly pleased to see her. And while Thisbe was glad to see her sister, there were so many unsaid things between them that Thisbe couldn't deal with right now. Especially with a war at hand. She turned her gaze abruptly to Florence. "I'm glad we found you," she called out as Gorgrun came to a stop on the ground. "It wasn't easy."

"Thisbe! I'm so relieved you're here," Florence said as

everyone disembarked the ghost dragon. Quince landed several yards away. "I nearly forgot you were coming. I mean, I know you said you were on your way, but with everything that has happened . . . time has flown by, and it's been a little hectic trying to keep track of everyone." She came forward to greet Thisbe and meet the others.

Sky ran up to Thisbe and embraced her, giving her a kiss on the cheek. But Fifer's approach was less enthusiastic. The twins exchanged a measured glance. Thisbe nodded.

"Hi," Fifer said. There was ice in her voice. Thisbe had left in the middle of the night without telling her a thing about her plans. That, to Fifer, was on the verge of being unforgivable. That's not how the twins had ever been. To make matters worse, Thisbe had told Aaron she was leaving. What if Thisbe had been killed? It was terribly hurtful to Fifer, and while she'd been able to tamp down those hurt feelings while facing Frieda's dissenters, they all came bubbling back up now.

Thisbe averted her gaze and took a nervous step back, then noticed Ava and Lukas, who were cowering at Florence's legs and staring at the ghost dragons. It was an eclectic, small group in this remote place away from Artimé. "What are you doing

LISA McMANN

here? Where is everybody else? We flew by the mansion, and it was so strange." A pang of fear, like the one she'd felt when she and Sky had stumbled onto Alex's grave, shot through her. "Is Aaron . . . and everyone . . . okay? They can't all be . . ."

"We think they're fine," Sky said quickly. She glanced from one twin to the other, noting the cold greeting and stepping in to explain a few things to the newcomers. "Alive, at least. We believe they're trapped in the remote rooms of the mansion." She explained the attack and Fifer's narrow escape. "The dissenters sent our frozen friends to the library and lounge and destroyed the main tubes so they couldn't return."

Thisbe stared. "Destroyed the tubes? That's ridiculous! So they're holding our friends as hostages and keeping us out of the mansion?"

"Yes," said Sky.

"Simber too?"

"No," Fifer said, lifting her chin and keeping her eyes narrowed, not quite looking at Thisbe. "He's trapped in the theater."

"What?" said Thisbe, incredulous.

Sky shook her head. "It's a long story."

"How did things get to this point?" Thisbe exclaimed. "I can't believe this is happening in Artimé." She turned to look at Rohan and Maiven and the others. "This is not the home I described to you. It's not the peaceful, beautiful land I know."

"We understand," said Rohan. "Really. None of this reflects poorly on any of you." He and the other black-eyed children were well aware of hardships in their homeland, so they could relate.

"I should introduce everyone," said Thisbe. She'd forgotten with all the tension surrounding her. "Maiven, you remember . . . my sister." Thisbe realized Fifer had no idea that Maiven was their grandmother. She didn't feel like mentioning it at the moment, but neglecting to would only cause more problems with Fifer down the road. "Fifer, we have some interesting news—Maiven is actually our grandmother. We'll explain everything later, but . . . I wanted to be sure to tell you right away." She tried not to sound defensive, but it wasn't really working.

Fifer's eyes widened. "Grandmother?" she whispered. "What?" She looked at Maiven, and they greeted each other with an awkward handshake.

"We'll have a good talk later," Maiven said. "I know this must be strange news at such a stressful time."

Fifer nodded.

"And . . . you know Rohan, too," Thisbe said to Fifer.

"Of course," said Rohan smoothly. He smiled and greeted Fifer, then quickly introduced everyone else, including himself to Florence, whom he'd heard so much about.

"Wait a second," said Fifer, suddenly alarmed and dropping her cold demeanor. "Where's Dev? Is he . . . dead?"

"No," said Thisbe. "At least we don't think so. But he's captured." She quickly brought Fifer and the others up to speed on what had happened, and how they'd been forced to leave Dev behind. Thisbe's guilt over it was evident.

"I'm sure he'll be fine," Sky said kindly. "He's gotten through everything else."

"I hope so," Thisbe said. She looked at the ground.

Fifer remained silent, and Thisbe could feel her sister's eyes boring into her. Did Fifer blame Thisbe for that, too?

Seeing the rising tension between the twins, Rohan stepped in again. "How can we help you, Florence?"

Florence pointed to the wall of the abandoned Quillitary

building, where an enormous drawing of double doors hung. "I think we've almost got this working, and then we'll have one more important player on our team. I hope so, anyway," she added. "Thisbe, how are your drawing skills? Fifer and I have painstakingly fixed a tear in this drawing to make the 3-D door pop out so we can get to the theater, where Simber is being held. But I think a tiny bit of the ink needs to be touched up, because it still doesn't work."

"I'm not as good as Alex was," said Thisbe. "But I'm not bad. Let me take a look."

"The ripped spot is at the top right corner." Florence gave Thisbe some of the drawing tools that she'd swiped from Claire and Gunnar's house. Florence knelt and invited Thisbe to stand on her bent leg so she could reach the top of the drawing.

After climbing up, Thisbe peered closely at the knot of wood in the drawing that Florence pointed out. She didn't see anything amiss at first. "You repaired the tear really well," she said. "I can't even see it. But I think maybe some of the ink in one part of this knot must have become too thin in the process of the tear and repair." She studied it for a long moment, looking at it from multiple angles, then considered the utensils in her hand. She selected the thinnest pen with the softest brush and uncapped it, revealing a narrow, feathery tip. She touched it to her sleeve to test it—she needed to know how much pressure it would take and if it would bleed into the paper. If she added even the slightest bit too much ink to the door, it would be ruined forever.

"I have some scrap paper you can test on," Fifer said gruffly, digging in her pants pocket for it. "We found it in Claire's house. It's the same thickness as the drawing."

"Thanks," Thisbe said, taking it. She tested the pen on the scrap, making a few broad strokes, then lightening the pressure until she felt like she had the right amount of ink for the job. Sweat beaded on her nose. She could feel an intense need to get this right, not just to release Simber but to prove to Fifer and Florence and Sky that she was here to help, to rise above her fight with Fifer and defend their land. "Okay," she said after a while. "Here goes." She lifted her hand and watched it tremble, then set her lips firmly, mentally telling herself to get through this.

Holding the pen poised, she brushed the air a few times to get the stroke at this angle and height, and then, without stopping the motions, let the pen lightly sweep across the knot of wood. Only once, and then she pulled back, expecting the door to come to life and push out from the wall. But it didn't. The drawing remained two-dimensional.

Thisbe blew out a breath, then repeated the action while everyone else watched silently. The door still didn't change.

Had she overdone it? Or did it still need something? Without having memorized the theater doors, Thisbe wasn't sure. She was only going on instinct—how should this tiny part appear? It didn't look too heavy, so maybe the knot should be even darker? Thisbe wiped the sweat off her face as the others continued looking on with strained expressions. Then she brushed the paper once more, ever so lightly, and leaned back, whispering, "Come on. Come on."

This time the enormous double doors pressed out from the wall, nearly a foot thick. The handles and hinges pushed out even farther. Thisbe stepped back and lost her balance, trying to get out of the way. Florence steadied her and helped her jump to safety. Then the two took another step back together. It was a stunning sight to see a drawing come to life—especially one so large.

The people from Grimere applauded. They'd never seen anything like it.

"Nice work, Thisbe," Florence said.

"Thanks," she said. "I didn't think I'd be able to do that." She caught Fifer's glance and they both looked away, but not before Thisbe saw that Fifer's expression had softened slightly. "Open the doors," Thisbe said coolly. "Let's get Simber out of there. Everybody stand back! And don't be scared," she added to her newest friends. "He looks frightening, but he won't hurt you."

Fifer grabbed the handles, turned them until they gave a loud click, then swung them open, revealing the backs of the theater seats in the dimly lit auditorium and a long, wide center aisle running toward the stage at the far end.

Halfway up the aisle, facing them, was Simber. The snarl on his face melted at the sight of Florence and two of his favorite humans, Fifer and Thisbe, and behind them two enormous ghost dragons, curling their necks and peering, fascinated, into the space. But then Simber's expression became pained, because he knew there was no way that he could help them.

Persuading the Cheetah

Simber came toward them and stopped at the theater doorway. Florence, Thisbe, Fifer, and Lukas and Ava gathered around to greet him. The black-eyed friends of Grimere stayed back near the dragons, cautious of the stone cheetah. They didn't remember the time they'd seen him before, because they'd been under the Revinir's mind control. And even though Thisbe had told them not to be afraid, it was hard to convince themselves of that once they saw the winged beast.

Florence ushered Simber out, closed the doors with a heavy thud, then loosened one corner of the paper border. The 3-D

LISA McMANN

door flattened immediately. Florence pulled down the rest of it, rolled it up, secured it, and slipped it into her quiver on top of the mage robe that Sky had brought back from the secret hallway.

The group of Artiméans began to explain to Simber everything that had happened. But before they could tell him much, Simber put a paw in the air to stop them. "Rrrememberrr, I worrrk forrr Frrrieda Stubbs now. You shouldn't be telling me all of this."

"Please," said Florence with disgust. "She locked you in the theater on purpose, Sim."

"She's destroying the mansion," Fifer said. "She trapped our friends in the remote rooms. Simber, she started a war against our own people!"

Sky's eyes flashed. "How can you stay loyal to her? I can't believe you're saying this, Simber. I'm . . . Alex would be so disappointed in you."

Simber turned sharply toward Sky, her words clearly cutting into him. "I was crrreated to be the helpmate of the head mage of Arrrtimé," he growled. "That duty courrrses thrrrough me. I don't have a choice."

"Nonsense," said Fifer angrily. "That's not the only thing

you're made of. When Mr. Today created you, he infused so many good things into you. Courage, for one, and a sense of right and wrong. You can't tell me that those things are less important than your duty to the head mage."

"Besides," Thisbe argued, "do you really think Mr. Today intended for you to be loyal to someone who is destroying the world he created to save Unwanted children? Be real, Simber."

"The twins are right," Florence said. "And if you don't see that, or feel it inside, Simber, then I have lost all respect for you. You may as well go back inside that theater and wait for your new master to let you out."

"Too bad Frieda doesn't have the 3-D door anymore," Fifer remarked. "You'll be stuck in there for good."

Simber began pacing, stewing over the words, and his low growl crescendoed into a frustrated roar. "You don't underrr-stand!" he said. "This isn't something I can change. It's the firrrst law of my existence! Therrre is no debating it!"

Fifer stepped forward and walked with him. "Simber," she said softly. "Have you even tried to think of it a different way?"

"Yes, Simber," said Thisbe, moving to stand with Florence. "You know in your heart, whether you admit it or not, that

Frieda Stubbs isn't the rightful mage. Only someone with Artimé's best interests in mind should rule this world. That's pretty basic. If Frieda keeps going, there won't be anything left of it." She paused. "I never knew Mr. Today, but I can't imagine that he would want you to be loyal to anyone who wishes to destroy everything Artimé stands for."

Florence closed her eyes and shook her head slightly. "The wisdom and maturity in these young women is the only thing keeping me from putting this door back up and shoving you back inside that theater right now, Simber. They're being way more patient than I would be."

Fifer couldn't help glancing sidelong at Thisbe after Florence's observation, but Thisbe pointedly didn't look Fifer's way and instead stayed laser focused on Simber. They may have been both making sense, but they were far from together on it.

Florence put her hands on her hips and stared at her friend. "Now, Simber. Where do you stand? After all of that, do you still declare your loyalty to Frieda Stubbs?"

Simber turned sharply and kept pacing. "I need to think!" he muttered.

Florence hesitated and glanced at Fifer, who nodded.

"Let's give him a minute," Fifer said. She retreated to allow the cheetah time without her breathing down his neck. Florence and Thisbe followed, and they all stood stonily and waited for the cheetah to come to his senses.

The agony on Simber's face was clear. He had been governed by a strict set of rules from the moment Mr. Today brought him to life. Loyalty to the head mage was his strongest instinct. But it was true he'd been struggling with Frieda Stubbs ever since Aaron had handed the robe to her. She wasn't a true head mage—her takeover had been manipulative and underhanded. And she didn't have the good of Artimé in mind. Simber doubted that Marcus would have ever imagined such a situation in Artimé, but here they were. Still, a right-hand cheetah statue had to follow the rules that were instilled in him. Didn't he? What would disappoint Marcus more?

Simber had already pushed the boundaries when he'd declared to Frieda that he wouldn't hurt her Artiméan adversaries. He'd said it, then thought immediately that he'd gone a step too far. But who had truly put these strict rules in place? Marcus had never once lectured Simber about any of the cat's

LISA McMANN

duties. But he *had* come to him for advice from time to time. He'd trusted Simber's competence in making wise and thoughtful decisions. He'd trusted his instincts and his ability to discern right from wrong. And his tendency to show compassion despite his gruff nature. Mr. Today had valued those traits in Simber, while never once demanding that Simber must be loyal to the head mage above all. It was just something Simber felt. Perhaps the severity of that rule had been self-imposed.

If Marcus were alive, what would he say to Simber right now? What would Alex say? Simber stopped pacing and dropped his gaze as shame filled him. Sky had said Alex would be disappointed. And he knew deep down that Sky was right. Admitting that stung the most out of all the arguments they'd made. Simber's greatest fear was disappointing people who counted on him.

Artimé was counting on him now.

Simber closed his eyes as heartbreaking pain speared through him. Thinking about Marcus and Alex was almost too much for him to bear. He felt completely lost in his current position with Frieda Stubbs, which made the memories of his former mages all the more precious. It didn't take much thinking to know what they would have him do right now.

But the fact was still true that Marcus, perhaps errantly, had instilled him with at least some sense of loyalty to the head mage. And that would be very hard for Simber to push aside. Could he do it?

His mind echoed the thought: Artimé was counting on him now.

He would have to use every bit of everything else Marcus had given him: Compassion. His sense of right and wrong. Kindness. And he must think of his loyalty as one to Artimé rather than some random person who undeservedly wore the robe of the head mage.

It would be a struggle. Simber's mind turned to Drock the dark purple dragon. Drock was struggling in a similar way, he realized. Struggling to fight the call of evil. While Simber empathized with Drock, there was something comforting about having him as a kindred spirit. When everyone else was compromised, Drock had chosen the harder path, the more dangerous fight. He chose to struggle against the inner pull to join forces with the one who called on him.

But there was some relief in fighting too. Simber hadn't felt comfortable with anything that had been happening. He knew what Frieda was doing was wrong in every way. He knew she would destroy Artimé. And he thought he had no choice but to go down with her. Loyal to the end. The way he was created.

Florence spoke near him. "You have the power inside you to override something if it turns out that it was a mistake," she said softly. "Marcus would be so sad to see you struggling like this right now. He would have done anything he could to change it. What a weight it would be on his heart, that he was the cause of your pain in this terrible time."

Simber turned his head. He'd been so lost in his thoughts that he hadn't realized she'd come over to him. His best friend, Florence, showing him a path to ease his pain. A road out of this internal turmoil that should not have existed in the first place. He glanced at Fifer and Thisbe and sensed their pain with each other. What would Artimé be for them if he turned away now? *Alex would be so disappointed.*

Simber moved toward the girls, head bowed. Then he sank to his haunches and lifted his gaze, catching Fifer's eye and holding it. He raised his paw, curled it into a fist, and tapped it against his stone chest. "I am with you," he said.

Army of Large

In the Quillitary yard, with Simber solidly declaring his opposition to Frieda, Florence gathered everyone together to assess their strengths. They were a strange group: Simber with his large body and huge wingspan, Florence standing miles above the rest. Two colossal ghost dragons. A queen with more weapons than Florence had ever seen anyone carry at one time. A tiny kitten. Fifer, Thisbe, Sky, and Rohan, plus their friends from Grimere, who all had varying amounts of dragon scales on their arms and legs, looked antlike in comparison to the dragons and statues. And young Ava and Lukas, miniature fighters growing hungry and cranky,

LISA McMANN

forced to go along for the ride, for no one in the group could be spared to stay back and watch them.

Florence scratched her head as she surveyed them, trying to determine their best strategy.

"The pressure of time is on all of our minds when we think of our friends," she said. "And that is the number one goal in what comes next. But I don't think there's a way to reach them without taking back control of the mansion. What's the best way to do that? Swiftly and forcefully." She turned to Maiven Taveer, eyeing her weapons belts again. "I assume you fight?"

"Yes, Captain Florence," said Maiven, standing tall and gazing at the warrior trainer with grave respect.

"The others have had some sword training," Thisbe told Florence. "And I've taught them a few basics in magic—glass, invisible hooks, the seek spell. But don't forget we are all part dragon and can breathe fire. And our scales give us some measure of protection."

"Not me, though," Rohan chimed in, shoving his sleeves up and showing his bare arms. He'd removed all of his fake scales by now and was the most ordinary one of all of them by looks. "I haven't taken in any of the dragon-bone broth.

But I've had a bit more sword training than the others."

"I'm impressed you've accomplished so much training in such a short time." Florence checked the sun's placement, which was fast approaching overhead. She wasn't sure yet how this group was going to successfully form a cohesive army and take over the mansion. "I need some time to assess each new member of our team and think through our strategy," she said. "We only have one chance to get this right. I know our friends are trapped, and those in the library will be feeling the discomfort of being without water by now. But if we fail in our takeover, they'll never get out." She hesitated, then continued. "If you're willing, I'd like to give you a crash course in fighting defensively against mages. Maiven, will you and your team work with me? I assure you I have your safety in mind."

"We'd be honored," said Maiven. "That is why we came." Rohan quickly translated Florence's request to the others, and they eagerly stepped forward, in awe of the giant warrior.

"We'll start by having you show me what your strengths are," Florence said to them. "Please begin warming up while I talk to the Artiméans for a moment."

The people from Grimere moved to an open area of the

LISA McMANN

Quillitary grounds to prepare. Florence turned to address Thisbe, Fifer, Sky, and Simber. "You four . . . while I'm assessing the others, I'd like you to sneak into the mansion. I need some very specific books from the Museum of Large library."

"Sneak in?" said Simber with a snort. "Me? How?"

Florence picked up one of the sacks of components that Sky had brought her from the previous trip. "Yes. You, Sky, and the twins will enter the mansion through Alex's . . . um, I mean through the balcony off the head mage's quarters. Get every book you can find on the mechanical workings of the mansion. We're going to need them later. There are a couple of specific titles that you absolutely must find. I'll write them down for you." She took some of Fifer's scrap paper and jotted down a few titles.

Fifer shifted uneasily. Earlier she hadn't wanted to go into Alex's apartment, but now it looked as though she wouldn't have a choice. And she would do whatever she had to do to save the others. She steeled herself for it—this was too important a mission to let something like that prevent her from being her best.

But Simber was still puzzled. "How am I supposed to sneak

in? I'm impossible to miss. You said they have guarrrds at ever-rry window. They'll surrrely see us coming."

Florence passed the sack of components to Fifer. "Invisibility paintbrushes," she said. "Take extra with you for your return flight. There are plenty of those components in that bag, and that's with assuming Simber will need three or four to com-pletely cover him each time. We'll have to work together to paint him quickly so the spell doesn't wear off before you get there. You three can paint yourselves on the ride to save time."

Simber wrinkled up his nose. He'd never been painted invisible before. And while most of the components weren't strong enough to do him any harm because of his large size and makeup, this was a defense component no one had ever tried on him before. After a minute he shrugged. "Verrry well. It's a good idea, Florrrence."

"I know," said Florence frostily. She gave him a side-eye and he snorted, and in that moment it seemed like their friendship was back to how it should be.

But Fifer and Thisbe's wasn't.

"Let's go," Fifer said, and Thisbe nodded tersely. There was no time to address their many issues, and frankly neither had the desire to do so—not with so many other people's lives at stake. They needed to gear up for a most difficult battle. But would they be able to overcome their limited abilities and resources? Fifer and Thisbe didn't need to be friendly to work together on this task. But they also knew that they could get everything right and still lose. The mansion, their friends . . . their homeland. When put that way, this situation wasn't looking hopeful at all.

Back to the Drawing Board

In the library, Ms. Octavia worked while the others slept—they'd stayed up searching for information until exhaustion set in and they could only guess whether it was day or night, for there were no windows in the remote rooms to let sunlight in.

Octavia was making strides. Instead of drawing a 3-D door with all of its dings and grooves and swirly wood knots, she'd decided on something a bit simpler—the window in her classroom. Every year with the new Unwanteds she'd taught them the 3-D door process by starting with that window. And while few over the years had accomplished bringing the window to

LISA McMANN

3-D life, enabling them to crawl through it onto the lawn, Alex Stowe had done it in his first year. He'd gone on to develop his phenomenal drawing skills, using this same drafting table to create a door that led to his twin brother Aaron's room in the university in Quill. That had caused a lot of problems, though, including exposing all of Artimé to the people who had sent the Unwanteds to their deaths. It wasn't exactly Alex's finest hour. But he'd turned out all right . . . and, in the end, so had Aaron. Octavia's heartstrings tugged as she thought about Alex, her most prized student, and she moved away from the table just in time for a tear to splash on the rug instead of on her drawing. It was never easy seeing one of her protégés leave them too early.

These memories churned through Ms. Octavia's mind as she sketched on the glass-top table. Gentle blue light shone up through it, creating a comforting glow and helping her make each stroke precise. This window was the octogator's best shot at performing such a difficult task from memory. Any other attempt would be fruitless—there was just no way to memorize all the minute intricacies of any door and retain them. Not at her age, anyway.

By the time Aaron got up to check on her progress, she had the window outline done.

"It looks great," said Aaron. "I'm amazed by your talent. I wish I could do it."

"Do what? Make a 3-D window?"

"Or simply draw anything."

Ms. Octavia looked at him. "Have you ever tried?"

"A few times. I wish . . . I wish I'd gotten the instruction that everyone else received."

"You're free to attend my classes anytime, Aaron. I'd say you developed your creative abilities quite well, though. You designed Lani's wheeled device. Fixed the tube on the Island of Shipwrecks. And built numerous constructions in Quill back when . . ."

"Back when you were evil," said Samheed from the darkness. Yawning, he emerged from between some shelves and ran his fingers through his hair to tame it. "How's it going, Octavia?"

Ms. Octavia raised an eyebrow at Samheed and didn't answer; her disapproval was evident.

"Sorry," Samheed muttered. "I'm just cranky because there's nothing to drink. Does anybody know the proper magic to build a water fountain? Claire has done it before, but I never paid attention."

"My skin is cracking from being out of the water for so long," Ms. Octavia admitted. "I've got seaweed dust flaking onto my drawing." She blew it off carefully. Though the octogator could survive without ever being in the water, she still went for a dip a couple of times a day to keep her skin moist. "To answer your question, I know how to do it. But we don't have the necessary components."

"What do we need?" asked Aaron.

"A few drops of freshwater, for one. It takes water to make water. And a structural element, like a basin component. We don't make them in bulk because they're rarely used."

"Do you happen to have any with you?" Samheed asked her.

"Again, rarely used. I don't clutter my pockets with such things unless I'm going on a journey, unfortunately."

"That should change," Aaron muttered. "Water is essential for humans. It's when we're totally without it that it's most necessary."

"That's obvious," Samheed remarked snidely.

Aaron ignored him. "Every human should learn the spell and carry one of the components with them."

"Florence doesn't need water, so maybe making extra components or teaching that spell wasn't high on her list," said Samheed.

"Water is also plentiful in Artimé," added Ms. Octavia, shooing the young men away from her table and going back to her sketch. "When we're not stuck in the library, that is. Who would have thought we'd be in need of it right here in our own mansion? And neither of you brought a canteen?"

Samheed and Aaron exchanged guilty looks. Like Ms. Octavia said, water was plentiful in Artimé, so there was no need to carry a canteen at home until now.

Clementi and Fox appeared from where they'd been napping in the stacks. "What's going on?" Clementi's stomach emitted a snarling growl, and she winced. "Any progress?"

"It's coming along," said Ms. Octavia. She didn't mention that she was beginning to struggle to remember the exact dimensions of the window frame—was it two and a quarter inches all the way around the glass, or two and three quarters? Back in her classroom she had the window in front of her to copy and measure if she needed to. Here she was constantly second-guessing herself. Things she'd been certain of before

LISA McMANN

she started drawing now seemed off. And the constant chatter wasn't helping her concentration. "Why don't you all do some more searching through the maps and books to see if you can find anything useful."

She emphasized the last word with a hint of impatience that sent the rest of them away to the various floors of the library. Samheed went to the Artiméan history section, and Aaron stayed on the third floor and scoured the construction and blueprints materials. Clementi and Fox descended to the section called "Mr. Today's Duplicate Library: Wisdom for All," which was almost the entire second floor full of the same books that were in the Museum of Large. He'd rewritten or magically reproduced the books he'd cherished so that people who couldn't access the not-so-secret hallway would still have full access to all the books in Artimé. His efforts were much appreciated at this time, perhaps more so than ever before.

Once the others had dispersed, Ms. Octavia pulled her glasses off her nose and rested her snout in two of her octopus arms, shaking her head slightly as overwhelming feelings of inadequacy swarmed her. She hadn't been prepared to do this. It seemed impossible. And if she didn't succeed, the humans could die.

New Life

I'd always wonderrred what it would be like to be invisible," Simber said wistfully, flying swiftly toward Artimé while Thisbe, Fifer, and Sky painted themselves invisible on his back. "I feel so frrree. Forrr so much of my life I've been pointed at orrr fearrred. People run away frrrom me scrrreaming. No one everrr says, 'Oh, I didn't see you therrre, Simberrr.' I'm impossible to miss. But now . . . I'm invisible. It's like I'm living a new and differrrent life. I'm starrrting overrr."

Sky leaned forward and hugged the enormous cat around the neck. "Being invisible has definitely changed your demeanor," she said. "You're practically—dare I say it? Practically chipper!"

LISA McMANN

"Yes, it's wonderful to see you—or *not* see you—so happy, Sim," said Fifer. She put the finishing touches on her invisibility as the mansion came into view. Then she steeled herself for the task ahead and prepared to go inside Alex's apartment.

"You just don't know what it's like," Simber went on, "neverrr being able to hide. Being too big to go places, like on the rrrescue mission in the catacombs. Surrre it's grrreat to be able to scarrre enemies, but I'm tirrred of frrrightening allies. Like new Unwanteds, or the black-eyed childrrren. Did you see them? They werrre cowerrring—cowerrring behind a *drrragon*, I might add. Am I morrre frrrightening than Gorrrgrrrun or Quince? I'm offended. That does bad things to my self-esteem, being morrre fearrred than a firrre-brrreathing drrragon."

Thisbe laughed, then lowered her voice to a whisper. "They just need to get to know you. They'll warm up in time. But I'm sorry you've felt this way. And I'm glad you have this chance to feel like you can sneak around for once. It's fun, isn't it?"

"Indeed," said the beast, lowering his voice now too. "I haven't had this much fun in quite some time."

Everyone became silent as they approached the second floor of the mansion. They were on the opposite side of the building from where most people usually gathered. It was known as the quiet side, and there was no one about. But they needed to be very stealthy, for the windows were all blown out in the entire mansion, and they could see dissenters stationed on the floor below, keeping watch. As Simber alighted on the balcony of the head mage's quarters and his riders carefully slid off, they could hear two dissenters below them talking with a definitive air of disgust in their voices.

"What is the purpose of all of this?" one said. "Are were supposed to stand here forever?"

"At least until Frieda gets rid of the Stowes," said the other. "She's mad we put Aaron in the library and destroyed the tube before she could get to him."

"He'll die in there soon enough. But about that— why does she hate them so much that she wants to kill them? I mean, Fifer's screams are aggravating and dangerous, and Thisbe is obviously a threat to be around with her firepower and explosions. But Aaron isn't even in control. He seemed happy to go back to the Island of Shipwrecks. Why not just let him go?"

The other one didn't answer immediately. Then she said, "I think Frieda initially had something against their mother. But that has escalated, and she seems to be taking things to the extreme. It's . . . making me uneasy."

"Me too. I'm not sure about this."

"Quiet—here comes whatshisname. Her new second-in-command."

The two fell silent. With the invisibility spells ready to wear off Sky, Thisbe, Fifer, and Simber, they contemplated that conversation while moving slowly and carefully inside the mage's quarters and continued through the apartment, to the door.

Fifer stopped there, and all four paused instinctively and looked around the room with heavy hearts. Would anyone worthy ever reside in this apartment again? Could anyone take Alex's place? They all said a silent thank-you to whatever powers had made it impossible for Frieda to see the secret hallway, for if she had moved in here and sullied all of Alex's things, they wouldn't have been able to bear it.

"Let's keep going," said Thisbe after a moment. It was weird being invisible, unable to see anyone but knowing they were very close. Of all the ones in the room, Thisbe felt the most uncomfortable being there, for she had not yet come to terms with the way she and Alex had spent their time together and how they had parted. She didn't know if she'd ever be able to address the complex feelings she had about him. Knowing Fifer had been given the chance to make up and become friends with Alex wasn't exactly sitting very well in Thisbe's craw right now either.

And now was not the time to start dwelling on those dark thoughts. "Come on," she whispered as their invisibility spells began to wear off. "We've got living people counting on us. We don't need any more empty rooms like this one to deal with."

One More Thing

They split up. Simber, Sky, and Fifer went to different sections in the Museum of Large library. Thisbe, still feeling out of sorts, went alone to check the tube in the kitchenette to see if it was working. To her great surprise, after having heard Fifer's account of the main floor tubes being destroyed, the control panel on this tube seemed fine and ready to take its next passengers wherever they wanted to go. Unfortunately, this tube only led to places outside the mansion, not to the rooms where their friends were trapped.

Thisbe knew where some of the buttons led to, and she and Fifer had been carefully taught which of the buttons were safe to use. One would take them to Gunnar Haluki's old house in Quill—that house was vacant now. Another button went to the jungle tube. A third would take them to the Island of Shipwrecks. The others led to places only Mr. Today knew, and no one had dared experiment with them to this day, for fear of the dangers they'd end up facing.

Thisbe eyed the button to the Island of Shipwrecks as she became fully visible. It would only take a minute to check on Kaylee and give her an update. Impulsively Thisbe pushed the button, and a second later she was there, stepping out of the tube and then running down the path to the sprawling, intricate rock structure that served as a home to the three men they called the grandfathers: Ito, Sato, and Ishibashi. All were well over one hundred years old but showed no signs of wearing out. They tended a greenhouse where Henry often visited to get herbs to make medicine. This was also where Aaron and Kaylee had lived for years, and their son, Daniel, had spent most of his life here.

"Kaylee!" Thisbe called out softly, not wanting to wake Daniel in case he was napping. She ducked into the structure, her footsteps loud enough to announce her location. She ran to the large gathering room and looked down the different hallways, wondering which one to search first. "Are you here, Kaylee?"

Ishibashi appeared from the hallway that led to the greenhouse. "Well!" he said with delight. "Thisbe! Is everything all right with Aaron?" The pleasure drained from his face, and worry filled it up.

"I think he's okay," Thisbe said, still panting from the run. "I just wanted to give Kaylee a quick update before I go back. Things are pretty bad. But nobody's dead or anything. Not yet, anyway."

"She's working in the garden," said Ishibashi. "I'll get her." He hurried as fast as his old legs could carry him. A moment later he returned with Kaylee, who was drying her hands on a towel. Her blond hair was tied back in a loose braid, and her pale skin was flushed pink from the sun. She had a streak of dirt on one cheek.

"What's going on?" asked Kaylee. "I've been so worried."

Thisbe quickly told her and Ishibashi about everything that had happened in the past couple of days, ending with the news that Aaron and everybody else were trapped. "We're forming a small but powerful army," she said. "Florence is assessing the new team members now while Fifer, Sky, Simber, and I are sneaking into the second floor to get some things." She took a breath. "I saw this tube was still working, so I thought I should give you an update while I had the chance."

As Thisbe relayed the story, Ito and Sato gathered and listened in. Now the four adults looked at one another worriedly.

"I'm going back with you," said Kaylee, determined. "I have to help."

Ishibashi spoke in Japanese to Ito and Sato, and they responded. Kaylee said something brief in that language as well, as she'd learned Japanese by now, after so many years with the scientists. They made a few more exchanges, then nodded in agreement. Kaylee turned to Thisbe. "Ito and Sato will remain here to care for Daniel. Ishibashi and I will come with you and fight for Artimé."

Thisbe turned and stared at Ishibashi. "You'll help us?" she said, her eyes misting.

"We are family," said Ishibashi. "I still have fight left in me." He smiled warmly. "I will gather my weapons."

"And I'll say good-bye to Daniel and get my weapons too,"

said Kaylee. She put her hand on Thisbe's shoulder and gave it a squeeze. "Thank you for coming to get us, Thisbe."

A short time later, the three of them were taking the tube back to the kitchenette. Thisbe arrived first, just as Sky was poking her head into the room trying to find her.

"Oh!" said Thisbe, worrying that she'd been gone too long. "Hi—I was just . . ." She stepped out of the tube and realized Sky's arms were laden with books.

"I was wondering where you were," Sky said, gratefully handing some of the books to Thisbe. "We could use your help. And we should be getting back to Florence."

Before Thisbe could explain, Kaylee and Ishibashi appeared and stepped out into the kitchenette, loaded with weapons and supplies. "Wh-what? How did you . . . ?" Sky sputtered. "Does this tube work? Did you ask them to come? Don't get me wrong, I'm thrilled—we need all the help we can get."

"I peeked in here and realized this tube wasn't broken," said Thisbe. "Since it's not connected to the main tubes in the mansion entryway, I figured I'd give it a try, and it worked just like always. I wanted to update Kaylee about Aaron," said Thisbe. "And once I told them what's happening, these two wanted to help. Do you think Simber can carry all of us? If not, a few of us can take the tube to the jungle and walk from there."

Sky's face exploded into a smile. "It's a short trip, so I think Simber can make it work. And we have enough invisibility paintbrushes for everyone." She let out a breath. "This is actually quite a relief to have reinforcements." She led the others out of the kitchenette and down the hall to the Museum of Large. There they found Fifer and Simber talking quietly in front of Ol' Tater. When the two heard the others coming, they turned.

"Now, there's a surprise," said Fifer. "Look who's here!" She ran to greet Kaylee and Ishibashi.

Thisbe explained her brief journey to Fifer and Simber. When everyone was caught up, Thisbe and Sky turned to collect the remaining books and return to the head mage's apartment to find a rucksack in which to carry them. "We'll get the invisibility paintbrushes ready," Thisbe called as they exited the museum. "Are you coming?"

"In a minute," Fifer said. She ran back to where Simber still stood in front of the old, dangerous mastodon. "Shall we take

LISA McMANN

the chance?" Simber asked Fifer. He pointed with his nose to one of the books on a small pile in Fifer's arms.

Fifer nodded slowly and opened it. "Is there really even a question?" She read for several moments, then looked up. "Thisbe and I have done this live spell before," she said.

"We don't need that one quite yet," said Simber. "How about the otherrr?"

Fifer continued to read, turning a page or two to make sure she wasn't missing anything important. Then she nodded slowly. "Yes," she said, then looked up. "I can manage that. Where to? The jungle? Or downstairs?"

"If we put him downstairrrs, they'll know someone's been up herrre again. I think we'd rrratherrr they didn't find that out quite yet. Trrransporrrt him somewherrre you can easily get to laterrr when it's time to activate him."

Fifer put her books on the floor. "Got it." She moved closer to Ol' Tater, then nervously put her hand flat on his cool, stone side. There were stories about him stomping around on the pirate ship during the battle Artimé fought when Fifer was two years old. He was very dangerous and didn't know friend from foe, so if they ever brought him to life, they'd have to be very smart and cautious about it. For now, getting him out of here and putting him somewhere they could access fairly easily seemed to be a good idea.

Fifer closed her eyes and drew in a breath. Letting it out, she envisioned a specific part of the jungle not far from Artimé's lawn but hidden from view, and near one of the wide paths that the rock had mown. It was important that Fifer place Ol' Tater far enough from where the little dog and Panther lived so they weren't squashed by his sudden arrival in case Fifer's aim was off. In her mind, Fifer stayed focused on the spot where she wanted the sleeping statue to land. Then she whispered the word few mages in Artimé had ever used in its magical form. "Transport."

The giant statue disappeared. Simber and Fifer waited in breathless silence, listening for any unusual shouts or screams or crashing sounds that would indicate a horrible mistake, but they heard nothing. After a moment, Simber nodded at Fifer with respect. "Well done. It took Alex a few trrries the firrrst time," he said. He hesitated but seemed like he was about to say more. But then he turned and didn't speak.

"Thanks, Sim," said Fifer. She gathered up the books and

started out the door, catching up to the others to get her invisibility paintbrush for the ride home.

Despite the danger at hand, a contented expression played around Simber's jowls as he watched her go. It was nice to be working directly with Fifer again. She'd handled the situation after Alex's death with poise that most thirteen-year-old humans didn't possess, and they'd gotten along so naturally, in a way that hadn't happened quite so early on with any of the former mages.

Perhaps it was because she was familiar. But Simber thought it more likely due to her inner strength and the leadership skills that came naturally to her. She was calm and collected when it came to big decisions and big, risky spells—much more so than Alex had been at this age. And there was no denying she was one of the most magical people Artimé had ever seen. If anyone could handle leading this group to victory over Frieda Stubbs, it was Fifer. She made Simber's decision to defy his ingrained calling a bit easier. Especially when he could envision the head mage robe on Fifer Stowe someday. He'd almost said so to her just now, but then he held back—he didn't want to put any undue pressure on her. Would Fifer even want it?

Or would she choose to follow her maternal ancestors back to the land of the dragons, like Thisbe seemed inclined to do?

The thought of both of them leaving Artimé was a hard one. But that could happen in the future. And there were things to overcome now. Simber knew that there would likely be many battles ahead of them. And he would be honored to fight alongside the girls at any step of the way. If they survived this one, anyway.

Growing Restless

I'm losing my mind," Ibrahim muttered to Seth. Both boys lay sprawled out on the lounge bar, staring at the ceiling.

"We could race with magic carpets again," Seth said listlessly.

"Thatcher said we shouldn't waste any more components," Ibrahim reminded him.

Seth grunted, too bored to say actual words. They lay there for several more minutes, listening to the conversations around them. There was an air of anxiety and despair in the remote room.

Nearby, Carina and Claire were attempting to create a new spell component to mimic the transport spell, only for living creatures. But they weren't having any luck, and not just because neither of them had ever done the transport spell in the past. "I don't think there's even a component for transport," Claire said. "I believe it's done through energy and thought, like the seek spell."

Lani looked up from her notes at the table next to them and confirmed it.

"Speaking of the seek spell, should we risk sending one?" Carina asked.

"All the seek spell will do is come out of the tube," Claire said, envisioning it. "It won't be able to point them to which remote room we're in, since the tubes don't work."

"Do you suspect Florence has figured out what's happened by now?"

"It depends if anyone got away."

"I'm hoping the others did."

Claire hesitated. She was more worried that Frieda had carried through with her threat against the Stowes. "Me too," she said after a moment.

LISA McMANN

Carina looked at her. "Do you think Frieda would actually . . . *hurt* them?"

Claire closed her eyes. "I'm definitely worried about it."

"And who else would be able to figure out how to fix the tubes besides Aaron?"

"We can hope for Thisbe to arrive, I suppose. Florence told me she was coming." The women grew silent.

At the bar, Seth sat up. "We're doomed," he muttered.

Ibrahim sat up too. "We're not doomed," he said sharply. "Remember who we are and where we come from. Our very nature, as Unwanteds, is one of survival."

"I've never actually been an Unwanted, you know," Seth said. He dropped his eyes, feeling suddenly inadequate among this group. He'd never faced being purged. He'd grown up in Artimé, free as anything, with little to care about except for missing his mother now and then when she left on journeys to rescue people in trouble. But then he brightened a little. "I did survive the great disastrous trip to the land of the dragons, though. And I actually didn't get very hurt—I was pretty much unscathed compared to Fifer and Thisbe."

Ibrahim gave him a sly look. "You also don't have black

eyes, so you weren't exactly a prized commodity over there."

Seth snorted. He hopped off the bar and looked around. "At least we have food. The only good thing about being down here."

From the floor, Carina called out, "Save the food please, boys! There's a limited amount of it, and we don't know how long we'll be here."

"I swear she has ears like Simber," Seth muttered. He looked around the lounge, feeling some level of depression floating about him. He needed to do something that would give him hope, but it was very hard to pull out of the bog of listlessness he'd plunged into after things began to look bleak.

Ibrahim jumped down too. "I feel like we're back in Quill with nothing ahead of us. It's stifling. We have to do something, Seth. Let's figure out how to get out of here. Come with me." He went over to the platform on which the lounge band played and started nosing around at the instruments. "We need to get our creative ideas flowing again. I feel like . . . maybe some music will help. That always gives me fresh ideas."

Seth shrugged. It sounded like a lot of effort. But he went with Ibrahim. Maybe his Unwanted friend was right—that

LISA McMANN

they needed creativity in order to feel creative. And maybe that would help everyone else, too. Music was a great way to stimulate ideas. Seth knew that well enough from his classes.

He picked up Fox's saxophone. It was quite small compared to the ones he'd played in Ms. Morning's classes because it had been designed for Fox. But it had a velvety sound. Seth played a few bars of a simple tune and saw Ms. Morning look up at him.

He blushed. Ms. Morning smiled encouragingly. "That's an excellent idea," she called out. "We could all use some music."

Ibrahim sat down at the drum kit. He was a dancer, so the rhythm and beat really appealed to him, and basic drumming had come easily to him. He could feel the beat like it was a part of him, like it was one with his heartbeat when he danced. Soon he and Seth were putting music together, and one of Ibrahim's sisters joined them to play the guitar and sing. Everybody in the lounge felt the tension melt for a short while. Soon others were clamoring to have a chance to play too.

Claire Morning brought the creativity-rebuilding session to a close with an oboe solo. It reminded Lani of her old friend, Meghan Ranger, who had been the most musical one of their original group of friends. The song brought tears to her eyes.

Meghan had loved Ms. Morning from the moment she arrived in Artimé. Lani looked over at Sean, Meghan's brother. His eyes were glistening too.

By the end, Seth felt a surge of life returning to him. He put the sax back on its stand, then went to sit under the bar between two stools. He closed his eyes, letting a rush of thoughts flow through his mind, so fresh he could almost feel their newness. This had been a good idea.

Seth turned his thoughts to every difficult situation he'd ever been in. He deliberately went through his solutions to them piece by piece. He'd used his wits before. He was smart and capable. And he didn't need Fifer and Thisbe around to save him from a jam.

After a while he opened his eyes, determined to figure out how to escape. There was only one problem: He still didn't have any ideas. But he was sure, now that his brain was moving again, that the ideas would come.

LISA McMANN

Preparing for a Journey

Dev woke up to the sun high overhead. He'd slept deeply, barely remembering anything happening since he'd closed his eyes the night before, other than dreams about the images that had flitted through his mind. He sat up gingerly and found that although Drock's prediction of him healing quickly had come true, his ribs still thrummed with a dull ache. But he could move a bit more easily now, and his other wounds were almost gone. "Too bad Drock's dragon breath only works on wounds he caused," Dev said aloud, his voice cracking after a long sleep.

"What's that?"

Startled by the voice, Dev turned and moved to the mouth of the cave he'd taken up residence in. Just outside sat Astrid, the same dragon from the previous night. She held a large fish wrapped in her tail. "Oh," said Dev. "Hello again. Astrid, isn't it?"

"Yes, I believe so," said the dragon, looking puzzled. She squinted at the sun, then said apologetically, "I've forgotten why I've come to call on you."

"Perhaps you're meant to give me that fish?" Dev said. "And start a fire?" He could get used to this kind of service, and he didn't mind if he had to work a little to get it.

"Of course," said the dragon. "At least I didn't forget to come at all."

"That's very remembery of you," Dev replied, nodding encouragingly as he eyed the plump makings of his next meal. His mouth watered. While he craved other foods sometimes, Dev never got tired of fish. It had been his go-to meal whenever Princess Shanti or the castle workers had decided to withhold Dev's meals as punishment for something Shanti had done. The river full of fish was the only loyal thing Dev had been able to count on his whole life.

LISA McMANN

Astrid started a fire for Dev, and while the fish was cooking, Dev went to get water. When he returned, the ghost dragon was surprisingly still there.

"Where do you live?" Dev asked politely, turning the fish.

"Oh . . ." Astrid gazed in the direction of the other caves. "Somewhere over there, I think. And you?"

"I—" Dev stopped abruptly. "I guess I don't live anywhere anymore."

"That must be nice," said the dragon wistfully. "It's what we ghost dragons all want. To disappear. Not to be stuck here in the cavelands forever. There's nothing to do. Endless waiting."

"I haven't exactly disappeared," Dev pointed out, but the dragon seemed lost in thought. "I . . . I still exist." Though for a split second, Dev wondered if it were true. If everyone thought he was dead, did he actually still exist? Who decided a person's status in life or death? The person himself? Or others who report it? The thoughts troubled him. He certainly felt like he existed, although insignificantly.

Abruptly Dev changed the subject, turning to some of the questions about the images he'd seen, figuring it was worth asking a ghost dragon about them. "Do you know where the big bulbous palace is? It's purple and orange and red, with gold that caps all of the turrets and rooftops. It's very beautiful." He pulled the fish off the fire and dropped it to the ground in front of him to cool, burning his fingertips in the process.

The dragon turned. "The palace," she mused. "I haven't thought of it in many years. Yes, it's just over there." She pointed with her tail to the south.

Dev turned to look, seeing nothing but cavelands and desert, and mountains beyond that. "Where?"

"On the other side of that mountain range, about a half day's journey. It's the land west of the crater lake, where Ashguard the curmudgeon rules. Surely you've been there."

"I may have been," Dev said, though he doubted it. "A half day's journey walking?"

"Flying," said the dragon. "It would take weeks walking there from here. The mountains would be nearly impossible to cross."

"Oh." Dev's heart sank. He was feeling better, but not that good. He didn't think he had it in him to walk and climb for weeks in his condition.

They talked about other things—sometimes the same

things they'd already discussed, due to the dragon's forget-fulness. But Dev didn't mind. He found it almost comforting. Astrid was pleasant, and it was nice to have someone big on his side for once.

As the morning progressed, he told her all about what the Revinir was doing in Grimere—twice, just in case it helped her retain the information. And he warned her to beware of the Revinir's growing power.

"Ah yes. I'd like to snap my jaws around that one," the dragon lamented, once she remembered who the Revinir was. "Too bad we can't. Won't anyone come and take back our land? Is no one left to free us? Allow us to go on to the next life? Doesn't anyone care about the land of the dragons? I fear we are a doomed species."

"There are plenty of dragons," Dev assured her. "They're just all under the Revinir's mind control, so they don't know that they should fight against her, not for her."

"What about that handsome dark purple specimen? Didn't he bring you here? My mind is fuzzy."

"Drock? Right—he's the only one who can resist it. He's different. Like me, I guess."

The dragon smiled, her cheeks pulling back to reveal fright-ful rows of sharp teeth. "What is your name, please?"

"I'm Dev," he reminded her, and grew bold. "From the line of Suresh. I—I think."

"And I am Astrid," she said with pride.

"Oh," said Dev, pretending not to know. "How nice to meet you. Would you like the rest of my fish?"

"How nice to meet *you*," said Astrid, accepting it. She swal-lowed it in one gulp, bones and all. "Have you heard about the evil Revinir?"

Dev blinked. "No," he said. "Tell me everything."

"I've just recently learned of her from another young man who was here." Astrid relayed the entire story back to Dev, missing only a few small points. It gave Dev a sense of relief and hope that she'd remember it.

By the time the fire was low, Dev looked in the direction of the palace, calculating what he'd need for his journey, for he was becoming more and more determined to find the palace that haunted his mind. "Does the river run all the way to the palace?" he asked.

"What palace?"

"The bulbous purple-and-orange one."

"Ah yes. With the gilded rooftops. Such a beauty."

"Yes, that's the one. Does this river run to it?"

"I believe it does. Though it's been some decades since I've been in that area."

Dev perked up at the news that the river would be accessible. That would help, at least. He could lie around in these caves in pain, or try to do something productive. There was little difference in his mind. And he could survive anywhere if the river was with him. "In that case . . . I may need to take my leave in the near future. I—I thank you for helping me. I'm feeling so much better."

"Leave?" said Astrid. She stood up and fire shot from her nostrils. "And just moments after we first met. That's a shame."

Dev ducked. "If you'd like," he said slyly, "you could go with me. We could fly there."

"Really?" Astrid exclaimed. "Where?"

Dev groaned inwardly but plastered a smile on his face. "To the *palace*. The purple-and-orange one. With the golden roofs."

Astrid smiled. "Why, Dev! I thought you'd never ask. I'd be delighted. I haven't been anywhere in ages." But then her face darkened. "We'll have to stay clear of Grimere, though—have you heard? It's been taken over by the evil Revinir."

On the Fly

S
imber and his full load of riders returned to the Quil-
itary yard, where Florence was demonstrating all the
fire-related spells she could think of to the black-eyed
children and Maiven Taveer. After Simber and his
team's invisibility spells wore off, Florence greeted them and
invited them to join in the training.

"Why is she teaching fire spells?" Thisbe asked Rohan in a
whisper as she took an open spot behind him.

"She thinks that because we already have the magical fire abilities of dragons, we might more easily pick up the fire-related magic.
She's been teaching us all sorts of amazing things! Everybody

except Maiven can do the fire-step one now. Even me."

Thisbe nodded in admiration. "I knew you could do it. You've been learning magic extremely well."

"Ahem!" said Florence, giving Thisbe a dark look.

"Sorry," said Thisbe, stepping back obediently. "I was just catching up."

"We'll have time for that later." Florence continued with her instruction, while Thisbe went through the motions in following her, since she already knew all of the spells that were being taught. She exchanged smiles with Ishibashi and Kaylee as they joined the ranks.

Ishibashi and Kaylee, both originally from the same non-magical world, were not at all successful in the art of magic. But under these dire circumstances they seemed willing to try again to see if any of these types of spells would work for them. When it became clear that they still didn't have any ability in the magical arts, they slipped away to a different corner of the yard and brought out their weapons.

Ishibashi began to teach Kaylee how to use small, flat, spiked discs he'd made from old broken weapons he'd found in one of the shipwrecks off the coast of his island. He said it resembled a throwing star. He gave her a fabric wristlet that would store a few of the stars, and he showed her how to use a single finger to pull one out so she could easily access and throw it in a split second. Then he showed her how to throw them. He pointed out a nubby growth on a nearby tree and sent a star sailing into it. The weapon stuck fast.

Soon Kaylee was getting the hang of it. "It's nice to have something that I can do from a distance," she said. "I'm great with a sword and dagger, but that isn't always useful on the back of a flying creature." She cringed, remembering the last time she'd fought with her sword on Simber's slick back and had nearly lost her life falling from a great height.

"These are lightweight and easy to carry," Ishibashi told her. "For an old man, they are easier than a heavy sword— they're the best weapons." He paused, then added, "I can still fight with my fists, though."

"I remember," said Kaylee warmly. "Just be careful. We don't want to lose you. Daniel needs his Papa Ishi." She loved the three scientists like family. As others did in Artimé, she'd wondered how the men had managed to live so long. They were the oldest people Kaylee had ever heard of.

"I will be very careful, Kaylee," Ishibashi told her solemnly, his eyes shining from the compliment. "You must trust me and not worry. And if my time in this world should end, I am ready for that." A troubled look crossed his face, but it soon vanished. He wasn't sure if he'd ever die. He and the other scientists had taken various doses of magical blue seaweed, and they had been responsible for giving some to Aaron as well to save his life long before they'd met Kaylee. Ishibashi knew that Aaron hadn't told Kaylee that he might be immortal because of it. The knowledge weighed heavily on Ishibashi's mind. He believed that Aaron shouldn't keep this information from his wife. But Aaron had told him once that it would only cause Kaylee pain to know it. And he'd made it clear that this information wasn't Ishibashi's to share.

"Well, I'm not ready for that," said Kaylee with a decisive note in her voice. "You're coming back home with me and Aaron when all of this is over."

"That is my plan too. But as we both know too well, we don't control much of anything."

Kaylee caught his gaze and held it. Then she nodded grimly and wound up and threw another star, hitting the target dead-on.

An Important Discovery

Maiven Taveer thoroughly enjoyed Florence's training sessions. "You are a great warrior," she said as they stopped for a break. "I should like to have you on my side forever, and would be fearful to oppose you." She nimbly climbed up onto Gorgrun's back to get the box of provisions they'd brought along.

"And you are surprisingly adept after being imprisoned for so many years," said Florence. "Thisbe told me that you'd been the leader of the military."

"Yes. Technically I still am." Maiven tossed the box down

to Florence. "However, my army has shrunk considerably." She pointed at the handful of Grimere children who were sitting in the shade of the Quillitary wall with Fifer, Sky, and Thisbe, waiting for the refreshments.

"Is this the extent of it?" asked Florence. She held out a hand to help Maiven to the ground.

"There may be a few more living in hiding beyond Grimere. I'm not sure. I searched one area, a palace where an old curmudgeon named Ashguard was last known to be. I suspected that area might be a hiding place for some of my people, but I didn't find anyone. And there wasn't sufficient time to check the village. I'll go back upon our return if there is time. We'll need all the help we can get to reclaim the throne."

"Much like us," said Florence wryly. "Do you think the Revinir will continue to destroy life as you know it in your land? How far does Grimere reach?"

Maiven took her dagger and sketched a map of her world in the dirt, putting it into four quadrants. Grimere, with the castle, city, and Dragonsmarche, was in the southeast quarter. The smaller village Thisbe, Fifer, and Seth had visited upon first arriving and searching for food and water was in the northeast quarter. These two quadrants were closest to the seven islands—the castle on the left and the tiny village on the right as one approached. Beyond them, the desert and cavelands where the ghost dragons roamed sat in the northwest, and the crater lake and vast land beyond where Ashguard had ruled was in the southwest. The great forest where the Artiméan rescue team had spent so much time was sprawled throughout the middle of the land, touching all four quadrants but much more heavily so in the northern two. Several rivers snaked through it.

"That helps me see it," Florence said. "Thank you." She studied it. "What is this land called?" she asked, pointing to the southwest, where Ashguard had ruled.

Maiven hesitated. "It was once part of Grimere. But the meteor that struck and created the crater lake divided the land, making it difficult to get to. One of the ruling black-eyed families lived in the palace—Ashguard Suresh and his kin. My family, the Taveer line, lived in the castle." She paused. "To answer your question, the land of Ashguard's palace doesn't have a name any longer, as the family was all but destroyed and it's a wasteland now. There may be one or two descendants among this group. I'm not sure if they even know themselves which family they came from. And it doesn't matter. We are all one family now."

Florence nodded. "I see." After a moment she took hold of the box of provisions and pried the lid open. "It seems hollow of me to offer, since I am likely of no use to you in your situation. But if there's any way we can help you, please let me know."

"Thank you, Florence. I will." Maiven began to hand out refreshments. "In fact," she said, looking over her shoulder, "I'll say it now. We will be needing your help."

"Fair enough," said Florence. "If we survive this, you shall have it."

Maiven nodded regally, and the deal was done.

Florence called Thisbe, Fifer, and Simber to join her and Maiven. When they had assembled, the warrior trainer laid out her plan for attack. The five of them conversed in serious tones, working out the kinks and adding a few extra flourishes to Florence's ideas. Even Thisbe and Fifer put aside their differences for the moment to discuss strategy. They ran through all sorts of scenarios, trying to find their flaws so they could fix them. By nightfall they felt they had a solid plan in place.

As the stars popped out in the sky, Florence brought everyone together, including the ghost dragons, for a final training session. Afterward she assigned duties to each of them and talked through what to do. Then she closed the session. "You all need sleep," she said. "We'll carry out our plans first thing in the morning. We can't afford to wait any longer."

Rohan and Maiven double-checked with the other children from Grimere to make sure they fully understood Florence's instructions. Before turning in for the evening, Rohan found Thisbe reading one of the books she'd fetched earlier. He sat down next to her.

"Here," said Thisbe, handing a second book to him. "We're trying to figure out how to fix the tube system. We're scouring all the books we can for clues. Would you mind looking through this one to see if there's anything about tubes?"

"I'm not sure I know what I'm looking for," said Rohan, whose only experience with a human-size transportation tube was the elevator in the catacombs, and that was hardly the same thing. "But it's easy enough for me to skim and look for the word."

"That'll do perfectly," said Thisbe. She smiled anxiously at him and linked her fingers in his. "We're so grateful to you and the others for helping Artimé. You have no idea how distressful this situation is in our peaceful land. We've never seen anything like it."

"There's no need to mention it," said Rohan. "Whether or not to help you was never a question in my mind. After what you did for us, it's the least we could do. And we're getting an excellent education in exchange. Like Maiven said, we needed to train before taking on the Revinir, and we can do that from a ghost dragon's back or anywhere else."

"You really are the best thing I've ever known," said Thisbe.

Rohan smiled and his eyes misted. "You don't know the half of it, *pria*."

"You are my *pria*," said Thisbe. She had an idea of what the word meant. She knew it was a term of endearment that Rohan had called her several times. The thought of her using it for someone felt bold. But Rohan was very dear to her, and that's exactly what she wanted to express.

Rohan chuckled. "That is not the right word to use for a boy," he said, his eyes dancing.

"What?" exclaimed Thisbe. "Why not? That's silly. There shouldn't be different words when the feeling is the same."

"You have words like that in your language."

Thisbe frowned. "Well, I'll change them, then."

Rohan tapped his lips. "Then call me *pria*, too," he declared. "I'm pleased to hear you say it. And I agree," he added. "I'd never thought about that before, but you're right. We shall change the language one word at a time."

"Yes!" said Thisbe. "*Prias* all around!" She leaned her shoulder comfortably against his, like they'd done so many times, and they paged through books under the light of a highlighter component.

Nearby, Fifer rested against Simber's side, reading as well, but she'd been listening to their conversation. Occasionally she threw glances at Thisbe, who looked very comfortable with Rohan. It was strange to see her twin so close with someone Fifer barely knew, and it reminded her of how much the twins had grown apart since their separation. And Thisbe had just called Rohan the best thing she knew, which meant Fifer had been put upon a shelf—not a surprise at this point. But would they ever be close again, like they'd been before going to the land of the dragons? Or, because of everything, had Fifer somehow lost out on that . . . to Rohan?

Thisbe and Rohan's clear physical affection for each other didn't bother Fifer, really—she was merely curious about it. It definitely didn't make her wish for someone to get cozy with. Simber was plenty cozy enough, and his stone side cooled her off when she got hot. He acted as more of a piece of furniture than someone to cuddle with, which was just fine, but emotionally, Simber was always there for her. She remembered the talk they'd had in the forest outside of Grimere after Alex's death, when Simber had told her that he believed in her. That had been the beginning of a strong bond that only grew over time. Fifer didn't need anybody else in her life if she had a companion like that.

There was one thing that Fifer thought was weird about Thisbe and Rohan, though. The two kept bumping elbows when turning pages, which was awkward. But neither of them moved aside to prevent it from happening again. If anyone ever got in Fifer's way, she usually moved or gave them a look so they'd move. Was it odd not to like having people touch you all the time? It didn't seem to Fifer like it should be. She liked having space. Maybe that was why she hadn't enjoyed dancing with Seth at the costume party.

After a few moments puzzling over this new revelation, Fifer returned to the important task of reading. She studied long into the night, even after Florence suggested she get some rest. Eventually Thisbe and Rohan nodded off, and soon only Fifer and the two statues remained awake. Knowing that people trapped in the library were suffering, Fifer fought sleep and other distractions. She paged through book after book that Mr. Today had painstakingly written about his many-years-long process of creating the various pieces of the world that Fifer had taken for granted until now. She scanned a thousand pages for clues, finding a few sections about the tubes and where they led, but nothing on how they were created.

Just before she could fend off sleep no longer, her eyes landed on a paragraph that seemed important, even though it wasn't about the tube system. Fifer jerked fully awake and sat up, reading it again.

Simber turned his head expectantly toward her. After a moment she looked up. "Hey, Simber, Florence," she whispered. "I think I found something."

Florence glanced over too.

"It's not about the tubes," Fifer explained, "but it's about the remote rooms. Apparently, because the kitchenette tube doesn't access the remote rooms, Mr. Today created a magical passageway from the upstairs secret wing that leads to each of the remote areas—theater, lounge, and library. He wanted to be able to reach them in a hurry if necessary."

Florence and Simber looked skeptical. "I've neverrr hearrrd of such a thing," said Simber in a low voice. "Though it wouldn't be the firrrst time I've discoverrred something new about the mansion. Marrrcus had his secrrrets—therrre's no denying that."

Florence came over to look at Fifer's book. "There's a passageway in the mage's living quarters we don't know about?" she asked. "I find that hard to believe. Simber and I know every inch of those rooms. The only hidden door I know about or have ever seen Marcus and Alex use is the one on the back wall of the office that connects it with the apartment."

Fifer found the place in the book and read, "'I made a mistake with the kitchenette tube, connecting it only to my distant friends and other places around the world. I forgot to add the remote rooms to that control system. Due to the intricacies of that particular tube's design, it made more sense to

LISA McMANN

simply create a different passageway from the secret hallway to the remote rooms so I could easily access them if necessary. As it turns out, I rarely use them, preferring to take the extra time to be visible and present in the mansion. I access those rooms now via the main tubes just like everyone else does.'"

Fifer looked up. "Do either of you have a clue what passageway he's talking about? Maybe there's a second secret door on the back wall of the office that we can find? Or inside the apartment somewhere?"

"Not that I know of," said Florence, mystified. "But Simber would know the apartment better than me."

Simber shook his head. "I can't think of anything. I neverrr saw him use a passageway. Everrr."

"Hmm," said Fifer, studying the book again. "Listen to this. It's a clue to locating it." She hesitated, then continued reading.

> *Right is left and wrong is right,*
> *stoop low to find the perfect height.*
> *Tiny eyes will serve you well*
> *To read your way into this spell.*

"Right is left?" asked Florence. "What?"

Fifer muttered the first line a few times. "Does 'right' mean 'correct'? As in, 'correct' is left? And wrong is right? Like there's a left and a right, and he's saying the one on the right is—" She stopped suddenly. "Oooh. Could it be?"

"Be what?" said Florence.

"Those *doors*? In the secret hallway?"

"Ah, Fiferrr," Simber said slowly. "Yes, I think that's it! I underrrstand now. That parrrt of it, anyway," He narrowed his eyes in thought, then said, "The two doorrrs in the hallway that we've all passed by a thousand times and wonderrred what's behind them. I'll bet my wings one of them is this passageway he's talking about."

Desperate Times

While Fifer's clue about the secret passageways was helpful, it didn't solve anything. Even though it appeared from Mr. Today's explanation that one of the doors in the secret hallway was this mysterious passageway he wrote about in his book, Simber, Florence, and Fifer still had no idea how to open it. Mr. Today had magically protected the doors in that hallway. He hadn't given the actual magical password in this book, which was typical style for the late head mage. He obviously hadn't wanted just anyone going anywhere they pleased without having to work for it. So that meant they'd have to find the proper spell on the door itself.

Simber and Florence knew that Alex had tried to open the doors several times over the years, with no success, but he hadn't had this poem clue. And the part about tiny eyes? That was strange, and it clearly meant something. But what?

Chances weren't great that they'd be able to figure it out in a short amount of time when Alex hadn't been able to do it in years. But at least it was something to offer a glimmer of hope that their friends weren't totally doomed. It was enough of a breakthrough for Fifer to call it a night. She needed rest to have a clear mind for the morning. With so many lives at stake, she couldn't afford not to be at her very best.

She stowed her books and supplies in the Quillitary yard near everyone else's, and hoped they'd all be alive to fetch them again when this was over. Then she lay down next to Simber and fell into a restless sleep, soothed by the sounds of nearby dragons breathing.

Before sunrise everyone was ready and anxious to go. Fifer had her hammock loaded with everything she needed, plus extra water for when, not if, they rescued the others. Her falcons flitted about, full of energy and eager to fight back against the ones who'd injured and killed their companions.

Florence, Kaylee, and Ishibashi planned to fly into battle on Quince and keep Ava and Lukas hidden on the dragon's soft back. It was nice for Florence to finally have something big enough to support her size and weight. She'd ridden on Pan before, but she'd never flown, so this was a new adventure. Florence carried her quiver and magic arrows as well as a mixture of spell components. Kaylee and Ishibashi were loaded down with weapons, including swords, daggers, and the handcrafted throwing stars that Ishibashi had brought from his island.

Sky, with her sword, and Thisbe and Rohan with theirs as well as some components, climbed onto Simber's back. And Maiven and the black-eyed children from Grimere took their places on Gorgrun. They carried melee weapons and whatever components they'd managed to learn in the short time Thisbe and Florence had been working with them. They also had their own fiery breath as an added secret weapon, which the dissenters wouldn't expect. And though they couldn't spray fire nearly as far as real dragons could, it was nonetheless dangerous. Slim lines of smoke drifted up from a few of the children's noses and mouths in anticipation. Now and then, as they waited for the signal to take off, they turned to the side to breathe a warm-up round of fire. Their eyes were clear, free from all mind control. Their hands were quick, their heads steady, their insides confident. They were ready for this battle. No matter what happened.

Simber walked with his riders to Fifer in her hammock. "You should say something to everrryone," he said in a low voice. "A speech."

Thisbe frowned. Why her?

Florence glanced at Simber curiously, trying to read his expression. Then she nodded. "Yes, Fifer. Give us some wise words and encouragement to build us up in this dangerous situation."

In the past, Fifer might have been struck with nerves and a feeling of inadequacy to do something like that. But not now. Not after all she'd been through. And not with Thisbe standing there—Thisbe who hadn't just been singled out by Simber as a leader in this group. Fifer had led a group before, and the role had become so natural to her that she barely blinked.

"Everyone," she called out, and waited for the group to quiet down and look at her. When they did, she continued. "Good morning, all. I hope you are feeling refreshed." She hesitated,

then dove in. "This is going to be difficult. Not only to succeed physically by taking back our land, but emotionally, too.
This is a complex situation, fighting against our own people.
No matter how mad they're making us right now, they've still
been a part of our lives for years, and this land on which we'll
be battling is our home."

She paused, trying to find the words to emphasize how
important everything was, and continued. "These factors can
affect the way we make decisions. I think it's obvious to the
ones who call Artimé home that the mansion we remember is
already in tatters, perhaps destroyed forever. And we will take
the time to mourn that like we continue to mourn for Alex."

Thisbe dropped her gaze.

Fifer paused, taking a moment to be sure her voice was
steady and strong. "But now we have to do our jobs without
hesitation. Without backing down or being afraid to . . . well,
to further destroy the possessions we love and the memories
we carry. We'll worry about restoring Artimé later. But for
now, we must focus on the people. We must press forward
knowing we have one chance to save them. Not just the ones
who are physically trapped, but those who are emotionally or

mentally trapped by Frieda Stubbs and her destructive words and deeds. We have one chance to take back the world that Mr. Today created for the Unwanteds—all of them, not a select few. We will not retreat!"

The group stood tall and cheered.

Fifer paused, letting the feelings of reassurance fill her up. "Also, let's not forget that this battle is only half of our task. This attack must be swift and sure, like Florence said. We must overwhelm them from the onset and drive them out before they know what's happening. Our friends are suffering, and time is of the essence." That last part, "time is of the essence," was a phrase Fifer had heard Maiven Taveer utter in the land of the dragons, and she'd liked the sound of it. "We must do what we need to do, and quickly. Is everyone clear on your tasks?"

"All clear!" shouted the group in one voice, which was a bit startling. Maiven had brought her military touch to this team in more ways than one.

Fifer's heart soared. She felt an ounce of hope that their small, strange army had a chance against a group ten times their size. Then she, with a tightness in her throat, made a fist and tapped her chest twice. "I am with you."

LISA McMANN

There was a split-second pause and a few strained looks. Thisbe stared hard at the ground, arms crossed. But then she and everyone else repeated the chest tap, some more heartily than others. With fervor, many responded to Fifer and all who surrounded them. "I am with you."

It came out as a whisper for Thisbe.

"Then," said Fifer, noticing it, "let's begin."

They wasted no time. Fifer whistled for her birds to take flight. Simber bounded and jumped, rising quickly with his passengers. Fifer and Simber led the charge side by side, while the pair of ghost dragons and their riders came right behind.

As they neared the mansion, Florence reminded the ghost dragons of their task in case they'd forgotten. Fifer and her birds, who had a different task, split off from the group, heading for the jungle. "I'll see you soon," she called out. "I believe in you!"

The rest of the group circled overhead. Simber and the dragons each belted out a mighty roar, giving fair warning of their presence to the dissenters in Artimé, and even waking up several of them who'd fallen asleep at their windows after guarding them all night. They stumbled into action and began firing components haphazardly into the air, missing wildly due to the distance of the attackers and the awkward angles at which they were throwing, upward and through the window frames.

Florence, taking point and calling the plays, kept one hand in the air for everyone to see. She made a motion prompting everyone to circle again, trying to coax the enemy out. When a few brave dissenters began climbing through the windows to get a better angle for attack, Florence dropped her arm and shouted, "Dragons, go! Carefully, please! Everyone else, use your rides as your shields and defend as necessary."

On Florence's command, the dragons split up and dropped to opposite sides of the mansion's vast roof. While digging their claws under the eaves and making a tremendous scraping sound that reverberated through the mansion, the dragons roared again, sending dissenters running in fear, in and out through the windows, unsure of where they would be safer. Thisbe and the other fighters on the backs of the fliers took careful aim whenever they saw opportunities to knock out dissenters without killing them. A few dropped. But not nearly enough.

Florence called out again to the dragons gripping the roof, and Gorgrun and Quince strained and pulled upward, sending showers of sparks and sprays of fire down on the mansion. With several earsplitting cracks, the entire roof broke off and wobbled in the dragons' grip, nearly plunging off one side to the ground. But Gorgrun adjusted and caught the corner with his tail just in time.

A moment later the dragons coordinated their moves and lifted the roof higher into the air, taking the ceiling and remaining chandelier chains and other fixtures with it. They carefully flew it to the ground nearby as people's voices inside the mansion exploded in fear and horror and protest. The ghost dragons returned to the space above the mansion with their fighters. Florence and the other riders leaned over and looked down inside the exposed second floor, where all of the living quarters were, and the breezy, huge entry area of the mansion, which had no upper level above it. Frantic dissenters were scrambling and running like ants whose farm had been uncovered. But there were few places to hide.

"This is shocking to watch," Thisbe said. She cringed as she pelted the people below. She'd known the mansion as her home for as long as she could remember. Now the dragons were taking it apart like it was some sort of construction game.

"Stay focused," said Sky, acting as a lookout. "Hold on to hope that we can restore it."

Florence watched the dissenters flood into the classrooms on the first floor, which offered them the most protection under the circumstances. "Just like we planned," she called to Quince. "This is our cue. Do you remember what to do? Take us right down into the middle of that big entryway."

Quince had a look of glee on his face as he prefaced his landing with a burst of sparks to push the remaining dissenters out of the way. Florence winced, hoping he hadn't set the whole mansion on fire, but all seemed okay. He centered himself over the space, then held his wings up and fluttered them to lower himself down. As he landed inside the once-beautiful structure, one foot hit the bottom part of the staircase and crushed a couple of the steps into powder.

Thisbe cringed, but she didn't stop taking shots whenever she could safely do so, all the while staying low on the dragon's back and dodging fire from the dissenters.

People in the upper-level residence hallways who'd been suddenly uncovered turned and ran into their rooms, locking themselves in. But of course they had no ceiling or roof overhead in there, either. They dove into tubes and closets and under their beds, but most were still visible to the fighters from Grimere above them.

Gorgrun hovered in place, positioning his black-eyed passengers to give them every advantage to take out the dissenters with their newly learned magic and dragon fire. All of them began shooting fiery blasts at the dissenters. Sometimes they started small blazes that would drive the people out of their hiding spots. Then they'd hit the dissenters with fire-step and minor explosion spells they'd learned from Florence. Once they cleared a section of rooms, Gorgrun would circle around and hover again over a different part. The black-eyed children would repeat the task, taking aim in every nook and cranny, spraying fire down every hallway from back to front, forcing the people to the balcony and down the stairs, leaving scorch marks everywhere but keeping the place from totally going up in flames.

Simber, dwarfed and almost nimble compared to the dragons, swooped down on the main floor with his magic- and sword-wielding riders and skillfully flew through the mansion's hallways, which by design were just wide enough for him. This was his territory, and he knew the main floor better than anyone in Artimé. Plus, his ability to see, hear, and smell was so far above the rest of theirs that everyone had full faith he would leave no stone unturned, no dissenter hidden. But where was Frieda? He hadn't spotted her yet.

The great cheetah twisted and turned through the halls, the vast kitchen, the classrooms, and the dining room, plowing down anyone in his way. On his back, Thisbe and Rohan pelted everybody they could reach with components and tried to keep themselves protected from getting struck by return components. Sky, leaning off to one side, took deep swipes and jabs with her sword at anyone trying to get past them. When Rohan got hit by scatterclips, he went soaring and slammed into the chef's giant pantry doors, sticking there. Simber quickly zoomed around, and they picked him up. Sky grabbed a few knives from the butcher block while they were stopped, and then they were off to gather up the hiding dissenters once more.

In the entryway, dissenters kept their distance from the dragon. Florence slid off Quince's back, and Kaylee and Ishibashi followed, staying close behind the warrior woman for protection from flying components. As they moved through the space, Florence held off anyone trying to rush at them,

LISA McMANN

and Kaylee and Ishibashi used their throwing stars to take down any menacing approaching attackers. Florence sliced the air with components in rapid succession, turning clockwise in a circle and striking dissenters at every tick. The panicked crowds that were rushing down the stairs from their rooms skirted around the enormous dragon and began clambering for the exits. Many of them crashed to the ground in mid-escape after being hit by a spell from Simber's team passing through.

When the enemy activity around Florence slowed down, Quince swiped his tail from side to side, rounding up enchanted dissenters and placing them in piles near the windows that faced the lawn. Florence and her team cautiously began picking up and tossing frozen and otherwise incapacitated dissenters outside in preparation for the next step of their plan.

Then Quince noticed a rogue group of dissenters whose spells had worn off trying to sneak back in through the door by the kitchen. Their sights were on Thisbe as she rode by on Simber, and they were poised to knock her flat and bring her to Frieda Stubbs, as the woman had requested. But Quince saw them coming and blew a huge fiery breath down the hallway in their direction. He turned them to charcoal and accidentally set the broken tubes on fire, requiring help putting it out from Gorgrun's team. After that, Florence sent Quince back outside to assist Gorgrun and the Grimere fighters.

Things were miraculously going better than expected, but there were two questions on Florence's mind: First, where was Frieda Stubbs? Florence had been searching for any sign of the woman, but found none. And second, why hadn't Fifer arrived yet? She should have been here by now. Florence desperately hoped that Fifer wasn't having any problems with her part of the plan—that could be devastating for more than just her. And now more of the frozen people were thawing, which meant Florence had to start fresh with a new round of freeze spells. With so few spell casters, things were getting dicey. If everyone started waking up at once, they'd have a brand-new battle on their hands, only this time they'd be scattered and without a plan. Florence dug in, pelting everybody she could find who was stirring, and wishing Simber would come back with Thisbe, Rohan, and Sky—she could use the help.

Luckily, one of Florence's questions was answered when fresh screams arose from the lawn. The mansion shook and rattled like it was sitting on top of a giant beating heart.

LISA McMANN

Florence rushed to the windows to see the rock barreling across the lawn from the jungle with Panther bounding beside her at a frantic clip. Following behind them was the source of the shaking—the stomping, roaring mastodon, Ol' Tater, whom Fifer had brought to life. Panther and the rock kept just out of Ol' Tater's reach, wanting the beast to follow them but knowing he would turn on them in an instant, for he had been created without any sense of right or wrong and would stomp on anything or anyone if given the chance.

High above Ol' Tater, Fifer and her birds were heading toward the mansion.

"Thank goodness," Florence muttered, laying down a row of dissenters who were struggling to their feet. "Simber!" she shouted, and in seconds the cheetah screeched around a corner and flew to Florence's side, his riders slipping and sliding as they tried to hang on. "It's time," Florence told him. "Leave Thisbe with me—you can keep Rohan and Sky, but Kaylee, Ishibashi, and I need a little more help here. Run out the back way and speak to Panther first. I'll set Fifer in motion."

"Got it," said Simber.

Thisbe slid off, and Simber galloped down the hallway

with Sky and Rohan past what was left of the smoldering tubes. Thisbe saw them and gasped. Could that situation get any worse? Now what were they going to do? There weren't answers. Instead, Thisbe turned her attention back to the dissenters, more of whom were thawing from being frozen.

"Help me keep them from escaping," Florence said, but Thisbe was already firing off components and freeze spells, inside and through the windows at the bodies on the lawn. Once Simber was outside, Florence signaled above to Fifer and her birds to be ready.

Fifer signaled back to let Florence know she understood. She shouted orders to her jungle companions.

In response, the rock came to a sliding halt near the fountain, sending a long ribbon of sod flying into the air and pelting disoriented Artiméans. Ol' Tater slowed down, then tried to stomp on the rock, but he couldn't lift his foot high enough. So he did no harm to the rock, but he continued trying, and the pursuit kept Ol' Tater occupied for the moment, which was helpful. The rock opened his giant mouth and waited for the plan Florence had talked to him about to begin.

Simber, with his passengers, ran up to Panther and touched

noses with her in greeting. Sky and Rohan eyed the black cat warily. Her fangs dripped with saliva and were a little too close for comfort. Rohan drew his legs up in front of him.

Panther was a bit of a wild card, but she listened to Simber. In Panther's ear he whispered, "Rrround up the fleeing ones and chase them into the rrrock's mouth. Trrry not to bite any-one unless they'rrre rrreally annoying."

Panther crouched and backed up. With an earsplitting screech, she sprinted into action, tearing across the lawn and circling around the dissenters. Ol' Tater saw her moving and gave up on stomping the rock. He pursued her instead and, in the process, essentially kept the dissenters from daring to make any moves at all for fear of him turning on them. Panther herded these captured foes toward the rock. With her fangs and ability to chase them down, combined with Ol' Tater stomping around and being terrifying, dissenters willingly jumped into the rock's mouth for their own safety, some of them surrendering once they realized everything they were up against.

Fifer directed her falcons to drop her into her room and invited them to remain there for safety's sake until they were needed again. She communicated with Gorgrun's team to make sure that, as they continued to sweep the upstairs, they wouldn't send any fire or spells at the birds while searching methodically for those who might be hiding. Seeing that the upper floor was under control, Fifer ran out to the balcony and downstairs to assist Florence, Thisbe, Kaylee, and Ishibashi on the main floor. Another wave of dissenters was waking up and struggling to their feet to try to fight off the intruders, and Thisbe and Florence had their hands full. Pelting the ones in her way before they could reach for their components, Fifer went to the window nearest Simber and called out to him. "Can you do without Sky and Rohan? We could use more help in here!"

Panther and Ol' Tater's herding technique was working well, and the outdoor team was fierce enough to make Sky's and Rohan's contributions minimal at best. Simber immediately flew the passengers to the mansion and dropped them off.

Fifer ran to confer with him. "What'll you do when the rock is full?" she asked. "Make a corral with the statues and dragons?"

"That's the plan," said Simber. He didn't stick around to elaborate and flew back to be a part of the circle that included

LISA McMANN

239 « Dragon Fire

the rock, Panther, and Ol' Tater. As Florence tossed people through the windows, Panther herded them, and the others moved fluidly based on Ol' Tater's whims to keep the dissenters surrounded but safe from the stomping mastodon.

"Follow me," Fifer told Sky and Rohan, helping them in through the window. "There are still plenty of people hiding in the cubbyholes and crevices, and we haven't found Frieda yet. Gorgrun and the Grimere fighters are covering the second floor, driving everybody downstairs. We'll join Thisbe and continue on the first." She started down the hallway, then ducked and hit the floor, crying, "Watch out!" Components came flying their way. Sky got hit by a backward bobbly head. Rohan released the spell, and the three scrambled to find cover before venturing forward again.

Florence saw them coming. "Good," she said. "I'm going outside to help make the corral. You three join Thisbe and keep sending frozen bodies out to us." She hesitated, then spoke quietly to Fifer. "The momentum is changing in our favor. But stay strong and be on your guard."

Fifer nodded, and they got to work. The ranks of dissenters had thinned inside the mansion. With the largest attackers having relocated outside—Quince, Simber, and Florence—some of Frieda's followers who were still in hiding crept out to see what was going on and to look for a means of escape. But Thisbe, Sky, Rohan, Kaylee, Ishibashi, and Fifer were on the move, hunting them down and making every attempt to attack before being fired upon. They forced them with swords to the windows or froze them and dragged them there, confiscating their components and tossing bodies one at a time onto the lawn for Simber and Florence to deal with. But there was still one person they hadn't run across yet.

Knowing Frieda wasn't a great mage gave them some hope that she wouldn't put up much of a fight once they found her. Unlike past enemies, such as Gondoleery Rattrapp and the High Priest Justine herself, Frieda Stubbs was an amateur villain. Thus, the group wasn't too worried about what would happen when she finally appeared.

That was probably a mistake.

Brought to a Boil

When Frieda Stubbs heard the attackers coming, she painted herself invisible and snuck out the back door of the kitchen, crossed the lawn, and climbed into a leafy tree on the border between Artimé and Quill, where she could watch everything that was happening. She was sure Garrit would bark out some orders on her behalf, and her people had been trained by the best—Florence. So she knew they'd fight for her and for their own peace and safety from the Revinir while Frieda planned her big move. Frieda hadn't expected the dragons, but they didn't seem to belong to the Revinir, so that put her mind somewhat at ease. And it was a bonus to have Thisbe show up. Perhaps she'd be able to do away with all the Stowes at once—it would certainly make her life easier. She worried for a while that Fifer Stowe wasn't among the outcasts who had attacked. But a short time later she saw the spitting image of Nadia Stowe coming from the jungle with her awful birds and that stomping mastodon statue.

With that creature about, Frieda decided to stay put for a while. Perhaps she'd let her enemies think she had run away. Of course they'd assume that, and they'd grow complacent and careless. Everyone underestimated her. But they were in for a shock, because Frieda was finally going to get revenge for what that awful pirate girl had done to her.

Life had been especially hard the past few years, seeing Thisbe and Fifer Stowe grow into young women. They looked more like their mother every time they came back from stirring up trouble in the land of the dragons. They had the same unusual black eyes and black wavy hair. Fifer, who wore her hair long, especially resembled Frieda's old neigh-bor who had come so abruptly and so suspiciously to Quill from a pirate ship.

Nadia had been aloof from the beginning, Frieda remembered. But she'd picked up on the rules of Quill quickly enough and tried valiantly to follow them. But the girl should have been declared Unwanted from the moment she'd stepped into the Wanted neighborhood where Frieda's family lived. Nadia didn't belong there. Frieda had known it from the start when she'd witnessed Nadia speaking to birds in the farm area of Quill. The birds seemed to speak to her, too. And there was a whole flock of them that fluttered high overhead, trapped outside of Quill by the barbed-wire ceiling that covered the island. They moved when Nadia moved. It was unsettling. And then there were the sparks that flew from her eyes, which she tried to hide. But Frieda had seen them.

Frieda shifted in the tree and drew her legs up out of sight when Simber flew a little too close for comfort. But he wasn't looking for her, and Frieda's time to shine hadn't come yet. So her mind wandered back to her nemesis.

Immediately after seeing the sparks, Frieda had reported Nadia to the governors, explaining that the new pirate girl was possessed. "Her eyes spark fire and birds follow her around," she'd told them. Sealing Nadia's fate, or so Frieda had thought.

LISA McMANN

It was such a strange claim that the High Priest Justine had called Frieda into the palace shortly before the Purge that year to question her. Frieda had felt a swell of importance. Surely she would be rewarded for this. But High Priest Justine grilled her with icy questions. And in the end, no matter how Frieda tried to defend herself, Justine declared that Frieda was telling tales. An illegal offense.

At the Purge, Nadia was declared a Necessary. And Frieda was named Unwanted.

It had been a terrible shock. The trauma of being declared Unwanted when she'd never been caught doing anything creative had scarred her. The shame of being shackled by the governors and the nightmares about being thrown into the lake of boiling oil lingered for years, even though she found herself in beautiful Artimé. It had been a horrible experience. She couldn't seem to get over the wrong that had been done to her. And it was all Nadia's fault. Later, Frieda often imagined Nadia's reaction to Frieda being called Unwanted. She knew the pirate must have been smug. The girl had been performing actual creative acts in plain sight, and she'd gotten away with it.

Frieda felt fresh anger bubble up. She'd hidden it for a long time. Tried to forget it and managed to do so for years. And when Alex became head mage, Frieda found that he possessed none of his awful mother's traits, so she accepted him. A few years later, when Nadia had died saving Thisbe and Fifer, Frieda felt a tiny bit of satisfaction. But over time, Nadia was considered some sort of hero. That burned. But Frieda held in her feelings then, too. At least there was Alex—the only good thing to come out of Nadia's existence. She steered clear of Aaron and the girl twins, warily watching them grow up.

But when Alex was killed and Artimé appointed Justine's successor, Aaron Stowe, to take his place, something had exploded inside Frieda. Not only were the twin girls a constant and growing reminder of Nadia, especially with Fifer's birds and Thisbe's sparking eyes, but Aaron was a constant reminder that the only decent one of them was dead. This time there was nothing Frieda could do to stop the rage inside her. She'd taken all she could handle of the Stowes. And she refused to live the rest of her life under the rule of people like Nadia.

The twin girls and Aaron would be the end of Artimé. They'd brought danger to the magical land already, and a great deal more was looming. And people had wanted to put their trust in Aaron? It was absurd. Frieda had to take matters into her own hands to save Artimé. She'd made it her mission to teach everyone about who the true dangers to the island really were. And it was working. Frieda was going to get rid of everything remotely related to Nadia Stowe once and for all, and save their world in the process.

Maybe not everyone saw it the way Frieda did quite yet, but most of them did. And her supporters were growing in number every day. In time all of Artimé and Quill would thank her, once all traces of the Stowes were erased from their island for good. There would be no one left for the evil dragon-monster, the Revinir, to come after. And Artimé would be at peace once more—this time for good.

Devastation and Loss

Astrid, the ghost dragon, and Dev, who now decidedly identified with the Suresh family of rulers, carried an air about them as they began their journey to the land where the palace stood. It was an air of distinction, perhaps. Or one approaching deservedness. They were going on an adventure to reclaim this closed-off, forgotten corner of the land of the dragons and the black-eyed rulers. They were going to see the shining palace of Dev's people.

As they flew, Dev let his imagination go wild. He pictured scenes in which his newfound family would run out of the purple-and-orange palace to greet him and welcome him into this beautiful place, saying lovely things like, "Our long-lost boy is home at last!"

The thoughts made his insides hurt a little. It also made him feel foolish that he'd spent any time imagining such a scene, which he knew in reality wouldn't happen. No one in the world cared a whit about Dev— the Revinir herself had said so. And not a soul in that palace would know him. If there even *was* anyone there. Dev would be a stranger barging onto the scene. The thought almost made him uncomfortable enough to tell Astrid to turn around and go back to the cavelands.

If not for the images, he might have. But somehow they seemed like proof of ownership. Why else would those scenes pound in his mind every time the Revinir roared, if the memories of such places didn't belong to him? What was his connection to them? He had to find out.

He wondered if Thisbe and the others had seen these same pictures. Thisbe had said something reassuring about them after his mind had first cleared. But so much had happened in those moments immediately afterward that Dev had been totally overwhelmed. Discovering Thisbe's return, being summoned to the castle, and Thisbe wanting him to act like he was still under the Revinir's mind control—it had been a lot. Enough that he couldn't remember any details of that part of the conversation if she'd given them.

Not long after that flurry of events, the Revinir had roared, and he'd been blinded with the images. Since then, the more ancestor broth he'd ingested, the less intense the images had been. And now, whenever the calls came, the pictures didn't totally overtake his senses.

Dev remembered his time in the tower. He recalled the look on the Revinir's face when she'd realized that the ancestor broth really did have an effect on him and the others. How he wished he hadn't inadvertently revealed it before she'd flung him out the window.

He shuddered.

"Everything all right back there?" Astrid called out. "Warm enough?"

"I'm all right. Do you remember where we're going?"

The dragon was quiet for a moment. Then she cleared her throat. "Errm. Not . . . quite."

Dev smiled and told her. Most of the time it didn't bother him that she and the other ghost dragons forgot things. It wasn't annoying unless the thing was very important or urgent. And at this point, Dev had nothing urgent on his agenda, which felt strange but nice. "Just don't go to Grimere," he said. Then he added, "My name is Dev, by the way."

"Short for Devastation, no doubt," Astrid joked.

Dev tilted his head, thinking about that and liking it. "Yes," he said with a laugh. "Short for Devastation. And don't you forget it."

"Ha-ha!" said Astrid with a glorious cackle.

The terrain below was desertlike until they reached a mountain range, where a stream passed through that was lined with trees. Dev was glad he'd asked Astrid to take him. Climbing the mountains would have been a challenge that Dev might not have been up for. His aching ribs seemed to be a pain that would never go away, and he'd only just learned to tolerate it.

The mountains below looked sharp and rugged and difficult. That explained why Ashguard's palace and the surrounding village was so closed off. There was no way to approach on foot from the north because of these mountains, and the crater lake was a barrier to the east of the land.

"What's to the south and west of the palace?" Dev asked presently.

"I don't recall," said Astrid, not surprisingly. "I'm feeling like it could be . . . water. Maybe? An ocean?" She paused, sniffing the air. "Or land. I don't know."

"Interesting," said Dev, trying not to laugh. "And beyond the oceans or . . . or land?"

"I doubt I've ever known that," said Astrid. "But clearly there are dragons beyond, if what you say is accurate about them having come from far and wide in response to the Revinir's call."

"They definitely have done that," said Dev. "Can you tell me why the ghost dragons aren't affected?"

"We hear the roar," Astrid said. "We just don't care. The only call we are willing to respond to is that of the black-eyed rulers."

Dev blinked. "What, you mean like me? Please. That's not even funny."

"You are the Devastator, after all."

Dev didn't tell her she'd renamed him wrongly from earlier. The two bantered a bit more to pass the time, and then Dev slept, but not for too long in case Astrid forgot where they were going again.

When she woke him, he sat up and looked down at the terrain. The mountains were behind them. Below, the remains of a city covered rolling hills. Bits of green growth showed through. There were some buildings and houses still standing, like a city that had been destroyed by a natural disaster. Dev glanced to the east, seeing the crater lake in the distance, and beyond that, the tree line of the forest and the promise of Dragonsmarche and Grimere. Astrid dropped lower and circled above a hill that had some sprawling structures on it. She had no problem finding a place to land.

"Are you sure this is right?" Dev asked her, bewildered. "You went to the place where Ashguard's palace was, right? The purple-and-orange bulbous castle with the—"

"With the gilded roofs," Astrid said. "Yes. This is the correct location. I'm sure of it. See over there?" She pointed through some tall, thick overgrowth, but Dev couldn't see anything orange or purple or gilded.

"I . . . don't . . . understand," Dev said, his voice faltering.

"I'll show you." Astrid landed smoothly and took several steps as Dev continued to try to make sense of what had happened here. The dragon pushed through the brush, trampling

LISA McMANN

it down to make a path. When the last trees parted, Dev spied a large building, mostly gutted but with a few enclosed spaces. And five smoke-stained towers with bulbs on top that were definitely not gold. Astrid continued toward it. "This is the palace," she said gently.

Dev's lips parted as he stared. When Astrid stopped in front of it, he slid down her wing and stood quietly for a long moment between two of the towers, looking into the deserted covered courtyard before him. No one came out to welcome him home.

Putting a Lid on It

Back in Artimé, above the mansion's new open-air, sunlit second floor, Quince and Gorgrun circled, ready to torch the place at a moment's notice, but trying hard to remember that, after accidentally setting the mansion tubes on fire, Florence the warrior trainer had asked them not to burn anything else down if possible.

Additionally, no matter how hard they tried, the ghost dragons couldn't tell which people running around the mansion and lawn were friends and which were foes. They were a smattering of good and evil. Some were more good than evil, others more evil than good, but the dragons knew full well that

LISA McMANN

that wasn't an indicator of anything regarding being on the *right* side of the war. It was never that easy. Even the black-eyed people were a broad variety of levels, so there was no putting humans into groups based on that.

So they decided to refrain from killing anyone unless called upon by the leaders they trusted: Thisbe, Maiven, and the great warrior woman. Instead they looked to help in other ways, like rounding up escapees, or assisting the black-eyed children and Maiven Taveer in hunting down dissenters in the maze of rooms on the second floor below them.

Since the doors to each Artiméan's personal room were locked, the dragons used their tails like ropes and ladders for the Grimere children, lifting them up over the walls to access the ones hiding in their rooms. And if the children were struck by a spell, Gorgrun and Quince picked them up and put them on their backs for safekeeping until the effects wore off or until someone was able to release the spell. Whenever one of the black-eyed fighters scared up a dissenter and identified the person as such, the dragons either chased them down the stairs to the spell casters working below, or they snatched them up in the curls of their tails or gripped them in their claws. Then they delivered them to the lawn for Simber to take care of.

Far down the lengthy hallways, the children from Grimere went in pairs from room to room, blasting fire at anyone hiding in order to flush them out. They used their fiery breath and the few spells they'd learned to defend themselves against dissenters who reached for a component and tried to fight. They shooed the people out into the hallway, and when a room was fully checked and cleared of all hiders, they cast glass panes in front of the doors so the dissenters couldn't easily get back in. Faced with the threat of fire, most of the confused and frightened dissenters put their hands in the air and pleaded for mercy as they backed down the hallway.

"We're going!" cried one. "Please don't hurt us!"

"We didn't want to have this war in the first place!" cried another. "I don't even like Frieda, and I *hate* fighting."

"She abandoned us hours ago!" the first accused. "What kind of leader does that? She was staring out the back door. Then she took out an invisibility paintbrush and applied it. I haven't seen her since. I'm sure she took off running into Quill like a coward."

The children from Grimere didn't understand much of

what was shouted at them, but Asha thought she understood the part about Frieda running to Quill, so she tucked the information away in case it would be useful to share with Thisbe later. She and the others held back from harming anyone who was going willingly to the staircase to be wrangled by the actual mages. For the most part, only a few fought back, and the rest surrendered . . . at least until they got to the main floor.

Down there, Fifer and Thisbe were whipping off freeze spells as more people were evicted from their hiding places and trying to make a run for it. Those who succeeded in getting outside without being hit by spells were stopped and corralled by Panther or the dragons. Florence continued to transfer the frozen ones from the mansion windows to the area around the rock outside, since his mouth was full by now.

Once things started to calm down, Florence called Gorgrun to assist on the ground. First she had him uproot a section of trees in the jungle and bring them to the lawn. Then she instructed him to lay four trunks lengthwise in an imperfect square around the dissenters. He stacked more logs on top of the first ones, building walls. They formed a pen with space at one corner for a door.

Once the structure was solid, Gorgrun and Quince picked up the mansion's roof, which they'd removed earlier, and set it on top of the pen to keep the dissenters from climbing out. Panther and Simber guarded the openings and methodically put more and more fleeing Artiméans inside, despite their cries of surrender and pleas for freedom. "You'll get yourrr chance to speak," Simber snarled at them. "But forrr now, I advise you to be quiet. Orrr else." His words were frightening enough to silence the group, at least for a while

Combing through the entire mansion took hours, and Fifer and Thisbe's team didn't work without sacrifice. Every human among them at one point or another had been frozen or scatter-clipped or backward-bobbly-headed or fire-stepped by dissenters who were still putting up a fight or trying to defend themselves from the small but increasingly effective army. Fifer and Thisbe did what they could to release the spells or revive each other and continue doggedly on, despite their growing number of bruises. Always at the back of their minds, keeping them going, was the reminder that their dear friends were suffering just a simple tube ride away. If only they could get it to work.

LISA McMANN

By the time they expelled and contained what seemed to be the best hiders and last of the obstinate stragglers, they had still not found Frieda Stubbs. With the place clear, though, there was no time to waste in trying to get to the remote rooms. They'd have to take the chance of running into a surprise meeting with the dictator and hope their training was enough for the best outcome. And who even knew if she was still in the building? Chances were great that she'd abandoned ship a long time ago. No one would expect anything else.

Thisbe and Fifer found themselves together with no one left to fight. Each offered a curt nod of congratulations, then went their separate ways, still unable or unwilling to address their differences with so many other things to tend to. While Thisbe took a minute to collect herself and check in with the others, Fifer slipped outside to see how things were going there.

"We're putting the last of them into the cage now," said Florence. She and Simber were extracting dissenters from the rock's mouth and making them go into the pen.

"I'll get started on Ol' Tater," said Fifer. "If we get him placed just right, he can serve as a door to the pen." She ran at the mastodon and jumped around to get his attention, then ran back toward the opening in the pen. Ol' Tater followed as expected, trying to stomp on her. When he was nearly in the place where Fifer wanted him, she began the spell that would put him back to sleep. Simber tossed the last dissenter into the pen, then helped to position the mastodon. Fifer sang, and the statue fell into a permanent sleep right in front of the opening to the log pen, his massive hindquarters blocking anyone from leaving.

With the dust settling and everything appearing to be under control, Fifer and Florence thanked the rock and Panther. The two took their leave and returned to the jungle. Simber stayed on the lawn to watch over the pen and the grounds and search for Frieda, and the dragons joined him there to keep the restless captives from trying anything.

Fifer and Florence hurried back inside to survey the damage to the tubes and try to get them to work. There they found Thisbe already tinkering with the tube that had suffered the least amount of fire damage. Rohan and Maiven stood just outside the glass, offering to help, but when they saw Fifer and Florence approaching, they parted and moved aside.

"Any sign of the Stubbs?" asked Fifer.

Rohan gave her a grim smile. "Asha overheard some of

the dissenters say Frieda snuck out early and left Artimé. She abandoned them all."

"I'm not so sure about that," muttered Thisbe. She gripped a small screwdriver between her teeth, and she was using both hands to pry up a corner of the control panel. She wasn't having any luck. "Time will tell."

"And what about the tubes?" asked Fifer anxiously.

"Not good," said Thisbe, looking up and pulling the screwdriver from her mouth. "It's not just that the panel is broken. Everything inside is smashed and melted. There's nothing we can do with this if we don't have a complete replacement, and I've never heard of any extra parts being stored anywhere, have you?"

"No," said Florence. "We've never needed them."

"And even if we did have a replacement," she said with a shake of her head, "none of us knows how to put it together. The only one who's ever fixed a tube is trapped in one of the remote rooms."

"I saw another . . . tube . . . in the kitchen," Reza said hesitantly.

Fifer and Thisbe looked at him, then at each other. They knew that tube well from their younger years. But like the one in the head mage's kitchenette, it had its own settings and rules for where it went. "Hmm," said Fifer. "That one doesn't run through these main tubes, though. I think it only has direct access to the living quarters for food delivery. Thisbe, do you remember if it also goes to the remote rooms?"

"I doubt it, but I'll check," said Thisbe. "I don't remember ever using the room service tube for anything except sending food to individual rooms upstairs." She slipped out of the main tube and ran to the kitchen, jumping over the debris that was scattered throughout the hallways. When she returned, her expression was grim. "That one has been smashed too. Only the tube in the head mage's kitchenette is functioning."

"Why did Frieda have to destroy everything?" muttered Florence. "It's senseless! It didn't work in her favor in any way. I can't believe this mess—I honestly don't know if we can ever repair these tubes." For the first time since the mission began, Florence's voice had become distressed. Everyone felt the same way—completely helpless. Their closest friends and family were trapped and wouldn't last much longer without water.

"In the world I come from, places have at least two exits," Kaylee said, feeling frustration boiling up. She knew that saying it couldn't fix the situation now, but she was stressed out and worried about Aaron, and felt like she had to speak her mind. "Maybe that would be a good idea going forward. Magic or no, stuff breaks." She frowned. "Sorry. I know that's not helpful at this moment. I'm just . . . scared." She tried not to let on how worried she was, but with the rumors flying that Aaron was one of the people in the library, she couldn't help but agonize over the fact that nobody had thought of a situation where the tubes would fail.

"Two exits! That reminds me of that passage I read last night," said Fifer, turning to Florence. "Let's have a look at those doors upstairs. I didn't bring the book with me, but I memorized the clue."

"What are you talking about?" Kaylee asked.

On the way up the broken-down staircase, with the sky overhead, Fifer explained to the others what she'd discovered the previous night. Then she recited the clue Mr. Today had written:

> Right is left and wrong is right,
> stoop low to find the perfect height.
> Tiny eyes will serve you well
> To read your way into this spell.

At the balcony, only Florence, Thisbe, and Fifer continued on, for they were the only ones who could see and enter the not-a-secret hallway. They did so without delay, leaving Kaylee, Ishibashi, and the people from Grimere on the balcony. While they waited, Ishibashi explained to the others how the secret hallway worked for those who possessed a certain level of magic. As they listened, Maiven, Rohan, and Kaylee kept watch, not forgetting that the person who had caused all of this devastation had reportedly escaped the mansion and could return at any moment.

"What else were the dissenters saying?" Kaylee asked the black-eyed children. "Did you hear anything?"

One of them spoke rapidly in her native language, and Rohan translated. "They didn't understand all of the words being said, but from their tones and gestures, the people seemed annoyed by Frieda," he reported. "Like they didn't want to be in this war in the first place. And they were angry that Frieda had abandoned them."

Just inside the secret hallway, Florence, who could see the Grimere fighters even though they couldn't see her, overheard what Rohan was saying and told the twins. Fifer and Thisbe, who were kneeling in front of the door on the left to look for the clue, nodded and kept looking for whatever Mr. Today had put there. "That's good that the people are angry at Frieda," Thisbe said as she scanned the wood surface. "Maybe some of them are finally coming to their senses. I'm not sure how we're going to figure out if the dissenters are safe now or not. And if not, what are we going to do with them? Do you have a plan?"

"Can't we just keep them in the cage?" Florence muttered. She was still angry about how destroyed the mansion was.

Fifer shook her head. "I've been thinking we should inter-view them with the dragons present to see what percent good or evil they are, and keep the good ones."

Thisbe looked alarmed. "Uh, I'm not sure I'd pass that test, so maybe step back from that a little."

Fifer glanced at her sister. "What?"

"It's a long story," Thisbe said. She shifted uncomfortably. "Are you sure the left door is the right door?" She peered all around the doorknob, seeing nothing.

"Pretty sure. That's the only sense I can make of 'Right is left and wrong is right.' But I'll check the other just in case."

"I don't see anything at all," said Thisbe. "And the other

door is the left door if you face the opposite direction down the hallway. So it's confusing. Which way was Mr. Today standing when he made that spell?"

Fifer sighed. She got up and crossed the hallway to examine that door, and scoured its surface for several moments. "I don't see anything here, either."

"Neither of you has tiny eyes," Florence remarked.

"No one I know of has tiny eyes," argued Fifer, "so there's not much we can do about that."

They searched a moment more. "Maybe we have to look farther down," said Thisbe. "It said stoop low, right? I assumed that meant to look below the handle, but maybe the clue is lower."

Fifer squinted and crouched, letting her eyes trace invisible lines across the entire door, dropping a little lower with each pass. "Still nothing."

"Same here," said Thisbe.

Fifer lay down on her stomach and squinted, looking for any sort of irregularity. "I see a scratch in the wood," she said. "And there's a little piece broken off the bottom corner."

"Is anything written there?"

LISA McMANN

"Not that I can see." She paused. "This is ridiculous. Who on earth has tiny eyes that Mr. Today would be referring to?"

"Who knows," said Thisbe. "It could totally be someone who no longer lives here. He could have written that book fifty years ago for all we know."

They kept at it. As Fifer rolled to her side, she felt something move in her hip pocket. She quickly lifted her body up, and Kitten pushed her way out.

"Mewmewmew," said Kitten angrily.

"I'm sorry if I crushed you!" Fifer replied. "I forgot you were in there."

Kitten folded her front paws and looked away in disdain.

Florence glanced over. And then she blinked. "Oh," she said. "Tiny eyes. I think we found our mystery helper."

Tiny Eyes

O f course!" cried Fifer. "How could we forget Kitten?"

The itty-bitty porcelain feline rolled her tiny eyes. This was not the first time the Unwanteds had forgotten that she existed. "Mewmewmew," she said, sounding sarcastic.

"What does that mean?" Thisbe asked. "We need Simber to translate."

"I'm not sure we want to know that bit," said Florence. "She seems angry. You two try to explain to Kitten what we're looking for. I'll go trade places with Simber and send him up here."

Soon Kitten was prancing around in front of the door, looking for clues and feeling important once again now that she knew Mr. Today had singled her out for this significant clue. She searched the door on the right first, where Fifer was. Mewing, but finding nothing, she and the twins moved to the door on the left. This time Kitten sniffed thoroughly, pointing out a small space under it, which the other door didn't have. Kitten peered up.

"I'm sure there's got to be something here," Fifer said to Thisbe. Then: "Kitten, can you see underneath?"

"Mewmewmew," said Kitten, sticking her head in the crack. Her voice sounded muffled.

"Good job, Kitten," Fifer said encouragingly. "But maybe you should come back out. Mr. Today left you a secret message on this door somewhere that will unlock it for us. Isn't this exciting? If you find it, we might be able to rescue Fox."

"Mewmewmew," said Kitten. She emerged from under the door and jumped at it, sinking her claws into the wood. Then she began climbing, holding her face close to the surface, looking for clues.

They could hear Simber coming. The big cat flew up over

the mansion wall and straight to the second floor, not wanting to add his weight to the staircase for fear it would come crumbling down. He frightened the children on the balcony in the process, which made him frown and wish for the invisibility paintbrushes again. Luckily the people of Grimere recovered more quickly than in the past, so that was an improvement at least. Though they still kept their eyes on him.

He landed and went into the head mage's hallway. "Tiny eyes," he said approvingly. "Of courrrse Marrrcus would have left something herrre forrr Kitten—she was grrranted nine lives, afterrr all, so she's got the best surrrvival odds of all of us. We should have known. I'm sorry I didn't think of you immediately, Kitten."

"Mewmewmew," said Kitten, sounding very put out again.

"I know, I know," said Simber, abashed. "I want to be a betterrr frrriend too."

The girls exchanged a rare glance but didn't dare ask for an explanation from Simber. Besides, they wanted Kitten to focus on the job and Simber not to growl at them for getting too personal with him, especially when he was being reprimanded.

Kitten seemed satisfied with Simber's answer, and she went

back to work, claws out, scooting around on the face of the door as if gravity had no pull on her. Back and forth she went until she reached a point about a foot below the doorknob and came to a stop. She put her eye to the wood and was quiet.

Fifer and Thisbe knelt, being quiet too, even though they could see nothing. Simber waited, his eyes narrowed to slits as if he were wishing them to be tiny too.

Kitten scrambled around and turned upside down. She studied the same spot while the twins held their breath. The sounds of the outdoors coming inside seemed strangely pleasant.

Before Kitten could speak about what she'd found, Simber turned his head sharply, hearing something none of the others could hear. His eyes darted, his nostrils flared, and he stood up. A low growl reverberated in his chest. Fifer and Thisbe looked wildly all around, expecting to see an intruder and grabbing for their components. But they saw nothing. Simber looked up and growled louder.

"What is it?" Fifer whispered. "Is it Frieda?"

Kitten turned too, then jumped down to stand by Simber and sniff the air.

"Someone's herrre," Simber said softly. "Above us. I can't see them."

"Can just anyone access this hallway now with the roof gone?" asked Thisbe. "Is the magical barrier only at the doorway?" Her answer came seconds later when dozens of huge magical sledgehammers began raining down on them, pounding and smashing everything in sight.

In one blink, both twins were slammed to the floor. Simber's tail broke off. And Kitten was smashed to smithereens.

LISA McMANN

One Other Way

Chaos erupted on the balcony as sledgehammers came pounding down on the ones there as well. Maiven Taveer's cap went flying, and she was thrown to the floor, followed by the rest of the Grimere team. They didn't know what had hit them, for they, like Fifer and Thisbe, had never actually seen the sledgehammer spell in use before.

"What's happening?" cried Rohan, who'd been struck hard in the thigh, causing a deep bruise and a momentary inability to walk. He dodged the hammer that continued coming after him and limped over to Maiven to help her to her feet. The rest of them scattered, running down the stairs or through the hallways, covering their heads and trying to escape the pounding sledgehammers.

"Take coverrr!" Simber shouted to the ones in the secret hallway, but it was loud enough for all to hear. "They'rrre coming frrrom above!" Without a roof overhead, and with no way to access the apartments without a dragon to lift them over the walls, there were few spots to hide. And the sledgehammers, like other Artiméan spells that were assigned a target upon activation, followed each person around, pounding and pounding relentlessly for several minutes before they struck their last blow and disappeared into the air.

Kitten's crushed body pieces magically pulled together, and she came back to life, only to be smashed to bits a second time. When she came alive, this time much the wiser, she dodged the hammer and flattened her body, then slid back into the tiny space below the secret door she'd been trying to open. She made it just in time and watched in horror as the sledgehammer, a hundred times bigger than her, pounded relentlessly, just barely nicking her front paw and turning her favorite claw and two of her whiskers to dust. She scooched farther into the slot and stayed put.

"Release!" cried Fifer, trying to get her hands on the

LISA McMANN

275 « Dragon Fire

constantly moving weapon so the release spell would actually work. "Release!" It wasn't easy, but finally she grabbed it and ended the spell, and the sledgehammer disappeared. "Who designed this terrible component?" she cried. She ran over to try to release the ones attacking Thisbe, who was still on the floor, knocked out.

"You can blame Florrrence forrr that one," said Simber, taking a running leap and beginning to fly, with sledgehammers chasing him. "She crrreated it when we werrre in Grrrimerrre. And it just happens to be one of the few that Frrrieda Stubbs is good at activating. Now, wherrre is she? She's got to be herrre somewherrre doing this." He soared around the tops of the walls, but he couldn't see or sense anyone.

Fifer finally managed to release all the sledgehammers attacking Thisbe, and she knelt next to her sister. "Are you all right?"

Thisbe groaned and opened her eyes, and the sisters locked eyes for a moment.

"Are you okay?" Fifer asked again, and she couldn't mask her concern.

"Hey," said Thisbe softly. "I'm all right. Go help the others. I'll be right behind you. Is Kitten okay?"

"Mewmewmew," whispered Kitten from her hiding place.

"Stay there, Kitten!" Fifer whispered back. She left Thisbe and ran out to the balcony, finding no one remaining there but hearing shouts from all directions and seeing a few bodies sprawled out on the main floor. She spied Ishibashi at the bottom of the stairs, fighting a sledgehammer with his fists, and went down to help him.

Another round of sledgehammers came sailing from somewhere above them. Fifer dodged and grabbed at them and tried to see what direction they were coming from. "Frieda Stubbs!" Fifer called out. "I know you're up there, you coward!"

"You're the coward!" shouted Frieda.

"I most certainly am not!" Fifer turned toward the voice and kept talking, hoping Simber, who was flying around above the mansion, would be able to pinpoint where she was. Fifer grabbed a sledgehammer handle. "Release!" she muttered under her breath, and continued with Frieda. "You destroyed this mansion, and you've left Artiméans to die in the remote rooms!"

"You're the one who did that!" shouted Frieda.

"What?!" cried Fifer. "How can you even say that?"

"How can you stand there and pretend like you aren't the

cause of all of this, Fifer Stowe?" cried Frieda. "You started all of this when you and your vagrant sister came to Artimé and terrorized us all with your dark magic."

For a split second, Fifer questioned herself. Was this mess truly Fifer's fault? Were she and Thisbe to blame? Before Fifer could retort, three heart attack spells came soaring down from the top of the wall, high above the classrooms. Ishibashi saw them and nimbly deflected two of them with his hands while Fifer dodged the third. But they did their damage. Ishibashi clutched his chest and crashed to the floor.

"Ishibashi!" Fifer rushed over to him to release the spells, but she knew he would continue to suffer for several minutes because of their severity. She dragged him under the staircase in hopes it would shield him from Frieda's view and aim. There was no way Fifer was losing Ishibashi.

Thisbe appeared on the balcony and limped down the steps, looking frazzled. The memory of Alex and the fear of Fifer dying had returned after the hammer incident, and she knew she had to make sure that didn't happen. She reached the main floor and discovered her friends from Grimere in various places, curled up and being beaten by magical sledgehammers or lying motionless. She scooted past Fifer under the stairs to get them to safety inside a classroom, but then stopped and turned back. She hesitated, then leaned in and whispered, "Frieda is a classic monster, Fife. I heard what she said to you. Remember, none of this is our fault. Rule number one of monsters like her? Always accuse your enemies of the crimes you've committed. That's what she's doing. I know her words probably hurt you, but don't let Frieda get to you. Just keep going." She hesitated as Fifer stared at her with an unreadable expression, but then she went on. "I'm going to get our friends to safety. Simber's up there, zeroing in on her location. And you . . . you need to take her out."

The weight of the moment, with Thisbe actually stopping to speak to Fifer despite their arguments, was a big one. And Thisbe was asking a lot. "What, you mean kill her?" whispered Fifer, aghast. "I don't know if I can do that. She's still an Artiméan. She's one of our people. I can just freeze her, and we can throw her into the pen with the others."

Thisbe gave Fifer a hard look. "Listen, Fife. You've got a lot more good in you than I do. You're so good that even I can sense it, and I'm only part dragon. But with Kitten losing two

LISA McMANN

lives back-to-back, she's too vulnerable to be hit by any more sledgehammers. And we need her. If we can't figure out how to use that secret door, I can think of only one other way to get our people out of the remote rooms immediately. Before it's too late to save them."

Fifer stared at her twin. "What do you mean? What way?" And then a flood of realization swept over her as she thought through the fallout if she took Frieda out permanently. "Oh," she said. And then: "Oooh. I see."

"I've got to go help the others," Thisbe said quietly. "Don't die, okay? At least not until after we figure things out. I can't stand to lose another sibling like that." She gave Fifer's arm a gentle squeeze and left her, rushing to aid her friends before they got pounded to death. Fifer's heart tripped in her chest and throttled her throat as she realized what a huge moment this was. What a large decision she was faced with. Barely able to comprehend the severity of it, Fifer helped Ishibashi sit up, all the while thinking hard about what she needed to do next. And exactly how she'd go about doing it. But could she actually defy her inner goodness and go through with it? Either way, this moment would be life changing. For better . . . or worse.

A Fatal Mistake

LISA McMANN

Fifer took an extra moment to care for Ishibashi under the cover of the staircase after he'd so valiantly stepped in front of two heart attack components meant for Fifer. All the while she frantically tried to plan her next move and attempted to not think about how her actions this evening would impact her life forever, no matter what she chose to do. As she helped the old scientist take a drink from his canteen and held his shaky hand, she thought back to the books she'd read over and over again when she was a child—the books Lani had written about the battles she and Alex and the older generation had experienced. Lani was one of Fifer's heroes, and she'd done some pretty brave and dangerous things. Things she'd performed selflessly and hadn't take credit for, like secretly helping to end the very first war in Artimé.

Sky was also someone Fifer admired, and if it hadn't been for her, Artimé might still be lost after the first time a head mage died. She'd helped Alex figure out how to bring the magical world back. And then there were Kaylee, and Alex, and Aaron . . . and Thisbe, for that matter. All heroes in different ways. They'd done incredible things. Made unbelievable sacrifices. Risked their lives for the sake of Artimé and its people. And . . . sometimes they'd taken someone's life in order to do it.

But none of these Artiméans had ever purposely taken the life of a fellow Unwanted. There was nothing to compare this moment to. Nothing to help Fifer come to terms with it, other than knowing Thisbe was for it. But Thisbe had more evil inside her than Fifer did, apparently. Fifer wrung her hands and peered out at the roofline.

Not to mention Frieda Stubbs wasn't exactly easy to target. She was invisible. She was most likely using invisibility paintbrushes to stay hidden up there on the wall. And probably moving around whenever Simber got too close. How was Fifer going to locate her? She wasn't sure, but she was going to use her best instincts to figure it out.

Ishibashi noticed the torment on Fifer's face. He put his other shaking hand on top of hers. "Is it a very difficult decision for you?" he asked.

Fifer gulped and nodded. "Yes. It's terrible."

"Your compassion is one of your many strengths, Fifer Stowe. You will know what to do when the time comes."

"Thank you, Ishibashi-san," Fifer whispered. Her eyes welled up. "I hope you are right."

"The older I get, the more right I am," said Ishibashi with a glint in his eye.

Fifer pressed her lips into a small smile. There was always something wonderful to be learned from the grandfathers. And though she still hadn't made a decision about what to do, she felt a little better about being able to make it if the time came.

Through the windows Fifer could hear a few dissenters in the cage outside, catcalling and chanting Frieda's name as Simber flew around above the mansion. And she could see the dragons circling the pen, keeping order. But the dissenters were getting restless. Fifer needed to make a move. Draw Frieda out so they could do something. With instinct guiding her, Fifer gave Ishibashi's hand a final squeeze. She stepped out from under the stairs and held her hands out, empty and visible. "Hey, Frieda! You nearly killed someone who doesn't even live here!" she called out. "How does that feel?"

"Ishibashi is a fraud!" Frieda called back. Her voice seemed to be coming from a totally different place now than it had been before. When Frieda spoke, the dissenters heard her and became louder. Fifer wasn't sure if they were encouraging Frieda or if they were angry with her, but they were being rambunctious enough that the dragons breathed a spurt of fire in through the doorway to help control them. Screams rose and died down, and Florence barked out a warning. Fifer cringed. She stole another glance out the window into the darkness, seeing that one wall of the makeshift corral was tipping precariously outward. Gorgrun was on the ground pushing it back in place with his head.

A single scatterclip whizzed past Fifer's ear in that distracted moment. "Die a thousand deaths!" Frieda cried, a bit too late to be effective. Fifer startled and realized that Frieda had tried to kill her for the third time. She wasn't hesitating.

"Nice try," Fifer said snidely after the clip harmlessly skittered across the floor. "I'm glad you're so terrible at magic. Did you run out of sledgehammers?"

"At least I still have other components!" said Frieda. Again, her voice seemed to be coming from a slightly different place. Fifer peered toward the spot, knowing that eventually the woman would run out of invisibility paintbrushes. Simber turned sharply in the air toward the head mage's voice. He swept along the wall, nice and low, trying to catch her or anyone who might be sitting on the top of it. But there was a scrambling sound that Fifer could just barely hear above the noises happening on the lawn, and a few pebbles and bits of silt filtered down in the front west corner of the mansion. Fifer turned carefully, catching Simber's eye and pretending she could see Frieda.

"Do you have her in your sights too, Simber?" Fifer called out.

"I do now," Simber said, playing along.

"You are a terrible liar, traitor!" shouted Frieda. More silt filtered down, this time from above the mansion's main doorway. "Everyone knows you are putting Artimé in danger. You won't survive this."

"You can surrender if you like," Fifer said calmly. "Or I can freeze you from here, and you'll probably fall to the ground and break into a thousand pieces. It's up to you."

"You're out of components!" Frieda cackled. "I hardly think you should be threatening me. A freeze spell? That's your answer? Weak."

There was another scraping sound, and then a flash of color. A tiny swath of Frieda's robe was in plain sight. Her invisibility spell was wearing off.

Fifer glanced at Simber, giving him a warning look, and he circled, pretending he hadn't seen it.

"Simber, you don't deserve to be the head mage's right-hand cheetah!" Frieda shouted angrily. She threw a handful of heart attack spells at the statue, but they didn't hurt him in the least. "You abandoned me. You turned away from the head mage. How could you fail so badly? What kind of servant are you?"

"The worrrst kind," said Simber, dolefully playing his part. "Apparrrently."

Fifer breathed a sigh of relief—Simber was nobody's

servant, and he was smart enough not to take the bait. But she knew Frieda's words must have hurt him deeply. "Simber's on the side of Artimé. We all are. All but you."

"What are you talking about, you silly little pirate child?" said Frieda with a laugh, but there was an edge to her voice. "You and your siblings brought the Revinir in sight of Artimé, ready to attack us with her dragons. This threat is all your fault, and I have the majority of the people on my side in agreement! Listen to them all rioting because of the way I've been treated!"

Fifer kept her expression stony and lifted her chin slightly, feeling a small surge of confidence. There was no rioting, only a few people shouting. She ignored the woman's name-calling. She could tell she'd gotten under Frieda's skin. And now, whether the head mage knew it or not, Fifer could make out the shape of her robe. If Frieda wouldn't surrender, it was almost time to make a move. Fear leaped into Fifer's throat, but she swallowed it back down.

Fifer knew she had to be cautious. Frieda had mistakenly assumed she was out of components, which was what Fifer had wanted her to think. But Fifer wasn't sure if Frieda had many

LISA McMANN

left, so she did some calculations in her head. The woman must have filled her pockets with sledgehammer components in order to release so many. Was *she* out of components? But then there was the head mage robe, which had pockets too. She could carry a lot of ammunition. Could Frieda have burned through all the components in her vest and the robe? It was hard to say, since Fifer hadn't seen the sledgehammer component before and didn't know its size in component form.

She recalled what Thisbe had whispered to her a few moments ago, about people like Frieda accusing their enemies of the very crimes they'd committed. Did that work for the situations they were in, too? Was Frieda accusing Fifer of being out of components because that was Frieda's way of foolishly telling Fifer that *she* was the one who was out? Fifer couldn't possibly know. But she didn't want to waste this opportunity. Who knew what would happen when Frieda discovered she was visible now. Fifer stepped out farther from behind the broken bannister, being careful not to reach for any components.

Simber saw her empty hands and growled a warning, but Fifer pretended not to hear him.

"Climb down, Frieda," Fifer said. "Let's talk this through.

I'm sure we can come together and figure out a way to end this standoff and free our friends from the remote rooms. Maybe you didn't intend to put them in such danger—if not, let's figure it out."

"Let them die there," said Frieda coldly, almost fully visible now but still not realizing it. "Then all I have to get rid of is your sister and you, and Artimé will be at peace again." She reached into her pocket and pulled out another scatterclip, turning it in front of her and letting the metal glint in the mansion light.

"You want all of those people in the remote rooms to die?" said Fifer loudly, hoping the penned prisoners were hearing all of this. "Are you really okay with that many deaths on your hands? I'm not sure the people of Artimé want that. Those trapped people are our most skilled fighters! They're our friends and relatives. They're the ones who have made sacrifices to save Artimé time and time again while people like you get to hide in your rooms. Without them, Artimé is vulnerable . . . especially if the Revinir comes back."

"You don't know what you're talking about," Frieda said. "The Revinir is afraid of me. And if I get rid of you, she won't have any reason to come back."

LISA McMANN

"Maybe," said Fifer. "Or maybe she was afraid of you when she knew you had a notoriously powerful group of fighters behind you. Remember, she's fought us before, and we beat her. Who knows what she'll think when she gets word that you've left your best fighters to die. She's more power hungry than you. If you think she's not going to come back to take over this island, you're dead wrong."

"Be quiet," Frieda said, her voice pitching upward. "You're a bore. Boring, screeching Fifer. That's my name for you." She pinched the scatterclip and held it up.

Fifer refrained from rolling her eyes at the ridiculous woman. Instead, seeing the move, she glanced at Simber and gave a slight hand signal. The cat blinked in response.

Without another word, Frieda wound up and threw the single scatterclip hard at Fifer, shouting the verbal component correctly this time. "Die a thousand deaths!"

On cue, Simber dove in front of it. It struck his side and bounced off, doing him no harm but shielding Fifer from the deadly hit and giving her a chance to aim with a weapon of her own. Simber swooped up and out over the wall.

Just as swiftly, Fifer raised her hand, needing no component for her plan. "I have a name for you, too," she said. She grimaced, her heart heavy and thumping wildly, and pointed firmly at Frieda Stubbs. As the woman gasped in anger and reached for another clip, Fifer shouted a phrase that hadn't been uttered in many years, first used by none other than her hero, Lani Haluki. "Evermore nevermore!" The power left her fingertips. Fifer ran straight for the nearest window and dove out of it.

The spell hit the head mage. She froze, shocked. A second later she slumped over. Her body deflated like a balloon. Soon all that was left of her was a flat rubber shape that slid and fell backward off the wall. Her head mage robe slipped off and caught the wind. It floated down to the beach. In that instant, everything in Artimé went black. And everyone who remained in every part of the mansion was flung together into the gray shack, all squashed on top of one another.

Regrouping

F ifer rolled to a stop on the hard ground where the
lawn used to be. She scrambled to her feet and turned
to see that the mansion was gone. An old, roofless
gray shack stood in its place.

Shouts rose up from inside it as people fought to get out.
More yelling came from the corral, for the mansion roof that
had covered the dissenters had turned into the much smaller
roof of the gray shack and had fallen in on top of everybody,
trapping them under its weight. The pen's log walls disappeared
in a puff of smoke, for even the jungle trees were magical and

had disappeared, with every vine and root going with them.

Nearby, Florence froze in place. And Simber, in mid-flight, came crashing down. He bounced and skidded on the harsh cement for twenty yards toward Quill, coming to a stop at the startled dragons' feet.

The sudden loss of the magical world caused terrible confusion, and people everywhere, covered in splinters of lumber and pieces of shingles or trapped beneath the roof, were certain they were close to death. Gorgrun and Quince rose up in confusion and began flying around in circles overhead, unsure what was happening but wanting to stay off the ground in case that disappeared too.

Fifer crouched in place and covered her head to protect it. When everything stopped changing or moving, she rose, shocked and bewildered by what she'd just done. She'd killed Frieda Stubbs. Ended a life—an Unwanted's life. The thought was horrifying. Fifer could hardly make sense of it.

The noise and confusion made everything worse. Fifer had never seen the magical world disappear before; she'd only read and heard about it.

"Thank the gods it's still daylight," someone nearby murmured, limping around bloodied and dazed. "This would be so much worse in the dead of night."

Fifer couldn't process any of it. A voice churned in her head. *You killed an Unwanted.* It made her sick. The satisfaction of doing something right was easily drowned out by the horror of doing something wrong. And now everything was complicated and overwhelming—what was Fifer supposed to do? She had to act before this scene got even further out of hand. After a second to gather her wits, she remembered the robe, which they'd need to restore the world. Fifer whirled around and located Florence, then went straight to the frozen statue and, in spite of her shaking limbs, climbed up on her back. She moved Florence's arrows aside, then shoved her arm deep down into Florence's quiver and pulled out the robe. She jumped to the ground and returned to the gray shack, searching the faces of the walking wounded as she went, desperate to see Aaron.

People were coming out of the doors and climbing through windows. "Is everyone okay?" Fifer called out. "Aaron! Is Aaron in there? Sky? Thisbe? Kaylee?" Her voice hitched with

LISA McMANN

a sob. "Seth! Where are you?" Now that Frieda Stubbs was no longer, Fifer felt all the emotions and stress of her friends' capture, combined with the fear and doubt of making the decision to take down Frieda Stubbs, come to the surface and let loose. She started shivering. "Ishibashi! Are you in there?"

In addition to Fifer's indecision about what to do with Frieda had been deep worry that her dearest ones might not survive being trapped. Or that the dissenters had used permanent spells on them. If they were alive, would they be injured? Wondering how these next moments would play out was paralyzing Fifer. And where was Thisbe? What if she wasn't okay? That thought sickened her more than ever. Their relationship had been in such a bad place. This couldn't be the way it ended.

"Thisbe!" Fifer screamed. "Aaron!" She stumbled to another window and spotted Rohan working to help people out of it. Then Fifer spied a few of the black-eyed fighters and Maiven, limping out of the shack's back door. "Thank goodness," Fifer breathed. It was a relief to see them—they'd been the ones Thisbe was tending to in the classrooms and kitchen. Then Fifer spied Sky and Ishibashi coming out the door together looking shaken but safe. She saw Kaylee climbing up and over the wall of the roofless shack and down the outside while simultaneously calling out the same names that Fifer was shouting. Fifer ran over to her. "Have you seen anyone from the remote rooms?"

"Not yet." Kaylee gripped Fifer's hand. "I'm so scared. What if—"

But Fifer gasped and pointed. Carina was exiting a window, and Seth was right behind. Fifer gripped Kaylee's shoulder. "They're going to be okay. They have to be."

"Go help Seth and Carina," said Kaylee. "I'll keep calling for Aaron."

Fifer nodded, feeling slightly more grounded now that her friends were surfacing. She ran over to Seth and threw her arms around him in a rare embrace. "I'm so glad you're okay." She searched his face. "Where were you? Was Aaron with you?"

"The lounge. We thought Aaron was with you," said Seth, wiping a trail of blood from a cut on his forehead. "What happened? Did he do this? Where is he?"

Fifer's heart sank. She wasn't prepared to answer that question yet. "I don't know. Help me find him." She searched the people exiting the gray shack, shouting, "Aaron! Thisbe!"

"Fifer?" Thisbe called out.

"Thisbe!" cried Fifer. She couldn't see her twin, but hearing her lifted her heavy heart. "Are you okay?"

"I'm fine. Did you find Aaron?"

"Not yet!" Finding Thisbe was one big worry to cross off the list. The confusion was becoming more manageable. "Aaron!"

"He's over here!" cried a different voice.

"Ms. Octavia?" said Fifer. She hopped up, trying to see over heads to find the short octogator.

"Yes, it's me!" said Ms. Octavia. "Aaron's alive. He can't speak just yet. We need water right away!"

Fifer hooked the robe she'd pulled from Florence's quiver over her forearm and reached around her back to make sure she still had her canteen, then started toward them. Ms. Octavia was trying to help Aaron out of one of the windows. He looked weak and was squinting in the afternoon light. Fifer grabbed his legs and assisted in getting him to an open space while Ms. Octavia turned to give Samheed and Clementi a hand. "I've got water," Fifer said breathlessly. She stripped the canteen off her shoulder strap and thrust it at Aaron.

He took it with shaking hands and swallowed some down. When Samheed arrived, Aaron passed it to him. Samheed drank gratefully and handed it off to Clementi when she collapsed next to them.

Fifer looked toward the area where she'd last seen Kaylee and called out to her, then beckoned her to come. Aaron returned Fifer's empty canteen, and Fifer remembered the extra canteens she'd left in the hammock. She called for her birds, hoping they'd safely flown out the top of the mansion before it turned into the gray shack. As Kaylee arrived and reunited with Aaron and the others, the birds fluttered down with the hammock. Fifer began passing around more water to the ones who needed it.

After a few moments, the last stragglers inside the shack made their way out. With the urgency lessening and things calming down, Fifer could feel her body start to shake again, as if it needed a turn to break down too. Thoughts of what she'd done to cause this haunted her, but she tried to push them aside. She took a few breaths. Hot tears pricked her eyes and threatened to spill over. Still shaking, she stepped away from the others for a moment to compose herself. The voice inside her head returned and kept reminding her *You killed an Unwanted.*

"I saved a lot of people," she whispered, trying to drown out the other voice. But it persisted. Fifer looked around at the devastated property and felt a heaviness she'd never known before. This place felt toxic in its current state, and she'd caused it by killing the head mage. "It's too much," Fifer murmured, clutching the robe against her chest. Then: "Get a hold of yourself."

Once things were restored to normal, Fifer knew she'd need someone to talk to who would support her and tell her she did the right thing. She looked for Thisbe, who was instructing the ghost dragons to lift the roof off the dissenters. If only the two were close again, Fifer could talk to her. She'd be the one who'd understand more than anyone. But things were too precarious right now, and there was no time to patch them up. Fifer blinked hard and turned away. Maybe the others were ready to restore the world so they could move on from this.

The people of Artimé had never been so prepared to bring things back to normal. They had the robe. They knew the spell. And everybody was out of the gray shack. Fifer returned to Aaron and her other friends to see how they were faring and gauge their readiness to take the next step.

Thisbe and Rohan arrived right after her, and before Fifer could say anything, Thisbe immediately started giving a report about the state of the dissenters, whom Fifer had hardly thought about until now. "There are some people with serious injuries under that roof," said Thisbe. "I told the dragons to move the roof onto the shack. We want to do that before we restore the world, right? Or else it would crush the people under it when it turns back into the mansion roof."

"Yes, exactly," said Aaron, still seated on the ground and looking dazed and disheveled. "Definitely put the roof back on before restoring the world so it'll transform with the rest of the mansion." His voice was gritty, and his normally clean-shaven face wore a thick stubbly growth.

"But won't the dissenters escape?" Fifer squinted at the people, many of whom were in no shape to run away. "Without Florence and Simber they are basically unattended right now. I don't want them getting away."

"We thought of that," Thisbe said coolly. "The dragons are handling it."

"Our people will help as well," offered Rohan.

"Great," said Aaron, closing his eyes.

The voice crept back into Fifer's head. Sure, she'd saved these people. But others had been hurt in the process. Had killing Frieda really been the only way to get the people out of the remote rooms? Had Fifer exhausted all other options? Couldn't they have tried once more to get the secret hallway door to work? Fifer pushed the voice away and watched Thisbe organize the other black-eyed children. They surrounded the dissenters, breathing warning blasts of fire at the ones who were trying to leave the area and letting the people know they meant business. Thisbe had arrived with an impressive team on dragons, and it was thanks to them that Fifer and the others were able to control the situation now. Thisbe had really become a strong and smart leader, and Fifer hadn't realized it until now. There was so much she didn't know about her twin. It made them feel even more distant.

Gorgrun and Quince placed the roof on top of the gray shack. Then the dragons returned to the ground and surrounded the dissenters with their bodies. Most of the dissenters were too dazed or injured to do anything, but a few of them, like Frieda's right-hand man, were yelling horrendous things in protest. Nevertheless, Thisbe and Rohan began assessing the

LISA McMANN

injuries, and soon Fifer spotted Henry, Thatcher, and Carina heading over there to help.

Fifer turned and saw that Sean had found Ava and Lukas. Quince helped them down, and Sean hugged the two tightly and listened to the story of their adventure on the ghost dragon's back. Fifer swallowed hard. Reuniting Ava and Lukas with their parents—Fifer had made that happen. That was worth something, wasn't it?

Feeling numb, Fifer looked away and tuned in to the conversation around her. Claire Morning and Gunnar Haluki had found Aaron and the rest. They exchanged quick explanations of which rooms they'd been in this whole time.

When Thisbe and Rohan returned, Fifer shook the wrinkles out of the robe and held it up by the collar, then draped it loosely over her arm. She glanced at Aaron. "Whenever you feel up to it . . . I think everything is in place now that the roof is there."

Thisbe turned toward her brother. "We should hurry so Henry can get to the medicine." She hesitated, then added, "I hope the inside of the mansion will be magically fixed too, like the tubes and staircase and everything. It was a real disaster in there."

Fifer nodded and stayed uncharacteristically quiet.

Thisbe noticed. She glanced at Fifer and said stiffly, "You did a good job. I was reviving Asha and Rohan in the kitchen, but I could hear you talking to Frieda and . . . well, you did everything right."

Fifer blinked hard. The lump in her throat stopped her from answering.

"Fifer, *you're* the one responsible for this?" Aaron asked.

Fifer eyed her brother, unsure how to take his question. Was he mad? Or just surprised? Her stomach clenched. What if he was mad? "Yes," she said quietly, then cleared her throat. "Simber helped. And Thisbe, obviously. And Ishibashi. And . . . well, everyone."

"Well done, Fifer," said Ms. Morning. "That must have been hard. Are you okay?"

Fifer wanted to say no. She wanted somebody to hug her. She wanted to crawl into her bed and never come back out. But she just stood still. "Yes. I'm okay."

Aaron looked up at Fifer. His lips were parched and peeling. "We didn't have much longer in there, if you know what I mean," he said earnestly. "Octavia was working hard on a

3-D window, but it kept going wrong. We were getting desperate for water. I kept fainting. If another day had passed, we might not have survived." He paused. "I know what you did was probably hard for you. But however it happened, it was the right thing."

Fifer's chin quivered and sobs threatened, but she held them back. "Thanks. I—um. Thank you." She held out the robe to him once more. "Are you ready?"

Kaylee stepped in. "Oh, no thank you," she said, taking Aaron's hands in hers so he couldn't accept it. "He's just fine without it."

Aaron gave a weary laugh and looked sideways at his wife. "Kaylee's right. No thanks. You're going to have to find a new head mage."

Fifer and Thisbe both stared. "You won't do it?" Thisbe asked.

"No way."

"Ms. Morning, then?" said Thisbe.

"Not me either, I'm afraid," said Claire. "My life is in Quill. There's got to be a better choice. Someone who is actually passionate about being head mage."

"How about Lani?" asked Fifer uncertainly. There had been a time when she'd wanted the job. Fifer squinted and looked around for the woman who'd inspired her actions that day.

"Again, no," said Claire. "Lani and I actually talked about it in the lounge while we were stuck in there. She told me that her time for that had passed, and she wasn't interested. She has a lot more on her agenda that she wants to accomplish, which wouldn't give her time for running things around here. So I think it's clear what that means."

Aaron nodded and looked at the twins. "Maybe it's time for one of you," he said.

The girls stiffened. "One of us?" echoed Thisbe. Her eyes widened as she imagined the prestigious job. Head mage of Artimé. Would she want to step into that role? Right now when everything crazy was happening in the land of the dragons? It was definitely tempting.

"But . . . ," said Fifer. "We just, um, *ended the career* of the last head mage."

"You did, you mean," Thisbe pointed out.

"And that would put you in some danger," Claire warned. "There are a lot of changes that have to happen in Artimé.

It's going to be a rocky time for a while, I'm afraid."

Immediately Thisbe's face grew worried—for herself and for her sister. No matter how mad she was, she didn't want Fifer to be in danger. They'd already had one head mage sibling die. It was hard to think of either of them taking over and being that vulnerable. Plus, for Thisbe, there was the Revinir to think about. And the dragon-woman had threatened to go after Fifer, too. No doubt she'd be returning sooner or later with her dragons. Fifer would be target number one on this island if she were the head mage. Thisbe frowned. Should she offer to become head mage in order to save her sister? She glanced at Rohan, who was giving her a puzzled look, as if he were wondering why she hadn't immediately turned down the offer. Thisbe closed her eyes briefly. He was right. Thisbe couldn't imagine doing it. She had another agenda entirely, and her other land was calling to her.

Henry shouted out from the area with the dissenters. "Can you bring the world back, please? We need supplies and medicine!"

Fifer felt sick thinking about being head mage. She wanted to shout "Yes!" to the skies. To slip her arms into the sleeves of that precious robe. But she had just *killed* someone—not just anyone, but the head mage, a former Unwanted, who the dissenters had supported. What would happen if Fifer said yes? Would the dissenters keep trying to come after her for revenge?

Aaron looked from one twin's face to the other, reading the signs. Thisbe gave a wan smile, then shook her head slightly. "I'm out. Thanks for thinking of me, though."

Sky gave Thisbe a nod. She knew that had been the right call.

"Fifer?" Aaron nudged.

Fifer sucked in a breath as the voice in her head returned. "I—I—what?"

"You seem like a good fit."

Fifer couldn't speak. Everything swirled in her mind. Good, bad. Good, bad. *You killed an Unwanted. You saved your brother's life.*

Thisbe closed her eyes, a pained look crossing her face as she imagined how hard things would be for Fifer in this role. Wasn't there anybody else who would do it?

"Why don't you want to?" Fifer whispered, glancing at her sister.

Thisbe hesitated. "I have other things I want to do. My work . . . and my heart . . . is in Grimere with our people and our land and the dragons." She glanced at Rohan as heat rose to her face.

Our people. Our lands. That included Fifer, and it gave her one more thing to feel strange about if she chose to do this. "But," said Fifer weakly, "what about *my* part in the whole land of the dragons . . . thing?" Her voice faltered and betrayed the truth—that she really wasn't very invested in the country of her mother's birth. The country where her grandmother should be queen. But none of that mattered. In that moment she knew for sure that her heart was here, in Artimé, in spite of the troubles this land and its people faced going forward. In spite of the danger she'd certainly face. Fifer wanted to be with Aaron and Kaylee and Seth, and all the others who were so special to her. The people she'd saved by ending the reign of Frieda Stubbs. And no matter what accusations the voice in her head made, Artimé needed her. It might take some time to convince herself of that after what had happened today, but Fifer had done what was necessary to save the world she loved.

Being head mage was also something Fifer had worked hard

to earn, though she hadn't realized it at the time. She'd fought Alex's rules to secretly train and take her place as a top mage on the rescue team. And she'd stepped up and led the charge to find Thisbe after Alex had been killed. She'd put her grief aside for the sake of the quest and had commanded people twice her age. Her team had found her sister and Sky and Rohan and Maiven, and they'd come out of a second fiery battle against the Revinir without losing anybody else. That was Fifer's success. Those were the battles she'd already won. When she thought of it that way, reuniting the people and reinstating the principles of Artimé didn't seem quite as hard as before.

Her gaze landed on the robe draped over her arm. She couldn't look Thisbe in the eye as all the confusing thoughts swirled around her mind. Was it wrong that Fifer felt so strongly tied to Artimé instead of Grimere? Should she be feeling bad about this in addition to her feelings about what had happened with Frieda? And, whether Thisbe wanted the role or not, would she make a better head mage than Fifer? She'd become a leader without anyone really noticing until now. Fifer glanced at Simber, frozen and splayed weirdly in the dirt, and remembered their short time working together in Grimere

309 « Dragon Fire

after Alex had died. Would the cheetah feel the same about Thisbe as he would about Fifer?

"Fife," Thisbe said, raising an eyebrow. "Let's be real. We both know you don't feel any particular pull from Grimere, and that's totally okay. But," she said slyly, "you could definitely be an ally as the ruler of Artimé, you know? Help us out a little, maybe? Once things are settled here?"

Head mage Fifer Stowe? It was everything Fifer wanted. She loved being a leader. But it was frightening, too. What would she do with all the dissenters? That was a big dilemma. Would they rebuild the pen and jail them there indefinitely? How would Fifer manage this new problem, which didn't go away just because Frieda Stubbs was taken down for good? Maybe Artimé would continue to be a world split apart, with Unwanteds fighting against one another. No one of sound mind would wish to inherit that. But it did spur Fifer on to want to fix it.

"I just . . . ," said Fifer. "There's so much . . . and I'm not sure how people would accept me."

"You are the best person to solve all of these things," Thisbe said, more earnestly than she'd spoken to Fifer in a very long time. "And you know who's more important than pretty much anyone, right?"

Fifer, still staring at the robe, wore an unreadable expression. She was having trouble catching her breath, and she realized she'd been holding it. She looked up. "Who?"

"Simber," said Thisbe. "Simber is more important than anything. He's the symbol of Artimé, more than the mansion or anything or anyone else. And Artimé needs him to be happy, or we all end up suffering." She paused for a breath, then lowered her voice. "And he wants *you*. He always turns to you. It's so obvious you'd be his number one choice. You two get each other." She studied her sister's skeptical expression. "Let's not let Simber down. Don't you agree with me?"

Fifer nodded. "I do," she whispered. "You're right. That's part of the scariness, though, that it does feel so right . . ." She knew she had a special bond with Simber. Even though he'd seemed to ignore her for a time when Aaron was head mage, she still knew he'd loved working with her. And he'd seemed to focus on her again ever since they'd sprung him free from the theater. Almost as if he saw her as his alternative to Frieda Stubbs. As the leader of this fighting group.

Sky grasped Fifer's arm. "We all believe in you. And we'll help you with all the problems we're facing. Bring Artimé back."

"You can do it, Fifer," said Aaron. "You've reenergized the core supporters of Artimé, and I know you'll be a superb leader. We'll help you if you need us. We'll protect you from the dangers." He paused, and they all heard a low rumbling in the distance.

"What is that?" asked Claire.

Aaron looked toward Quill. "Right on cue," he muttered. "It's the people of Quill coming to complain. No doubt they're annoyed to have lost their world too. We don't need them muddying things up here—let's get this world fixed and turn them all around so we can help the injured ones."

Thisbe's earnest look didn't waver. "So you'll do it?"

Fifer nodded slowly. "We've already got enough of a mess in Artimé without Quill barging in and being obnoxious." Tamping down the voice in her head, she slipped her arms into the robe and fastened it around her neck. She looked up, her face aglow. "Okay, team. Let's make this happen."

Restoring

With her mind made up, Fifer walked over to the back step of the gray shack. She still had so many questions about how she would handle the clash between the dissenters and the other Unwanteds. She still had doubts and the constant reminder that she'd killed a human being. But she knew that things would only get worse the longer they had to live without the comforts and necessities of Artimé. Being reminded that Quill was also wiped out made Fifer want to get things up and running. Pronto.

She stood squarely in the correct spot. After a quick tutorial

LISA McMANN

from Aaron, and with the friends she'd rescued standing all around her, she concentrated and carefully recited the spell that would bring Artimé back. She could feel each word deeply in her core: Imagine. Believe. Whisper. Breathe. Commence. Then she repeated them two more times. At the end, after a whispery moment in the eerie gray world, everything began to change. Colors reentered, and the mansion spun back into existence, with the roof in the correct place. The lawn reappeared and spread under everyone's feet, and fountains sprang up in the usual places. The jungle sprouted and grew to maturity, and the world was repopulated with beavops and owlbats and rabbitkeys and platyprots and squirrelicorns once more. The lifeless statues stirred.

"You did it," Aaron whispered in Fifer's ear. "I'm really proud of you. We'll talk soon about how Kaylee and I can help you. I won't leave you stranded."

"Thanks, Aaron," said Fifer, hardly able to believe what was happening. She'd really done it. And now she was head mage of Artimé, looking at her magical world. Her eyes traveled to Simber, halfway across the lawn, his face still smashed into the ground but his hindquarters in the air now as he pushed himself to his feet. How would she explain things to her new number one companion? She started toward him.

Simber groaned as the grass grew up around his face and tickled his nose. He snorted and stretched his limbs and neck, then shook the dust and dirt off. He lifted a paw to his chin and rubbed it, feeling the new scrapes there. "What the—" he said, looking around to figure out where he was and how he'd managed to land so ungracefully. He'd experienced this strange feeling of having missed something important a few times now. This time it didn't take long to understand what had happened. And for once he wasn't forced to experience the growing feeling of horror and dread coming over him that he'd lost another companion, which was a relief. "Did Fiferrr succeed? I think she actually did it," he muttered to himself, remembering his final move before everything went blank. "I knew she could." His heart swelled, and he looked around to see who had brought the world back. He wished he'd said something to the humans before all of this happened about who he'd have chosen if given options.

Then Simber noticed Aaron alive, safe, and moving to the fountain for freshwater. He wasn't wearing the robe, which

LISA McMANN

was a surprise. "Then who . . . ?" Simber's gaze swept the area, anxiety growing as he saw Ol' Tater stomping and splashing at the edge of the sea. The mastodon statue always came alive when the world was brought back. But who had restored it, if not Aaron? Claire, perhaps? That would be okay with him, though he knew she didn't want to be the head mage.

But what if something else had gone wrong, and the head mage was someone horrible? He had no idea how much time had passed. It could have been minutes or days. When his eyes alighted on a young woman coming toward him wearing the head mage's robe, Simber blinked. And then his face broke into a rare, wide grin. "Well," he said, shaking his head. "Well, well, well." He almost wasn't sure how to feel about it at first, for he didn't know how the decision of who would bring back the world had come to happen. Were there arguments over it? It didn't matter much, at least at the moment, for an overwhelming joy took root in Simber's soul and grew. He'd seen something in Fifer. They'd already experienced times of true companionship. She'd helped convince him to free himself from his attachment to Frieda Stubbs. And she'd led the team to victory. Now Fifer was his new head mage companion. After a tumultuous year, things were finally looking up for Simber.

He loped toward Fifer as she was nearing him. He could see the flush of success on her face and the light in her eyes. It seemed right and good.

"Simber," said Fifer. Merely mentioning his name almost choked her with emotion. This moment . . . this . . . this *thing* . . . It meant something so great and deep and surprising, so far beyond her own comprehension. She thought about all the passages she'd read in which Mr. Today and Simber were together. And so many more about Alex and Simber. And now it was her turn. "I— Hello, Simber. Hi. So . . . this happened. Just a short time ago. Today." She searched his face. "You helped. We did it together. Do you remember?"

Simber couldn't hide his pleased look, and he didn't really want to. But he said in his usual gruff voice, "You could have waited to end herrr until I'd landed on the grrround, you know. I think I've chipped a tooth."

Fifer smiled. "Just trying to keep you on your toes," she said. The two gazed self-consciously at one another, a bit overcome in the moment. And then Fifer slipped her arms around the cheetah's neck and stroked the scrapes on his chin. "I'm glad you're not too banged up. I'll get it right next time." They both paused, thinking and wondering about what next time would look like, and Fifer realized that if next time came and Simber was transformed into a frozen statue, that would mean Fifer had been the one killed. "Uh," Fifer said, editing her previous statement, "next time we fight an enemy together, I mean."

"Rrright. I knew that's what you meant."

"Heh. Anyway, we'll need to fix your tail and your tooth and those scratches on your chin."

"Florrrence can do it. Or Aarrron." He hesitated. "Was everrrything all rrright with him?"

Fifer nodded. "They're all okay. And . . . yeah. So . . . this robe and I seem to be okay with everyone in our group . . . I think." She looked at him expectantly.

Simber let out a soft growl that was almost a purr, and Fifer knew that meant he was happy. They looked up as Carina approached. She congratulated Fifer. "I just spoke to Florence. She's figured out it's you."

"Thank you," said Fifer. "I'm starting to realize how difficult it will be to reunite Artimé after . . . everything. But I want to get it right." She cringed as the voice in her head reprimanded her again, and she glanced at Florence. The warrior trainer was directing the dragons to keep the dissenters contained, as if nothing had happened. "Florence has them under control."

"Yes," said Carina. "She told me to tell you to come see her when you have a moment. Also, Ol' Tater is at it again. Do you want me to send Sean over there to put him to sleep?"

"I'll take care of him," said Fifer, glancing at the beast, who was harmlessly splashing at the shore for the time being, thanks to one of the dragons swatting him with his tail when he strayed too close to people. "And then I'll talk to Florence." It felt official—Florence, the great warrior, was summoning the new head mage to discuss the next steps. Even though Fifer had led a team before, this was different and strange and monumental, because Florence hadn't been there. And this time it was permanent.

"Did Kitten make it out all rrright?" Simber asked Carina.

Carina nodded. "She and Fox have been reunited. Everyone on our team is tending to the injured."

"Simber," said Fifer, "could you check with Kitten and find out how many lives she has left? I believe she lost two in this battle."

"Of courrrse."

Fifer started toward Ol' Tater. "I'll be right back." She hastily left Simber and Carina and went down to the shore. When she was close enough for the mastadon to hear her, she thanked him for his help, then, with a pang of sympathy, sang the song that would put him to sleep.

As before, Ol' Tater's movements ceased. Fifer went up to him and touched his side, then concentrated and transported him magically back to his spot in the Museum of Large.

Once that was taken care of, Fifer went over to Florence. A sudden feeling of inadequacy came over her, for she still had no idea what to do next, and she hoped Florence wouldn't demand any answers quite yet. But it was clear the dissenters needed tending to—the injuries they'd sustained were significant from the shack roof dropping down on them. Fifer spotted Henry, Thatcher, Lani, Samheed, Seth, and several others moving through the corralled group with medicine from the hospital ward now, trying to make the people more comfortable.

Fifer was struck by the scene. A pang of emotion ran through her for her friends. Despite the dissenters attacking them, there was no question that Henry's team would care for them when hurt. This was what Artimé was supposed to be like all the time. This was what Fifer wanted to bring back to this magical land: Love. Kindness. Peace. And a renewed appreciation for the reason Mr. Today had created this world in the first place. But was that possible after what had happened? After what Frieda had done to create the frenzy and after what Fifer had done to stop it? Had things gone too far to turn back? Some of these dissenters were responsible for destroying the tubes, knowing full well that people were trapped inside. Could they ever be forgiven? What punishment should they face? And . . . would they accept Fifer as their head mage? She knew some of them wouldn't.

"Congratulations, Fifer," Florence said warmly, though she held her hand out as a warning to the dissenters to stay in their places. "That robe looks just right on you."

"Thanks. It's a bit too long in the sleeves, but Sky can tailor it for me later," Fifer said. "How are things going here?" She lowered her voice and eyed the dissenters, continuing to wonder how they felt about another Stowe being the head mage—one that had ended the life of the leader they'd followed. Had

LISA McMANN

they heard what had happened yet? Did they know Fifer was responsible? At present no one was outright challenging her.

But the whispers among the captured ones had begun now that the world was restored and they saw Fifer wearing the robe. Fifer shifted uneasily, wondering what the people were thinking about her. Did they hate her because of all the lies Frieda had told them? Did they still resent her for the once uncontrollable magic she possessed and the danger she'd put them in for years just by existing? It was unfortunately likely that both were true. Fifer nodded primly to acknowledge the dissenters' looks and whispers, then stood up straighter and lifted her chin. She was their leader now, and she wasn't going to be intimidated. But standing here, looking at them in their pitiful state, gave Fifer an idea. She was, in fact, planning to do something that might surprise them. She was going to show them how a real Artiméan should behave. Maybe they'd learn something.

"I think I know what we should do," Fifer said to Florence. "We can bring the dissenters into the hospital ward to make it easier to treat them. By doing that, we'll keep them all contained in one space. We'll post guards at the exit. And . . . ," she continued, thinking hard, "no one gets released without a thorough interview, conducted by me and others of my choosing."

"An interview?" asked Florence, sounding unsure.

"Yes. We'll need to ask each one of them where their loyalties lie and what their intentions are going forward. Find out how they feel about what they've done."

Florence tapped her chin thoughtfully, waiting to hear more. "Some of them have done great harm," she said. "What about them?"

"I'm not sure yet," Fifer admitted. "But Thisbe, being part dragon, has a new sense that I think will help us understand their hearts. Maybe, if she's willing, she can help us decide if we can believe what the dissenters say."

Florence nodded. "That's the beginning of a sound plan," she said. "Very fair and kind, I think. Maybe a little too kind, but I admire that in you. I think even though we're in the minority, we have such a great, strong team who already trusts you. I feel certain they'll buy into this idea."

"We don't actually have a lot of other options. What else are we supposed to do? Banish them?"

LISA McMANN

"Maybe."

"To where? The Island of Graves to get eaten by the saber-toothed gorillas? Or to live in the underwater Island of Fire? None of our other island friends would want them." Fifer gave a grim smile. "Besides, it's the way things should be around here. Compassionate. I'm going to show them what they never showed Thisbe and me. Maybe we can turn this around if it's not too late."

"You've always been good-hearted," Florence said carefully. "But don't fall over backward trying to make them *all* comfortable. They need to feel some shame. And some need to pay for what they've done."

Fifer nodded, but she wasn't sure about that. What about herself? Did she deserve to be banished after what she'd done? She was certain some of the dissenters would think so. "I hear you, Florence," Fifer said, but she was still conflicted.

She took a step toward the mansion, then hesitated. She wanted desperately to talk to someone about everything, and Florence had always been there for Fifer. But now wasn't the time to be selfish when people were in pain. "Thanks," she said instead. "I'll go assign duties, then check on the hospital ward." She wrinkled her nose. "I hope everything inside the mansion was magically restored to its usual splendor. But somehow I fear it won't be."

"Henry said the hospital ward is in good shape," Florence said. "He'd made it small when things started to ramp up with Frieda. So hopefully if you extend it to its largest size, most of the things inside it will be intact."

"Good," said Fifer. "Keep things under control out here. We'll talk later once we get everyone settled. I'll let you know when the hospital ward is ready for patients."

Fifer walked briskly to the mansion, her new robe swishing around her ankles. She opened the main door a crack, then cringed. She pushed the door farther and saw the entirety of the mansion's enormous entryway. It was as she'd feared: just as destroyed as they'd left it. They'd have a lot of work to do on the structure *and* the people before things would be back to normal. It was clear that bringing the world of Artimé back was just the first step in a huge process, which was revealing itself little by little as an enormous never-ending task. And Fifer, finding herself in a very sticky situation, wanted desperately to stay focused, reestablish Artimé's policies, and show the people how things were going to be from now on. Somewhere in there she would have to find a friend she could confide in. But without Thisbe at her side, she felt isolated and lonely amid a sea of friends. It seemed like things were growing more difficult by the minute.

Palace in Pain

D ev wasn't sure what to think as he and Astrid roamed the palace property, taking it all in. Set within a mysterious fog was the debris-covered land: uprooted pavers everywhere and an immense dead garden covered in spider webs. Rising above the fog were the palace's towers, the largest in the center of a covered court-yard and one at each of four corners surrounding it. All of the towers were topped with weather-beaten bulbs like enormous onions, and all but the middle one had cracked and split. Two of the bulbs had fallen into such disrepair that they were in pieces that hung down like petals, revealing glimpses of ruined interiors. The whole property was an old, decaying mess.

It had been completely abandoned, or so it seemed. From the looks of it, nobody had lived here in a long time. The correct shapes were there to match the image in Dev's head, but the palace was otherwise hardly recognizable from the glorious purple, orange, and gold image that had danced around the edges of Dev's mind ever since he'd taken in the ancestor broth. All the splendor had drained out.

"I keep wondering what happened here," he said softly, overwhelmed with disappointment. He berated himself for getting his hopes up so high. He never used to do that. Turning to his ghost dragon companion, he asked, "Do you remember what went on to cause this?"

Astrid sat on her haunches. The low part of her ethereal body blended in with the fog. Her neck curved around and downward, as if she were bowing to this mess. "Seeing it like this brings back the memory of those terrible days," she said slowly. "I'd forgotten them for a blissful little while." She paused, then added, "Sometimes forgetting is nicer than remembering."

"What days?" Dev pressed. "Are you saying you know

what caused this? You must tell me!" He was somehow devastated by the deterioration of this strange place, even though he had no memory or connection to it other than the image and his expectations. But he felt a strong tug at his heart when looking at the palace and property. This place was connected to him somehow. He'd never felt anything like this before. "I'm almost certain my ancestors died here," he blurted out.

He didn't know what had prompted him to say it. He'd been a slave in the castle Grimere his entire life and had never known his parents. He'd spent his years as a companion and whipping boy for Princess Shanti for as long as his memory served him. He'd known zero information about his mother and father, much less anyone else in his familial line who would have been alive when this place was destroyed. All he'd had were his black eyes to give him a clue. Until now.

There had been an image of a gray man in his mind too. Hunched over a small desk, his white-and-charcoal beard hanging down. Deep wrinkles in his gray-brown face. Ashes were sprinkled over his gray robe. Before this moment, Dev hadn't focused on that image—the man was so gray and boring. Besides, Dev had no idea who he was. He'd chosen instead to dwell on the beautiful palace. But now the gray man came forward in his mind. Who was he? Why didn't Dev have any memory of him, either?

There was something inside him that was stronger than his memory, though. Something about that ancestor broth was trying to nudge him toward information about his family, and Dev desperately wanted to learn it. It was as if he needed something to grasp. Something to hold on to. Like his entire life had become literal when the Revinir had told him nobody cared about him and then tossed him out the window. Falling, falling, with no purpose and no good end.

He hadn't realized it until recently. His whole life he'd gone about his daily tasks, working and suffering and hoping for a hot meal and some water once a day or so. There was nothing else to it other than looking on as the princess experienced the good life.

It had seemed like enough. It had been easy, back then, to ignore the tiny thoughts that something wasn't quite right. That life could be different. Better. That he didn't deserve what he'd been dealt. But ever since Fifer had said so bluntly that Shanti hadn't been a good friend to him, Dev had been dying a little inside. He'd denied it over and over, in his dreams and

LISA McMANN

his work and his precious quiet moments before drifting off to sleep. But Fifer's words pounded louder and louder in his ears, like the sound of an approaching horse that had been spooked.

Dev realized and acknowledged that Fifer's statement was true. Shanti, the only family Dev had ever known, hadn't thought of him as a brother. Dev was her slave. The one she called on when she wanted something. The one who was punished for her wrongdoings. The one constantly scrambling to hang on to the security of a terrible life, because the alternative could be worse.

He felt so stupid about it now that the truth about Shanti had been revealed. But how was he to have known? He'd never experienced life differently until meeting the people from Artimé. Fifer and the rescue team had taken him in. And before that, Thisbe in the catacombs. Despite that she'd left him to rot with the Revinir, she'd taught him so much. He'd never felt true kindness from anyone until Thisbe had wrapped her arms around his sobbing shoulders in the catacombs kitchen. And then . . . he'd never felt comradeship, true brotherly companionship, until Drock the dark purple dragon had told him they were alike. And that he was worth saving.

Now, with the images of the palace and the gray man so present in his mind, Dev felt a connection to this place like he'd never felt anywhere in his life. It was so strong it made him ache. Tears from the pain of it—the pain of being alive yet feeling dead for his entire fourteen years—sprang to his eyes. He felt the ache build and wasn't sure if he'd ever be able to push it away.

Eventually he realized Astrid hadn't answered his questions. She was continuing to stare at the palace, lost in her memories. "What happened here, Astrid?" he asked again, more gently now that he saw the pain in her eyes. "Will you tell me?"

Astrid glanced at Dev, mildly startled to be reminded that he was there. Then she stood and took a few steps into the covered courtyard, the ceiling of which was the sagging second floor of the palace that connected the four corner towers. "Even the gold is gone," she said. "I suppose it was only a matter of time."

She was right. The bulbs at the top of the towers had been stripped of the gold that had plated them. The warm, bright colors had muddied, faded, and peeled off, and heavy mold grew in patches on the stately facade.

"Do you think someone stole the gold?" Dev asked. That made the most sense to a person like him. He might have tried the same thing, had he known about it and possessed the proper tools to extract it.

"Likely. Pirates, I suppose."

"The Revinir has gold," said Dev suspiciously. "A lot of it."

Astrid shook her head. "I doubt it was her. She's only been around for a short time. I expect this happened sometime after the war. It's been . . . many years."

"Forty, I think. Will you tell me about it, please?" Dev asked for the third time. He could see she was working hard to come up with the details.

Astrid kept walking slowly toward the center turret, like she was trying to identify the different parts of the property that she remembered from long ago. "It's been so long since we spent any time around here. Since the meteors hit. Forty years wandering around in the cavelands, waiting," she said. "I almost can't believe it's been that long."

"Waiting . . . to die?" asked Dev.

"Waiting to die," Astrid confirmed.

There was silence for a moment. Astrid peeked inside a

broken window in the tower and sniffed. Then she began a longer answer to Dev's question.

"Once upon a time," she said, "two black-eyed families and a council of dragons ruled this land in peace and abundance, and everything was good."

Astrid Remembers

T he Taveer family ruled in Grimere," said Astrid. "Maiven Taveer was the queen and commander of the army there, and a smart army they were. Precise and beautiful and full of life—oh, my dear boy, you should have seen them shine with pride as they marched the road to the square. The leading dragons in formation along with them. I can still picture it. And Maiven—I'd forgotten about her until we arrived here. What a noble queen! But I'm afraid she's been dead for many years. No one has seen her since the uprising."

"She's alive," Dev said breathlessly. He felt a rush of joy

to bring such news to the dragon. "She was in the dungeon of the castle all this time! I fed her with my own hand. And now I believe—at least, I think—she has escaped. There was a fire in the castle recently, you see, though I don't remember it because the Revinir had most of us black-eyed children under her mind control. But Thisbe—she told me a few things about what happened."

"That's incredible news about the queen," said Astrid, though she sounded a little like she didn't believe it. "If true, perhaps something good will come of it." She stopped abruptly and turned to look at Dev. "How many of you are there? Enough for an army? And how many dragons in Grimere at present, not counting the ghost variety?"

Dev wasn't sure. "Seven or eight children, I think, plus Maiven. And Thisbe and Fifer. And, um . . . there's one good dragon we can count on." He frowned. "Probably."

Astrid turned her head and blew a breath of fire, clearing the fog from the courtyard. "That's not many," she said.

"It's a very small army," agreed Dev, almost apologetically. "Though—" His face clouded. "The others have left. It's only me still here in the land of the dragons. So I guess that would be one dragon . . . and one human." He dropped his chin. "That's not really any, when you come to think of it."

Astrid didn't answer right away. Instead she started walking again, circling the center tower and looking around. The courtyard appeared to have been an open-air living and dining space with a fireplace and a clay kitchen that had been stripped of everything valuable. The ceiling of the courtyard was the base of the second floor, stretching to all four corner turrets around the center one. There were more floors above it, but they were in terrible shape. Some had collapsed, but the second floor seemed to be holding up all right, other than bowing a bit.

Dev noticed that each tower was its own enormous, tall home with a separate doorless entrance. While Astrid took a break to think some more, Dev looked inside each of them. The metal-and-stone staircases in three of the towers seemed to be the most solid and unharmed parts of the property. But the two towers with bulbs that had split were unclimbable due to the large pieces of debris that had fallen inward and blocked the way.

Dev and Astrid met back in the center of the courtyard and

LISA McMANN

went up to the large tower. The huge, arched doorway had been stripped of its door, and the space was open for anyone to enter. When Astrid ducked her head inside, a family of foxes with young kits skittered out from under the staircase and ran toward the overgrown bushes to the south.

Astrid backed out of the doorway so Dev could see inside. The stone spiral staircase was built off to one side. "I believe Ashguard lived in this one," Astrid said. Then suddenly she poked her snout through a second-floor window to look down at Dev. "It's not nothing."

"What isn't, please?" asked Dev, poised on the first step.

"One dragon and one human. It's not nothing. It's something."

"Oh." Dev felt his face grow hot. "Well, yes, I suppose so." He didn't elaborate on the fact that there was literally nothing he and Drock could do to stop the Revinir. "Thank you," he added, then chided himself for thanking the dragon for calling him "not nothing." He knew he was something. It was just hard to remember that sometimes.

Dev climbed a few steps in the dark entryway and peered up the spiral. The tower was lit only by sunshine coming through filthy panes of glass high above him. He could see long cob-webs hanging down, like something had broken through them. "Would you like to tell me what happened forty years ago?" he asked Astrid.

"Oh, yes." She paused. "The meteors, of course. There were two of them that I saw. Others say more, but they must have landed far away, because I didn't see or feel them hit. One after another those two came, slamming into the ground between here and Grimere. They formed the crater lake near Dragonsmarche. You've seen that, haven't you? The impact cracked the earth and caused a big leak—water and fire came spurting up around the meteors to form the lake. And that volcano grew quickly."

"Yes, I've seen it," answered Dev, climbing slowly and stopping at the second floor, finding it in appalling shape. He leaned out the window. "So both meteors hit in the same place? That explains why no one could say where the second one hit. They stacked up." He'd heard rumors about the meteors when he worked at the palace. People had said the impact caused their world to split off from the world of the Seven Islands, where Thisbe, Fifer, and Seth lived. They had a volcano there, too—perhaps that had come from one of the other meteorites that people had seen.

"Yes," said Astrid. "The ground rumbled and groaned for hours. And it cracked somewhere beyond the castle, deep down under the sea where the rock was weaker. After a day or two, it gave way and split our world in half."

Dev nodded. That's what he'd heard. He went back down the steps, then exited into the courtyard. "But that didn't cause *this*, did it? Wasn't there some fighting? How did this happen?"

Astrid sniffed the air for a few moments, looking puzzled, then sniffed the ground near Dev's feet. "There was an uprising," she said when she was done. "A group of rogue soldiers who'd wanted to take charge and oust the black-eyed ruling families. They'd been building their faction for years, I think. Slowly but steadily. They never would have been able to succeed if it hadn't been for the meteors and the earthquake. People thought it was the end of the world. And the sea . . . It bottomed out and left that big gaping chasm, with the castle barely on the stable edge of it. The queen's ships were lost, falling forever."

The idea of that was unfathomable. "So this group of

usurpers saw the people's panic as an opportunity?" Dev knew full well who'd led them. It was the king, Shanti's father. And he definitely wouldn't have called himself a usurper. His version of the story was very different from Astrid's. And even though the dragon's memory was faulty, Dev believed her over the king.

"Yes," said Astrid, who was finally finding momentum in telling the story now. "Immediately after the meteors hit, the rogue soldiers captured several black-eyed children and forced them—by threatening their parents' lives—to kidnap their friend Nadia, the queen's daughter. The children obeyed, and the usurpers sold the young princess to pirates for a ridiculously large sum, which sent the black-eyed royalty into a tailspin. We believe the pirates escaped with Nadia to the land of the Seven Islands before that world broke off from ours."

Dev stopped exploring and faced her, wide-eyed. "Then what happened?"

"After Queen Maiven sent her fleet to stop the pirates, the great split under the sea happened, and she lost most of her ships. The queen's personal ship hadn't sailed yet, and she made it to safety when they felt the first ominous shivers.

The rogue group saw their chance to seize the castle and capture the queen. I thought they'd killed Maiven. All this time I believed she was dead—everyone else believed it too. That she's alive, as you say . . . Well, it's the best news I've heard in a long while, I'll tell you that."

Dev smiled but said nothing because he didn't want to interrupt her story now that it was moving along so swiftly.

Astrid paused a moment to think. "Once they took possession of the castle, they spread the false rumors that the world would end under black-eyed rule, and they blamed the dragons for the natural disasters that had happened. The usurper group's support grew wildly, but they knew they needed to possess the rest of the land in order to retain power long term. Days later they and their growing military marched the streets, fighting off dragons and steering around the crater lake and over the mountains to this kingdom. Many of the black-eyed people from both families had found safety here until the new king's army arrived. There was no place for them to run to from here. Ashguard Suresh's palace was overthrown. The village was torn apart."

Dev pressed his palms against his temples in shock. He'd

had no idea about much of this. "So why is it deserted now, if the rogue group took over?"

"They only wanted to destroy the lines of black-eyed rulers, not take the land. No one wished to be so isolated way out here, far from Grimere. Plus, the formation of the crater lake blocked easy access to this area. The new rulers recklessly killed your grandparents and took their children as slaves. They probably enslaved one or both of your parents, and traded you away soon after you were born. It was a game to them. Trading black-eyed children became a valuable practice."

Dev was quiet for a long moment as he remembered when Thisbe and Fifer were first captured and sent to be auctioned at Dragonsmarche. He hadn't seen it happen, but he'd helped Fifer in the aftermath. Had he been auctioned off in that same horrible way? And what had happened to his parents? Dev could hardly handle thinking about them after that news. It was easier to believe he had none than to get his hopes dashed again.

"What of the ghost dragons? How do *you* fit into the story?"

"At that time my generation of rulers, the elder dragons, were preparing to pass on to the next life. But without our

LISA McMANN

co-ruling humans in control of the land named for us, our chance to transfer power peacefully to the next generation was put in jeopardy. Because of the rumors that the rogue group had started about us, many of the younger dragons were killed or cast out. Hundreds fled to find other lands that weren't so dangerous to be in.

"To preserve our rightful ownership and ensure a smooth transition, my generation of dragons was forced to live on. Slowly we turned to ghosts, and now we haunt the cavelands while we wait for the proper human rulers to take back the power, and for our dragons to return—physically *and* mentally. Whenever that happens, we can go peacefully, leaving our bones to be buried alongside the bones of our ancestors. But until it does, we are cursed to the cavelands to wait."

"Cursed," said Dev as he crossed the covered courtyard to a different tower and peered inside. "Like the rest of the dragons are now."

"They are being controlled by the Revinir, which is indeed a curse," Astrid said. She walked over to the corner of the palace to peer into the turret that Dev was climbing up.

"At least the dragons are here in this land again," said Dev, hooking his arm outside a window halfway up to the onion bulb. "Isn't that a good thing? If we can break the Revinir's curse on them, they can help Drock and me fight to take back our land." He paused, then added, "Unless they think we're the enemy when they wake up. I imagine they won't know where they are if the mind control is broken. Like what happened to me."

Astrid was silent for a moment. Then she sighed. "Time will tell, I suppose. That's really all we have."

Discovery and Longing

S omeone has been here recently," Astrid called out. She returned to the main turret and sampled the air inside the window now, rather than outside it as she'd done before. "Someone almost . . . familiar. I've been trying, but I can't quite . . . Hmm."

Dev came over from the turret he'd given up on, careful not to trip on the uneven floor. A few stubborn trees had grown inside the courtyard where they ought not be, pushing up between the loose pavers. As he strolled, Dev turned again to the images he'd seen and asked abruptly, "Who is the gray man?"

"What's that, my boy?" Astrid sniffed again, her face

pressed against a window whose glass had been broken out long ago.

"The gray man. All bent over, with a long beard. I have his image in my mind, and I think he lives . . . lived . . . here."

"Ahhh," said Astrid. "That would be Ashguard Suresh. He was the black-eyed ruler who owned this palace, and the leader of the Suresh line of people. He was a good friend to the dragons, though a bit harsh to the humans around him, especially after the attack stripped him of his family. He survived the usurpers through wits alone, but few others did. Once they left, he hid here for many years after the attack."

"So he became a curmudgeon after everyone else was killed? He wasn't always that way?" Somehow this felt important for Dev to know.

"That is how I remember him," agreed Astrid. "Very kind in his youth. And always good to us dragons. Treated us like royalty in all things, especially when it came to making decisions about our land." She pulled her snout out of the window. "You should go back up in this one and explore. Someone was here, but they're not here now."

"Okay." Dev thought that pretty much anybody would

LISA McMANN

be a curmudgeon if they lost their entire family and people. And their palace that they'd probably worked really hard on. It made him feel warmer toward the gray man, knowing his kindness never wavered toward the dragons. If Dev were a ruler, that's how he'd want to be too.

Dev reentered the middle turret that Astrid was looking inside and stopped at the bottom of the staircase to let his eyes adjust. He sniffed the air, like Astrid had done, but his dragon senses weren't even close to being fully developed, and he didn't smell anything but the foxes. As he waited, he ran a hand over the scales on his arm, thinking about what it would be like to have *all* of the dragon senses and abilities, rather than just the scales and the fiery breath and an occasional premonition. Being able to see in the dark would be nice.

When he could make out the steps, he started climbing, following the spiral. Sometimes he'd look down over the railing at the floor below to see that Astrid was still there. He passed by the entryway that led to the second floor, which was stripped of all decor and whose rotted floor didn't look safe to walk on. But the stone steps seemed stable, so he climbed them. He passed the third floor, and the fourth, and the fifth, all of which were similar to the second floor. Finally he rounded the last curve of stairs, which meant he was entering the bulbous top part of the turret. He looked up at an unusually small opening, like a large trapdoor. Continuing up, he poked his head through and discovered himself at one side of a huge, round room. The walls curved around to form a point far above his head.

It looked like the inside of an onion, but it smelled like books. As Dev climbed the last steps and reached the landing, he noticed it *was* a trapdoor—he could close and lock it from the inside if he wanted to. He kept moving and could make out in the shadowy light that this tower was very different from the castle Grimere's tower that he'd been trapped in. This turret was an incredible library. There were more books than Dev had ever seen before in his life, even in the castle. They lined the walls from floor to ceiling and all around the widest part of the bulb. Shelves loaded with books even hung on rusty chains from the ceiling, though they were way too high for Dev to reach.

On the floor were stacks and stacks of books, and around the stacks were several pieces of furniture. Four old claw-foot chairs, a number of small sofas and fainting couches, some of which had fabric that was decayed and disintegrating. There

LISA McMANN

was an ancient-looking harp on one side of the round room, surrounded by several smaller instruments. A big wooden desk that looked like it was too enormous and heavy to be moved stood on the other side. More books were on top of the desk, and some of them were open. There was a candelabra there too, in the center of everything, but no apparent way to light it. Dev went over to it and pursed his lips, concentrating and waiting until the heat boiled up in his throat. He blew a steady, narrow stream of air, and fiery bits came out with it, igniting the wicks and illuminating the desk.

This room had been gorgeous once, that much Dev could tell. He wondered why thieves had taken the time to painstakingly loot the gold off the bulbous turrets and all the other places, but had left all these beautiful books and instruments just sitting here. And then, after a minute, he didn't wonder anymore. The furniture and large items couldn't fit down that hole of an entrance. Ashguard must have built that trapdoor after everything was already up here. Perhaps he did it when he lived alone, fearing attack.

Not to mention that, as a practiced thief, Dev knew that people who would loot an entire palace full of priceless decor weren't the types of people who would steal books. A book thief was likely either in search of acutely necessary information or in need of mental or emotional escape. Not monetary profit. They were desperate rather than greedy.

Dev had stolen a book once. Of all the things he'd stolen, it was the only one that he regretted. Probably because books had souls. They weren't inanimate and uncaring, like nuggets of gold or jewels. Books had feelings. But the stolen book had helped him learn to read when he was forced to sit through Shanti's lessons with her, so he could almost forgive himself for tucking it inside his cloak one day and keeping it in his tiny, cold room near the dungeon to give him comfort whenever he'd had a spare minute. It had probably burned up in the castle fire, he realized suddenly. The thought of that put him in a melancholy mood.

"Have you seen this place?" Dev called down to Astrid a while later. "It's amazing up here! I think this is where Ashguard must have lived after everything else was destroyed." He ventured over to the desk and ran his forefinger over a few of the volumes that were open and faceup. He was surprised to find almost no dust had collected on the pages. "Some of these books have been opened recently," he shouted. As Astrid had suspected, someone had indeed been here, but only the books knew who it was. Dev gazed at the pages, startled and disappointed to find them written in a language he didn't know how to read. The font was fancy and full of curls, and because of that the letters were hard to decipher, in addition to the words. After a minute of trying to pronounce a few of them, Dev shrugged and gave up. Hopefully not all the books were written like that. He went to the east window and looked out over the path Astrid had trampled for them and beyond.

"I can see the crater lake from up here!" he reported. Astrid hadn't been answering, so he wasn't sure exactly where she was or if she could hear him from this distance. His voice echoed through the empty spaces. "This is a really great lookout tower. These windows have glass in them." He hesitated, and fear seized him. "Where are you? Astrid?"

Astrid poked her head through the doorway at the bottom of the stairwell and called up to him. "I'm still here. It's a shame everything is destroyed."

Dev breathed out in relief. He'd had a split second of panic, thinking Astrid had abandoned him or gotten captured or something. Not that he didn't like this place—he loved it. He just didn't like being alone. "Oh, Astrid, you're wrong!" he said. "Not everything is destroyed." He moved swiftly back to the hole in the floor and looked down over the railing at the stairs, barely detecting her face at the bottom. "This tower is an enormous library. The furniture is falling apart, but there are a lot of books here, and a fireplace with wood, and musical instruments. And no wild animals that I've noticed so far, though there are bound to be bats. It's actually . . . quite nice, I think. In a run-down sort of way. Better than no home at all, that's for sure." He noticed how suddenly chatty he'd become, which was unusual for him. He'd just never been excited about a place before. Or been given the opportunity to gush.

"Speaking of home," Astrid said, sounding mildly anxious, "I'm sensing we should head back. Something feels off here. And it's getting late."

"Oh? What feels off? You mean with the smell of whoever was here before?"

"Maybe," she said, but she didn't sound sure at all. "I can't quite detect it. But it's there." She pulled her head out of the turret entrance and disappeared.

Dev stayed in place, hovering over the trapdoor a moment longer in case Astrid was going to say something more. But she didn't. He took a moment and tried to sense danger on his own, but nothing felt off to him. Everything here felt exactly right. Reluctantly Dev glanced over his shoulder at the library and at the instruments. His scales were flat on his arms and legs. No images were pounding his vision. The Revinir didn't seem to be very angry or active at present. In fact, he realized with a start that he hadn't heard a single roar from the Revinir since right before she threw him out the window and left him for dead. It made him wonder briefly what she was up to. But just as swiftly the thought left him. He gave one last longing look, then slowly went down the staircase to the ground to join Astrid.

She'd nodded off, and when Dev woke her, she seemed surprised to see him, but in her usual, forgetful way. Dev must have spent a little too much time out of her sight. "Hello!" she said, "And . . . . what . . . exactly . . . ? Hmm." She looked around, confused.

"I'm Dev." He smiled and gently explained, "You brought me here, and a short time ago we were talking and you said you wanted to go home. Back to . . . the cavelands." His face fell when he pictured the terrain. The cavelands were so boring. But Dev needed to stay out of Grimere. He'd promised Drock he would, and Drock was someone Dev didn't want to let down—not after what the dragon had said to him. He also wanted to be there in case Drock returned, looking for him. In case there was news from . . . anyone.

A pain shot through him. The thought of Drock never returning with news was high on his mind. The fact that he might never see Thisbe and Fifer again was a little too much to take. But what was he going to do? Sit around in the cavelands with a bunch of forgetful, roaming ghost dragons and wait for something that might never come?

Or . . . was there another option? Dev had developed a kinship with this land and palace, decrepit though it was, in the short time they'd been here. What if . . . ?

"Of course. Dev," said Astrid, remembering. "My special friend Dev. Short for Devastation. Yes, you are a gem, I think. Or at least leaning that way, as my senses tell me."

"Oh, really?" said Dev, tapping his lips. "Thank you."

"Well, climb aboard. We mustn't dally. It's a half day's journey if memory serves. Home awaits."

Dev's heart sank as he stood next to the dragon. His feet felt like cement. But when Astrid knelt down, Dev did as she'd asked and climbed aboard. Once he was settled in the cushiony hollow between her wings, he gazed at the grounds. The spider-webbed garden was horrifying. The foxes barking and scurrying around the main-floor staircase were unsettling. And the palace was doomed to collapse entirely after a few more years of neglect. Yet he couldn't take his eyes off it. From Astrid's back he could see a river snaking through the back property, swollen as if it had recently rained here. The picture of the river reminded Dev of the third image in his mind from the ancestor broth, and he wondered again if it was trying to tell him something about his past. He knew that having a river nearby was the most important thing about settling down. He'd always known that. But Drock might be coming back for him in the cavelands. And here, if he stayed, he'd be all alone. Conflicted, Dev closed his eyes and brought the image of the beautiful palace to the forefront of his mind.

Astrid, with her great wings outstretched, began to run and flap them, creating a *whoop-whoop-whoop* sound as they sliced the air. She lifted off with Dev aboard. He opened his eyes and turned to look over Astrid's side at the broken-down palace, so different from the image in his mind. Yet he couldn't shake the strong pull of it. He couldn't stop thinking about it.

Astrid cleared the treetops and kept flying. Dev's chest tightened, and the ache in his ribs, which had been forgotten most of the afternoon, returned. He turned to watch the grounds grow small but felt his eyes closing again, as if unable to look. A sick feeling rumbled through his gut. In that instant he knew that, despite everything, he belonged here. Not in the cavelands. Not in the forest or in Grimere or anywhere else. And maybe that meant he'd be alone, like old, gray Ashguard Suresh, the curmudgeon. Maybe it meant Dev would become a curmudgeon too, but none of that mattered. Astrid was taking Dev away from the only place that had ever felt like home to him, and everything about that was dead wrong.

"Astrid!" Dev called, desperation evident in his voice. He rose to his knees, hanging on with one hand to her pillowy skin and pleading, "Please turn around. Please! I . . . need to go back. I need . . . to go . . . home."

An Unwelcome Visitor

I f Drock comes to the cavelands with news of the other black-eyed people, you must tell him where I am," Dev told Astrid as she prepared to leave for the cavelands again, this time without him. "Can you remember to do that?"

"I promise," said Astrid.

Dev found it hard to believe her. "Wait. I'll tie a ribbon of grass around your claw."

"A ribbon of grass?" said Astrid, completely befuddled. "Why would I want that?"

"It'll help you remember," said Dev. "Stay here. I'll be

right back." He ran out toward the river, where the grass grew long and sturdy, and plucked three pieces of equal length. He tied off one end, braided the strands tightly, then tied off the remaining end and brought it back to Astrid. "Hold out your talons, please," he said.

Astrid obliged. Dev knelt and tied the grass ribbon around her smallest claw, making several knots to keep it from slipping off or untying. "Whenever you look at this ribbon, you will think of me," said Dev. "And you'll remember that you need to tell Drock where I am. Okay?"

Astrid frowned. The grass ribbon felt like she had something undesirable stuck between her claws, and she didn't really like it. "Okay," she said doubtfully. "If you say so." She didn't seem sure of this plan at all.

"I believe in you," said Dev. "And . . . thank you, Astrid. For everything you've done for me. I'm very grateful."

"Take good care of yourself," said Astrid. "I've grown fond of you since the moment I first discovered you in Ashguard's tower. I knew there was someone up there. Did I tell you?"

LISA McMANN

Dev smiled uneasily but didn't correct her. He worried that a grass ribbon around her claw wasn't going to help her one bit. But it was something. "I've grown fond of you, too. Don't forget me here."

"I could never forget you, ah . . ." She blinked.

"Dev," said Dev.

"That . . . was a joke," said Astrid slyly.

"Oh," said Dev, trying to laugh but failing miserably.

"Good-bye, Dev," said Astrid. And with that, she took her leave.

Dev waved until she stopped looking back, and then he shielded his eyes from the sun and watched until she grew small. He thought he saw a tiny something drop from her claw to the ground below. Dev shook his head and sighed. Hopefully, if Drock asked about him, that would jar Astrid's memory. But if not, Dev would have to deal with whatever came his way indefinitely. Alone.

The thought made his stomach churn. He hadn't spent much time alone, and he didn't like it. He'd told Fifer as much when he'd joined her rescue team, and he wasn't used to making his own decisions after a life of having someone dictate his every move. But he was ready now. Or at least he hoped he was.

» » « «

An hour later Dev had caught, cooked, and eaten a fish. He found a couple of buckets, which could come in handy for fishing in the future. And he stumbled across a well in a corner of the courtyard that had a hand pump. After a few minutes of pumping, the water turned clear and tasted good. He didn't even need to go all the way to the river to get a drink. That seemed like a luxury.

Soon he returned to the center turret and climbed up to the bulbous library tower. He looked around more thoroughly and began to count the volumes of books, but gave up after a few minutes. Then he tried out all of the sofas to see which would make the best and softest bed and beat the dust out of it. While the dust settled, Dev went over to the corner to check out all of the instruments and tried playing each one. He made a loud racket but didn't care.

Before sunset he looked through an entire section of books

and found several in a language he could read. As he settled down on his sofa, facing the window that looked to the east, he smiled contentedly. This broken-down mess of a palace was all his. Not just because he'd decided to stay since he felt a calling to this place. But because his inner sense told him he was the rightful owner. Dev was of the line of Suresh—there was no question in his mind anymore. Ashguard had been one of his ancestors, perhaps even his grandfather. The ancestor broth that Thisbe had fed him told him so.

Sure, there was a lot of work to do if Dev ever decided to restore this land and these structures. But he didn't need a whole palace, or even very much of it. And he didn't need to fix anything at all if he didn't want to. He had everything he could ever want: a river, a sofa, and books to be his friends.

As he stared out the window, watching the sky lose its light, he saw a spot like a fly on the windowpane. But it grew larger, and more spots appeared. Dev got up and went to the window, then squinted through it. Was it a flock of birds?

They grew larger still. Very big birds? Some of Fifer's falcons, perhaps? Had she sent them with a message? What was happening?

The darkness fought against Dev's vision, but soon the spots in the distance grew large enough for Dev to recognize without the need for direct sunlight.

They weren't birds.

His chest tightened and his breath ceased. It was a posse of dragons, with the Revinir in the lead. And they were coming straight for Dev's palace.

An End of Something

The long day stretched into night in Artimé, and Fifer and her team were hard at work in very different ways. By the time all of the dissenters had been moved from the lawn to the confines of the hospital ward, other things were progressing as well.

Florence sent Seth with the two ghost dragons back to Quill to fetch everyone's things that they'd left in the Quillitary yard. When they returned, the dragons were content to fish in the sea, then rest on the lawn and munch on the herbs from Henry's garden while they waited for their next assignment. Seth went inside to help others with cleanup.

Inside Ms. Octavia's classroom, Aaron studied various books, trying to find out how to fix the tubes or make new control panels. Carina, Sean, and Samheed worked on repairing the staircase so it wouldn't collapse, and then they started fixing all of the broken spindles and sections of railing. Henry and Thatcher handled the injuries in the hospital ward, with Crow and Scarlet helping out. Florence assisted Simber in guarding the entrance to the ward. Seth, Kaylee, Ishibashi, Sky, and Ibrahim cleared out the debris scattered throughout the mansion, repairing what they could and magically making the rest disappear.

Fifer and Lani talked through the current status of the dissenters while magically replacing the chandeliers. Then they sealed the top of the mansion walls to the roof all the way around, so that whenever rain was scheduled it wouldn't leak inside. Clementi moved from window to window on each floor, painstakingly reciting permanent glass spells at each for what everyone hoped would be the last time.

Thisbe officially introduced Maiven Taveer, Asha, Prindi, Reza, Rohan, and the rest from Grimere to the mansion. And later, while Thisbe instructed the black-eyed children on how they could help and invited them to explore the mansion, Fifer introduced Aaron to Maiven, his grandmother. The three talked through that surprise, and Maiven shared how they'd come to learn the truth. Then, with pressing duties awaiting them all, they agreed to talk more when there was time.

Kitten and Fox went together to the secret hallway so Kitten could continue looking for Mr. Today's clue. There was no doubt in her mind that if she found it and tried to tell anyone, they would ignore her mews as usual. But it would be good to have the information whenever the humans got around to waking her up and asking for it.

Once Fifer left Aaron in Ms. Octavia's classroom, she returned to the hospital ward. She was still trying to figure out the best way to handle the dissenters. Several of them expressed gratitude for being let inside and for the comfortable beds in the ward. And many seemed remorseful about fighting against the other Artiméans. But not all. Garrit and a few others were furious. And Fifer knew that Florence had been right. There had to be consequences for their actions.

Fifer addressed them sternly. "What you have done to Artimé is unforgiveable," she said. "You put the lives of your fellow people in grave danger by following the leadership of a madwoman. There is no excuse for your behavior. If you would like to remain in Artimé, you'd better start thinking about what you plan to do to improve yourselves and this world going forward. Or be prepared to part ways and leave this island."

She paused her speech to gaze from one bed to the next and from chair to chair. Everyone was unsurprisingly quiet in this moment, even the angry ones. "I'm going to start interviews tomorrow," Fifer said. "So be prepared to show me and the others that you can be trusted." She turned to go. "Now, get some sleep. We can all use it."

Especially Fifer. She was feeling exhaustion set in, but she still had a few things to do before she could rest. And part of her didn't want to rest, because that would just open her mind up to spin around all the problems with Artimé, with Thisbe, and with herself. At least for the moment she could cast those aside. Being busy had its advantages.

The crew of statues fixing the mansion continued to work while Fifer went upstairs to expand the hallways and add new apartments for all of their guests. By the time she finished showing their Grimere friends where they would sleep, she was exhausted and ready to collapse. She went straight to her room and found Thisbe there already, unpacking her things in the bedroom.

"Oh," said Fifer. "Hi."

"You moved me back in," said Thisbe, looking up. "I tried the other room—the one you threw all my junk in front of last time I was home—but the door didn't know me anymore."

"Yeah . . . I didn't want all of your stuff to sit out in the hallway forever after you left without telling me."

Thisbe pressed her lips together and sat on her bed. "I see." She folded her arms over her chest. "Do you have anything else you'd like to say?"

Fifer sighed. She knew she shouldn't start this right now when she was tired. That was never a good idea. But she'd been feeling bad for so long that it just came out. "I feel like you intentionally misunderstood me."

"What? When? Today?"

"No, not today. Right before you left. You kept finding things to get offended about as you walked around here with your . . . your attitude. Like you were more important because you had a mission in the land of the dragons, and I was just being silly because I believe people need fun in their lives. And water. Remember that time you yelled at me because I said people should have canteens, of all things?"

Thisbe burrowed her fists into her eyes. She could feel a quick anger rise inside her. "You *were* being selfish." She let out an exasperated breath, overwhelmed with all of the misunderstandings and how to address them. "Look, we're both exhausted. Can we talk about this later?"

Fifer clenched her teeth and nodded primly. "Are you staying here? In this room?"

"May I, please, your head mageship?" Thisbe said sarcastically.

"Are you jealous of my position?" asked Fifer, narrowing her eyes. "You said you didn't want it!"

"No, of course not!" yelled Thisbe, throwing her hands up in frustration. "It seems like a terrible job, if you ask me. All I was saying is that this is still my room too, isn't it? Besides, I figured *you'd* be the one to move out."

"Me? *You're* the one who left!"

"Yes, you! You're the head mage now. You have your own special apartment."

Fifer gasped. The words hit like a slap. Moving to the head mage's quarters hadn't crossed her mind yet, and it felt horrible thinking about taking over her dead brother's apartment. "Oh, Thisbe," said Fifer, her throat tightening. Tears sprang to her eyes, and she turned swiftly so Thisbe wouldn't see them.

Thisbe stood up, immediately remorseful. "Ugh, I'm sorry. I didn't think." She wrung her hands. "I knew I shouldn't have opened my mouth tonight. Please . . . I'm begging you. Let's go to bed and talk about this when things settle down. Before we make it worse."

Fifer nodded, not trusting her voice. The two got ready for bed in silence, both of them upset and wanting to turn the light off as soon as possible so they wouldn't have to see each other.

Once in bed, Fifer stared at the ceiling in the dark. Everything was tumultuous. She could hardly wrap her mind around all the changes. And now, before she could even catch her breath, she and Thisbe were in an all-out war. This was so foreign—the twins used to agree on everything. Tell each other all of their secrets. Have great conversations before drifting off to sleep.

How Fifer longed for that to happen again, but there was so much junk piled up between them that it felt insurmountable. She missed the way things used to be, but she didn't know how to get them back there. For someone in control of an entire community, she certainly seemed out of control of this situation. Would she and Thisbe ever be the same again?

On the other side of the room, Thisbe turned to her side and pulled the covers up around her ears. She didn't like how things had gone. She'd expected Fifer to thank her for returning, not attack her for leaving. After all, Thisbe had gone with Drock back to captivity to save Artimé! It had been such an unselfish act, and Fifer was mad about it? That was pretty rude. And pretty typical of how Fifer had been acting since before Thisbe and Drock had left. The two just didn't see eye to eye anymore. And it seemed like it wouldn't be long before they were going their separate ways for good. The thought was painful.

The girls, both restless and lost in their thoughts, didn't speak, though they could tell the other was still awake. It was the opposite of how they used to act. Everything was so strange. And neither girl was certain their relationship could survive it.

Revinir on the Move

Dev watched the Revinir coming closer and tried not to panic. She was still very far away. Wouldn't she, of anyone, know that this palace was deserted? She must have been here at some point in the past ten years since she'd arrived in this world. She probably stole something from here—Dev wouldn't put it past her. So why was she flying out this way? Did she know Dev was alive and hiding out here?

His heart stopped for a second, and he couldn't think straight. Had she gotten to Drock now too? Is that how she found out that Dev was here? "Oh no," Dev whispered. "Oh, dear gods, *save* me. What am I supposed to do now?" After such a short respite without any worries, all of Dev's fears came rushing back. And here he was, alone, to face them.

"Think, Dev!" he said. "If Drock finally succumbed to her call, then he would have told her I was in the cavelands, not here. Plus," he said, feeling a small surge of hope, "she hasn't roared at all since Drock rescued me, so he wouldn't have had any of her calls to respond to. So that means Drock is still safe. Right?"

He turned back to the window to see if Drock was there with her, but it was too dark to tell. The Revinir and her posse of dragons were definitely getting closer, though, and they seemed to be heading straight for the palace. "They might not be looking for me," Dev muttered, "but even if they're not, I definitely don't want them to *find* me. I need to hide."

The thought of finding a hiding place in this dark, unfamiliar, run-down, falling-apart property with animals and bats and spider webs was almost enough to make Dev want to walk out right now with his hands in the air and give himself up. But if there was still a chance the Revinir thought he was dead, he had to keep that lie going as long as possible. He stumbled through the dome, snuffing the candles and wondering if there was anyplace safe to hide in the library.

"They can't get into this room," Dev murmured. "They're too big to fit up the stairwell or through the windows." And he knew he could lock the trapdoor. But his expression soured. A trapdoor and too-small windows wouldn't stop dragons. "The Revinir wouldn't think twice about knocking a tower down or torching the place to flush me out. If they set fire to this palace, there's no escape for me." He started down the stairwell, convinced that the library was not the place to be.

By the time he exited into the courtyard, he knew he couldn't hide anywhere inside the palace. If they caught wind of him, they'd burn it all down. And Dev couldn't bear to lose this place that he already thought of as his very own. He had to hide somewhere away from the palace. Somewhere they wouldn't be able to track his scent. Or see him. Or search for him . . . or whoever it was they were looking for. He started running south across the courtyard.

It has to be Thisbe and the others they're in search of, Dev thought as he slipped through the overgrowth of bushes and saplings. The fog had returned, and the grass was damp with dew. Concluding that he wasn't the hunted one, whether true or not, calmed him slightly. He was glad for himself. But he was also glad for Thisbe that the Revinir, for whatever reason, had chosen to come this way instead of toward her home island. Maybe the Revinir was thinking only a fool would go back to hide in the same place she had hidden last time. If so, Thisbe had outplayed the dragon-woman again.

Dev couldn't see the Revinir and her dragons very well from the ground because of the trees and brush, which made their impending arrival that much more ominous and frightening. He reached the spider-web-covered garden and stopped, feeling his heart pounding in his throat. Should he crawl under the webs and hide in there?

But no—just because Dev found it to be a scary place didn't mean dragons would be scared of a few thousand spiders. They'd probably tromp right through it without noticing. He had to think like a dragon. Where could he go that they wouldn't search? Or, more importantly, where they wouldn't be able to smell him?

Dev's breath became labored, and his mind went blank. He felt like a frightened rabbit, frozen with fear. And then he bolted, running crazily across the property in the dark, stepping on any number of painful things but barely feeling them pierce through his worn-out shoes. He couldn't process anything. He couldn't decide what to do. He could only remember the fleeting feeling of being free for those few hours, and now the threat of being caught was a hundred times worse than it had ever been before.

He tripped and dropped to his hands and knees. "No!" he sobbed. "I'm not going back!" Shaken from the fall yet even more resolved, he got up and kept running.

When he ran out of breath, surrounded by overgrowth and fog, he knew he was lost. He glanced at the sky, wondering if the Revinir had landed yet. He didn't see her or any other dragons. Would he feel their impact when they hit the ground? He listened, and in that moment of stillness, he heard a familiar sound.

"The river," he whispered, and the image of the rushing river with the forked branch sticking up jumped to the forefront of his mind. He took a few breaths, trying to calm down and think through his options. Was the image of the river coming from his ancestors, trying to tell him something?

When the ground shuddered, signaling a dragon landing, and then shuddered again and again, Dev knew he didn't have a choice. He tore through the growth. Branches swatted at him, cutting his face and body, and he knew the scent of blood wouldn't help him outwit the dragons.

The sound of the river grew louder, and he ran straight for it. Down the bank he went, leaping over the soft, wet mud that lined it, so he wouldn't leave footprints. Then he sloshed through the water, waist deep, heading upstream, away from where the palace stood.

Every now and then he could hear a dragon snort. He could see flames shooting through the night air behind him. Dev kept moving, pushing against the current and constantly turning to see if the dragons were following the scent trail he'd left behind on land. He tried to take comfort in the fact that the river was a smart choice. His only choice.

The riverbed shook with dragon footsteps. Dev turned to see an enormous, unfamiliar red dragon approaching the bank. The boy sank down to his neck in the freezing water and continued moving, searching for something to hang on to. But the dragon drew closer and began to drink. Dev took a deep breath

LISA McMANN

and slipped under, trying hard to stay still, keep a foothold, and not get swept away by the current.

Underwater, while his breath ticked away bubble by bubble, Dev had thoughts. *I should have gone downstream. If I lose my footing, I'll be swept right past the dragon. I should have known they'd want a drink after flying all this way. I should have gone into the spider garden. I should have gone back to the cavelands with Astrid when I had the chance.*

And then: *I should have stayed in the cavelands and never come here at all. Who am I to think I deserve a palace? That I deserve anything at all?*

It was the last thought that had Dev sobbing underwater. And the only problem with sobbing underwater is that it requires an intake of breath.

He twisted his head—he had to, or else he'd suck in water and start coughing, and then he'd for sure be caught. He drew in a breath, two breaths, then three, unable to stop once he started. On the fourth breath he opened his eyes, almost not wanting to see what he was certain was directly on top of him.

An enormous dragon's face was only tens of feet away, its nostrils flared. It was solidly bent down with front legs in the river, fishing. Behind it, several feet from the bank in the overgrowth, was a smaller dragon, barking instructions and demanding water and fish. Her iridescent scales caught the starlight. The Revinir.

Dev's life was almost over. He knew it. And soon the dragons would know it too. He took another breath as silently as possible and slipped his head under the water again, feeling the sand and rocks start to shift under his feet because of the current. He swam farther, feeling around for anything to grab on to to help him stay in one place or propel him upstream, all while listening to the slightly muted voice of the Revinir talk about what sort of fish she wanted the red dragon to catch for her.

Why not just catch your own fish? Dev wondered. Didn't she know how? Or maybe she just liked bossing other dragons around? She'd certainly liked bossing him and the other slaves. . . . Dev's thoughts became thick and slow, for the water was cold enough to make his body and fingers numb by now. He surfaced to take one more breath, and that's when he saw it. A long, thin, dark V in the moonlight in front of him, coming up from the riverbed. Dev submerged and inched forward, reaching blindly in front of him, and grabbed on to it. A forked tree branch? His fingers were too numb to tell, but the image flashed before his eyes. The thing was solid and would secure him in place. He hooked his arm around it.

Dev could hear splashing behind him. Muffled snorts. And occasionally a flash of dragon fire illuminated the water around him. Despite his angry lungs, he pulled himself down farther, hoping no part of his body or clothing would be visible. Wishing he could hold his breath for longer, like Thisbe and Fifer and Seth had said they could do. He knew that the pressure in his chest and the black spots in front of his eyes would only become worse with every throb of his heart. He could feel the need for air pulsing angrily in his face, his neck. He couldn't tell if his arm was holding on tightly anymore. He couldn't feel his feet at all, and it seemed like his body was floating up to the surface, though he tried his best to sink. No matter what, though, there was no way Dev was going to stand up or even turn his head for another breath. It was a miracle the dragons hadn't seen him the last time.

If Dev was about to die, it would be on his own terms. He'd rather drown than be eaten by a dragon. He'd rather suffocate than go back as a slave to the Revinir. As long as he could convince his body not to panic and rebel, the better his chances of getting through this.

Eventually the blackness overtook him. His arm loosened on the underwater branch. His legs slacked and his feet lifted and he breathed water into his lungs. The rest of his body popped up to the surface as he writhed and choked and rolled down the river on the current until it deposited him on the opposite bank in a heap.

A Study of One

When Fifer awoke early the next morning, she remembered that she was the head mage. Then she remembered what she'd had to do to get there, and a wave of nausea washed through her. Even though putting an end to Frieda Stubbs had been the right thing to do in order to save all of those people from the remote rooms, it was still hard for Fifer to admit that she'd done it. She'd traded a single life for many, which seemed like it would be an easy decision, but it wasn't. Logically it made sense. But part of her wished the events of the previous day had all been a dream. Or . . . more like a nightmare. She blew out a quiet breath and sat up. Mostly she was glad Aaron and Clementi and Samheed hadn't died of thirst. She had to focus on that.

She stretched and saw Thisbe still asleep in her bed. At the sight of her, the memory of their fight came rushing back, and Fifer's already unsettled stomach tied up in knots. Was it possible that today would be even harder than yesterday? With so many things up in the air and so many conflicts to resolve, Fifer wasn't sure where to start.

She thought about Sky—maybe she could give Fifer some guidance. Sky was always steady and calming during a crisis. And she'd been there for Fifer when they went to Warbler to collect Queen Eagala's things. Which reminded her that those materials were still in the skiff, anchored just offshore. Fifer would have to fetch them and bring them in for Thisbe. Though a tiny part of her didn't feel like doing anything generous for her sister at the moment.

Fifer got dressed and brushed her hair. She slipped the robe on over her clothes and vest and tiptoed out of the bedroom, pausing for a moment in the living quarters when she noticed a new note on the blackboard. Desdemona had put

LISA McMANN

up a congratulations card for Fifer, signed by all the other blackboards in Artimé. It gave Fifer mixed feelings, bringing a sentimental tear to her eye alongside a chill of worry. But it also reminded her that there was so much to accomplish today. And that sending a general blackboard message to everyone in Artimé was probably something she should do to ease some of the questions people might have. She'd talk to Florence about what to say.

Perhaps that note could wait until after Fifer started releasing dissenters, if that was what she decided she ought to do. . . . She was still conflicted about how to punish them. She went out into the hallway and saw Sky exiting a room down the hall. Fifer waited for her.

"Hi," said Fifer, feeling a bit awkward in the conspicuous robe.

Sky smiled and came up to Fifer, giving her a warm embrace. "How are you?"

Fifer gripped Sky tightly, almost as if holding on for dear life. When Sky tried to pull away, Fifer didn't let go.

"Oh, Fifer," said Sky, hugging Fifer again and patting her back. "This has been rough, hasn't it?"

Fifer kept her face pressed into Sky's shoulder. She couldn't speak for a moment. But then she took a deep breath. "I'm struggling with some stuff."

"Tell me," said Sky.

Fifer released the embrace and pressed her lips together, lifting her eyes to meet Sky's encouraging gaze. "There's this voice in my head . . . my conscience or whatever. It keeps reminding me that I killed a fellow Unwanted. I feel terrible about it, and I can't seem to tune it out."

Sky turned, and the two started walking down the hallway toward the balcony. "I can imagine that must feel very strange," she said. "But let's explain the facts to your conscience. From what I heard, you weren't even close to figuring out Mr. Today's clue. Do you know how long it took me and Alex to figure out how to bring the world back the first time with one of Mr. Today's little clues?"

Fifer looked up. "How long?"

"Days," said Sky. "Many days. If you'd stuck to the route of figuring out this clue and it also took you days, guess what?"

"Aaron would be dead."

"And he's not the only one. Clementi and Samheed would

LISA McMANN

be too. And it's not like Frieda would have given you time to work on it. Fifer—she tried to kill you! Multiple times! You acted in self-defense, and your quick moves and bravery make you a hero. You saved the lives of people who were unfairly trapped by that dictator and her followers."

They reached the balcony and stopped at the railing. Sky's words acted like a salve to the critical voice in Fifer's head. "She did try to kill me," Fifer admitted. "Four times, I think it was."

"Let me ask you something," said Sky. "If you could have killed the Revinir as she attacked Alex, and you knew it would save him, would you have done it?"

"Of course!" said Fifer, indignant. "I'd do anything to save Alex! I'd do anything now to bring him back!"

"And do you feel that same fierce love for Aaron?"

Fifer stared. "Yes," she whispered. "Probably more. If I'm being honest." Aaron had always been there for Fifer, while her good relationship with Alex had just begun when his life was taken away.

"Please, Fifer," said Sky. "Just think about how life would be today if Aaron were dead. If Clementi and Samheed were dead. Imagine that for a moment. And then think about if one of Frieda's lethal spells had hit you. Killed you." Sky was quiet for a long moment as tears came to her eyes. "Think about Thisbe. Think about me! And Lani. Henry and Thatcher. Think about Seth. And Dev. And everyone here who has ever crossed paths with and had their lives made better by you or one of the others."

Fifer closed her eyes as tears dripped down. Her heart ached as she thought about finding Aaron and the others dead instead of alive. She could hardly bear it.

"Fifer," Sky went on more forcefully now, "Frieda Stubbs was just as much an enemy of Artimé as the Revinir is. And you have delivered this land from her." She sniffed, then added, "I want you to wear that robe with more pride than any other head mage has ever worn it, for you have done more to earn it than anyone who came before you. Do you understand me? Are you listening?"

Fifer opened her eyes. She lifted her chin, and though it quivered, she kept it high. "I am listening," she said. What Sky had told her made Fifer see everything differently. It eased her biggest worries. And while she imagined that voice would never go away, Sky's words had just cut it down to a whisper. "Thank you."

LISA McMANN

Sky wiped her eyes and smiled. "If you ever again feel like you're doubting your actions and your right to be in this position of leadership, come talk to me. And I'll set you straight as many times as I need to, until you can let go of that awful voice in your head and see your bravery for what it is—true dedication, selflessness, and heroism."

Fifer nodded. "I will."

"Good. Now . . . is there anything else you need to talk through before we start our day?"

Fifer thought about mentioning Thisbe and their fight. But that felt wrong. Not only was Fifer spent after all they'd worked through so far, but more importantly she didn't feel right about bringing it up when she and Thisbe had agreed to talk things through. "I think that's it for this session," Fifer said with a small smile.

"Good," said Sky, giving Fifer another hug. "Let's hit this day hard." With that they descended the stairs. "This place is looking better," Sky said with a critical eye sweeping over the main entry area. "Someone was working overnight."

"The statues, no doubt," said Fifer. She hastily wiped the last of her tears with her sleeve and took a cleansing breath.

They found Simber guarding the doorway to the hospital ward. People were talking and moving about in the room. When they saw Fifer pass by, a couple of them started shouting. "Let us out of here!" and "We said we're sorry!" and "We want our rooms back!" Then one, accusingly: "Did you kill Frieda Stubbs?"

Fifer felt a chill go down her spine. Sky squeezed her hand to remind her of their talk. Fifer squeezed back and exchanged a glance with Simber. "I'll return shortly," she told him.

"Take yourrr time," Simber drawled. "They arrren't going anywherrre."

Though Fifer had expected the dissenters would soon discover that she'd been the one to put an end to Frieda Stubbs, the first accusation of it out loud had been jarring. "Let's step outside," Fifer said smoothly. "We have some things to collect from Scarlet's skiff."

"Indeed we do," said Sky.

Fifer and Sky continued out the front door and to the shore. "Are you okay?" Sky asked.

"I will be," Fifer said. "I'm . . . trying to be." They waded out to the skiff, which had only been slightly damaged during the battle due to its location away from the action. Thankfully, the books and supplies they'd gathered from Eagala's throne room were unharmed by the battle and just as they'd left them.

Fifer and Sky brought them into the mansion and dropped them off in Ms. Octavia's art classroom for Thisbe to study later. When they entered that room, they were surprised to see Aaron, looking disheveled, curled up and reading in a comfortable chair in the corner.

"Have you been here all night?" Fifer asked him. She and Sky set their piles of Eagala's journals on a table.

"Yes," Aaron admitted. "I dozed a little. But I found some pamphlets that Mr. Today wrote regarding the installation of the tubes. They were folded and tucked inside a different book that I found in the Museum of Large library. The good news is that I think I know what to do now. It might take me a while to rebuild the control panels, but I have the tools I need over at my island." He looked at Fifer. "Did someone say the upstairs kitchenette tube is still functional?"

"Yes," said Fifer. "That's how Thisbe went to get Kaylee and Ishibashi."

"Great. Well, you can put a tentative checkmark next to

'fixing the tubes' on your list, because I'm making progress." He smiled wearily. "How are you? Did you sleep well?"

"Yes," said Fifer, even though she hadn't. "I was really tired. But now . . ." She glanced out the classroom door and across the entryway to the hospital ward, where the few troublemakers were growing louder, protesting their restrictions and shouting out about Frieda's death. Fifer took a deep breath and let it out, remembering what Sky had said. "I need to make some decisions. I'm going to do interviews, but I also feel like I shouldn't be naive and start trusting them all. They did some pretty horrible things."

"And some of them are threatening you for doing the right thing and saving Artimé," said Sky. "That is not okay."

"Do you feel like any of them are sorry for what they did?" asked Aaron. "Are there any who didn't really take part?"

"Some of them," said Fifer, "but does that mean we should just forgive them and be okay with it?"

"We shouldn't excuse complacency," said Sky.

"I think I know what I want to do with the worst of them," said Fifer.

Aaron gazed pointedly at his sister, as if willing her to

LISA McMANN

remember something about his past without him having to say it. He'd made worse mistakes than these dissenters . . . who just happened to be the very people who hadn't been able to forgive him. As if on cue, Samheed walked in. Aaron shifted his gaze out the window.

"Morning, everybody," said Samheed. He glanced behind him as Thisbe and Rohan appeared together and joined them.

"What's going on?" Thisbe asked. She didn't look at Fifer and took a seat at a nearby table, sipping occasionally from a steaming-hot mug.

"Impromptu meeting?" Rohan, also carrying a mug, sat down next to her.

"It appears to be," said Sky. "Before I forget, Thisbe, we brought you some things." She pointed at the stacks that she and Fifer had carried inside, but didn't elaborate, and Fifer didn't add anything. While Thisbe glanced curiously at the journals and papers, Sky studied Aaron, then glanced at Samheed. She wondered how the two had gotten along stuck in the library together. "Fifer, how can we help you with this dilemma? I think Aaron could serve you well in the interview process."

Fifer nodded slowly. "Yes, you may be right. I was thinking several of us could be on a panel. Lani too, maybe?"

Samheed nodded. "She's coming down shortly."

"Great," said Fifer. "This feels like we're getting somewhere. Maybe we could give the people a preliminary quiz. Like, 'If you could choose any head mage, alive or dead, who would it be?' And if they write down someone awful, that would tell us something."

Samheed raised an eyebrow. "Maybe make it multiple choice. Put Frieda on there."

"And all the other head mages," said Aaron, turning his head. "Mr. Today, Alex, me, and Fifer. Might want to put Claire on there, too." He laughed sardonically. "I'm certain none of them will choose me."

"That sort of test could be disconcerting for the current head mage," Rohan said quietly, looking at Fifer. "You may wish to prepare yourself for some surprise answers."

"It's fine," Fifer said. She knew she was in for some rough times ahead. At the moment, after her talk with Sky, she felt somewhat prepared. "I know a lot of them wouldn't prefer me, especially after that unfortunate glass-breaking incident at the costume ball. And, well, I killed their leader. Obviously that's on many of their minds." A shadow crossed her face, but she continued. "I've dealt with people in Artimé running away from me my whole life, and talking disparagingly about me and Thisbe. I think . . . I can take it."

Thisbe glanced at Fifer and caught her eye for a brief moment before Fifer looked away. They'd both been the source of much scorn over the years. That didn't make it hurt less, but it had taught them to deal with adversity. It made them both think about how they needed to stick together, especially during tough times like these. Yet . . . they had to figure out how to get back on the same page first.

Lani came rolling down the staircase and curved into the classroom nibbling on a fruity pastry. Samheed quickly filled her in.

"Oh yes," she said, when she heard about Fifer's panel idea. "I want to be a part of this. And all of us have different perspectives on people. Samheed and I have had some of them as students, and we know them in that capacity. Others have been aggressive toward Aaron. It'll be hard to admit them back into the mansion unless they show true remorse."

"And if they don't?" Aaron asked. "Then what? Banish them? Put them in confinement like they did to us? Are people allowed to have differing opinions in Artimé? Where's the line?"

The questions were met with uncomfortable silence. After a minute, Fifer spoke. "I don't want a jail here in Artimé. And of course we wouldn't banish anyone for having a different opinion. I'm talking about the people who intentionally endangered your lives and who continue to be a danger to Artimé. After thinking about it overnight, I'm not opposed to sending the worst of them to another island for a while."

"Which one of our allies do you want to terrorize?" asked Samheed, sounding a bit condescending. "That hardly seems fair."

Fifer crossed her arms and looked hard at her former instructor. "I wouldn't think of terrorizing our friends," she said. "There's an island that's currently unoccupied."

"Which one? The volcano island?" asked Lani.

"No. The Island of Dragons."

Samheed's jaw dropped. And then he gave a wry smile. "Never underestimate a Stowe," he said. "When will I ever learn?"

Aaron gave him a pained stare. "Clearly never."

Everyone else remained quiet, thinking about the logistics of turning the Island of Dragons into a temporary holding place. It made sense—there would be easy access to food and freshwater. And it wouldn't be hard for Simber to glide over there now and then to check on them.

Then Aaron spoke gently to his sister. "I appreciate that you want me on your panel," he said. "But I will decline. I've caused too much contention with the dissenters already. You'll present as a more unified jury without me in the mix."

Samheed frowned, but then his face relaxed, and he said with a hint of kindness, "I think you're right, Aaron. That's big of you to see it that way. But"—he stiffened slightly, as if regretting his generosity—"your opinion of the questionable ones will actually be valuable."

"I agree," Fifer said, turning to Aaron. "Will you at least be nearby to listen in?"

"So now we have spies?" asked Aaron sharply.

Fifer's lips parted. Then she closed them. "Yes, Aaron. I've got no problem with spies. This is a serious situation. And we have precedence for that. Charlie and Matilda spied on you in Quill for years."

Lani laughed aloud.

Aaron's lips contorted as he tried not to. "Good point. Very well, then. I will be a spy."

Thisbe stayed quiet, sipping her tea. Then she offered, "One Stowe on the panel might be enough."

Fifer glanced up. "You don't want to help?" she asked.

"That's not what I said," Thisbe replied. "I just think the panel needs to be more impartial. If we put the whole family up there, it could be seen as unfair. I think having you is enough."

"That's an excellent point, Thisbe," Lani said. "This isn't a family rulership, and we don't want to paint it as such. Fifer alone is in charge. No one should think otherwise."

"Oh," said Fifer, feeling torn. "Yeah. I see that." She was losing important panel members left and right. "But what about the dragon knowledge you have about the good and evil levels? Rohan, can you do it?"

"I don't have any dragon qualities," Rohan reminded her. "Not to mention I need to be invested in my training sessions with Florence and the others. And remember that just because someone contains more evil than good, that doesn't necessarily make them a bad person." He glanced at Thisbe.

LISA McMANN

Thisbe shifted uncomfortably. She felt self-conscious about that. Like people didn't really understand what that meant—even *she* didn't really know. But it wasn't as simplistic as it sounded. She frowned as she thought. "I agree that having insight like that could be useful. Why not use an actual dragon? I think Gorgrun and Quince would feel honored to help, if you ask them."

"Over and over, since they won't remember," said Samheed under his breath. Lani gave him a look.

"That's . . . actually a great idea," Fifer admitted. "They'd be good to have around anyway—not only are they wise, but they're intimidating, and they'll provide an extra element of seriousness to this."

"If I may make a suggestion," said Rohan, "perhaps Maiven Taveer would be an excellent impartial judge of character as well."

"Now, that's a fine idea," said Samheed, sitting up. "She's a wonderful human being."

Lani agreed. "She'd be perfect."

"She's . . . also family," Aaron pointed out.

Fifer frowned. "She doesn't really feel like family to me. Not yet, anyway. I'm keeping her on the panel. She'll have valuable advice." She tapped her lips, feeling a bit better now that things were falling into place. "So it's me, Lani and Samheed, Maiven Taveer, one or both of the dragons . . . and Aaron as a spy hiding out in here? Maybe Seth and Carina and Claire can sub in if someone needs a break."

"And Simberrr," came an unmistakable growl from across the mansion. Of course Simber was listening in. With his acute hearing, when was he ever *not* listening?

"Yes, Simber," Fifer called. "Of course." She stood up, indicating the meeting was adjourned. "We'll set up in the entryway. Gorgrun and Quince can gather outside the front door and poke their heads in." She let out a deep breath. "I'm beyond ready to bring normalcy back to Artimé."

Then she accidentally caught Thisbe's eye. *Maybe not that ready*, she thought.

Second Chances

When the sun spilled color at the edge of the sky, Dev choked and coughed and threw up all over himself. His body was numb from the cold, and he just wanted to sleep. But he'd been cold before, back when he'd occasionally been locked out of the castle at night. So he knew that sleep was the worst thing he could do. He groaned and steeled himself, then pushed up on one elbow and promptly wretched again. The pain in his ribs cut through the numbness.

Mustering strength, he looked around, even though his head felt like it weighed as much as a full broth of kettle from the catacombs. With relief he discovered there were no dragons around. No Revinir. He wasn't sure what had happened or how he'd escaped them. Perhaps the gods of mercy had been on his side again. First Drock catching him. Now this. It made him wonder if he was meant to live.

He also wondered if the Revinir's distance from the edge of the river had distracted the red dragon enough to allow Dev to float by unnoticed in the dark. Why had she stayed so far from the water? In Dev's experience, dragons spent plenty of time in the water, because it was their main source of sustenance.

Whatever the case, Dev was alive. And smelly. Very smelly. And now his throat hurt from vomiting. But he was conscious, and not captured, and very, very cold. His teeth chattered. His face felt puffy, and his hands were wrinkled like an old person's. He was sopping wet. And he knew he needed to find shelter and get dry before he froze to death.

With another deep groan he pushed himself to his feet, feeling terribly unsteady. "Where am I?" he whispered. The effort of talking made his throat sting even more. He stumbled on the bank and slipped to one knee, but caught himself and took in his surroundings as the sky grew brighter. The river

LISA McMANN

was flowing downstream to his left. That meant the palace was somewhere on the other side of it. He'd have to cross.

Tears pricked his eyes, and he wanted to give up. This was just one more difficult thing thrown at him. He felt like he might never make it in his condition. And he was so tired of fighting. Always, always fighting against the elements. Fighting for food. Fighting for shelter. Fighting dragons and fighting sleep and fighting images in his mind, just to have one good, decent thing in his life. And now here he was, on the wrong side of a river, freezing and weak and not sure if he could fight the current.

The image of the river and the branch came back to him. That scene had happened in real life. To *him*. Had it been a gift from his ancestors? It made him feel encouraged, though only slightly. Maybe he really was meant to be alive.

He hugged himself, then slapped his arms and chest, trying to garner some warmth but only making his skin sting. Bolstered, he let out an aggravated sigh and sloshed into the water. He used his anger at the disparity in life to propel him forward, slogging across the river one hard step at a time. In the middle he had to swim. The current swept his feet from under him, and he swirled once and went down. But then his feet found the bottom again, and he bobbed back up and pressed onward. Finally he made it out the other side.

He wanted to shout in frustration, but he couldn't. He wanted to scream at the sky, at the ground. At the river. At the distance he'd have to walk and the flights of stairs he'd have to climb and at everything else that stood in his way of his being dry and comfortable. At the castle and the king and Princess Shanti. At the Revinir for making his already miserable life even worse than he'd ever thought possible. At the red dragon for not choosing a different place to stop and fish.

And at Thisbe for abandoning him. "How could you do that?" he cried, clutching his sodden shirt and plodding onward, his expression filled with agony. She'd left him for her own safety. And she hadn't come back. Dev remembered what the Revinir had said. *Not one person in this world cares about you.*

Dev pressed forward between bushes and trees, looking through tears and a blinding sunrise for anything that seemed familiar, knowing this was the right direction. Looking for onion bulbs against the sky. And finally, through the brush, he saw them.

Somehow he made it there. Barefoot, for apparently he'd lost his ragged shoes in the river. He entered the center tower and scared off the foxes. Then he crawled up the spiral staircase, six flights to the top. He threw himself onto the floor and slid over to the fireplace on torn, bloody hands and knees. Every movement made him cry out in pain. He grunted as he tossed a log into the fireplace, clutched his side as he took a deep breath, and blew fire at the kindling until it caught and he collapsed. After a moment he got back up, took off his wet clothes, ripped the fabric off one of the rotting sofas, and wrapped himself in it. He lay down by the fire and stayed there for hours. Maybe days, he wasn't sure.

The world had come after Dev for the hundredth time. It still hadn't broken him completely, but it had come closer than ever before. And he knew he might not survive when it came for him again.

Lose You Forever

H ey, Fife?" said Thisbe as the others dispersed from the meeting. "Can I have a minute?" Rohan hesitated, a question in his eyes, but Thisbe urged him on, so he left.

"Hey, Thiz," said Fifer. "Uh . . ." She looked out the doorway like she had to be somewhere. She wasn't sure she was ready to tackle this problem too.

Thisbe eyed her. "Do you have another meeting?"

"I was just, um . . ." Fifer tapped the corner of a table. "No. I guess I can let Lani and Samheed set up the panel."

"Do you want to talk about . . . everything?" Thisbe seemed

LISA McMANN

as hesitant as Fifer felt, but in a way Fifer was glad Thisbe was pressing to talk.

Fifer nodded. She closed the classroom door so they would have privacy. Then she turned and studied her sister. Thisbe was taller and more muscular than she'd been the last time Fifer had really looked at her. "So . . ." Fifer swallowed hard and cringed. This was not going to be easy. Where should they begin?

"You've changed," Thisbe said.

"You mean *you've* changed," said Fifer defensively.

"Fair," said Thisbe. "That's true. Being held captive as a slave does that to a person."

Fifer blinked. Did this argument go that far back? She had to think hard about when they'd begun to grow distant. She pinched the bridge of her nose and remembered when they'd been separated in Dragonsmarche: Thisbe to captivity in the catacombs and Fifer pelted with shards of glass. She'd nearly died, and Simber had taken her home, leaving Thisbe behind. Things hadn't been the same since way back then. "Oof," said Fifer, sitting down heavily. "This is going to take more than a few minutes, isn't it."

Thisbe offered a crooked smile and sat across from her. "I was just thinking the same thing. But . . . I'm here for it. If you are."

Fifer looked up and held Thisbe's gaze. For the first time in a long time, she got a glimpse inside her sister's heart. "I want to get you back," she said. "I miss you so much."

Thisbe's bottom lip quivered. She reached out a hand. "I can't stand the thought of losing you forever. Let's figure this out."

They talked through everything. Instead of telling each other all the things they'd done and all the hard times they'd experienced that the other one hadn't, they told each other how scared they'd been without the other. "I was so lonely and afraid," Thisbe confessed. "I saw that glass shatter and hit you, and then I was taken down into the catacombs—it was horrible. My biggest fear was that you were dead, and I didn't know for such a long time if it was true."

"Mine was not knowing where you were once we returned for you," Fifer said. "I felt so helpless in that forest. Like I was failing you every moment. And then, when you weren't in the catacombs and Alex died . . ." She shook her head. "You think someone is invincible, and they're gone in an instant? It felt like I couldn't catch my breath for weeks. Everything hurt. And I still didn't have you. It was such a dark time."

Thisbe thought about when she and Sky and Rohan had found Alex's grave. She was still struggling mightily with how she felt, and all she could do was repeat a phrase she'd said before. "I'm sad I didn't get to know him like you did." It came out a little stiffly, but it was the best Thisbe could do on this topic.

"Me too. I think you would have liked him."

Thisbe wasn't sure about that.

They talked on, but they also listened to each other. They let each other speak, even when the words didn't come out quite right. And they apologized and vowed to be better to each other. To not jump to conclusions. To ask more questions and listen more. To not always accept the surface response as the true answer, but to dig deeper until their vulnerabilities were exposed. That was how they'd been before. That's how they wanted to be again.

"It'll be different, though," Fifer mused. "Before, we were

two menaces in the eyes of Artiméans, united by being out-casts. Hopefully, they don't see us like that anymore."

"Ah," said Thisbe, looking at her sister with a gleam in her eye, "but now we'll be two menaces against the world, united in eliminating tyrants. So it's still kind of the same."

"Kind of," said Fifer with a half smile. And even though they both knew that change was inevitable going forward—big, massive changes as they pursued their new roles—they agreed to do better in sharing their goals and desires with each other. Not to compete, but to support. They knew being twins was always going to be something most people didn't have the luxury to experience. But they also knew that they had to work on their special bond in order to keep it.

Eventually they ran out of problems to fix between them, and the air felt clear once again. Both of them sat with their feelings for a moment, exhausted but content that they'd said all they needed to say to put the fights and hurts behind them and attempt to move toward a closer bond once more. It wasn't going to be easy. But it was going to be.

"Let's connect soon, like old times," Fifer said to Thisbe. "Walks on the shore. I want to get to know you again."

"I'm in," said Thisbe. She stood up and went around the table. "Are you okay with a hug?"

Fifer nodded, and the sisters embraced. "I'm here for you," Thisbe whispered.

"I'm here for you, too," said Fifer. Things weren't back to normal between them. But they were finally headed in the right direction.

Trial by Jury

After Thisbe and Fifer ironed things out between them, Thisbe pointed to Queen Eagala's books. "What are these?"

Fifer quickly explained Queen Eagala's journals and how she and Sky had obtained them. When Rohan returned, he and Thisbe started reading through them, looking for clues that would help them understand the Revinir.

Fifer left them and joined up with her fellow panelists, who'd gathered in the entryway. They talked through their strategy, then went to work interviewing dissenters, starting with the ones who seemed to have done the least amount of damage and appeared the most remorseful.

Over the next several days the panel drilled the dissenters one at a time about their roles in the civil war. Sometimes Seth or Carina sat in to give one of the others a break, but Fifer wanted to hear from each person herself. Simber, Florence, and the dragons had a pretty good idea of who the bad seeds were, having watched over them since the battle began. Their true colors showed through the longer they had to wait to be interviewed. There were several who were more than a little angry at Fifer. And some who threatened her for what she'd done.

Aaron traveled back and forth between the Island of Shipwrecks and Artimé, fetching tools and bringing materials he found from ship wreckages to reconstruct the three tube panels that had been destroyed. As promised, he listened in on the interviews without being seen, and gave Fifer feedback whenever she asked for it. Simber listened in as well from his spot in front of the hospital ward. Every now and then Fifer would catch Simber's eye and nod or frown, and Simber would respond nonverbally to indicate his opinion. Gorgrun and Quince gave their verdicts about the hearts of the people, and Maiven proved to have the most poised and thoughtful questions to get at the heart of the individual's motivations. There was something about her royal presence that brought many of the dissenters to understand what serious harm they'd done and show deep shame for it.

It was a relief to discover that many of them were sorry for their actions. They'd gotten caught up in it, they said. Interview after interview, that was the common thread. Looking back at the way things had escalated, they couldn't believe they'd let Frieda's fear- and hate-based momentum carry them to do such awful things to their fellow Unwanteds. Many of them confessed to not wanting to participate in the siege but also not knowing what to do about it at that point. Things had gone too far. They feared for their own lives, if Frieda had discovered that they wanted out.

Several of the dissenters begged to speak to the ones who'd been trapped in the remote rooms so they could confess and apologize. Others wrote letters to the ones they'd harmed.

"I froze Seth and put him in the tube to the lounge," sobbed one man. "I'm so sorry. I used to help care for him when he was a little boy, while Carina was gone with Alex rescuing people. I can't believe I did it. I don't know how I turned into this person."

"I was responsible for pushing the frozen mages out of the tube onto the floor of the lounge," said a woman. "Neighbors from my own hallway whom I've lived near for years. I'm ashamed of myself."

"I'm the one who destroyed the last working tube with magical sledgehammers," confessed another. "Everyone was in a frenzy, and Garrit was screaming at me to do it! I couldn't think! And I couldn't sleep after that. I don't deserve to be an Unwanted anymore. I accept whatever punishment you see fit to give me."

But some weren't so remorseful. One of them rushed the table that the jury sat behind, trying to attack Fifer. Simber flattened him in an instant before he could do any harm, but it rattled Fifer and the rest of them. They locked him back up in the hospital ward until all the interviews were finished.

As the days and processes continued, tears were shed across the panel and throughout the mansion. In the end, most of the dissenters were allowed to stay and were sentenced to labor around Artimé, fixing and cleaning up the things they'd destroyed. Seven unrepentant dissenters, including Frieda's friend Garrit, were sentenced to the Island of Dragons for a time to be determined, with no means of escape. Quince offered to deliver them as soon as the interviews were over, and Simber flew alongside in case Quince forgot what he was supposed to be doing.

At long last, Fifer put out a statement through the blackboards:

Dear friends, it read. The world of Artimé is in a period of mourning and reflection. We have heard from all of you, and I, as your head mage, feel compassion for the stories you've shared. We appreciate your cooperation and expect you to begin your assigned duties immediately. If you have any last words to say to the panel, please come forward today.

After dinner that night, as Fifer waited for Simber and Quince to return, she found Thisbe and Rohan on the lawn, resting near Gorgrun. She took a breath and ventured toward them, wanting to follow through with her agreement with Thisbe to be purposeful about reconnecting, and wanting to get to know

Rohan a little better. "Am I interrupting?" Fifer asked.

Thisbe smiled and patted the grass next to her. "I was just thinking about you. We saw Simber and Quince take off with the prisoners. It must have been hard to banish people, but I'm especially glad you sent that Garrit guy away. He was the worst."

"Here's hoping he doesn't do anything to mess with Pan's island, or she's going to be really mad. If she ever comes home, that is." Fifer sat down wearily next to her sister and leaned back on her elbows. "I'm glad we're finally done with this so we can get on with fixing things," she said. "It went all right, you know? Better than I expected. Maiven is a champion. I'm so glad we had her help."

Rohan smiled. "I saw her head to her room this afternoon once you finished with everyone," he said. "She said she had a splitting headache after all of that drama. The chefs prepared something mysteriously fragrant and effervescent in a tall glass for her to take with her."

"She deserves whatever treat that was," said Fifer with a laugh. She sank back into the grass and closed her eyes. "I still can't believe our grandmother is a queen. Did I tell you Aaron flipped out when I introduced him to her?"

"You told me. They have lunch together every day now," said Thisbe. "It's very cute."

"I love that. I can see them getting along really well." Fifer paused. "How is training with Florence going for everyone?"

"Great," said Thisbe. "Rohan is turning into one of our superstars."

Fifer opened one eye. "Oooh, really?"

"Yes. He reminds me of Ibrahim and how quickly he picked up the art of magic," Thisbe said. "Plus, he's got really fluid moves like a dancer."

"*Are* you a dancer?" Fifer asked Rohan, sitting up. "You might have heard about our yearly costume ball."

Thisbe groaned in jest. "We're *not* doing another ball."

Fifer ignored her. "Dancing is . . . well . . . encouraged. Unless you're me." She laughed a little too hard, from exhaustion but also remembering her fight with Seth at the last ball. "Never mind about that."

Thisbe shot Rohan an amused look. "I'll tell you all about it later," she said.

"Yes, later," said Fifer. "Please don't recount it in front of me." It still bothered her a little. She'd felt pretty isolated and

LISA McMANN

purposeless for a while. But that was quickly changing. She had almost too much responsibility now. "Where is Seth, anyway?"

"He's been a bit scarce," Thisbe said. "But he joined us in training the last few days. I think he wanted to get a little refresher course."

"I need to talk to Florence about starting up a session for other mages feeling the same way," Fifer mumbled. She was too tired to move now. "I'll do it tomorrow."

"What's the occasion for that?" asked Rohan. "Is it common practice for the skilled mages to train randomly?"

Fifer sat up. "We do refresher sessions now and then, but especially when we anticipate any sort of unrest." Her mind felt suddenly weary too. "Like . . . with you and the land of the dragons. Florence and I want to be able to help you. When the time comes, I mean." Hopefully, Fifer would have plenty of time to get things in order here and rejuvenate first. A year or two sounded about right. She couldn't stand the thought of leaving again so soon.

"Really? Is that right?" Rohan seemed extraordinarily moved by the sentiment.

"I told you," Thisbe said to him. She leaned in and pressed a kiss on his cheek. "Our people care about this situation. They're going to help us when we go back."

"Um, right." Fifer gave a wan smile. She hadn't exactly agreed to help them *that* soon. But they would cross that bridge when they came to it. She was just becoming friends again with Thisbe and didn't want to jeopardize that, especially while things were still a bit shaky between them.

"That's very generous," Rohan said. "Especially after what you've been through. We're so grateful for your help. Truly."

"Mmm. No problem," Fifer said. She was starting to feel a bit overwhelmed. And then she added weakly, "After all, you just helped save Artimé, and we couldn't have done it without your team. It's . . . the least we can do." But Fifer could feel a weight pressing inside her chest at the thought of one more wearying journey and dangerous fight to add to her list of things to do. She couldn't stand to think about it now. Not when this job was so new and Artimé still so fragile. It was all too much to handle.

Growing in Power

Once things began to resemble normalcy in Artimé, Kaylee and Ishibashi went back to the Island of Shipwrecks. Aaron finished his work on the tube control panels and, with a little magic, repaired the three main tubes and got everything running smoothly again to the remote rooms.

Lani, Fifer, and Simber found Kitten so they could make another attempt at figuring out Mr. Today's clue. As they ascended the stairs, the three of them who weren't Kitten recollected that she had five lives remaining. But Kitten insisted it was only four. And though the others couldn't come up with one of the instances of her death, they took her word for it—perhaps she'd been crushed at some point alone with no one else around to notice.

In the secret hallway Kitten showed the others where to find the tiny clue on the door, which was indeed the one on the head-mage-apartment side of the secret hallway. As it turned out, only Kitten could open it with a mew spell. She did so, and Fifer swung the door wide. Inside was a small vestibule with magical panels labeled THEATER, LIBRARY, and LOUNGE. "Well, what do you know," said Lani. Merely pressing a button next to each made the panels melt away and allowed one to step directly into the remote room.

Fifer, Lani, and Kitten went into the lounge via this method and noted that the placement of the secret panel was on the back wall by the band stage. They searched the area around the panel and discovered a tiny nub of a button that blended into the paneling, situated above eye level. No one had ever noticed it before. All they had to do was tap it to open and close it. "I can't believe this was here all along," Lani exclaimed. "We sat down here for days, and that button was there all this time. It's maddening! We should tell several

LISA McMANN

key people about it so they know it's an emergency exit."

"I'm not so sure I want to do that," said Fifer. "I can see the reason why Mr. Today kept this a secret. It would allow anyone who knows about the panels to access the secret hallway, even if they aren't magical enough to enter it from the balcony. That could be dangerous."

"Hmm," said Lani. "I hadn't thought of it that way. But at least a few of us know now. That should be enough to prevent a disaster in the future."

The three of them went on to find the doors in the other two rooms and locate the tiny buttons. Then they returned to the secret hallway, where Simber was waiting. "Do we need to keep this main door to the alcove locked magically?" Lani mused. "It would be annoying to require Kitten's presence in order to open it. I recall Mr. Today used to carry Kitten in his pocket in the early days, so it made sense for him. But maybe it's not a problem, since we won't need it often."

Fifer considered the options. "While it would be easier to remove this alcove door completely, I trust Mr. Today's original intentions. And I want to preserve the traits of the secret hallway as much as possible. Kitten is usually pretty easy to find."

"All fair points," agreed Lani. "We'll keep this new information close."

"Kitten," Fifer instructed, "please use your best instincts when deciding whether to open this door. I trust you."

"Mewmewmew," said Kitten.

With that settled, Lani turned to Fifer. "What's next on your list?"

"I need to locate an extra head mage robe to keep in Florence's quiver. That worked so well as a storage place."

"I know exactly where Frieda's robe ended up," said Lani. "Let's go knock this one out too."

While Fifer was slowly crossing off tasks on her New Head Mage List of Things to Do, Seth, Ibrahim, and Clementi joined Thisbe and the others from Grimere on the lawn every day to learn from Florence. Sometimes Carina and Samheed participated too, as well as Sean, Scarlet, and Thatcher. Even Henry sat in on a few trainings when he wasn't busy in the hospital ward.

The black-eyed team trained physically and magically, honed their weapon skills, and grew stronger. They worked harder than they'd ever worked before, knowing the future of the land of the dragons was in their hands, and it could slip through their fingers if they didn't do this right. Getting their land back was up to them. And if they didn't succeed, they would not only be failing themselves as leaders, but they'd be failing a nation of people and a league of ghost dragons who were waiting to die. Everything rested on their ability to take down the Revinir for good. "We have one shot," Thisbe announced, and she reminded them of it daily. It became the mantra of her people. One chance to get it right.

In the evenings, Seth and Rohan worked together to teach Artiméans and those from Grimere to speak the other land's language. Thisbe and Fifer often sat in together to absorb this knowledge, and before long the groups were communicating much better than before.

One morning Florence took Thisbe aside. "I want you to have these," Florence said, and handed her four tiny boxes that fit easily in the palm of Thisbe's hand. "These are obliterate spell components," she said. "They are individually packaged for safety's sake." She trained Thisbe on how to use them, and how not to. "We'll use one for practice," she said. "The rest are for you, and you only. Understand?"

Thisbe understood.

Then Florence and Thisbe took a day trip out to sea in one of the pirate ships that was big enough to hold Florence's weight. With them they towed an old boat that was no longer seaworthy or of use to the people of Artimé. They stopped near a sandbar some distance off the northern coast of Quill and maneuvered the old boat onto the sand. Then they sailed a short distance away. When they'd gone far enough, Thisbe removed one of the four components from its box and held it tightly in her hand. She concentrated as Florence had instructed and threw it with all her might.

"Obliterate!" she cried. She and Florence hit the deck and covered their heads with their hands. The component found its mark. An explosion roared, shaking the ship and rattling through Thisbe's chest and ears. Splinters rained down on them. When it stopped, Thisbe and Florence gingerly went to look out over the water. The boat—and the sandbar!—were completely gone. Only tiny bits of wood floated around them.

"Oh my," said Thisbe under her breath. "Everything is . . . gone."

"That's how powerful the obliterate spell is," said Florence.

"I wanted you to see it. And I hope you never need to use it."

"That was such a wide area of coverage," said Thisbe. "Good in a few situations, I suppose. But not in others. I'll definitely think hard about using something like this, Florence. You can trust me to be careful."

"I do trust you," said Florence, "or I wouldn't have given them to you."

They returned to Artimé as the sun set. Thisbe carried her three remaining obliterate components in their little indestructible boxes inside her vest. As they anchored the ship in the lagoon, they could see a group of former dissenters carrying out their sentences, working to swab the decks on the other ships. There was another group digging on the lawn near the existing garden, creating a spacious new extension for Henry's herbs and other medicinal plants.

"Looks like Fifer came up with some good sentences," said Thisbe.

"Do you wish you'd stepped into the role?" Florence asked her.

Thisbe hesitated. Sure, she'd thought about it. More as a way to protect Fifer from the people who were threatening her than because she wanted to rule Artimé. She still couldn't shake her feelings about how she'd lost Alex and the guilt that had come with that, and she couldn't stand the thought of losing Fifer the same way. At least the twins were on the road to healing their relationship. But Thisbe continued to fear for Fifer's life in the role that had taken one Stowe already.

"Sometimes I think about that," Thisbe said carefully. "But not because I want to run this land. My heart is in Grimere. But I can't stand the thought of those prisoners on the Island of Dragons coming back after they've served their sentence and doing something . . . terrible."

Florence nodded. "I'm worried about that too. I want you to know that Simber and I will be acutely aware of that when the time comes. None of us want to lose another Stowe."

Thisbe grimaced. Her feelings about Alex began churning again.

"What is it?" Florence asked. "Did I say something wrong? Would you rather I didn't mention Alex anymore?"

Thisbe tried to smile. "It's not that," she said quietly. She almost confided in Florence, but she felt too much shame and guilt to admit to the warrior that she thought she wasn't

LISA McMANN

grieving properly because she just hadn't felt much love for her brother. Especially when she knew how much Florence had loved him. "It's just . . . I'm just dealing with some stuff. About . . . that." She frowned and shook her head. "I don't really want to talk about it. Okay?"

"Okay," said Florence. "I'm here if you ever change your mind."

"Thanks." Thisbe was quiet for a moment. "Fifer's perfect for this role. She's the right person."

"She's going to do just fine as head mage," agreed Florence. "I know things are a little stressful right now. But if anyone can overcome adversity and turn people's scorn into admiration, it's Fifer. I look forward to a long and prosperous reign."

Thisbe nodded, but her expression remained troubled. There was something ominous about Florence's words. *A long and prosperous reign.* Thisbe didn't like to tempt fate—not after what had happened with Alex. And with everything the Stowes had been through, Thisbe of all people knew there were no guarantees of anyone surviving the enormously tough job of head mage of Artimé . . . with the added duty of being ally to the black-eyed people of the land of the dragons.

Solitude and Peace

Dev recovered and his strength returned as many uneventful days passed. The palace began to feel more and more like it belonged to him and him alone. He started fixing little things here and there, caring for the place. He honored the way it had once been but knew it would never return to that glamour—not with him the only one working on it, anyway. But that was okay. Dev didn't need things to be fancy. He cleaned up the library, dusting everything, straightening the books, and sweeping the carpets with an old broken-handled broom he'd found in a storage closet in the courtyard's open-air kitchen.

He'd found some other things by now as well that no one else over the years had deemed valuable enough to steal. Some random pieces of clothing that he'd discovered wadded up in a laundry room were a bit big for him, but a welcome addition to his limited and deteriorating wardrobe. Shoes, too, that appeared to be in a style Shanti might have worn. Dev didn't care what they looked like as long as they protected his feet and stayed on without giving him blisters.

His best clothing prize was a long, brown woolen skirt with a useful gold pin in it to adjust the fit. The skirt was warm and soft and very comfortable. He wasn't sure if the pin was real gold or just gold-coated, but it was definitely his most valuable find so far, and he was pleased that the looters had overlooked it. He took pride in wearing the pin at his hip and made sure to flash it to the family of foxes whenever he went by. It was a great relief to replace his old rags, which weren't going to last much longer.

Now that his feet had healed after his mad run over sticks and stones, and now that he had new shoes, he explored the four smaller towers, confirming his fears that they were uninhabitable. Two of the staircases weren't safe to climb at all due to heavy debris and towers that were caving in. In one, a few of the metal stairs inside had melted. He wasn't quite sure what could have caused such a disaster but wondered if it had been the result of dragon fire. In the base of that tower he noticed a few large, black, porous rocks that held on to a terrible stench. Had some smaller bits of the meteors landed here and begun the destruction of this once-beautiful place?

Dev ventured farther outside every day as well to get fish from the river, even though revisiting the place where he'd nearly died made his body shake uncontrollably. He didn't like to be away from home for too long, preferring instead to be in the cozy library tower with his lookout windows in all directions and his warm fire—he couldn't seem to get enough of the fireplace lately after his lengthy experience in the cold river.

His ribs healed. Each day was a little better, and Dev grew curious about what lay beyond the palace grounds. On his walks, with his new brown skirt brushing the tops of the long grass, he found several kinds of trees that bore fruit. There was an apple orchard south of the palace that was flourishing, apparently oblivious to the death and destruction surrounding it. Fruit rotted on the ground between the trees, and small animals seemed to enjoy snacking on it without taking too much notice of the new human who roamed about. Dev only collected what fruit he needed for a few days, plus a couple of extra pieces to leave for the foxes. He was careful to respect the animals' space and tried not to tread on their paths or scare them away.

Daytime was easier for him. At night he looked fearfully out of the windows for splashes of fire in the darkness or other signs of the Revinir. In between these mild panic sessions, Dev tried to soothe his fears by playing the various instruments. He wasn't very good at any of them, but he was learning how they worked and getting better a little at a time. And he found books that showed pictures of them so he could learn what to call them. Lyre. Piccolo. Sitar. Mandolin. Kanjira. They had regal-sounding names that seemed to fit in with this formerly glorious place.

Dev talked to himself as he went about his daily chores to keep himself company. Not too much to be annoying, for he found he really enjoyed the quiet. But sometimes he preached elaborately to an invisible Thisbe about how she'd abandoned him and tried to plot out what he'd actually say to her if he ever saw her again. Sometimes he was angry with her, but more and more often as time passed he came up with valid reasons for her to have left Grimere without him. He would be hurt, yet understanding.

"Perhaps you *have* returned to Grimere and you're looking for me now," he mused. "How would I know? Maybe you're feeling terrible about everything. Maybe you can't sleep at night because you're worried."

That's the thought he preferred to dwell on when he went to bed. For some reason it brought him comfort when he felt most alone and scared. "Yes," he said sleepily as he turned in one night. "I see you are very sorry. I understand you had to sneak the others out when you had a chance. Oh? You returned the next day but heard rumors that I had perished? That makes sense."

What didn't make sense was that the Revinir was out roaming different parts of the land of the dragons. He hoped she hadn't gone to the cavelands to terrorize the ghost dragons. But there probably wasn't much she could do to them. They couldn't kill her, but they could drive her away easily enough. Why had she come all the way out here to the palace only to leave soon after? Who was she looking for? He couldn't stop making guesses. She might have been searching for him, but then again maybe she wasn't. Did she still believe him dead? Or had Drock been forced to spill the beans on that? And speaking of Drock, would he ever figure out where Dev was? Would Astrid remember to tell him if he showed up looking for him?

It was a concern for Dev, but not nearly a big enough one to make him want to find out the answer by physically going anywhere. These peaceful days, after the world had tried for the umpteenth time to do him in, were a welcome relief and a much-needed respite for a boy who'd been a slave all his life.

He could get used to this solitary way of living. He could even find it in his heart to forgive Thisbe if she had a good enough reason for abandoning him. But the more days that passed, the more Dev got a feeling that something bad was coming again. Dread was his primary emotion. It was the only thing he could count on.

The fact that the Revinir hadn't roared in weeks was of growing concern. What did it mean? Had something happened to her? Or was she doing it on purpose to hide her whereabouts? She was the most devious creature Dev had ever known, so of course he had to imagine the worst. "What *is* the worst thing she could do?" Dev wondered aloud. "And where is she? How in the world is anyone going to be able to stop her?" With that familiar feeling of dread, Dev realized the future of this land might really be up to him and Drock. It gave him nightmares.

That night he dreamed of the most horrible thing he could ever imagine—the Revinir returning and capturing him, then imprisoning him in the castle dungeon and torturing him to the edge of his life. The nightmare was so powerful it made him sweat and cry out and fall off the sofa.

He knew he wasn't safe here. He wasn't safe anywhere. He may as well give himself up rather than live with this fear all the time. Maybe the soldiers in the catacombs would take him back and let him work there quietly. He knew how to use the elevator entrance in Dragonsmarche—he'd seen the soldiers do it. Could he just slip down there in the middle of the night? At least the Revinir and her mind-controlled dragons couldn't get to him down there.

In the morning, Dev dressed in his long skirt and a jacket and packed up his few extra pieces of clothing. He cooked and ate a fish and filled his canteen and an old wineskin he'd unearthed with water. Then he returned to the library and stared out the east window in the direction of the crater lake and tried to talk himself into setting out for the one place Drock had warned him not to return to.

But his lead feet wouldn't walk. His soul had attached to the library, and his heart to the land. He wasn't going anywhere.

It was a decision he would soon come to regret.

Growing Restless

Over time, Thisbe and Fifer naturally fell into a practice they'd begun in their childhood, meeting up with Seth on the lawn after a long day and taking a walk along the shore to the lagoon. Seth was busy today, which was fine, because Fifer and Thisbe were ready for a break from the constant activity of the past weeks and hoping for a little quiet twin time. They were still trying to navigate the changes each of them had experienced since they'd been torn apart. And trying to patch up the broken parts. They'd grown closer during these weeks together. That was comforting after all they'd gone through.

LISA McMANN

"How is your team coming together?" Fifer asked.

"Better than I expected," said Thisbe. "Everybody's making progress. Maiven is picking up techniques from Florence and vice versa. Those two have become best friends. And the others are the strongest I've seen them." She paused. "I think we're almost ready." Thisbe felt a flicker of sadness at the thought of leaving, but at the same time she was more than eager to go.

But Fifer felt a wave of panic. Almost ready? What did that mean for her? But she remained quiet. Maybe Thisbe would sense that it wasn't quite the right time for Artimé to step in. But Maiven and the children and ghost dragons had unselfishly left their chaotic land to help Artimé. Fifer felt like she couldn't refuse to do the same whenever they felt like it was the right time to go.

Thisbe went on. "It's been monumentally helpful being here and training. The others learning magic was something I never imagined they could do, so that's been great. And we're all stocked up on components and learning how to make a few too. I think we have everything we need. The new message spell and the obliterate components, among everything else. Thanks for letting us use your lawn to practice everything."

Fifer laughed. "It's not my lawn, but you're welcome." They strayed to the water's edge, feeling the cool waves splash their feet. "Florence told me that the remake of the obliterate spell turned out to be even more powerful than the one Alex used years ago. That seems a bit scary."

"Yeah, it was pretty shocking to see how destructive it is," Thisbe admitted. "Even for me." She patted her interior vest pocket, to which she'd added a flap and button to keep its contents extra protected. "I'm hoping we never need to use them."

Fifer agreed. Then, to get a better sense of Thisbe's thoughts on timing, she ventured a few questions. "I was wondering, now that we've got the majority of the dissenters back on good behavior, if you'd like Florence to start training our Artiméan team in any specific way. What would be most helpful? And . . . um, what sort of timeline are we looking at?"

"Hmm," Thisbe said, sensing something in Fifer's question and throwing a curious glance her way. "I guess Florence's usual training would be best, along with more combat training."

"Kaylee could help with that," said Fifer. She kept her eyes down, but she could feel her shoulders tensing.

Thisbe nodded, but she didn't take her measured gaze off Fifer. "I've been turning this over and over in my head, and I'm still not sure how we're going to take the Revinir down. Or . . . when would be the best time for you to come to our aid. Rohan and Maiven and I have been discussing it. We haven't come to any hard conclusions yet, but we absolutely don't want to go at her half-prepared. We want the full force all at once. It's the only way to beat her."

"Oh, okay," Fifer said, feeling a bit of relief.

"I'm not convinced that'll be anytime in the next few weeks. But once we're ready, it'll have to be go time."

Fifer blew out a silent breath. "Got it. We'll . . . get ourselves prepared."

Thisbe paused, then laughed. "We sound so old, planning attacks like this."

Fifer glanced at her sister. "I think we were forced to grow up fast. Just like our brothers."

Thisbe stopped laughing. She stepped over a rock along the shore. "Do you still miss him?"

"Who? Alex?"

"Yeah."

"I do," Fifer said. "A lot. We really got to be friends there at the end."

Thisbe was quiet for a moment. "I'm glad for you."

A pang of sorrow pierced through Fifer's chest. "Thanks. But I'm sad for you. You must still be really conflicted about it."

Thisbe took in a sharp breath. "I am. I'm not sure I'll ever get past my weird feelings about everything. It was . . ." She blew out the breath. "Good grief, it was so hard."

"Because . . . ?"

"Because . . ." Tears sprang to Thisbe's eyes. "Because I don't know how to grieve for someone I didn't . . . really . . . like."

"Oh, Thisbe," said Fifer, turning to her.

"I . . . have so much guilt about it. And I'm jealous of you, in a strange way. Not because I want to hurt like you're hurting—obviously no one wants that. But because I guess I wanted to have the thing that came before the hurt. The love that caused the pain." She was quiet for a moment. "I don't have that. And I feel terrible about it. Like I missed out on something that I'll never be able to get back."

Fifer didn't know what to say. "I don't think there's a rule about how to grieve, Thisbe," she said gently. "I just remember something Florence told me once, that all feelings are valid, no matter what they are. Whether they seem appropriate or not, you have a right to feel them. Knowing that has made it easier for me."

Thisbe wiped her eyes on her sleeve. "That's good advice," she said. "I'm struggling through it. It'll be manageable, I think. Eventually."

Fifer took Thisbe's hand, and they walked together like they'd done so many times as children. But this time, a spark of energy pulsed between them. Thisbe's confession had made Fifer feel closer than ever to her. It was such a relief to have her sister confide in her again.

Soon they reached the jungle and continued along the sea to the lagoon. After a while Fifer asked, "What's it like holding hands with Rohan?"

Thisbe kept her gaze on the sand. "It's . . . nice. Warm. He was there when Sky and I found Alex's grave. He's been really . . . I don't know. I feel like he's a part of my soul that had been missing my whole life. We're so connected. So close. I can't really imagine life without him."

The words stung Fifer in a way she hadn't expected. She tried to swallow the jealousy she felt. Did Thisbe mean that she was closer with Rohan than with her? And if so, why did that bother Fifer so much after all the healing they'd worked hard to do?

Thisbe glanced at Fifer and saw her expression. She hastened to explain. "When I was all alone in the catacombs, Rohan and I went through so much together. You know? Our lives will never be the same after what we experienced. Maybe a little like how you and Alex bonded. Or you and Seth when you were searching for me. Or . . . Dev, even." She grimaced.

"I never wanted to kiss any of them," Fifer blurted out. She glanced sideways. "You kiss him on the lips, right? What is that like?"

"Yes, a few times." Thisbe could feel the heat rising to her face as she remembered her first awkward kiss with Rohan when they were sitting together in the tunnel between their crypts. "It's softer than you'd expect. It's . . . nice. I like it."

Fifer didn't even like hugging all that much, and she couldn't imagine kissing anyone. It didn't sound nice at all. "So what about Dev? Do you like him?"

"I . . . not like *that*, but yes. Don't you?"

"Sure, but, well, you know—it's Dev. He's not exactly trustworthy."

Thisbe nodded, but she realized that her impression of Dev had changed slightly over time. "He's gotten easier to be friends with," she said. "And now I just feel so bad for the way we left him. He's the one reason why I think we need to go back to Grimere sooner rather than later. I have to find him."

Fifer stiffened. "Remember, you can't let those feelings get in the way of your plan to be prepared. Don't go back too soon just because of Dev."

"I know. I know."

"Where do you think he is?"

"Back in the catacombs, probably. Doing all the work by himself. Ugh, I'm a terrible person."

Fifer made a face. "The catacombs? That's the last place I'd want to go."

"I don't feel like I have a choice. We need to find him. He really sacrificed everything for us to escape. We owe him— and so do you. Without him, our team wouldn't have been here to help you. I just hope . . ." Thisbe didn't continue.

"Hope what?" asked Fifer.

A platyprot in a tree nearby called out, "Hope what? Hope what? Hope what?" and exploded into giggles. Startled and a bit annoyed, Thisbe guided Fifer away from the creature before she answered so it wouldn't continue mimicking everything they were saying. She frowned and looked at her arms. Her scales were standing up, probably from being surprised by the birdlike creature. She smoothed them down and finished her thought. "I hope he's not dead."

Fifer gave Thisbe a solemn look. "Me too. We'll . . . you know. We'll find him together whenever you're ready." She cringed. "I'm committing to that."

Thisbe noticed Fifer's expression and bit her lip. "I've been wanting to talk to you a little more about that. Are you sure you're able to leave Artimé so soon after taking over? You have a huge new job here, and I was wondering if maybe you feel like you should stay here."

"Thisbe," said Fifer. "I want to help."

"I mean," said Thisbe, "obviously I want you to help us too. But you have to tell me if the timing is wrong. Seth and Ibrahim and Clementi are all on board to help me. Some others, too." She paused, then continued more gently. "Don't make me count on you if it's not possible. We'll figure it out."

"Seth and Ibrahim and Clementi?" said Fifer, her voice hollow. She'd been so busy as head mage that she hadn't heard about her Artiméan friends officially joining Thisbe's brigade. It made her feel a bit strange. Like maybe she wasn't part of that group of friends anymore now that she wore this robe.

"I'm serious, Fifer," said Thisbe. "As much as I need you, I want to let you off the hook. You have a lot going on."

Fifer studied the ships in the lagoon, unsure how to feel. "Well, thanks. That's nice of you to be thinking about that, and I understand the predicament I'm putting you in if you can't count on me when you need me. I've been thinking hard about this situation too. Things here are pretty far from settled. But they are smoothing out."

Thisbe stopped to look at Fifer. "You are more important than anything. Let me know soon. It'll be okay either way."

Fifer smiled. "Thanks." She felt a wave of relief flood her. Just knowing what Thisbe expected made everything seem more manageable. And to have a way out . . . it allowed her to take a few easy breaths before things got difficult again. The

LISA McMANN

pressure was off to go with Thisbe, but now it was on Fifer to make the decision. In Fifer's limited experience, sometimes life was easier if someone made the decision for you.

They kept walking around the curve of the lagoon, both a little on edge about what the future held. "Have you uncovered anything good from the journals?" Fifer asked after a while.

Thisbe nodded. "Interesting stuff, personality-wise. I'm not sure how useful it is, though." Her scales rose on her arms again, and this time she stopped walking and looked up anxiously, her eyes darting in different directions. "What is going on?" she muttered. "Now it's happening when I'm just talking about her?"

Fifer frowned and looked up too, but there was nothing unusual—just some birds. "That must feel strange. Do the scales ever fall off?"

"Not so far." Thisbe turned and peered into the jungle. "Does Panther or the scorpion ever come all the way out here? Sometimes other kinds of lurking danger make my scales stand up."

"I don't think so," said Fifer. "Definitely not the scorpion. He hates the light."

Thisbe didn't detect anything in the jungle except the platyprot, which followed them and alighted on a nearby branch. But Thisbe's scales told a different story. "Something's off," she said quietly. "Maybe we should go back."

"Go back. Go back. Go back," said the platyprot.

"Is it the platyprots that are causing your scales to do that?" Fifer studied her sister and grew worried. "Do you want me to call my falcons to take us home quickly?" she asked.

Thisbe snorted. "Seriously, Fife? The birds? What do *you* think?" But Thisbe's laughter soon died in her throat, for there was a disturbance inside the jungle near the treetops. Then a large shadow passed over them.

The twin leaders looked up. And then Thisbe yelled, "Run!"

One False Move

The Revinir swooped down at the twins from her hiding spot above the jungle trees. Instinctively both girls tried to run into the jungle to make it harder for the dragon-woman to catch them. But the Revinir was too fast. She reached out with her powerful hind legs and clamped down on Thisbe and Fifer, hooking her curling talons around their arms and piercing holes into the backs of their vests and through Fifer's robe. She rose with one in each claw, lifting them up into the air.

Thisbe twisted and squirmed and sent burning spears of lightning at the Revinir's claws, working her way loose, and fell a heart-stopping distance into the water below.

LISA McMANN

"Thisbe!" Fifer cried, and tried to worm her way out of her robe and vest, but the claws had pierced through and she was stuck.

When Thisbe surfaced, the Revinir swooped down and snatched her up again, letting out a strange little scream as she grabbed her and dragged Fifer through the water too. This time the Revinir dug her talons in deeper and rose even higher. Thisbe cried out in pain, and bolts of fire shot from her eyes and fingertips, hitting the Revinir but doing no harm.

Fifer began flinging deadly spells at the dragon-woman with her free hand, even though she knew that the Revinir didn't seem to be affected by anything. Then Fifer screamed for her birds, who came flying in from the jungle and soared at the dragon-woman. But the birds were like flies to her. She batted them away with her front legs and her wings, killing several each time she swatted at them.

"Retreat!" Fifer ordered. "Get Simber!" Shimmer and the remaining birds retreated and flew toward the mansion as the Revinir soared away from it.

Seeing that her spells weren't working against the dragon-woman, Thisbe quickly scribbled a help message on the new send spell and sent it to Florence. But before the girls could attempt to do anything else, the Revinir swooped low and signaled to the sea below her.

The surface erupted. Six red water dragons exploded from below, where they'd been lurking, hidden from view and waiting for their cue. They rose up, water spraying everywhere, and flanked the Revinir, snarling at Thisbe and Fifer. As darkness fell over the land of the seven islands, the Revinir and her mind-controlled dragons flew in formation to the west, heading for the world she ruled. As she went, she flipped the girls upside down and shook them. Components rained down into the sea. The girls tried to catch them and managed to save a few. Fifer saved more than Thisbe because she'd loaded up her vest and her robe. But there was nothing else they could do. They gave up fighting with magic. It wasn't worth wasting the components they had left.

"Why can't you leave us alone?" Thisbe shouted to the Revinir when she was upright again.

"Because I need you," said the Revinir. "I can't take over the land of the dragons without the black-eyed rulers on my side. Don't you know that by now?"

"You think kidnapping us is going to bring us over to your side?" Thisbe asked.

"You'll come around. There will be so many benefits for you. I'll tell you about them in time."

"Then why aren't you kidnapping all of the other black-eyed people?" Fifer retorted.

Thisbe gave her sister a panicked look. She didn't want the Revinir to know the others were in Artimé too. But it turned out not to matter.

"If I have you two, the others will follow," said the dragon-woman. "They'll go along with whatever you say, because people care about you. You'll see. Thank you for sending your little spells to summon them, by the way. That was helpful. They'll all come to me in Grimere, and we can fight it out on my home turf with all of my dragons. Nice and tidy."

"You'll never take over this world or the land of the dragons," Thisbe growled. Furious, she sent more fiery blasts at the Revinir's underbelly, trying to find a weak or sensitive spot. At least she didn't run out of this kind of weapon as easily as she used to. And she didn't need a component for it. But that didn't help if it was totally ineffective. She thought about the three obliterate components in her inside vest pocket and hoped they were still there. It wasn't safe to use one on the Revinir now, with Thisbe and Fifer attached to her. They'd all be annihilated. But if she saw her chance . . . she wouldn't hesitate.

"I'm already taking over everything," the Revinir said, starting to sound impatient. "I don't think you understand that you're my secret weapon, Thisbe. And Fifer is a bonus. For some reason," she added sarcastically, "unlike Dev and the other slaves, a lot of people seem to care about you. You make great bait. Really, you should just join my side. Both of you. That's all it'll take to reclaim the land for the black-eyed rulers. And if you join me and we successfully take over the land of the dragons, maybe . . . I'll do something nice for you."

"You're horrible," said Thisbe, spitting fire.

But Fifer narrowed her eyes. What had the Revinir just said?

"Our time together could have been so much better," the Revinir went on. "If you'd joined me from the start like I told you to, Thisbe, things would have gone very differently. But you'll own your evil side one of these days. It's in your makeup. You don't have a choice."

LISA McMANN

"Stop saying that!" Thisbe spewed more of her magic fire-power at the dragon-woman.

Fifer had had enough. "Just shut up!" she shouted at the Revinir. "You don't know the first thing about her. She does have a choice!"

"Typical outburst from someone like you who knows nothing. I can't fathom how you ended up as ruler of Artimé. You must have drawn the short straw for that undesirable job."

Fifer ignored her as an idea began to churn. The Revinir hitched her painfully tighter in her grip and glanced back. "Nobody's even coming yet," she said, sounding disappointed. "Here you are, the leader, and nobody even cares that I've abducted you—that's not how I thought it would go, to be honest. But I'm not worried."

"You are a monster," Thisbe muttered, letting her limbs flop. She couldn't beat the dragon-woman with magic or fire and gave up trying for the moment to regain her strength. This wasn't how Thisbe had planned it. Now everything was going wrong. Their "one big attack" plan was foiled. While she caught her breath, she studied the dragon's scales as carefully as she could while dangling from this frightening height. Was there a worn spot anywhere? She had to come up with an alternative plan.

"You're right," the Revinir admitted. "I'm a monster. You're absolutely correct about that. But I have feelings too. In fact, I'm almost sorry I killed your friend Dev. But that's what monsters do sometimes."

Fifer gasped.

"What did you say?" cried Thisbe.

The Revinir cackled. "You heard me correctly. He didn't want to give you up, but he couldn't help it. You lied to me about the ancestor broth, Thisbe. Lied to my face." Her laughter faded. "And I believed you. I need a good liar like you on my team. I mean it—I've got the dragons and, as one of them, I'm a rightful ruler too. You've got the black-eyed people. Together we can declare that the land is back in the right hands! But I've got to break you first, I see. Luckily, I know just how to do it."

Fifer and Thisbe, still strung painfully tight in the grips of the dragon-woman, looked at one another in horror, unable to comprehend what the Revinir was talking about because of what she'd said about Dev. He was dead?

Dev. Their friend. She'd killed him.

In that life-altering moment, another electric connection

passed between the girls like what had happened before when they were walking. Only this time they weren't touching. It was a feeling, like tiny pulses in their chests, that brought their minds to connect for the first time in their lives. It reminded Fifer of what Alex and Aaron had once felt. The way they'd described it. It was the thing Fifer had felt so inadequate about when she was searching for Thisbe back in the forest of Grimere and been unable to feel if Thisbe was nearby. And now, with her sister just feet away but with no ability for them to speak freely, they had become one.

We aren't going to survive this, thought Thisbe, looking into her sister's eyes.

Fifer could hear it like a whisper. But she didn't answer right away, for something else was already brewing deep inside Fifer's mind. She stared at Thisbe hard, thinking intensely about something the Revinir had said. Trying to work out this thing that wouldn't quite come together. But feeling that if she were patient, if she just thought a little longer . . . maybe it would. After a moment, Fifer pulled out one of the few remaining send spell components that hadn't been dumped into the sea. She tapped it, producing the pencil, then wrote:

Florence,

Call Simber back. Keep the people from Grimere safe. Don't come after us. And don't reply. Trust me.

—Fifer

Fifer sent the message, and it went soaring away, lighting up the night.

"Ha!" said the Revinir. "Getting a little worried? Wondering why they're not coming? There's no one back there. Not one person or ghost dragon or flying cheetah chasing after you." The dragon-woman laughed again, but this time her voice sounded strained.

"You're right," Fifer said, trying to sound devastated. "Maybe they don't care about us after all."

Next to her, wild with angst, Thisbe searched Fifer's face. "What are you doing?" she mouthed.

Fifer pressed her lips together in a line, then concentrated, trying to send a message to Thisbe like Thisbe had sent, perhaps by accident, to her. *Don't despair. Remember the fights we've won.*

In the Quiet

Dev had pleasantly lost track of the days. Every morning he woke up to sunshine streaming into his library and had to remind himself that he was free to do whatever he wanted, or to do nothing at all. This was his home now—all his. This life was definitely something he was getting accustomed to. Being a little bit lonely sometimes? That was a bargain of a trade for his old life.

He was still worried about the Revinir returning, but that fear lessened over time. He could think of a lot of reasons why she wouldn't. Obviously, she must think the palace was abandoned—there was no way any normal person would live here, and she saw that for herself recently. Plus, the whole village around the palace was deserted. She couldn't possibly imagine that this was a good hiding place for whoever she was looking for. It wasn't convenient to anywhere, and there was no easy way in and out of this corner of the land with the crater lake on one side and the mountains on another.

Eventually Dev was convinced that the Revinir had been looking for Thisbe and the others and hadn't found them. Or . . . maybe she was exploring what was beyond this land to the west and found it totally desolate with nothing to conquer. It was reasonable to believe she'd never be back.

As Dev's confidence increased, his explorations grew wider. He visited the small deserted village beyond the apple orchard a few times. Some of the homes were structurally sound, but all of them were cleaned out—looted of anything valuable. Dev thought about hiding in one of them if the Revinir ever returned. She'd be less likely to find him unless she and her dragons searched through the narrow streets, which they'd have trouble fitting through without completely knocking down walls and other structures. And while that wouldn't be difficult for them to do, it would be time consuming and a waste of effort for no good reason . . . unless they expected to find someone there. The fact that they'd been gone so long without returning gave Dev more hope every day that they'd lost all desire to spend another ounce of time in this isolated place.

After his nightmare that had left him on the floor and packing for the catacombs, Dev had returned to his senses. Leaving his bulbous library would be a big mistake if there wasn't a need to do so. He loved it here. He had a sofa to sleep on, a fireplace to warm him at night, and books and instruments to keep him company. He had all the fish and fruit and wild plants he could eat just steps away. And he could fix things around the property whenever he felt like it, a little at a time. Even the fox family that had found shelter in the entryway to the stairwell got used to him coming and going, and soon the young kits were big enough to venture out on their own. One of them liked to follow Dev up the stairwell, though its mother always barked at it to come back.

Dev hadn't heard or felt a roar from the Revinir in all this time. And although he could call up the ancestor images anytime he wanted to, and marvel over how one of them had saved his life, the pictures offered no answers that he didn't already know. So Dev used his imagination to create his own explanation about what these pictures meant for him.

Astrid had seemed quite certain that the gray man was Ashguard Suresh, the curmudgeon who had lived in this palace long after all his people had been killed or captured by the usurpers. But Dev added on to the story, turning Ashguard into his grandfather. Dev imagined that this dear relative had granted this property to him in a very important document. That he'd been summoned to take care of it.

Thinking about that made him wonder which of his parents was a direct descendant of Ashguard. What had they been like? How did they live? And how did they die? Dev had all the time in the world now to make up answers to the questions he'd barely had time to think about his entire life.

To help in his attempt to clean up and fix bits of the property, Dev continued to collect potentially useful items whenever he ran across them, whether in the village or around the palace. He had quite an assortment of long, flat boards, as well as two buckets and two ropes. He'd even found some sheets of chain-mail mesh in a small building at the back of the palace that he called the foundry. Dev used the chain mail to make a fishing net, which would be easier than the hook-and-line method. And with the leftovers, he fashioned a chain-mail shirt to go under his regular cloth shirt, which would protect him from being stabbed by a sword or knife in case intruders ever came. One couldn't be too careful when one was all alone. Besides, wearing it made him feel stronger.

This particular day began with a startlingly bright sunrise that streamed in through the newly cleaned east window onto his face, waking Dev up. He went to the window to watch it rise, bumping his nose against the glass and leaving a smudge.

"Oh, glorious sun," he said in praise. He loved how it lit up and made colors with the clouds in the sky. After breakfast he tinkered around the palace, then decided this would be the day to try to reach a little alcove that he'd seen from one of the turret staircases but couldn't access because of the rotting floors. He went to the foundry and gathered up two long boards and a rope. Then he ventured out across the courtyard to one of the small corner towers, whose staircase hadn't been mysteriously melted, and climbed up and around the debris to the fifth floor.

He looked around for something solid and sturdy to anchor

himself to. He was suspicious of the leaky ceiling, so he tied one end of the rope around the bannister at the top of the stairs. The other end he secured around his chest as a safety measure. Then he surveyed the great room that stretched out before him. There was nothing in it. In some places the floor had caved in from rain and rot. There was a gaping hole directly in the center of the room, below the point of the onion spire, where leaks had been causing deterioration for years. The floor joists showed through in places, but at the edges of the room they looked relatively solid.

The prize Dev was after was a small alcove on the opposite side of the great room, which had some interesting things in it. With the rope around him, he wouldn't fall far if those joists were rotten too and gave way under his weight.

He placed the first board on top of the exposed floor joists and tested it gingerly. It held him. He walked across, laid the second board down and stood on it, picked up the first board, and repeated the process, all the way around the edge of the great room to the alcove. As Dev drew closer to it, he could see more clearly what was in it: a small writing desk like the one in his mind image of the gray man. Next to it was a large metal box.

Once there, Dev stepped inside the space, which seemed to be in much better condition than the great room. He eagerly lifted the cover off the box and searched through it. But its contents were disappointing. One by one Dev pulled out several fairly useless, heavy knickknacks that seemed to be of little value, though they each were engraved with a diamond-shaped symbol containing the letter S. Probably for Suresh, Dev surmised. No wonder no one had stolen these—it wouldn't have been worth the weight to lug them around, and everyone would have known they were stolen from a ruler.

Dev put everything back in the box, but then he paused and removed an old beer stein that seemed like it could be useful for him to drink out of. In addition to the diamond S symbol, it had an unusual engraving on it that he liked. The engraving was a quote, written with curly letters in the same language he'd seen in the books left open on the big desk in the library. He couldn't read the quote, but it felt important.

Dev turned to the small desk and ran his hand over the smooth surface. Then he opened the narrow drawer, expecting it to be empty. To his surprise, lying flat inside it was a small stack of sketches and paintings. On top was a watercolor of a little girl. The painting had once been quite colorful but had faded over time. As Dev studied her, his scales prickled and a few of the images flashed in front of his eyes. This was someone important, he thought. Important to him.

Carefully Dev checked the rest of the drawers, finding them disappointingly empty. He rolled the stack of drawings and slid them into the mouth of the stein, then painstakingly made his way back to the stairwell on the boards. He untied the rope and gathered up the boards, then descended the stairs with his new possessions. He returned the boards and rope to the foundry and went back to the library.

With his beer stein and the art pieces in hand, Dev sat down at the huge desk. He gazed at the etching on the stein, then paged through the big book on the desk to see if he could match up the words. When nothing jumped out at him, he pushed the book aside and looked through the sketches and paintings. He went back to the first one, which was the best of the lot, and smoothed it out to study it. It was simple: The girl stood outside with trees behind her. Soon Dev realized with a start that the backdrop of the sketch was the flourishing orchard. This little girl wasn't a random painting bought on a whim at the market. She had been sketched not far from here. Perhaps she'd even lived here—that made the most sense. And Ashguard, or someone, had commissioned her painting. Dev knew all about such things. Shanti had had her portrait done every year around her birthday, and she'd hated it because it took so long to do. She always made Dev accompany her to keep her entertained, which was exhausting for him because she was so cranky.

This girl wasn't cranky-looking, though. She looked sweet and familiar, though he couldn't quite figure out why. The drawing was old—this person must be forty or fifty years old by now. If she'd survived, anyway.

Dev glanced out the south window toward the orchard. From this height he could look down on the tops of the gnarled apple trees beyond the overgrowth that surrounded the palace. Maybe one day he would chop all of the weeds and bushes so he could see the orchard even better.

As he turned back to study the drawing, his eye caught movement out the east window, directly in front of him. He froze, hoping it was just a bird like it had been all of the other times he'd been startled by movement outside that window since the Revinir had come. But this bird wasn't flitting about. It was coming straight on.

Dev's breath grew shallow, and an old familiar sense of dread washed over him like the river. He went up to the glass and used his shirt to wipe away the smudge he'd left earlier, then peered through the window. His scales lifted on his arms and legs. Fear seized his lungs, his brain. He couldn't move or think or even make a noise. All he knew was that the thing that had terrified him most was happening again: The Revinir and her red dragons were coming, this time in broad daylight. And soon they'd be close enough to see him if he made a move.

Dev stared, slack jawed, as his gut churned. He couldn't stay here. He shoved the drawing of the girl inside a book, gathered up his bag and canteen, and skidded down and around the stairs. He exited the tower and ran for his life across the courtyard and down the hill toward the orchard and the village. All the while he hoped and prayed that the gorgeous sunlight, which he'd praised just that morning, wouldn't be the foil that betrayed his existence to the worst enemy the land of the dragons had ever known.

Acknowledgments

S ome of you have been reading this series for a very long time, since you were in grade four or even earlier, and now you're older, in high school or beyond, and you're still reading it. Thank you so much for staying with these characters and this world! I love meeting you in person and on Instagram and Twitter (@lisa_mcmann) and learning what you love about the Unwanteds and Unwanteds Quests series. Your steady support over the years makes me excited to write more!

I want to thank my editor, Liesa Abrams, for always knowing exactly what my manuscripts need and helping me put the best story into your hands. And my agent, Michael Bourret, who has been my guide and my friend throughout this wonderful career for over a dozen years.

I also want to give a huge shout out to Owen Richardson and Karin Paprocki for the beautiful cover art and design of all of these books. Dragon Fire is quite possibly my favorite cover of all time. (I exclaim this loudly every time I see a new one, though.) And I'd also like to acknowledge and thank my son, Kilian McMann, who gave me the idea for the Unwanteds when he was twelve-years-old and has been drawing and designing things for the series ever since—you can find his work on TheUnwantedsSeries.com.

To all the people who give their time and talents to making this series, I am eternally grateful for your tireless work and dedication. Thank you from the bottom of my heart.

ABOUT THE AUTHOR

Lisa McMann lives in Sacramento, California. She is married to fellow writer and musician Matt McMann, and they have two adult children. Her son is an artist named Kilian McMann and her daughter is an actor, Kennedy McMann. Lisa is the New York Times bestselling author of over two dozen books for young adults and children. So far she has written in genres including paranormal, realistic, dystopian, and fantasy. Some of her most well-known books are the Unwanteds series for middle-grade readers and the Wake trilogy for young adults. Check out Lisa's website at LisaMcMann.com, learn more about the Unwanteds series at UnwantedsSeries.com, and be sure to say hi on Instagram or Twitter (@Lisa_McMann), or Facebook (Facebook.com/McMannFan).

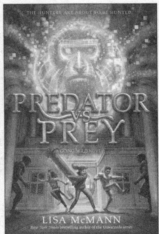